PRAISE FOR

# A WHISPER IN THE DARK

"An exciting, fast, page-turning read that promises . . . and delivers."
—*Fresh Fiction*

"A fine thriller . . ."
—*The Best Reviews*

# DEPTH PERCEPTION

"A tightly written novel of romantic suspense by an author at the top of her game."
—*All About Romance*

"An exciting page-turner, *Depth Perception* will appeal to the fans of Beverly Barton and Iris Johansen. This tense thriller will keep you up way past midnight."
—*The Best Reviews*

"A fabulous, taut paranormal thriller that grips readers . . . The story line is action-packed and filled with atmosphere that has the audience gasping as the tension mounts . . . exciting . . . a terrific read."
—*Midwest Book Review*

"Explosive . . . deep [and] emotional . . . a riveting adventure."
—*The Romance Reader's Connection*

# FADE TO RED

"Castillo is pushing the envelope. And she is doing a very convincing and, yes, disturbingly good job . . . This is not a book for the faint-hearted . . . If you like nothing better than an adrenaline rush and a hero and heroine possessing multiple character layers, then be assured that *Fade to Red* will be exactly what you are looking for and so much more."
—*A Romance Review*

"Enlightening and original."
—*The Romance Reader*

*continued . . .*

"A throwback to the old days of romantic suspense . . . chilling . . . Great character development [and] an ability to totally immerse the reader into the sleazy underbelly of porn and cause a shiver or two."    —*Romance Reviews Today*

"Chillingly graphic—romantic suspense at its best."
                                                    —*The Best Reviews*

## THE SHADOW SIDE

"An electrifying chiller rife with action and passion . . . splendid."                    —*The Dallas Morning News*

"*The Shadow Side* is exhilarating romantic suspense . . . never slows down until the final moment. Read this thriller."                    —*Midwest Book Review*

"Stunning. A masterpiece of suspense polished off with a raw romance. This book, the best romantic suspense I've ever read, knocked me out. The characters were hot, the story was downright chilling . . . but so compelling. The pace constantly keeps you on the edge . . . giving you twists and turns and never giving you any clues as to what's going to happen next . . . until the very last minute! Don't miss this thriller; you'll be sorry if you do. They don't come any better than this."    —*Romance and Friends*

## THE PERFECT VICTIM

"Castillo has a winner! I couldn't stop turning the pages!"
                                                    —Kat Martin,
            *New York Times* bestselling author of *The Fire Inside*

"*The Perfect Victim* is a gripping page-turner. Peopled with fascinating characters and intricately plotted . . . compelling suspense that never lets up. A first class reading experience!"                    —Katherine Sutcliffe,
        bestselling author of *Darkling I Listen* and *Obsession*

# OVERKILL

## LINDA CASTILLO

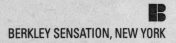
BERKLEY SENSATION, NEW YORK

**THE BERKLEY PUBLISHING GROUP**
**Published by the Penguin Group**
**Penguin Group (USA) Inc.**
**375 Hudson Street, New York, New York 10014, USA**
Penguin Group (Canada), 90 Eglinton Avenue East, Suite 700, Toronto, Ontario M4P 2Y3, Canada
(a division of Pearson Penguin Canada Inc.)
Penguin Books Ltd., 80 Strand, London WC2R 0RL, England
Penguin Group Ireland, 25 St. Stephen's Green, Dublin 2, Ireland (a division of Penguin Books Ltd.)
Penguin Group (Australia), 250 Camberwell Road, Camberwell, Victoria 3124, Australia
(a division of Pearson Australia Group Pty. Ltd.)
Penguin Books India Pvt. Ltd., 11 Community Centre, Panchsheel Park, New Delhi—110 017, India
Penguin Group (NZ), 67 Apollo Drive, Rosedale, North Shore 0632, New Zealand
(a division of Pearson New Zealand Ltd.)
Penguin Books (South Africa) (Pty.) Ltd., 24 Sturdee Avenue, Rosebank, Johannesburg 2196,
South Africa

Penguin Books Ltd., Registered Offices: 80 Strand, London WC2R 0RL, England

This is a work of fiction. Names, characters, places, and incidents either are the product of the author's imagination or are used fictitiously, and any resemblance to actual persons, living or dead, business establishments, events, or locales is entirely coincidental. The publisher does not have any control over and does not assume any responsibility for author or third-party websites or their content.

OVERKILL

A Berkley Sensation Book / published by arrangement with the author

PRINTING HISTORY
Berkley Sensation mass-market edition / October 2007

Copyright © 2007 by Linda Castillo.
Interior text design by Kristin del Rosario.

ISBN: 978-0-425-21829-7

BERKLEY® SENSATION
Berkley Sensation Books are published by The Berkley Publishing Group,
a division of Penguin Group (USA) Inc.,
375 Hudson Street, New York, New York 10014.
BERKLEY SENSATION and the "B" design are trademarks belonging to Penguin Group (USA) Inc.

PRINTED IN THE UNITED STATES OF AMERICA

10  9  8  7  6  5  4  3  2  1

This book is dedicated to Barb Hansch, Appaloosa enthusiast, therapeutic riding coach, horse trainer extraordinaire and friend; Kim Hansch, who rides a mean barrel pattern and makes it look easy; and the late Doug Hansch, husband, father and friend. Thanks for all the fun times at the barn, guys.

# ACKNOWLEDGMENTS

A book is an undertaking of monumental proportions that hijacks a writer's life for months on end. It is an endeavor that entails hundreds of solitary and sometimes frustrating hours of work, countless sleepless nights, and the whole heart of anyone crazy enough to call himself or herself an author.

I have people to thank for helping me complete this book in record time. First and foremost, I'd like to thank my husband, Ernest, for all of those evenings when you came home to find the house dark except for my office and didn't try to coax me out. For my critique group—Jennifer Archer, Marcy McKay and April Redmon—whose unflagging enthusiasm, humor and support kept me going when the going was tough. Thanks for the Wednesday night Marty marathons, guys. To Ronda Thompson and the rest of the Amarillo writing community for welcoming me to the Texas Panhandle with smiles and open arms. And to all of the wonderful ladies at the barrel races. You gals are awesome!!!

# PROLOGUE

*The sign quivered in a brisk southwesterly wind, welcoming weary travelers to Caprock Canyon, Texas, population 3500, where, evidently, one could find the best vistas in the state. The cheery signpost looked out of place among the scrub and prickly pear that dotted the bleak landscape of the high plains.*

Despite the sign's message, Marty Hogan didn't feel very welcome. The truth of the matter was she didn't want to be here. She didn't have any interest in the town, its citizenry or her new job. She sure as hell didn't have any inclination to take in the goddamn views. But then that fickle bitch Fate was funny in the way she doled out wisdom. In the last six months, Marty had had enough wisdom shoved down her throat to last a lifetime.

Sighing, she put the Mustang in gear and started toward the main drag. Downtown Caprock Canyon was the length of a football field and just as uninteresting. The redbrick storefronts included Jeb's General Store, Hawkin's Hardware, a Western outlet advertising Wrangler jeans, and the

Wagon Wheel Diner, where you could get a biscuits-and-gravy breakfast for $1.99. Outside the barbershop, two grizzled old men sat in matching metal chairs, smoking cigarettes. On the street in front of the diner, three men in cowboy hats climbed into a big Ford pickup where a fat border collie waited in the bed.

Born and raised in Chicago, Marty might as well have landed on foreign soil. Or maybe Mars. But after thirty-five resumes and thirty-four thanks-but-no-thanks responses, she figured she was lucky to have a job at all. After a single desultory phone interview, the Caprock Canyon PD was the only department willing to hire a has-been, renegade cop with a bad reputation and a semitruck full of emotional baggage.

Just Marty's luck she would end up in Bumfuck, U.S.A.

Six months had passed since the incident that thrust her into the national spotlight—and to the very top of the media's hit list. A hostile media that took what should have been an obscure story and ran it into the ground. Marty Hogan became an overnight sensation, going from street cop to the most hated police officer in America.

Depending on your point of view, of course.

Her indiscretion put the phrase *police trauma syndrome*—an axiom coined by psychiatrists after the Rodney King debacle in LA—back in the limelight. But Marty had heard the other not-so-clinical names, too. Rogue cop. Fascist bitch. Nutcase. The labels shamed her with a passion she could not express. She wished fervently she could dispute them. But like her former partner, Rosetti, always said . . . if the straitjacket fits . . . In this case, she thought, the fit was perfect. Just ask the amateur videographer who'd caught the whole mess on tape and sold it to the highest bidder. The son of a bitch was probably sipping mojitos and soaking up the sun in Cancun.

In less than twenty-four hours, patrol officer Marty Hogan became Chicago's new obsession. For weeks, those awful clips filled the airwaves from Bangor to San Diego and every podunk town in between. Love her or hate her, everyone had an opinion about the female cop who'd gone off the deep end and beat a male suspect to near unconsciousness.

It didn't matter that the bastard had shot and killed a little girl. A nine-year-old hostage guilty of nothing but being in the wrong place at the wrong time. How horribly ironic that a kid's murder didn't garner even half the coverage.

Goddamn vultures.

Even now, Marty still received letters—and threats. She got so much mail, in fact, that she'd changed her address to a post office box, mostly for personal safety reasons. She'd changed her phone number, too. Three times, to be exact. But the diehards still found her. In a bizarre twist, about half of the people who took the time to contact her praised her actions on that fateful day. People were tired of crime. Tired of criminals getting away with murder. Now was their chance to chalk one up for the good guys. Give the girl a promotion. Pin a medal on her jacket.

Reality hadn't been so kind.

Six days after *The Incident*, Marty was fired from a career she'd spent eight years building. She'd been charged with felony assault. A serious offense that could have garnered hard time and a ten-thousand-dollar fine. But after an expeditious trial, the jury had taken into consideration the extenuating circumstances and the charges were ultimately dropped. Of course, that didn't help when the threat of a civil suit still hovered over her head like a pall.

Sometimes the irony of the whole thing was just too much.

Now, having faced professional ruin, incarceration, financial devastation and public ridicule, Marty almost wished Caprock Canyon *was* on another planet.

Shoving thoughts of the past aside, she idled down the main thoroughfare, which was aptly named Cactus Street.

The old pang sounded in her belly when she passed the police station. That same emotion twisted inside her every time she so much as looked at a cop or a black-and-white. She could only describe it as a longing for something that was lost. Dreams were so damn hard to let go of.

She watched as a young officer with the requisite crew cut and Arnold Schwarzenegger physique crossed the sidewalk to a white Explorer emblazoned with the Caprock Canyon PD insignia. He looked sure of himself. Cocky. Happy and secure in his job. A young person with his entire future before him.

Marty had been him a lifetime ago.

*Don't screw this up,* she thought, but cruised past the building, hating it that she didn't have the guts to pull in. Berating herself for putting off the inevitable, she turned around in a Lutheran church parking lot and sped back through town. The young officer and his cruiser were gone when she reached the police station. Pulling into the empty space, she studied the redbrick facade. The structure was a neat, one-story building with double glass doors and five reserved parking places in front. She thought about the chief of police and wondered what kind of man would hire a cop with her reputation.

A schmuck, probably.

Gripping the steering wheel, Marty broke a sweat beneath her wrinkled khaki slacks and jacket and tried not to hear the little voice in her head telling her this was a bad idea. She needed to go inside; she was already ten minutes late. Not a great way to make a good first impression. But she was nervous, seriously depressed, and for the first time in a long time, she was scared. Really, really scared.

The irony of that burned. Up until that day six months ago, Marty had never been afraid of anything. She could walk into a dark warehouse with nothing but her Glock to back her up and barely raise her heart rate. She could approach a car full of suspected gang members in the dead of night and not feel the shaky stab of terror she felt at this moment.

Now fear seemed to be the overriding emotion that drove her every move. It was her best friend and her worst enemy. She second-guessed every thought, every decision, and every action. Not a good state of mind when you were a cop. Unless you had a death wish. If Marty wanted to be honest, she'd considered that, too.

Sick and tired of the incessant thoughts pummeling her beleaguered brain, she climbed out of the car and stepped into sunlight so bright it felt as if it might burn her eyeballs right out of their sockets. She fumbled for her shades, shoved them onto her nose. Around her, Caprock Canyon was as hushed as a ghost town out of some melodramatic Italian Western. She almost couldn't believe it when a tumbleweed the size of a recliner rolled down the street. The only thing needed to make the scene complete was a gunslinger with a poncho, a six-shooter and a flat-crowned hat.

The day wasn't over.

Taking a deep breath, Marty smoothed wet palms over her slacks and started for the entrance. She could hear the zing of her pulse as she pulled open the glass door and stepped inside.

The smell of cigarette smoke hovered in the air. Seated at an ugly metal desk, a round-faced person of indistinguishable gender and frizzy brown hair eyed her over the top of a computer monitor. The little creature wore a turquoise jacket with silver conchos and thick-lensed bifocals that made watery blue eyes look huge, and had the most wrinkled skin Marty had ever seen on a living being. Relief skittered through her when she spotted the brass plate mounted on a chunk of walnut identifying the person as Jo Nell Mulligan.

"Hep ya?" the woman asked.

"I'm here to see Chief Settlemeyer."

"You Hogan?"

"The one and only."

"Thought you might be her." The receptionist looked her up and down, a potential buyer eyeing a beef cow, trying to decide if it was fat enough to get her family through the winter.

Marty resisted the urge to squirm.

"Smaller than I thought, but I guess size ain't no issue when you're pissed. Heard you broke your hand." A raspy sound that might have been a chuckle rattled from her throat. "Fed that sumbitch a sandwich he ain't gonna soon forget."

Marty glanced toward the door, wishing she could run, knowing once she started she might never stop. She didn't want to talk to this rude little creep. She couldn't give a shit about the job. The problem was she had no other prospects and absolutely nowhere else to go.

The woman was still talking, but Marty had tuned out the brunt of it. ". . . you got that look about you. Cop look. Guys here all got it. You'd think each and every one of 'em was Dirty Harry hisself." Phlegm rattled in her throat when she laughed. "Never seen it on a woman before, but it suits you just fine."

"What suits whom just fine, Jo Nell?"

Marty turned at the sound of the deep male voice. Surprise rippled through her when she found herself looking at a tall man leaning against the doorjamb of the rear office, taking in the scene as if he were watching some amusing sitcom. His arms were crossed. A toothpick jutted from the corner of a mouth that curved up in a half smile. But what was most surprising about this man was the black Stetson perched on his head. A born-and-bred city girl, Marty wasn't used to seeing men in cowboy hats. She sure as hell wasn't used to cops wearing them. She knew it was silly to let that intimidate her. But it did.

He shifted and the nameplate affixed to the wall behind him came into view. *Chief Clay Settlemeyer.* Marty couldn't believe he was the man she'd talked to. Over the phone, Clay Settlemeyer had seemed soft-spoken and . . . civilized. The man staring her down didn't appear to be either of those things.

He stood well over six feet tall, but with the hat it could have been twenty. His skin was tanned and far from smooth, but every line only served to make his face more interesting than any male face had a right to be. A day's growth of stubble gave him a rough-around-the edges look. His eyes were as dark as the West Texas sky at night, an unusual shade of gray with a hint of starlight. His mouth seemed to curve easily into a smile. But Marty got the impression he could snarl just as readily.

He wasn't a handsome man; his mouth was too thin. His eyes were too intense. His brows too heavy. His face was as hard and angular as the foothills to the west. But the package as a whole stirred something inside her she couldn't name. Something that made her pulse quicken, her heart flutter uneasily in her chest. Marty had experienced the sensation before, and recognized it as a reaction to danger. Of course, that didn't make sense. She wasn't in danger. Damn it, she wasn't some fragile debutante who shrank away from a dangerous-looking man. She'd grown up with cops. Hung out with them most of her life. She could hold her own in any situation—just ask the poor bastard she'd put in the hospital six months ago.

But this man unnerved her in a way she'd never been before. His stare penetrated her cop suit of armor with the proficiency of a double-edged sword, tore away the facade she used to protect herself. He made her feel stripped bare, because he was looking at her as if she were a woman at the end of her rope and facing a very long fall.

"I was just about to buzz you, Chief."

"My office is ten feet away and my hearing's just fine, Jo Nell."

"Guess I'll yell next time."

He sniffed. "You've been smoking again."

"I have not," she said, deadpan.

Marty couldn't help it; she snickered, drawing a dark look from the chief—and a wink from the very busted Jo Nell.

He pointed at Marty. "You're late."

Six months ago, a smart-assed reply would have sailed off her tongue with the ease of a bird taking flight. Today, she had to work at it for a full two seconds. "Traffic," she said.

Clay Settlemeyer stared at her for what felt like a full minute, his heavy, black brows riding low over those weird gray eyes. His mouth remained as flat as the Texas plain. Marty was usually adept at reading people, but this man's expression revealed none of his thoughts. Fearing she'd ticked him off, she was considering another tactic when he shook his head and let out a chuckle.

"In that case, come on in." He motioned to his office.

Squaring her shoulders, Marty gathered the jagged remains of her composure and entered, keenly aware that he was right behind her.

"Have a seat," he said.

She lowered herself into the vinyl chair opposite his desk and tried to relax.

Closing the door, he rounded his desk. "How was the drive?"

The fifteen-hour drive had been long and boring, and Marty had had way too much time to think—something she tried not to do too much of these days. A recent insomniac, she'd left at midnight and driven straight through. "No problems."

"When did you get in?"

"Ten minutes ago."

"You find a place to live?"

"Rented a house on the south side."

"Nice area. Close to the canyon. You'll get some wildlife out there."

Since the extent of Marty's experience with wildlife centered around the occasional bar fight or domestic dispute, she had to ask. "Wildlife?"

"Deer mostly. Coyotes occasionally. A few skunk." He raised a brow. "If you own a cat or dog, you might want to keep them inside at night."

She found herself thinking of the .22 mini Magnum revolver she'd packed in her trunk. "I don't have any pets."

"Probably a good thing. Old man Hardeman'll be a good landlord."

She wanted to know how he knew who her landlord was when she hadn't even told him where she'd be living. But Marty figured in a town the size of Caprock Canyon, you didn't need a genius power of deduction to figure things out. It freaked her out a little to think of living in a place where everyone knew everyone else's business. More than anything, Marty craved anonymity. She had the sinking feeling it was one of many things she wouldn't find here.

She watched as he pulled a manila folder from his desk drawer. Her eyes went to the tab, found her name printed in bold blue on the label. She wondered what was in the file, if he'd done his homework, and she tried not to fidget.

"So what made you accept a job here in the Texas Panhandle?"

The word *bumfuck* floated inappropriately through her mind. Marty smiled, but she wasn't the least bit amused by any of what was happening. "You're kidding, right?"

His eyes narrowed, sharpened. "It's a simple question."

She reminded herself he'd already hired her. She hadn't signed anything, but as far as she knew it was a done deal. Still . . . they hadn't talked about *The Incident*. Surely he knew about what happened in Chicago. Didn't he?

"I was ready for a change." Trying to play it nonchalant, she lifted a shoulder, let it drop. "I sent out quite a few resumes. You made the best offer." The only offer, she silently amended, but decided it probably wasn't a good idea to point that out.

"Going to be a big change for you."

"I'm getting that." Realizing that sounded flippant, she nodded. "Like I said, I'm ready for something different."

Reaching into the breast pocket of his denim shirt, he removed a pair of reading glasses, then opened the folder. "In case you're wondering, we have television here in Deaf Smith County." He looked at her over the tops of his glasses. "We also have cable TV, satellite TV and newspapers. Most of us can read, too."

All Marty could do was stare.

"I saw the video," he said softly. "I talked to your superiors. I know what happened."

"So why did you hire me?"

"Any reason why I shouldn't?"

She couldn't curb the laugh that broke from her throat. "For starters, I beat the hell out of a suspect."

"Jury evidently didn't see it that way."

"I can only assume they took into consideration the extenuating circumstances."

"Must have been a fair-minded jury." Frowning, he leaned back in his chair. "For future reference, just because this is a small town doesn't mean we're dumb hick cops."

"I didn't think that."

"Yes, you did." He said it without rancor.

Because he was right, Marty looked down at her hands, willed them not to shake. But she could feel her temper winding up. Nothing new there; she was like a walking time bomb these days. She hadn't driven all the way from Chicago to Texas to get raked over the coals for some penny-ante job where she would more than likely spend as much time herding wayward cows as she did directing traffic.

Settlemeyer turned his attention back to the file. "You have good credentials, Hogan. SWAT experience. Your marksmanship scores are off the chart." He glanced at her over the top of the paper he held. "I talked to the chief of detectives of the Fourth District."

"I'm sure he had some interesting things to say."

"As a matter of fact, he did."

*Here it comes,* she thought, *the deal killer.* Her heart plummeted into her stomach. James DeLuca hated her; there was no way this man would hire her after speaking to DeLuca. He'd wanted to crucify her, her partner and another first responder who'd been on the scene that day. He'd called for a Division of Public Integrity investigation. The next day he'd demanded her resignation. Lucky for Marty the jury had been in a charitable mood when she'd had her day in court or she'd have been sitting in a jail cell right now. DeLuca and the rest of the suits hadn't been quite so forgiving.

She stared at Settlemeyer, knowing he was about to drop the hammer. The son of a bitch had changed his mind. He was going to fire her before she even had the chance to prove herself. If things went south here, she'd have nothing. No job. She'd broken the lease on her apartment in Palatine, forfeited the deposits. Now, she had no place to live. No way to pay her bills. Or her lawyer. Her only friends were cops, most of whom wouldn't be caught dead associating with her. Marty was poison to the world right now.

Fuck Clay Settlemeyer. Fuck DeLuca. Fuck them all.

Heart racing, Marty shoved away from the desk abruptly, her chair screeching across the tile floor as she stood. She stared at Settlemeyer, knowing now was the time to say something. To defend herself. Her actions. At the very least she should tell him to get screwed for letting her drive fifteen hours only to have this last chance yanked out from under her.

But Marty's throat was so tight she couldn't speak. There were so many emotions jamming her brain that she couldn't begin to identify them or put them into words. Not that anything would make a damn bit of difference now.

"Thanks for your time." Turning, she started for the door.

"Hogan."

Marty didn't stop until she put her hand on the knob. Even then she didn't turn to face him. She didn't want him to see what she knew resided in her eyes. Didn't want him to see just how much this opportunity meant to her.

"Just so you know, DeLuca gave you a favorable recommendation."

She heard the words, but the only thing that registered was the hard pound of her heart, the heat leaching into her face, the tingle in her fingertips as she gripped the knob.

Holding herself together by the sheer force of desperation, Marty turned. "What?"

Settlemeyer's chair creaked when he leaned back. Lacing his hands behind his head, he studied her as if she were some lab experiment that wasn't quite coming together the way he'd envisioned. "I don't know if this matters to you, but I'm one of those people who believes in second chances."

Something akin to panic fluttered in her gut. Marty was adept at keeping a handle on her emotions. She'd been doing it for too many years to count, and couldn't remember the last time she'd cried. Certainly not throughout the fiasco of the last six months. Growing up with two older brothers and working in a male-dominated profession, she'd learned early in life that tears never accomplished a damn thing. Most law enforcement types saw them for what they were: a sign of weakness. Marty was a lot of things, not all of them good, but she wasn't weak.

But certain things had a way of wearing you down. It was ironic, but most often it was common kindness that undid Marty. She wasn't sure what that said about her as a person.

She stared at Settlemeyer, not sure what to say. But she knew what she felt. Another swirl of panic went through her when telltale heat surged behind her eyes.

*Not now, damn it.*

"I don't need your charity." The words came out surprisingly strong. She wanted to add some smart-assed reply, just to show him none of this mattered. She wasn't some emotional basket case. She could start over. Maybe in security. But for the life of her Marty couldn't find the words.

"This has nothing to do with charity," he said. "I need a cop. You've got the credentials. A good recommendation. As far as I'm concerned, those two things override what you did six months ago. As long as you can keep a handle on your temper, the job is yours."

"I'm a good cop."

"That appears to be the general consensus."

"There's more to what happened six months ago than the media reported."

"Sometimes the whole story doesn't sell good airtime." He took off his glasses. "So is that a yes or a no?"

"I need the job."

"I'll take that as a yes." Reaching into a drawer, he removed a .40-caliber Glock, a leather holster, an antiquated cell phone, and a shiny new badge and laid them on the desk. "Get your uniforms from Jo Nell. I think there's a form or two you'll need to fill out. Taxes and health insurance and such. You start tomorrow, second shift."

Marty stared down at the badge and gun, hating it that the images wavered through unshed tears. Her hand trembled when she reached for them. When she looked at Settlemeyer, his eyes were already on hers.

"I've already got a cell phone," she managed.

"Now you have two. That's the one I'll be reaching you on 24/7." He closed the drawer. "Any questions?"

Marty shook her head.

"Shift starts at 4 P.M. and ends at midnight. Half hour for dinner. You'll be riding with someone for a few days until you get your feet. For starters you get Monday and Tuesday off as well as one Sunday per month. Friday is payday. You getting all this?"

"I got it."

"In that case, welcome to Caprock Canyon, Officer Hogan." He stuck out his hand.

Forcing her gaze to his, Marty took his hand and pumped it twice. She got a fleeting impression of calluses and restrained strength before he released her.

"See you tomorrow," she said.

"Watch that traffic." He softened the words with a half smile. "And don't be late."

"I won't." Turning, Marty started toward the door and hoped she could keep her word.

# ONE

*Through the dust-coated glass of his office window, Clay* watched his new recruit cross the sidewalk to her car and assured himself hiring her hadn't been a mistake. She had impressive credentials, after all, better than any of the three men who made up his small police force. She had eight years on the street in South Chicago, a tough district that would send a lot of cops scurrying to the nearest door.

He wasn't buying it.

No matter how you cut it, Marty Hogan had screwed up royally six months ago. She'd lost control and used the kind of judgment that gave all cops a bad name. Clay had watched the video a dozen times. Like tens of thousands of others, he'd been disgusted and sickened by the images of a cop beating a bound suspect. And yet after learning that the suspect had murdered a nine-year-old kid in cold blood, Clay had silently, perhaps wrongly, applauded her.

He'd been shocked as hell when he'd received a resume from her three weeks ago. It had taken him all of ten minutes to call her and conduct a phone interview. She'd handled herself well and answered all of his questions in just the right way. Despite her past mistakes, he decided Marty Hogan deserved a second chance.

But now, after meeting her, Clay doubted his initial assessment. He could spot baggage a mile away. No matter how hard she tried to conceal it behind that thin veil of tough, the woman was carting around enough emotional luggage to fill a 747. Clay ought to know; he was the proverbial expert on the subject.

Not wanting to examine his own past too closely, he watched her pull away and tried not to acknowledge the possibility that he'd messed up. Over the years he'd seen more than his share of cops in psychological distress. During his stint in the Middle East as an MP, several of his counterparts had been held in the vise grip of post-traumatic stress disorder. In the years he'd worked as a patrol officer in Dallas, he'd seen young cops just one moment of bad judgment away from eating a bullet.

Marty Hogan was a cop on the edge of a very precipitous drop. She wouldn't admit it; he'd seen the denial in her eyes. But he'd recognized it because he'd seen it before in his own eyes. She was as shaky on her feet as a person could be—and still be standing.

"So why the hell did you hire her?" he muttered.

Clay knew the answer to that question, too. Right or wrong, or some ambiguous place in-between, he'd been compelled to give her another chance. Someone had done the same for him a long time ago. If Clay hadn't taken it, he might have been one of those unfortunate young cops who couldn't take the stress and stuck a gun in his mouth.

He wondered if Marty Hogan had slipped that far.

Unfortunately, her frame of mind wasn't the only thing bothering him about the newest addition to his force. He wasn't sure why, but he hadn't expected her to be attractive. He knew that was a sexist attitude that had nothing to do with whether or not she was a good cop. Clay had always considered himself an enlightened and open-minded man. Damn it, he wasn't sexist; he had nothing against female cops. Some of the best cops he'd ever known were women.

But whether he wanted to admit it or not, the way she looked would impact the department. It would change the dynamics of his team. It would change the way he viewed his own job. Clay would just have to be careful to keep things in perspective. Keep them on an even keel. Simple. The way he liked them.

As he pushed away from the window and watched her Mustang disappear down the street, Clay had a sinking feeling it wasn't going to be easy. Life rarely was. In fact, nine times out of ten it was complicated as hell.

Marty Hogan had complicated written all over that shapely body of hers. Clay had never been good at complicated. Just ask his ex-wife. As he rounded his desk and sank into the leather chair, he had the terrible premonition he was about to get a crash course.

*The house sat on an overgrown lot across the street from* a furniture store that had long since closed and a fire hydrant that had been run over by something big and never repaired. Next door, a rusty horse trailer with a flat tire stood alone in a vacant lot where hip-high weeds jutted from cracked asphalt. Beyond, the vast yellow plain stretched as far as the eye could see. Evidently, the Realtor hadn't been exaggerating when he'd told Marty the house was located on the edge of town.

She parked the Mustang curbside and tried not to be disappointed. She wasn't that picky about where she lived. As long as the place was relatively clean, had running water and air-conditioning, she could eke by. Well, as long as there were no mice or bugs.

But as she climbed the crumbling concrete steps to the

wooden porch, Marty wondered if even those basic criteria would be met. An old-fashioned wooden screen door screeched like a cat in heat when she opened it. Checking the lopsided mailbox mounted beside the door, Marty found the key, shoved it into the lock and opened the door.

The odors of dust and old wood with an underlying hint of mildew greeted her when she stepped into the living room. Olive green shag carpet stretched the length of the room like trampled grass. The sofa and chair spoke of a bad trip back to the 1970s, replete with orange stripes and armrests as big as a man's waist. The off-white paint helped bring it all together, but as Marty made her way to the kitchen, her hopes of finding something neat and pretty were dashed.

Yellow and white tile countertops glared at her like a judgmental mother-in-law. An almond-colored refrigerator groaned and rattled as if gasping for its last breath. Peeling yellow linoleum floors creaked beneath her feet as she moved down the narrow hall toward the bathroom, where she got yet another unpleasant surprise. Pink tile covered the walls of the tiny space. Not a subtle, eye-pleasing pastel, but a slap-in-the-face freaking *Pink* with a capital P. Some tasteless soul's idea of art deco. Probably never been to Miami. On second thought, he'd probably never been out of this godforsaken town.

Marty stood in the doorway and took in the scene like a bystander watching a train wreck. If she hadn't been so damn depressed she might have laughed. But it was either that or cry. And she didn't want to cry. Once she started she might not be able to stop.

Letting out a passable snort, she explored the rest of the house, which took all of five minutes. In a nutshell, the place was a two-bedroom, one-bath nightmare. Perhaps this was God's way of punishing her. Since a sympathetic jury hadn't seen fit to incarcerate her for her transgression, this would be her prison. Her purgatory.

For now, it would have to do. After all, a former cop with a bad rep and shaky state of mind couldn't be too picky.

Back at the car, Marty unloaded her suitcase and laptop case and lugged both to the house. She unpacked her clothes and put them in the single chest of drawers. Next came the mini Magnum five-shooter and ankle holster, which she placed in the top drawer of the night table. She should probably go to the grocery and buy some staples, but she didn't feel like it.

She was on her way to the back door to check out the rest of the lot when her cell phone vibrated against her hip. The loneliness and depression pressing into her vanished when she saw her former partner's name pop up on the display.

Grinning, she sat on the stoop and hit the Talk button. "About time you called."

"How ya doin', kid?" Steve Rosetti's voice rolled through the line like tires over gravel.

"Frickin' peachy, Rosetti."

"Missin' the traffic and crime, huh?"

"Or maybe I'm just missing you."

"Ah . . . be still my heart." They both knew Rosetti was a happily married man. "How was the trip?"

"Long." She paused. "Too much time to think, but you know how that goes."

"Don't want to get that brain working too much. How's Texas?"

"I saw my first tumbleweed today."

"Holy shit." He chuckled. "Did you shoot it?"

Marty really laughed for the first time since arriving in Caprock Canyon. "I feel like I've landed on Pluto."

Rosetti paused. In the background Marty heard a car horn, and she knew he was out patrolling. A pang rolled through her belly hard enough to make her close her eyes. God, she missed riding with him.

"So how you really doin'?"

"I think the change is going to be good."

"Jesus, you're a bad frickin' liar, Hogan. You gotta work on that."

"This place sucks. The job sucks."

"Sounds like frickin' home to me."

She laughed again. "I knew you'd cheer me up."

"Yeah, that's me. Mr. Fuckin' Cheery Shit."

In the background, another horn blared. Rosetti cursed. "Hey, kid, I gotta go. Some hurry-up dipshit just ran a light."

Marty closed her eyes again. "Go get 'em, Rosetti."

"You, too."

The line clicked and filled with silence. That same silence seemed to fill Marty, echoing a loneliness so deep her bones ached with it. Snapping her phone closed, she blinked back tears, wishing she was anywhere but here.

*Radimir Ivanov stood in the secure visitor area of Build*ing Nine of the Rochester Federal Medical Center in Minnesota and waited for the clinical director. Around him, corrections officers and medical personnel eyed him with the disdain of the enlightened. As if he were just another lowlife off the street here to visit some piece-of-scum convict.

If only they knew . . .

Let them believe what they will, he thought. Sooner or later, they would learn the truth. He would show them all. Filthy American *svinyas. Pigs.*

Someone called out his name. He turned to see an overweight young doctor approach wearing green scrubs and a harried expression. A name tag pinned at his shoulder read *Dr. Blessi.* Beside him, a buff corrections officer stared at Radimir with unconcealed hostility.

"Right this way," the doctor said.

Radimir followed them down a wide hall tiled in non-descript gray, with doors spaced every twenty feet or so. Some of the rooms were darkened, but a few were lit enough so that he could see the immobile forms lying in the beds. One patient was cuffed to the rail and eyed him with the hatred of a tethered dog. Another writhed and moaned as if someone had doused his body with acid.

They walked past a brightly lit nurses station where two additional corrections officers drank coffee from foam cups.

"Right here." The doctor stopped outside Room 381-B, checked the chart and scribbled something on the page.

Bracing, Radimir peered into the room. He could see his brother Rurik beneath the layers of white sheets and blankets. His hand dangled listlessly over the side of the bed. A polished steel handcuff encased his wrist. From his left arm, an IV line dripped like intermittent tears.

"Is he going to be all right?" Radimir asked the doctor.

"We repaired the ruptured bowel this morning. He has a severe concussion, a few broken ribs, but no other major injuries."

*No other major injuries.*

*Sooksin,* Radimir thought and imagined himself cutting the doctor's throat.

Rurik had suffered injuries no man should ever have to endure. The Aryan Nation inmates had beaten him with the makeshift weapons cons were so adept at making. Once his brother was down, they took turns kicking him, as if he were nothing more than some mangy dog. Once he'd been semi-conscious, they'd proceeded to rape him with what-ever object they could get their hands on and with such violence that they'd perforated his rectum.

How dare the doctor intimate that he had no other major injuries. His brother had sustained the worst kind of wound. The kind a man couldn't see with his eyes, but felt deep in his heart. The kind of harm a man took with him to the grave. No one walked away from an ordeal like that un-scathed.

Radimir's only consolation was the knowledge that the perpetrators would pay. Every single one of them, no matter how long it took. After all, he had connections. Powerful connections. Not only inside the prison itself, but the Federal Bureau of Prisons.

"He's sedated. You can stay for ten minutes." At that the doctor nodded to the corrections officer, then left the room.

Radimir entered the room and stared at his brother's form. Rurik's face was almost unrecognizable. Black stitches ran like tiny railroad tracks over his right eyebrow all the way to his temple. The left side of his head had been shaved and more stitches stood out stark and black against the white flesh of his scalp.

Just when Radimir thought he'd seen the worst of it, his brother opened his one good eye. Within its pale blue depths, Radimir saw the extent of his pain. The magnitude of his humiliation. The kind of shame that cut to the bone and went all the way to a man's soul.

"*Pizdets.*" Rurik whispered the Russian term for a bad situation without a solution.

"There is a solution, my brother."

The pale blue eye rolled back, landed on him, focused. "*Pizdy vlomit.*"

"I know. They beat you. How many?"

"Six or seven."

"Do you know their names?"

"Some."

"I need names. Get them."

The immobile man nodded, then looked away, the pale blue eye filling with tears. "I am their *shestiorka*."

It was the worst thing a man could be in prison. Unable to hold his brother's gaze, Radimir looked toward the window. "I'll take care of it."

"How, my brother?"

*"Vziatka."*

"Bribe whom?"

"Let me worry about that. You rest now. Get strong." Radimir bent, put his mouth close to his brother's ear. "I'll get them," he whispered. "All of them. Including the *gaishnik* bitch who put you here."

His brother sighed. *"Chuchka derganaya."* Crazy bitch.

"This is her fault. What she did to you for all of the world to see caused this."

*"Promudobliadskaja pizdoprojebina."* Fucking bitch.

"She will pay. I will make her my *shestiorka*," Radimir promised. "And then I will put a bullet in her brain."

"Kill her in my name, my brother. For I am already dead."

Radimir wanted to tell him that was not the case. But they'd always been straight with each other. He knew unless his brother found an ally in prison—or joined one of the many gangs—he would most likely never see the end of his sixteen-year sentence. The most he could do was assure him that his death would be avenged.

Radimir picked up his cell phone and wallet at the security window and dialed the number on the way to his car. "Pack your bags," he said when the familiar voice answered. "We have some killing to do."

# TWO

*The moan of the prairie wind had to be the loneliest* sound on earth. At least in Chicago the hiss of traffic, the din of arguing neighbors and barking dogs reassured Marty that she wasn't the last person alive.

She lay on the lumpy, twin-size mattress and tried not to think of the state of her life or the downward spiral of her career. She tried not to think of tomorrow, her first day on the job, or that she simply didn't have the energy to muster any enthusiasm.

"Hogan, you are frickin' pathetic."

Sitting up, she threw her legs over the side of the bed and put her face in her hands. She rubbed her eyes, almost wishing she could cry just to get the feeling of sand out of them. The alarm on the nightstand mocked her, telling her Father Time didn't give a damn that she wasn't going to get any sleep again tonight. Three A.M. and going strong. Like the Energizer Bunny on speed.

Rising, Marty padded to the kitchen. She hadn't made it to the grocery. Hadn't bothered with dinner. But she had brought with her from Chicago the one thing that might get her through the night.

Standing on her tiptoes, she reached into the cabinet above the refrigerator and pulled out the bottle. At the sink, she found the drinking glass she'd turned upside down earlier, and she carried both to the table. Sitting, she broke the seal and poured.

She knew drinking straight vodka at three o'clock in the morning was not the answer to her problems. In fact, Marty was smart enough to know that alcohol, no matter how carefully or therapeutically administered, would only make everything worse. Just ask her father, who'd been a functioning alcoholic—and drank himself to an early grave.

If only she could turn off her mind . . .

"Here's to you, Dad." Marty drank the vodka straight down. She was in the process of pouring another when the wall phone trilled loud enough to make her jump. The first thought that popped into her mind was that one of her cop buddies from Chicago had been hurt on the job. Nothing good ever came from middle-of-the-night calls.

She snatched up the phone on the second ring. "Hogan," she snapped.

No response came, but she heard the hiss of an open line. Holding the phone snug against her ear, she listened, certain the caller was still there. She could hear the faint whisper of his breathing and some background noise she couldn't identify.

"Is someone there?"

The instant the words were out, Marty knew they were a mistake. It had been a while since she'd received a late-night call from her underground fan club. Had some fruit-cake tracked her all the way from Chicago to Caprock Canyon? Or had some local passerby seen her lights on and decided to call the infamous Marty Hogan for a little late-night entertainment?

"Wrong number, asshole." Shaking her head in disgust,

Marty hung up with a tad too much force and went back to her vodka, the tumult of her thoughts, and the incessant cry of the midnight wind.

*"Watch this."*

"Holy crap! She freaking *tased* him, man. He's goin' down!"

Marty stood in the hall between the reception area and the break room of the police station and tried not to panic. She couldn't believe her soon-to-be coworkers had recorded the worst moment of her life and were now watching it as if it were some raunchy and hilarious sitcom.

Break out the popcorn, everyone. Now showing, *Jackass Meets COPS*, starring the one and only Marty Hogan.

How the hell was she supposed to handle this?

*"Powee!"*

Someone hooted like the Hollywood version of an Indian on some hokey late-night Western. "Look at that! She knocked that dumb ass for loop, didn't she?"

"Hell of a right hook on her, that's for sure."

"She ain't that big. Look. The poor idiot's trying to defend himself. Bam! He gets a right in the chin for his trouble."

"I read somewhere that she broke her hand. Crazy bitch."

"Don't mess with frickin' Hogan, man. She'll Rodney King your ass." This followed by a whistle.

"I heard she put him in the hospital."

"Fucker deserved it. Killed a little kid."

The break room atmosphere sobered at the mention of the real victim, but within seconds the colorful commentary resumed. "Look at her go! She's wailing away on that guy like freakin' Mike Tyson!"

"Blammo! Pow! Duck, you dipshit! Oh, you can't. Your hands are cuffed."

Another round of raucous laughter erupted.

Backing more deeply into the hall, Marty stood there with her back against the wall and tried to decide the best course of action. An experienced police officer herself, she knew many cops tended to be politically incorrect with regard to humor. They saw too much, too often, and they became immune to the things that would send your everyday Joe Blow running to his mommy.

Marty herself had partaken in her fair share of bad behavior. But to hear coworkers she had yet to meet hooting it up at her expense was like a sucker punch to the solar plexus. They were ridiculing her. Laughing at her. Making fun of her when she'd been at her lowest, caught up in a moment that would haunt her the rest of her life.

She couldn't let this stand. Unless she wanted to spend her tenure here in Caprock Canyon on the receiving end of cruel comments and back-room jokes, Marty was going to have to put a stop to this before things got to that point.

She knew how to look out for herself; she'd done so many times over the years, facing down far worse characters than these milk-fed farm boys. Still, the thought of confronting three men she didn't know—cops she would soon be working with—thoroughly unnerved her. But what was the alternative? Sit back and let them ruin any chance of peace she might find here?

Her heart pounded like a piston in her chest as she started toward the break room. Acid churned in her stomach when she stepped inside. Three sets of male eyes swung around to face her, widening as if she were some South Side Uzi-toting gangsta. For the span of several seconds no one moved. No one spoke. Except for the hard pound of her heart, you could have heard a pin drop.

Marty's legs shook as she crossed to the coffee station, but her hand was steady as she reached for the carafe and poured. Behind her, she sensed her counterparts signing messages to one another, trying to figure out how to handle their gargantuan faux pas. Six months ago she would have been pissed off, but mildly amused, and would have shot off some remark that might have cut just as deep.

This afternoon she felt humiliated and quietly enraged, with no outlet for either emotion.

"You must be Officer Hogan."

She forced herself to take a sip of coffee before turning to face the man with the tenor voice. He looked end-of-shift worn, still wearing the navy departmental uniform. She guessed him to be twenty-five years old. Muscle just starting to turn to fat. She guessed he was married. Too well fed to be single. He was just starting his life. Maybe a kid on the way or a little one at home. His wife wore the pants. A fact he tried hard to hide from his cop pals, but never quite managed.

Marty looked into his eyes and took another sip of coffee. "You should be a detective." She tapped the name tag pinned to her breast. "Your powers of deduction are pretty goddamn amazing."

He held on to his smile, but some of the I-wasn't-part-of-that facade slipped. "Hey, I'm just trying to be friendly."

"Yeah, that was some real friendly commentary I heard when I walked in. I especially liked the part about crazy bitch. Was that you?"

"No."

"You sure about that?"

"We were just goofing off. No harm done, okay?"

Marty was an expert on harm. She knew she should let this go. But her temper was like a wild beast, teased by a cruel master and straining against its chains. She let her eyes skim the other men, both of whom were watching the exchange with unconcealed anticipation. Everyone loved a good knock-down drag-out, especially a bunch of bored cops. "Anyone got the balls to fess up to the crazy bitch line?"

"Come on, we were just kidding around."

Marty smiled, praying her lips didn't tremble. "Don't

worry. I promise not to use my right hook. Look, I don't even have my Taser on me."

A buff young officer put his hands on his hips. "It was me. But like Dugan said, we were just messing around."

She looked at his name tag. Jett. "Next time you have something you want to say to me, *Jett*, you can say it to my face." She scanned the other men. "That goes for all of you."

Jett's cheeks reddened. His eyes flicked to the other men and Marty knew this was no longer about her; it had suddenly become a matter of pride. Jett's pride. And she knew he wouldn't back down in front of his cohorts. "Look, I said I was sorry."

"No, you didn't."

His cheek twitched. "We tried to apologize. If you're not going to accept that, fine. But we don't need you walking in here like you're some kind of pseudo-celebrity and breaking our balls."

"I didn't realize anyone in this room *had* any balls."

Smiles fell. Booted feet shuffled. Tension sucked the air out of the room, like in the seconds before an explosion. A thin man with a pasty complexion, pockmarks and blue black hair stepped forward. His name tag told her he was Smitty. "You think that little video clip and your big city credentials give you license to strut in here and cut us down?" He motioned toward the small television where the worst moment of her life had been played out just minutes before. "Let me tell you. It makes me sick to watch it. Makes me ashamed to be a cop."

Marty looked him up and down. "Makes me ashamed you're a cop, too."

If she was good at anything, it was finding people's hot buttons and pushing them. Smitty hadn't been too hard to figure out. One-up him in front of his cop buddies and he was frothing at the mouth. She knew the type. Hell, she'd *been* the type once upon a time.

Marty could feel her temper winding up, a jet engine

barreling down the runway, seconds before takeoff. In the eight years she'd been a cop—and aside from *The Incident* six months ago—she'd never gotten into a physical confrontation with a fellow officer. But this snot-nosed, wet-behind-the-ears little shit didn't realize he was walking a minefield.

"You know what you are?" he snarled. "You're a fucking disgrace. The only reason you're not in jail right now is because you're a woman."

Marty didn't defend herself. She'd tried too many times and it never worked. Instead, she stood there and watched the sweat bead on his forehead, and she found herself wishing he'd take a shot at her so she could punch him between the eyes.

"You *tased* the guy," he said. "You cuffed him. When he was down you beat the shit out of him. Don't walk in here like you're some kind of high and mighty robocop and—"

Marty wasn't sure who moved first, but the next thing she knew she had her forearm against his chest and was shoving him against the wall. She gave him points for not fighting back. For not doing what he wanted to do and punch her lights out. Had she been in his shoes, she probably would have. He might be a smart-assed idiot, but his mother had taught him well.

"You weren't there," she snarled. "You don't know what went down."

"You think you're the only cop who ever had to face something tough?" He shoved her back hard enough to make her stumble. "Get over yourself."

Vaguely, Marty was aware of another officer putting his hand on her shoulder. "Come on, Hogan. We were just goofing. Let it go."

But it was too late. The fury that had been boiling inside her for so many months gripped her with such ferocity that for a moment her vision went black and white, tunneling on the other man's face. She could feel her heart rate jacking into the red zone. Every muscle in her body going rock hard. Adrenaline running like acid through her veins.

She lunged at him. The hand that had been placed so gently on her shoulder scraped down her back. Her mind's eye blinded her with images from that day. The sight of the girl lying in a pool of blood on the backseat of the car. The blowback from a horrific head wound sprayed on the window like red paint. Marty had forgotten who she was and went after the killer with everything she had. Now she was taking that pent-up rage out on this bozo and would probably pay another hefty price.

At the moment, she didn't care.

*"Hogan!"*

Clay Settlemeyer's voice cut through the fog of rage like a gunshot. Marty had drawn back to hit Smitty. The realization of what she was about to do jolted her, and she froze. Abruptly, she was aware of strong hands digging into her arms, pulling her back. A soft male voice telling her to take it easy. Let it go. Cool down.

Glancing over, she realized one of the other officers had grasped her arm and was hauling her back. He talked to her as if she were some nutcase wrapped in a straitjacket about to hurl herself off a bridge.

It wasn't too far from the truth.

"In my office." Settlemeyer stepped between her and Smitty and motioned angrily toward the door. *"Now!"*

Marty shook off hands that were reluctant to release her and struggled to pull herself together. She could hear her breaths rushing from between clenched teeth. Her pulse hammered like fists inside her head and against her ribs. Without looking at either man, she brushed past them and strode into the office.

"Sit the hell down."

She turned to see Settlemeyer and Smitty enter the room. It didn't elude her that both men watched her the way an animal trainer might watch a lion that had just mauled its handler.

She was too keyed up to sit; her heart rate was still in the red zone. But one look at the chief's face and she knew it wasn't a request.

Taking the farthest chair, she fixed her eyes on the floor at her feet. Next to her, Smitty plopped into the chair and proceeded to squirm like a recalcitrant teenager in the throes of being grounded.

The chief yanked out his chair and settled behind his desk. "Let me start by telling both of you you're an inch away from getting your walking papers."

Smitty pointed at her. "She waltzed in like some kind of hot shot and shoved me!"

"This isn't grade school and you're not a sixth grader!" the chief shouted, one-upping him in the decibel department. "You're a cop. Act accordingly." He shot a dark look at Marty. "Both of you."

Marty returned her gaze to the floor. Ashamed. Humiliated. Still pissed.

"Hogan, what happened?"

She raised her head and met Settlemeyer's gaze, wondering why he'd decided to get her version first instead of one of his own officers. "I walked in to start my shift and your crew was camped out in the break room." The rise of fury came so quickly, she lost her breath and fell silent.

Settlemeyer waited.

A breath shuddered out of her. Grinding her teeth, she forced out the words. "They were watching the video. The clip of what happened in Chicago. Making all sorts of inappropriate comments about me."

Settlemeyer sighed and turned his attention to Smitty. "That true?"

Smitty glanced out the window, then back to his boss. "Well, yeah."

"How did you think that was going to go over with Hogan? Or me?"

Smitty gave her a scathing look. "She was frickin' early. We didn't think—"

"That's my point, you didn't think. It's not the first time." Sitting back in his chair, Settlemeyer shook his head. "Which Einstein brought in the tape?"

Smitty tightened his lips.

The chief came forward in his chair. "Spit it out or you're fired."

"Dugan." Smitty met his boss's steely gaze. "Look, it was a joke. We didn't mean anything."

"You see anyone laughing?"

Dropping his gaze to his feet, he shook his head.

"Who threw the first punch?" the chief asked.

"She did," Smitty spat.

Settlemeyer pointed at Marty, and she braced. "Your probationary period just went from thirty to ninety days, Hogan. You so much as look at one of my officers like you want to hit them and you're out of here. You can go back to Chicago and take your bad attitude with you. You got that?"

"I got it," she said between gritted teeth.

"Right answer." Rising, he walked to the door and swung it open. "Get the hell out of my office before I change my mind and fire both of you."

Marty rose, unduly relieved she still had a job. If she'd been in his shoes, she probably would have ended it right then and there. Especially considering this was her first day on the job.

She waited until Smitty left, then started for the door. Settlemeyer braced his arm in front of her, blocking her way. "Not you."

Surprised, she stopped and looked up at him. In the back of her mind she wondered if he'd changed his mind, if he was going to fire her after all. "Why not?"

"You're riding with me today. Get your gear and meet me in the cruiser. You've got ten minutes."

# THREE

*Marty wasn't sure of a whole hell of a lot these days.* One thing she was utterly certain of at the moment was that she did not want to ride with her boss.

"You a small or a medium?" Jo Nell's chicken-scratch voice tugged her from her thoughts.

"Small."

"Thought so." The woman thrust a plastic-wrapped uniform at her. "Locker room's there." She gestured toward a door at the end of the hall, her arthritic finger bending slightly to the right. "Seein' how we don't have no female cops on the force, guess we got us a unisex locker room now." She leaned forward and spoke in a conspiratorial voice. "If I was you, I'd use a shower stall."

Nodding, Marty started toward the locker room, hoping she'd find it empty.

No such luck.

Steam swirled and the sound of running water filled the air when she pushed open the door, telling her one of the other cops was using the shower. If the chief wasn't waiting for her outside, she would have turned around and left. But he was, so she didn't have a choice but to get dressed pronto.

A dozen beat-up lockers lined the tiled wall to her right. A wooden bench that was bolted to the floor ran parallel with the lockers. Two shower stalls—one of which was in use—two urinals and a toilet stall comprised the opposite wall. At the far end of the room, a sink, mirror and soap dispenser crowded into a too-small space.

Her old precinct in Chicago had separate facilities for male and female officers, so the unisex locker room had never been an issue. It was definitely an issue now. Not that Marty was unduly modest; she wasn't. But she would never put herself in a vulnerable position. That included dressing around her fellow cops. Especially the bozos who'd been hooting it up at her expense.

Hefting the new uniform, she stepped into the single vacant shower, closed the door behind her and slipped into the clothes in record time. Not a great fit; Marty had dropped a good fifteen pounds since being fired. Along with the pounds, she'd lost what few curves she'd had, leaving her with narrow hips, a skinny waist and size A bra cups.

She was still tucking her shirt into her uniform slacks when she yanked open the shower door and stepped out. Only then did she notice the running water in the stall next to her had gone silent. Before she could get out of there, the shower door swung open, and Smitty stood naked and dripping in front of her.

Marty was twenty-nine years old; she'd seen naked men before. She'd had two serious relationships and a single, loveless affair in her lifetime. She'd dealt with more than one drunken suspect who'd thought it might be funny to take off his clothes and run from the cops.

But seeing a fellow officer—a coworker and total stranger—naked and staring at her with open hostility in his eyes was something else entirely. Marty would have preferred another verbal confrontation. At least she would have known how to respond.

Unnerved, she averted her gaze and headed toward the door. Smitty made no move to get out of her way or cover himself as she passed. Out of the corner of her eye, she saw the pink flash of his tongue as it flicked between his lips. She heard whispered words that could have been "suck this, bitch." But her heart was beating so hard and fast she couldn't be sure.

Six months ago she would have shot back something about shrinkage or maybe she would have just pointed and smirked. Today, the disrespect, the disdain, tore down her defenses. Marty didn't respond. She didn't look at him. And she didn't get too close as she headed toward the exit.

She hit the locker room door with both hands. Jo Nell looked up from her desk and muttered something about paperwork. But Marty didn't stop.

She shoved the front door and sent it flying. Outside the bright sunlight hit her eyes like a supernova. Though it was barely over eighty degrees, she broke a sweat beneath her uniform. A nerve sweat that slicked her neck and back like ice water. She sucked in a breath, only to have her lungs seize. She could feel herself shaking inside and out. Rage and what she could only identify as fear pulled her in different directions.

"Son of a bitch," she panted. "Son of a bitch."

Willing her heart to slow, she set her hand against the brick and leaned. Two breaths and her head began to clear. Her pulse leveled out. If only she could . . .

"Hogan."

She glanced up to find her new boss standing a few feet away, his expression perplexed and concerned, and all she could think was *shit, shit, shit.* Busted.

"You okay?" he asked.

"I'm fine," she muttered.

"I can tell by the way you're holding on to that wall."

"I said I'm fine." As if to prove her point, she removed her hand from the brick and straightened.

"You want to sit down for a minute?"

"No. I just . . . need to work." She gave herself points for holding his gaze.

Frowning the way a father might frown at a child who'd just lied to him, he gestured toward the white Explorer parked curbside. "In that case, let's go."

*Clay had seen a lot of different forms of emotional stress* in his years as a cop and MP. He'd always believed he was adept at recognizing the signs, no matter how well hidden by the individual. Not the case with Marty Hogan. She'd fooled him during the initial phone interview, answering all of his questions with the skill of a master interrogator herself. She'd almost fooled him again during their first meet.

But when she'd walked out of the police station a moment ago, when her guard was down, he'd caught his first glimpse of the troubled woman beneath that tough facade. Clay hadn't liked what he'd seen. In the few moments she'd thought she was alone and unobserved, he'd seen just how close she was to the edge. He'd realized just how precipitous and slippery the slope. And he knew she was going to be a problem.

He wanted to believe he'd missed the signs because of her qualifications or because she'd come with a personal recommendation. Or maybe because he thought she deserved a second chance. But deep inside Clay knew those weren't the only reasons he'd taken her on, and he wasn't the least bit proud of his other, less-than-noble motives. Motives that had little to do with her marksmanship skills or SWAT training or big city experience—and everything to do with those big, vulnerable eyes and the way that uniform swept over a body he had absolutely no business noticing. The truth of the matter was he was willing to look the other way because she was a woman. Because she was attractive. Because that facade of tough she wielded with such proficiency appealed to him on a level he wasn't prepared to ignore.

"You jackass," he muttered to himself as he opened the driver's-side door and slid behind the wheel.

Annoyed with himself, Clay started the engine. He was keenly aware of Marty sliding onto the seat next to him and cast her a sideways glance as he put the Explorer in gear and pulled onto the street.

She sat quietly, looking out the passenger window. Though she showed no outward signs, the tension came off of her in waves. He'd come down on her pretty hard—and rightfully so—but she'd seemed to take the dressing-down in stride. That made him wonder if something else had happened between the time he'd ordered her from his office and the time she'd gone to the locker room to dress. Clay didn't like the answers that popped into his head. Smitty liked to shower after his shift. Had the two partaken in another altercation?

"You want to tell me what happened in there?" he began.

She shot him a startled look, but quickly masked it. "What do you mean?"

"Don't play dumb, Hogan. I saw the look on your face when you walked out."

She dropped her gaze a little too quickly. "Nothing happened."

"You sure about that?"

"I'm sure."

Clay didn't believe her, but didn't push the issue. She didn't know the dynamics of the department. The new kid on the block, she didn't want to earn the reputation of being a stool pigeon, running to the chief every time one of the other officers offended her. Clay understood that. But this wasn't the first problem he'd had with Smitty.

Harlan "Smitty" Smith had been with the Caprock Canyon PD for nearly six years. Early on, Clay had believed the man was a good cop. But Smitty had a mouth on him. As Clay grew to know him, he soon realized his senior officer had a temper—and a streak of mean in him as long as the Texas state line. Not a good combination for a small town cop. Clay had talked to him about it, and Smitty had assured him he'd keep his temper in check.

But an incident the year before had given Clay reason to doubt his word. Smitty had stopped a young female driver on a back road in the dead of night for a faulty taillight. According to his report, Smitty smelled alcohol on her breath when he'd asked for her driver's license and registration. In turn, he'd asked her to step out of the car and submit to a field sobriety test. That was where his report and her account of the incident went in opposite directions.

According to Smitty, the driver had become belligerent and refused the test. When he detained her and attempted to place her under arrest, she'd fought him. An altercation ensued, and Smitty was forced to subdue the subject for her safety and for his. She'd sustained a bruised knee and an abrasion on her forehead in the scuffle.

That was the story he'd told, anyway.

The young woman told a very different one. She claimed Smitty had pulled her over, kicked out the taillight, then ordered her from the car. When she exited the vehicle, she claimed he'd cuffed her and proceeded to grope and touch her inappropriately. It was her word against his. Because Smitty had a spotless record at the time, Clay had believed his officer.

By the time the blood alcohol test was administered, there were no traces in her system. Clay had always assumed it was because so much time had elapsed. But a seed of doubt had been planted in his head. Doubt that, over the following months, made him remember other incidents in which Smitty had skated a thin line.

Now he wondered if his senior officer had mouthed off—or worse—to Marty. She was no hapless suspect and could hold her own as well as any man. Still, she was new to the department. She'd arrived with a dust storm of ignominy hanging over her head. She deserved a work environment that wasn't hostile. It was Clay's responsibility to make sure she got it.

He was going to have to have another talk with Smitty. Hell, he was going to have to talk to Hogan, too. The last thing he needed was discord among his officers. Or a rogue cop running around.

"If you have any problems with Smitty, I want to know about it," he said.

Questions rose in her eyes, but she didn't voice them. "Okay."

They rode in silence for several minutes. Clay took her through the tiny downtown district, past the historic courthouse, over the railroad tracks at the edge of town, and left the city limits. As they passed lake-flat land covered with miles and miles of yellow prairie grass, Marty took in the scenery with all the enthusiasm of a bored teenager.

"So, are you taking me out here to rake me over the coals about what happened back there or are you just going to shoot me and get it over with?" she asked after a moment.

Clay couldn't help it; he smiled. "Since I already raked you over the coals, I thought I'd ask you if you want to talk about it."

She lifted a shoulder, let it drop. "I'd rather let it go if you don't mind."

"You talking to anyone?"

She swung her surprised gaze to his. "You mean a shrink?"

"Call it what you like. Shrink. Therapist. Psychiatrist. Psychologist. Pastor. Anyone but some imaginary friend."

"I'm not nuts."

"Nobody said you were nuts."

"Smitty did."

He frowned. "Look, you've been through a traumatic ordeal."

"I'm handling—"

He cut her off. "Nobody handles seeing a kid's brains blown out."

She turned back to the window. "I guess you did your homework."

"I read the reports." Clay said the words gently, but he could feel the walls going up around her. The tension leaking out, filling the spaces between them. "Sometimes stress takes on forms that we don't recognize or understand. Depression. Anger. Isolation. If you need to talk to someone—"

"With all due respect, Chief, I've had just about all the psychoanalyzing I can take. Work is the only therapy I need right now."

"Just trying to figure out where your head is."

"My head is right here."

He'd been hoping she would be more open, more receptive to talking about what had happened in Chicago. Didn't she realize he couldn't turn her loose on the public if he couldn't trust her state of mind? Talking with her was the only way for him to get to know her. It was the fastest way for him to figure out if hiring her was a mistake. Since she wasn't cooperating, he would have no choice but to take appropriate action.

*They ate burgers at the Dairy Dream and were back on* patrol by 6 P.M. Marty hadn't spoken since they'd rounded up several head of Dick Crowley's livestock that had escaped their pasture. She hadn't complained, but Clay could tell she hadn't liked it. That was fine with him. If she couldn't hack rural police work, she could go back to Chicago.

But he had to admit, he liked her. She had a quick wit and a relatively healthy sense of humor that leaned toward the dry. More than once he'd found himself watching her. He was glad he'd taken the time to ride with Marty and gotten to know her a little bit. But he'd resolved that this would be the last time. He didn't like the way he was reacting to her. Better for everyone involved if he kept his distance.

At dusk he headed south on the farm-to-market road.

"Where are we going?" she asked, as they passed by the city limit sign.

"I thought I'd show you the canyon. The places where folks are most likely to speed. We'll drive by a couple of problem areas."

"What do people do around here, anyway?"

"Ranching and farming are the mainstays. Not much manufacturing or white collar here. We've got the farm store. The John Deere dealership off the main highway. There's a feedlot fifteen miles to the south."

"Feedlot? That's not a restaurant, is it?"

"It's where cows are fattened up for market. You don't want to be downwind."

"Gotcha."

"There's a grain elevator between here and there." He shrugged. "Pretty exciting stuff."

"Crime rate?"

"Nil. The occasional DUI or bar fight. Those are about the only incidents that occur on a regular basis." He glanced at her, but she was already looking out the window, ignoring him. "We've got some badass cows in this county, though. You ever get into a tussle with a cow?"

She turned to him and blinked. Then her lips curved.

"Not since that biker chick on the Fifty-seventh Street Beach."

She had a pretty mouth. Very white teeth. This time, the smile reached all the way to her eyes, and for an instant, Clay couldn't look away.

"I'm betting she lost," he said thickly.

"She did."

"Speaking of cows, have you ever been to a rodeo?"

"Do biker bars count?"

Now it was his turn to smile. "There's one at the sheriff's posse arena this weekend, if you're curious. Might be a good way for you to get out and meet some people. Get a feel for the community."

She didn't reply, and he wondered if she already had plans. If maybe she was going to fly back to Chicago. If maybe she had a boyfriend there . . .

Before he could order himself to stop, Jo Nell's voice crackled over the police radio. "Chief, you there?"

Recognizing his dispatcher's tone, he quickly reached for the mike. "I'm here."

"I just got a call from Nola Miles a minute ago. We got a disturbance again over at Foley's Bar."

Annoyance swept through Clay. Foley's Bar was Caprock Canyon's main drinking establishment and a magnet for thirsty troublemakers countywide. "What kind of disturbance?"

"How do I know? Some kind of ruckus. Nola was screamin' her head off and didn't give too many details."

"I'm on the way."

Racking the mike, he made a U-turn in the middle of Cactus Street and hit the gas.

"Trouble?" Hogan asked.

Clay didn't miss the anticipation that jumped into her eyes. "Bar fight."

She arched a brow. "Really?"

"Don't get too excited, Hogan. You're going to sit this one out."

"Good to know you have such faith in my policing skills, Chief."

Clay shot her a sideways glance and frowned.

"So, do you get many calls like this one?"

"We average a call a week from Nola, the bar owner. Everything from fights to fires to bathroom drug deals and prostitution."

"Wow, I'm impressed."

"Foley's Bar is pretty much one-stop shopping. You get that when you mix booze, boredom and discontent."

"I'm starting to feel right at home."

Clay cut the conversation short when he turned into the gravel parking lot of the bar in question. Pickup trucks of every shape and size, a single car of indistinguishable origin and a row of a dozen or more chrome-laden Harley-Davidson motorcycles formed a haphazard line outside the front door. It was one of only a handful of drinking establishments in Deaf Smith County. The music and booze and lure of the occasional female drew cowboys, bikers, wayward teens and the unwary traveler from miles away.

Gravel spewed as he slid to a stop next to a pickup truck where four scruffy Australian shepherds stood erect, their combined attention focused on the front door. Clay and Marty slid from the Explorer simultaneously. Two pickup trucks down, a man in a black leather vest and suede chaps had fallen to his hands and knees and spewed vomit onto the gravel.

"Pretty glamorous place you got here, Chief." Marty stepped around the downed man, giving him a good bit of room. "I'll bet you bring all the girls here."

"You think the parking lot is nice, just wait till you see the inside."

"I can hardly wait."

Walking into Foley's Bar and Grill was like entering a cave replete with intoxicated cavemen, wild monkeys and the occasional cavewoman. Clay paused just inside the front door and gave his eyes a moment to adjust to the dim light and the onslaught of stimuli to his senses. From speakers the size of refrigerators mounted above the bar, Eric Clapton belted out a song about an illicit narcotic. The bass drums rattled glasses and bottles with the violence of a small earthquake. The odors of cigarette smoke, hard liquor and spilled beer mingled with the darker scents of unwashed bodies and marijuana.

Clay didn't have to ask where the problem was. A crowd had gathered between the two pool tables at the back of the room, all eyes on some commotion just inside the wall of bodies. A couple of dozen men wearing everything from cowboy hats to black leather hooted and cheered and shouted the occasional obscenity. It didn't take a rocket scientist to figure out what had them so excited.

"Catfight," Clay muttered.

"Still want me to sit this one out?"

"Yeah, I do." He cut her a hard look to let her know he wasn't kidding. He knew some of these people. Knew how to handle them to keep the situation from escalating. "Call Jo Nell," he said. "Tell her to get Jett out here pronto."

Marty didn't look happy about being relegated to the sidelines, but she reached for her mike and relayed his request. As they started toward the crowd, he saw her slip into cop mode. Eyes hard and watchful, her hand resting easily on her expandable baton, she scanned the room, an occasional glance over her shoulder. A cop through and through. He wasn't exactly sure why, but he felt confident he could count on her to watch his back.

"Fucking *bitch*!"

A series of earsplitting shrieks ripe with expletives exploded from a female mouth somewhere in the melee.

"Police. Step aside." Clay fought through the throng of

people, toward the nucleus of the fight. "Come on, folks. Let me through."

He heard Marty behind him, echoing his words, stronger than he would have liked, but backing him up the way he'd asked. "Police! Move it! Now!"

Two dozen undulating bodies crowded into the small space between the pool tables. Clay pushed forward. Marty brought up the rear. So far so good.

A man as wide as a barn stepped aside, and Clay caught his first glimpse of the fracas. Pale flesh and black leather and long strands of blond hair clutched in a fist. Two women grappled as if in fast motion on the stained linoleum floor, in a blur of fists and hair and bare flesh.

"Get off me!" one of the women screamed. "Get the fuck off me!"

Clay didn't wait to hear more; there was no way he could wait for backup. He knew from experience that this was the kind of situation that could escalate quickly. He had to defuse things before everyone in the place started punching everyone else.

Bending, he caught a skin-and-bones brunette beneath the arms and attempted to haul her back. "Police. Let's go."

She snaked around, bared tobacco-stained teeth and snarled like a dog. "Get your hands off me!"

"Not in this lifetime."

She twisted her head to one side. Clay jerked his hand away just in time to avoid what would have been a nasty bite. "Have it your way, sunshine," he growled. "You're under arrest."

The cuffs were midway from his belt when someone bumped him from behind. Clay didn't know if the shove was on purpose or by accident, but it was hard enough to send him to his hands and knees. The brunette scuttled away. Quickly, he glanced over his shoulder to see a bald man the size of a woolly mammoth start toward him. Clay recognized him; he'd seen him before in this very bar, as a matter of fact. Had a weird name for such a big oaf. Timmy or something. And Clay knew from experience that, despite his size, Timmy was relatively harmless. But this time he looked pissed.

Clay got his legs under him, scrambled to his feet. "You need to calm down," he warned.

"I ain't gonna do nothing," the man said. "Just don't want you getting rough with my woman."

The way he was coming toward him, Clay wasn't so sure of Timmy's claim. Just to be safe, he set his hand on his baton. "Back off now."

The flash of blue uniform seemed to come out of nowhere. He saw lips peeled back in a snarl. Determination etched into a pale face. The black steel of a baton being snapped to its full, effective length. Marty, he realized. And all he could think was that Timmy had just bitten off more than he could chew.

# FOUR

*"Drop the weapon!"*

"Huh?"

As if watching a scene from some second-rate action flick, Clay saw Marty slam the baton down between the man's shoulder blades. Her voice rose above the bawdy shouts as she ordered him to put his hands behind his back.

Evidently, Timmy had other ideas.

An animalistic howl erupted from his throat as he spun. Hogan, a foot shorter and a hundred pounds lighter, dropped into a street fighter's stance. To Clay, she looked like a house cat about to square off against a rogue pit bull bent on having her for lunch.

"That hurt, you bitch cop!"

"Drop the weapon! Do it now!"

Hit-or-miss teeth clenched in an alcohol-induced rage, the man lunged at her.

Dancing back a few steps, Hogan swung the baton a second time. Barry Bonds slamming in a home run. The weapon connected with the man's shoulder, so hard Clay heard the slap of steel against flesh and muscle.

It wasn't enough to stop Timmy.

"Get down on the floor!" Hogan shouted. "*Now!*"

It was as if Clay were stuck in slow motion. The crowd's attention had shifted from the fighting women to the female cop about to face off with a man twice her size. Clay couldn't move fast enough to stop any of it. Snapping his own baton to its full length, he lunged into the crowd and began pushing his way toward them.

Through the throng of bodies, Clay saw the man swing at Marty. Not the jab of some staggering drunk. But a bone-crunching, roundhouse blow that could have launched even the biggest man to kingdom come. Clay didn't want to think about what it might do to a 110-pound scrap of a woman. Knock her head off, maybe.

But Marty seemed prepared and ducked right with the prowess of a boxer. Before the man could line up for another shot, she pulled her pepper spray canister from her belt and blasted the man's face with capsicum acid.

"Get on the ground now! Put your hands behind your back!" She didn't wait for him to comply, and drew back the baton a third time.

Clay used his shoulder to get through the final line of bystanders separating them. From ten feet away he saw what was going to happen next, and knew he couldn't get there in time to stop it.

The brunette came at Marty from behind, screaming as if she were on fire. Marty raised the canister and sprayed the woman in the face. Screeching like a set of bad brakes, the woman went to her knees, clawing at her face.

"Hogan!" Clay yelled a warning.

But he was too late. She spun back to Timmy, but the man was already too close and lined up for another punch. His fist shot out like iron from a cannon. Marty raised the canister and sprayed, but she wasn't fast enough. The stream of capsicum acid hit Timmy between the eyes right about the same time his fist connected with her cheek. The impact snapped her head back. She reeled backward. Her legs tangled. She hit the floor hard on her back and lay still.

"Hogan!"

Clay broke through the crowd. Fury infused his body as he rushed toward her. The knowledge that the situation was now officially out of control rushed his mind. Before he even realized what he was going to do, he found his revolver in his hand, leveled at the man.

"Get down on the ground!" he shouted. "Do it now!"

A few feet away the man clawed at his eyes and bellowed a curse. "It burns!"

When the man didn't move fast enough, Clay shoved him to the floor. Once he was down, he quickly snapped the cuffs on wrists the size of tree trunks, then turned to help Marty.

He gave her points for getting to her feet. She stood next to the bar, head down, leaning heavily against it. Nola Miles, the bar owner, gripped her biceps. One look, and Clay knew she'd been clobbered a good one. A cut stood out stark and red on her cheekbone. Her left eye was already beginning to swell. It would be black by the time they got back to the station.

Damn it.

"Hogan," he said, surprised to find he was still out of breath. "You okay?"

"As soon as I find my eyeballs, I'll be just fine," she said.

Even Nola, who was as hard and dry as the Texas plain, looked shaken. "He hit her hard, Chief. She's going to have one hell of a shiner."

"Thanks for pointing that out." Marty gestured toward the cuffed man. "He's got a weapon."

Clay cocked his head. "A gun? Knife?"

"I'm not sure. But I saw it. In his waistband at the small of his back. He reached for it."

"I ain't got no fuckin' gun," the man growled.

Frowning, Clay knelt beside the man and yanked the hem of his shirt from his pants. "Where is it, Slick?"

"I ain't got nothin'!" he spat. "Get this shit out of my eyes! It burns!"

Clay felt around the waistband, pulled out a wallet and checked the driver's license. "Timothy Burris. Tucumcari."

"It ain't against the law to be me, is it?"

"Only if you hit a cop or have a gun on you without a conceal carry license."

"I ain't got no gun."

Roughly, the chief turned him over, checked the front of his pants, his pant legs, even his shoes and socks. "You got any warrants, Timmy?"

"I ain't got nothin'." He glared at Marty. "She's lyin', man."

Clay made eye contact with Marty, pleased that she held his gaze. But the initial fingers of doubt walked down his spine. Rising, he approached the bar owner. "You know that guy?"

"Been in before. Comes in every so often with some biker types from New Mexico. Usually keeps to hisself. Don't know what got into him today."

"I think it's called alcohol."

The bartender chortled.

Raising his head, the man glared at Marty. "She's what got into me. Hit me with that damn stick."

Clay ignored him. "He won't be back for a while."

"We ain't going to miss him none."

Clay turned to Marty, caught a glimpse of the cut on her cheek and had to bank the rise of protective instinct. She was a cop. He had to keep that in mind. But the man had hit her hard. Broke the skin open on her cheek. She would, indeed, have a black eye. "I'm taking you to the clinic."

"I don't need to go to the clinic."

"Yeah, I can tell by the way your eyes are crossed." He

was about to hit the mike clipped to the lapel of his jacket to check on backup when he spotted Jett coming through the front door.

Clay did a quick scan of the place. The skinny brunette was nowhere in sight. Probably halfway to the New Mexico state line by now. Some of the bystanders had decided now was a good time to leave. The rest had lined up at the bar for another round. A catfight and an arrest all in a single day were about all the excitement they could hope for.

In any case, the situation was under control. He supposed he could type up his report when he got back to the station.

Now all he had to do was deal with Hogan.

*"The good news is you're not going to need stitches. The* bad news is you're going to have one hell of a black eye."

"That's what everyone keeps saying." Marty sat on the gurney in the exam room of the Caprock Canyon Medical Clinic and tried not to fidget. She'd never liked doctors, especially when she was a patient. But Clay had ignored her protests and brought her here anyway.

Doc Harrigan was almost interesting enough to make her change her point of view. He was ninety years old if he was a day, with wrinkled brown skin and long white hair he kept pulled into a neat ponytail at his nape. His brows were the color of a raven's wing and rode low over dark, intelligent eyes that made him look much younger.

Doc made a sound of annoyance, and it was clear he was more distressed by the notion of a male assaulting a female than a drunken hoodlum slugging a cop. "I hope the perpetrator is in jail."

"He is."

At the sound of Clay's voice, Marty glanced toward the door to see him leaning against the jamb with his arms folded, a toothpick jutting from the corner of his mouth.

He didn't look too happy to be here, either. Judging from the silent treatment she'd received on the drive over, she was probably going to get another lecture on the way back to the station.

The way her day was going, he might even fire her.

But she'd been *certain* she'd seen a weapon. When the suspect shoved Clay, his shirt rode up, revealing a dark object in his waistband.

So where the hell was the gun?

Clay's eyes were on the doc, but she could tell his attention was on her. "She going to be okay?"

"I butterflied the cut." He looked at Marty and smiled. "Advil or Tylenol for pain. Ice for the first twenty-four hours, then heat, if you need it."

She nodded. "I'll do that."

"Moral of the story, young lady: don't pick a fight with someone twice your size."

"I'll try to remember that."

The doc turned back to Clay. "Give her the rest of the day off, will you, Chief?"

"I don't think that'll be a problem." Clay's expression made her wonder if maybe he was going to give her the rest of her life off. "We all done here?"

"She's good to go."

Clay pointed at her. "Let's go, Hogan."

Marty slid from the gurney and thanked the doc on her way out. She was surprised to see that dusk had fallen. Even more surprised to realize she was only midway through her shift. She felt as if she'd pulled a double. Her head was beginning to pound. The left side of her face felt as if it were twice its normal size. One look at the chief's expression, and she had the sinking feeling things were going to get worse before they got better.

He didn't speak until he pulled onto the highway. "How's the eye?"

"It only hurts when I blink."

"Try not to blink." He glanced at her and frowned. "Did you really see a gun?"

She met his gaze evenly. "I saw him reach. I saw something in his waistband. I drew the logical assumption."

"You saw me search him, Hogan. There was nothing in his waistband."

"I saw something." But she could tell by the look in his eyes that he didn't believe her. That hurt more than she wanted it to. "Maybe he ditched it."

"It's possible. He would have had to do it fast. Kick it away or hand it off when we weren't looking, then have someone snatch it up for him."

"Maybe someone did."

He returned his attention to his driving. Marty didn't know what to say. But her heart was pounding. Her mind was racing. She'd come into this with a shadow of scandal hovering over her head. Combine the incident from this morning with her fellow officers and the fiasco at the bar, and she couldn't blame the chief for doubting her.

"What the hell were you thinking jumping on that guy, anyway? We had no backup. He had a hundred pounds on you. You thought he had a weapon."

"He had a weapon. I know you don't believe me, but I saw him reach."

"So why didn't he use it?"

"You know the type. Not a cop killer, but willing to go to great lengths to avoid jail time."

"So where's the gun?"

"He ditched it."

"No one saw it."

"Except the person he handed it off to." She grappled for patience that had long since worn thin. "How many times are we going to go over this?"

"As many as it takes." Clay pulled over.

Marty hadn't realized he was driving her home. They were parked outside the house she'd rented. She wasn't sure why, but it embarrassed her. The place was a dump. She was a mess. And her head was pounding like a damn jackhammer.

"You can type up your report tomorrow." Without speaking, he got out and crossed in front of the car. Realizing he was going to open her door for her, Marty reached for the handle and swung it open herself.

He stepped back and watched her exit the Explorer. She tried not to wince when her head felt as if it wanted to split open, but wasn't sure she succeeded.

"I'll walk you in."

"That's not necessary."

He made no move to go back into the Explorer. Feeling awkward, Marty started for the house, trying not to notice the cracks in the sidewalk or the little swirls of dust kicked up by the wind because there wasn't a stitch of grass in the yard. She walked slightly ahead, refusing to acknowledge the clumsiness of the moment, and tried not to look at the peeling paint or the grimy windows.

On the porch, she fumbled for her key, stuck it in the lock. The door opened to the same drab living room she'd left earlier in the day. In the back of her mind, she wondered if Clay was trying to work up the nerve to fire her.

She turned to face him. "I think I can take it from here."

He stood just inside the door, his expression inscrutable. Jesus, she was going to have to learn to read him. Not knowing what he was thinking could drive a girl nuts.

"If I didn't know better, I'd think you were trying to get rid of me," he said.

"I'm not. I just . . ." Her words trailed when he moved more deeply into the house. At first Marty didn't know what he was doing. Then she realized he was heading toward the kitchen. That he'd spotted the bottle of vodka on her kitchen table. And she knew he was going to ask her about it.

She trailed him as far as the kitchen doorway. He didn't

go directly to the bottle. Instead, he went to the back door and looked out at the bleak landscape beyond.

"I don't believe you about the gun," he said.

Six months ago Marty would have given him an argument he wouldn't soon forget. But because her confidence was at an all-time low, she suddenly felt uncertain. Had she seen a gun? Or had she merely caught a glimpse of a wallet or cell phone and let her imagination take care of the rest?

"You think I'm lying?"

"I think you're mistaken."

Because she wasn't sure which was worse, she didn't respond.

He wandered to the kitchen table and picked up the bottle of vodka, which was just over half-full. "You drink alone often?"

"No," she lied.

"You just think it makes a nice centerpiece?"

Marty's heart rate picked up. The throb in her temples joined in until her head felt like a gong.

Setting the bottle on the table, he walked to the sink and picked up the towel. He sniffed it, then crossed to the refrigerator and opened the door. "You might want to hit the grocery tonight. There's a Super Value out on the highway. Not too fancy, but they carry all the staples."

"Okay."

He reached into the freezer and withdrew a handful of ice cubes.

"I can do that," she said.

"I'm not finished talking to you. Might as well kill two birds with one stone."

She wondered if she was the bird he was going to kill.

He pulled out a chair. "Sit down."

Never taking her eyes from his, she sank into it.

"I'm faced with a real dilemma here, Hogan."

"Dilemma?"

"Do I send you packing? Call it quits? Send you back to Chicago where you'll be lucky to land a third-shift security job at the local storage facility? Or do I try to make this work and hope you don't screw up again?"

"With all due respect— "

"Let me finish." Taking his time, he carefully folded the towel around the ice. "If I choose the former, we both lose. I lose a person I feel could be a decent officer. You lose what is probably one of best offers you'll be able to get at the moment. If I decide to go with the latter, I'm not going to be able to do it alone."

"I'm a good cop." It galled her that she felt the need to say it. "I need this job."

He contemplated her with those intense gray eyes, then set the ice pack gently against her cheekbone. Though his voice was rough, his hands were gentle, his touch soft. "I guess the real question is whether or not you're willing to do your part."

"I'm willing."

His gaze held her with unflinching intensity. "You could have gotten yourself killed today. You reacted. You didn't think things through. You took a stupid risk."

"I thought I saw a gun."

"You don't sound very certain of that."

Marty didn't know what to say. At the time, she'd been so certain. Now she wasn't.

"You screwed up, Hogan. This isn't the first time, is it?"

Marty wanted to dispute his words, but couldn't. Screwing up seemed to be her middle name these days. The one thing she could swear to was that she was a good cop. Damn it, she was.

"I know what it's like to make a mistake," he said. "Believe me, I've made my share. Not just little ones either. I've made the kinds of mistakes that changed people's lives. Changed my own life." He paused. "Taken a life."

She stared at him, shocked.

"I'm not going to fire you, so you can stop looking at me that way."

Because she didn't know exactly how she was looking at him, she didn't move, didn't change her expression.

"But this is the way it's going to be." He pointed at her, a gesture she was beginning to recognize as his undivided attention. "I'm assigning you Rufus the Police Dog duty."

"What?"

"Like a lot of towns and cities, the Caprock Canyon PD has its share of PR problems. A lot of our citizens don't trust us. Some think all we do is hand out tickets and eat doughnuts. I've been working on a PR campaign to show them that's not the case."

"You might have noticed that I'm not very good at PR."

"Evidently you're not very good at patrolling, either."

Marty dropped her gaze, saw that her hands were knotting nervously in front of her and quickly stilled them.

"Rufus the Police Dog visits area schools. Elementary. Middle. High school. You'll be talking to kids about their personal safety, stranger danger, traffic safety, Internet dangers, drugs."

"I don't know anything about kids."

"You were one once, weren't you?" He crossed to the window above the sink, glanced out, then turned back to her. "I'd also like Rufus to visit some of the area clubs and businesses. For example, the 4-H Club, Boots and Spurs, I think, is the name of the chapter. The FFA. Rotary Club. Lions Club. Kiwanis. Some businesses might want us to speak to their employees about how to keep their homes and businesses safe. Business owners might want to know how to avoid employee theft. Private citizens will want to know how to prevent crime in their home. Highway safety. Phone scams."

She was still trying to absorb all of that, wondering how a town the size of Caprock Canyon could have so many clubs and organizations. On a deeper level, she wondered if he was trying to push her out the door. Or maybe he was just trying to save her cop's soul. "So where does the dog part come in? Do I have a Labrador as a sidekick?"

"Actually, there's a Rufus costume we keep in a locker."

A ripple of horror went through her. She'd seen cops in those kinds of uniforms before, and she'd laughed her ass off at them every time. "I guess I've officially arrived in hell," she said.

"I guess that depends on your perspective."

# FIVE

*They arrived in Chicago with the first deep freeze of the* season. Radimir had picked up his sister, Katja, at her row house apartment in Brooklyn. The trip from Brighton Beach had taken fourteen hours, and they'd driven straight through.

They rented a two-bedroom house with a basement in a decrepit neighborhood on Chicago's South Side. A place where no one would pay attention to the comings and go-ings of a young Russian couple. Katja went to the hardware store to buy the tools they would need for the job. Radimir met with the man from Kiev he'd spoken to before they left Brighton Beach. He was a distant cousin and cut them a deal on a 9-millimeter Beretta, a Russian-made Dragunov assault rifle, and a shotgun with a sawed-off barrel. The amphetamines came from a Romanian contact down in Gary, Indiana. Radimir paid more than he should have, but the man explained the drugs were pharmaceutical quality and no longer easy to come by. The local PD had been cracking down.

Once preparations were complete, Katja and Radimir

had lunch at a quaint Armenian restaurant just off North Michigan Avenue. Katja browsed the jewelry at an upscale boutique, and ended up buying a dress and shoes at a shop inside the Water Street Mall. Radimir drank tepid coffee and watched the American women to pass the time.

At darkfall, they were ready.

Katja wore the glittering red dress and heels she'd bought at the mall, and let her long brown hair cascade over her shoulders. It was too cold for strapless, but she didn't seem to mind. Even to Radimir, her brother, she was the epitome of sex.

They'd grown up together in the old neighborhood in Brighton Beach, but there were times when Radimir felt he didn't really know his sister. Even some of the hard-core gangsters kept their distance from her. Over the years, Radimir had heard rumors that she was only his half sister. Their mother had an affair with a Jewish man who'd later left for Israel, leaving her pregnant. Radimir had been three years old. But he and Katja and Rurik had been raised as full siblings, and their mother never told them differently.

But Katja was unlike any woman he'd ever met—and he'd met a lot of women in his thirty-two years. Despite her striking beauty and a body made for sin, Katja possessed the mind of a man. She liked sex—liked it, perhaps, a little too much—and made no bones about going after what she wanted. Even more unusual was her capacity for violence. It was an aptitude that was not hindered by conscience or emotion. When it came to killing, she was as methodical and precise as a sniper's bullet. She once told Radimir she liked killing as much as she liked sex. He'd never talked to her about it again.

But he heard the stories. And at the age of twenty-nine, she had become one of the most valuable members of the Red Mafia. A secret weapon of sorts that had led more than one man to his demise.

Steam billowed from the gutters into the frigid night air

as they idled down a back street of Chicago's South Side. Most of the merchants in the area had already closed down for the night. The hookers, petty thieves and drug dealers who took over after dark roamed the streets like beaten-down predators.

This was the neighborhood where they would find the cop. According to the information Radimir gleaned from his contact inside the department, the pig worked second shift. He was patrolling alone tonight.

Next to him, Katja rolled silk stockings up her thighs and secured them with the snaps of her lace garter. "I am ready," she said.

Radimir pulled into an alley next to a newspaper kiosk and shut down the engine. He turned to his sister to see her glide a tube of lipstick over her lips, turning them the color of blood.

"You sure about this?" he asked.

"Why wouldn't I be?"

"This man, he's a cop. He's not stupid."

"Maybe not, but he's a man. That makes him predictable." Her huge, dark eyes gleamed just a little too much when she raised them to his. "I want this American *svenja* to pay for what he did to Rurik."

Nodding, Radimir made a fist. "For Rurik, then."

Katja closed her eyes and braced. He punched her as hard as he could. His knuckles connected with her cheek with such force that he heard them crack. Her head snapped back and hit the passenger window. Before she could recover, he reached out and tore the front of her dress so that she had to hold it up to cover her breast.

Tears of pain glittered in her eyes when she looked at him. "My mouth, too," she said. "Don't break my teeth."

He slapped her with an open hand, hard enough to sting his palm. When she turned back to him, a small trickle of blood oozed down her chin, but it was tempered by a strange light he didn't understand in her eyes. "More."

Suppressing a rise of revulsion, he raked his knuckles hard across her cheek, marring the white flesh.

"Again," she said.

"Enough."

"*Ootebya nyet yayeesav.*"

"I have balls," he snapped. "I just have a brain to go with them."

That made her laugh, but he could tell she was still angry. Crazy woman.

It took them nearly three hours to find their target. A Crown Victoria city car with all the trimmings. The cop was alone. Katja swallowed four aspirin, but didn't clean the blood from her face.

Radimir followed the police cruiser at a safe distance for another half hour, waiting for the right moment. When the cruiser stopped at an all-night diner, he parked in an alley half a block to the south.

Donning the long coat she'd purchased at the mall, Katja got out of the car and bent to peer in the window. The coat was open, and Radimir could see her breast from where he sat, and tried not to stare. The blood on her mouth glittered black in the dim light coming off the streetlamp.

"I'll wait until he comes out," she said.

"Get him away from his cruiser quickly. Lure him down this way. Try to keep him off the radio."

Her teeth gleamed white against the red of her lips. "He's as good as dead," she said and slammed the door.

Radimir watched her walk with long, purposeful strides toward the diner where their target sat in a booth, alone, huddled over a bowl of something hot.

Stupid cop didn't have a clue he was about to die a long and terrible death.

It was an excellent location for an ambush. The diner sat on a corner at the intersection of two relatively quiet streets. Two doors down, a narrow alley laced with fire escapes made the perfect staging point. The cruiser was parked illegally near the mouth of the alley. The cop would have to walk that way to get to his car. So far, so good.

It took the cop nearly twenty minutes to gobble his slop. He flirted with the waitress another ten minutes before leaving. When he stepped out of the diner, Katja sprang into action.

Radimir watched her toss the coat. She emerged from the alley at a lurching run. Arms outstretched, she stumbled toward the cop, glancing repeatedly over her shoulder as if someone was chasing her. Even in the dim light, Radimir saw surprise on the cop's face. Radimir smiled when he thought of how many more surprises the night held in store for him.

Twenty feet before reaching the cop, Katja went to her knees. Looking left and right, the cop rushed to her and stooped to help. He set his hand on her back, tilted his head as if listening to whatever story she'd invented to draw him in. She pointed in the direction of the alley, laying it on thick. God, she was the best liar in the world.

The cop helped her to her feet. Katja put her arm around his shoulder. The flap of fabric slipped, exposing her breast and the ruby bud of her nipple for just the right amount of time. They began moving down the sidewalk, with her leaning heavily on him.

"Come on," Radimir whispered. "Do it. Now."

Sometimes Katja liked to cut things too close. Take things too close to the edge. Reckless bitch, he thought, but he smiled.

He squinted into the darkness, watched her hand disappear into the fabric of her dress. She and the cop were almost to the cruiser now. Ten yards away from where Radimir sat in his car. Katja collapsed. The cop bent to help her. Knowing that was his signal to disembark, Radimir left the car, walked to the rear and opened the trunk. He could hear her voice now, as sultry and warm as a summer night. Using the shadows and dark as cover, he kept his head bent toward the open trunk, stealing looks at them over his shoulder.

Katja pulled the stun gun from beneath her dress and thrust it at the cop's chest. The electrical charge snapped and flashed white in the darkness.

The cop went rigid, then went down like a bull. He rolled, then reached for her, but Katja was ready and hit him with the stun gun again. The cop's body jolted and went still.

Radimir darted to them. Looking left and right, he took the man's shoulders. Katja lifted his feet. They carried him to the car and tossed him like a slab of meat into the trunk. Working quickly, Radimir yanked the handcuffs from his coat pocket and cuffed the man's hands behind his back, cranking the cuffs down tight. Katja tore a length of fabric from her dress and jammed it into the man's mouth, then set a length of duct tape against his lips and wrapped it around his head. Before Radimir closed the trunk, she spat on the cop.

"You're dead," she said to him in Russian and they got in the car.

*Marty couldn't remember the last time she'd been so* utterly humiliated. Well, that wasn't exactly true. She'd been pretty damn humiliated when she'd caught her coworkers hooting it up over the video. Not to mention the fiasco in Chicago. The hearings. Her termination. The Cook County prosecuting attorney playing the video for the jury during her trial.

Wearing the Rufus the Police Dog gear wasn't that bad. It was nice and cool outside, after all; she was relatively comfortable. The ventilation was pretty good. Marty was learning to look at these things in a more positive light.

By far the best thing about being Rufus the Police Dog was that no one could see her face. No one ever had to know who she was. Marty found the anonymity incredibly liberating.

Clay had assigned her crosswalk duty this morning. All she had to do was don the Rufus suit and make sure traffic came to a complete stop for the crosswalk in front of the Palo Duro Elementary School while the kiddies crossed Cactus Street. As Rosetti always used to say: *Piece of frickin' cake.*

Next, the chief had assigned her the "Arrive at School Safely" program that was being implemented statewide by the Texas attorney general. In a nutshell, Marty would speak to several different elementary grade levels—both children and their parents—about back-to-school safety. It was her job to get the word out. Keep the kids safe. Entertainment at its humiliating best.

"Officer Hogan?"

Marty looked up to see second grade teacher Nancy Combs stick her head out the door of her classroom and smile. "You look great."

"I've always looked good in fur," Marty muttered.

The teacher motioned her into the classroom. "We're ready."

"Just let me get my head on."

The teacher laughed and ducked back into the classroom.

Sliding the Rufus head over her own, Marty stepped into the room.

In the course of her career, she'd spoken before all kinds of groups countless times. She'd always thought cops made the worst audience. They could be rude, loud and downright obnoxious, especially if they were pumped up or bored. But there was something disproportionately intimidating about kids.

A collective gasp of pleasure erupted when Marty walked into the classroom. She'd never been a big fan of kids. They were little and weird and invariably seemed to say things she didn't know how to respond to. But as she walked to the teacher's desk and turned to the class, she had to admit it was fun to watch their faces light up. She'd become so jaded over the years, she'd forgotten innocence was still alive and well. It was nice to have it proven to her that such things still existed.

"Hi," she began in her best dog voice, "I'm Rufus the Police Dog, and I'm here today to tell you all about Run Away, Shout It Out, and Tell a Grown-up. Do any of you know what that is?"

A little girl in a plaid skirt, ill-matched sweater and dark tights stood up. "Recess!"

A few chuckles rippled through the kids. Marty would have joined them, but she knew just how easy it was to lose your audience when they were already thinking about recess.

"Run Away, Shout It Out, and Tell a Grown-up are three things you need to remember to keep yourselves safe," she said. "For example, if it's recess time and you're playing by yourself, and an adult you don't know walks up to you and tells you he lost his puppy or that he has candy in his car for you, what do you do?"

"Run Away, Shout It Out, and Tell a Grown-up!" a little boy hollered.

"That's right!" Marty woofed a couple of times and brought her paws together. "Let's say it together. Run Away, Shout It Out, and Tell a Grown-up! Run Away, Shout It Out, and Tell a Grown-up!"

The kids began to chant.

"Good!" She pointed at the little girl who'd stood up with the recess crack. "What do you do if a stranger approaches you when you're walking home from school?"

"Run Away, Shout It Out, and Tell a Grown-up!" the little girl yelled.

"Good job!" Marty crossed to her and gave her a high five with her right paw.

Back at the teacher's desk, she glanced down at the notes she'd spread out. "How many of you walk to and from school?"

About half the kids in the class raised their hands.

"Did you know that Rufus the Police Dog thinks you should walk in groups?"

A little girl in pigtails and blue jeans raised her hand.

Marty pointed with her paw. The kid looked familiar, but Marty didn't think she'd ever met her. "Yes?"

"My dad says if a bad guy tries to grab me I should kick him in the penis."

Marty choked back a laugh and grappled for a proper adult response. Nothing appropriate came to mind, so she stuck to the tried and true. "Remember, Run Away, Shout It Out, and Tell a Grown-up!"

"I know who you are," the girl said.

"I'm Rufus the Police Dog."

"Uh uh. You were bad. Willie Stubblefield told me you're the lady cop who beat up a spect and he had to go to the hospital."

Marty's first impulse was to correct her by telling her there was no such thing as a spect. It was a *suspect* she'd beaten the hell out of. Get it right before you go shooting your mouth off, kid.

Stumped, Marty glanced toward where she'd last seen the teacher, only to realize the woman had flown the coop. Probably in the teacher's lounge smoking a cigarette. She turned back to the class, and to the little girl. Brat, she thought and looked down at her notes.

"For today, I'm Rufus the Police Dog." She scanned the children's faces, wondering which boy was Willie Stubblefield, wondering how her boss would feel if Rufus drew down on him. Knowing that wouldn't go over well with the chief, she decided the correct course of action was to let it go.

"Does anybody know what to do if a stranger offers you a ride?" she asked.

A dozen hands shot up. Marty didn't call on the little girl with the pigtails.

She was midway through the program when movement at the door snagged her attention. She glanced over to see Clay and the teacher watching her with unconcealed amusement. Knowing they couldn't see her face, she grinned.

"That's it for today, guys." She woofed. "Does everyone remember what Rufus the Police Dog says?"

"Run Away, Shout It Out, and Tell a Grown-up!" came a chorus of voices.

Gathering her notes, Marty headed toward the door. Mrs. Combs giggled and stuck out her hand. "Thank you, Rufus."

Marty thought about growling, but touched the teacher's hand with her paw and headed toward the door. The chief moved aside to let her pass. In the hall, Marty removed the costume head and tried not to think about what it had done to her hair.

"Not bad for a cop from Chicago," Clay said.

Marty held up her paws. "Don't get any ideas about making this a permanent thing."

"Aw, come on. You're a natural."

"I'll become a natural pain in the ass if I have to do this much longer."

"Sorry about the suspect comment."

"Par for the course," she said. "Kids hear talk from their parents. They repeat it."

"She didn't hear it from me."

Realization stunned her to silence. "That's your little girl?"

Marty could tell he tried not to grin, but he didn't do a very good job of it. The kid wasn't merely his daughter, she was his pride and probably the love of his life. For a split second, Marty found herself inexplicably charmed.

"She's kind of outspoken," he said.

She gave him a closer look, realizing the girl had the

same gray eyes. The same direct way of speaking. The same thin mouth that could go from smiling to snarling in the blink of an eye. She stared at his mouth, wondered what else it was capable of, and quickly banked the thought that emerged.

"Don't worry about it," she said.

"I'll talk to her about it tonight."

"She wasn't exactly stating an untruth," Marty pointed out.

"No, but she's old enough to know what's appropriate and what's not."

Marty didn't know the first thing about kids, so it wasn't like she could offer an opinion. Instead, she concentrated on shedding the Rufus costume. "Anything in particular bring you here?"

"You."

She stopped what she was doing and looked at him. "I'm not in trouble again, am I?"

"I don't know. Are you?" When she had to think about it, he chuckled. "Jesus, Hogan, associating me with your being in trouble is getting to be a learned response with you, isn't it?"

"It's that Pavlov's dogs thing, I guess." She glanced at the uniform and chuckled. "No pun."

"I came by to see your presentation."

"Oh," she said and did her best to hold back the blush that crept up her cheeks.

"I needed to pick up Erica, anyway. This is her last class of the day."

Marty sensed there was something else coming her way, but for the life of her she couldn't figure out what.

"I wanted to remind you about the rodeo this weekend."

She made an attempt to cover the fact that she'd forgotten, but he was too quick. "Uh, I'll be there."

"You forgot."

"I wrote it down." *Somewhere.*

"The whole department is going."

"Oh boy. Definitely don't want to miss out on seeing the guys."

He frowned. "In any case, we're going to cheer on the kids, eat some hot dogs, drink some beer later. I thought you might like to join us."

"You're not going to make me wear this goofy costume or ride a cow or something, are you?"

He laughed outright. "Not unless you want to."

"I don't."

"Probably a good thing."

"In that case, I'll be there." Marty folded the costume and proceeded to stuff it into its canvas bag.

"Where are you headed next?" Clay asked.

She glanced at her watch and frowned. "Rufus stint at the Rotary Club."

"You'll knock 'em dead."

"Somehow I don't think Rufus is going to be quite the hit he was here."

"Everyone loves Rufus."

Marty had just dug her car keys from her pocket when her cell phone vibrated against her hip. Tossing Rufus's head into the bag as well, she fumbled for her phone, snapped it open. "Hogan."

"Hogan."

Surprise rippled through her at the sound of Patrick "Peck" O'Connor's voice. He'd been her sergeant back in Chicago, and a quiet supporter after the fiasco that had ended her career. Marty had wished he'd been more vocal in his support of her. He hadn't, choosing his own job over hers, but she didn't hold it against him.

She grinned. "Don't tell me you called to tell me the suits have decided to reinstate me."

"Uh . . . Marty."

She knew something was wrong when she didn't get an immediate raucous and politically incorrect comeback. "Peck? You there?"

"Goddamn it, Hogan."

The initial fingers of uneasiness pressed into her, sharp nails of apprehension raking down her skin. "What's wrong?"

"Rosetti is dead."

Marty did the only thing she could and choked out a laugh. Surely this was a joke. Rosetti couldn't be dead. She'd just talked to him a couple of days ago. Peck was full of shit. Playing a cruel joke on her.

"That's bullshit," she heard herself say.

"I wish it was." He sighed heavily. "He's dead. No one can fucking believe it."

As if from a great distance Marty heard the canvas bag she'd been holding hit the floor, followed by her car keys. Her mind reeling, she leaned against the cool tile wall, denial taking her through all the reasons why this man would be lying to her. Revenge or some cruel joke prompted by the embarrassment she'd brought to the department.

But in some far corner of her mind, she knew no matter how far she ventured into denial, it wasn't going to change what had been said. She knew Peck wouldn't lie to her about something so serious.

"Are you sure?" she managed after a moment.

"Yeah."

"My God. How?" she asked, imagining a car accident, a heart attack or maybe some dipshit gangbanger with a gun.

"You don't want to know."

"Peck, tell me what happened."

A wheezing breath shuddered out of him. "Details are sketchy. The brass ain't sayin' much, but the cops who were on the scene are saying all kinds of weird shit. It's bad, Marty. Worse than anything I ever heard in my life."

"Bad like what? What happened to him? Was he murdered? What?"

For an interminable moment the only sound that came through the line was the sound of his heavy breathing.

Peck was a big man. He was tough, too. Marty had never seen him show any emotion but anger. To hear his breath hitching like a scared kid's frightened her more than anything he could have said.

"Here's what I know. When he didn't show up at home this morning after his shift, Eileen called in. She thought maybe he'd gone out for a beer with the guys. He didn't. No one knew where he was. Some of the guys started looking. Making calls. A couple of hours later an anonymous call came in. Some foreign-sounding motherfucker. Told dispatch where to find him. Called him by name."

Keenly aware that she was gripping the cell phone so tightly her knuckles hurt, Marty tried to relax her hand, but couldn't. In her peripheral vision, she saw that Clay had noticed something was wrong and moved closer. He cocked his head as if to get a look at her expression, and she tried hard not to let the horror gripping her show.

"You know Rolly Martino?" Peck asked.

"No."

"Well, he found Rosetti's body about an hour ago." His voice broke and he whispered a curse. "They cut him up. Into little pieces like a fuckin' fish. I heard they tortured him. Tortured Rosetti, man."

"Who?"

"No one knows. I'm looking at his caseload now. But this ain't no normal shit, let me tell you. These sick fucks took their time with him, Hogan. They're professionals. They hurt him bad and they did it for a long time."

"Peck . . ." She choked out the name. "Why?"

"I don't know, and no one's talking."

He was silent for so long, Marty thought he had disconnected. "Peck?"

"I gotta go. It's all over the news up here. Cops are pissed and the brass are shitting their britches."

"Call me if you find out anything more, okay?"

"Yeah."

The line clicked.

Marty wanted to pretend the phone call had never come. She wanted to deny that one of the best friends she'd ever had was dead. That a part of her life she would always treasure was gone forever.

"What happened?"

Clay's voice reached her as if from a great distance. Marty tried to clip the cell phone to her belt, but missed. She stared at her hands, unable to believe they shook so badly, unable to believe they were hers.

*Rosetti is dead.*

Peck's words rang in her ears like the memory of a nightmare. Disbelief was a weight on her chest. She couldn't believe he was gone. She *wouldn't* believe it. Not until she flew back to Chicago and saw his cold dead body for herself.

*They cut him up. Into little pieces.*

What in the name of God had happened to Rosetti? Who was responsible? Why would they torture a cop?

She stepped away from Clay, only to realize the outer fringes of her vision had grayed. Reaching for the wall, she leaned. Her stomach knotted, and for a moment she feared she might be sick. She could feel her heart pummeling her chest, her breaths rasping from a throat that was suddenly parched.

"Hogan. Come on. Take it easy. Talk to me. What happened?"

The dizziness passed. Numb with horror and grief, she finally looked at Clay. "Rosetti," she croaked. "My partner. He's . . ." She couldn't say the word. All the while, in the back of her mind she desperately hoped Peck had made a mistake. That he'd called her prematurely. That she would receive another call any moment letting her know that all was well.

"Your partner from Chicago? Was he hurt? What?"

"Killed." She put her hand on her forehead and pressed

hard with her fingertips, trying not to imagine Rosetti suffering a terrible death. Even though they hadn't talked often since she'd moved to Caprock Canyon, just knowing he was in Chicago, keeping the criminals on their toes, was a huge comfort.

"Murdered," she whispered.

He stared at her with those hard gray eyes. She couldn't imagine Clay Settlemeyer offering platitudes. But that was what people did when someone died.

"That's tough. I'm sorry." As if realizing there was more happening than she was saying, he tilted his head, forcing her gaze to his. "What else?"

"I don't have details. I guess it just happened. But it was bad."

His eyes held hers. Within their depths she saw him trying to read between the lines and decipher what little information she'd given.

"Tortured," she forced out.

"Jesus."

Marty wanted to cry. She wanted to rant and scream and throw things. Why the hell did Rosetti have to be dead?

She looked at the floor, saw the canvas bag and stooped to pick it up. She couldn't believe that just a few minutes earlier, she'd been worried about something as trivial as wearing a silly costume. Now her best friend was dead, and she would never have the chance to tell him how much he'd meant to her.

"I have to go." Blinking back tears, she reached for the bag. "I can't do the Rotary Club."

"I'll have Dugan cover for you." He took the bag from her. "You want me to drive you home?"

Marty didn't want him to. She didn't want to share her grief. Her rage. Having been raised by males, she saw grief as a private thing, not to be coddled or fawned over or even acknowledged. But while she had been raised by males, she was a woman with a woman's heart. Right now, that heart was breaking.

"No," she said, her voice coming surprisingly strong.

He never took his eyes from hers, a man looking for a lie, a denial, and getting both. "You sure?"

Unable to speak, she nodded.

He handed her the keys he'd picked up off the floor.

Marty gathered the shattered remnants of herself and fled.

# Six

*Marty couldn't cry. On the short drive from the school*
to her house, she tried. Anything was better than having so
much turmoil building inside her with no escape. But it
was as if a giant fist had been jammed down her throat and
snatched her lungs from her chest. The sensation was so
powerful, a choking sound tore from her lips as she unlocked the door and stepped into the living room.

She wasn't sure why she'd come here. She hated the
place—hated just about everything about Caprock Canyon—
but this was her only refuge. More importantly, this was
the place where she could get information. And a drink.

Closing the door behind her, she went directly to the
spare bedroom, pulled the laptop from its case. While the
computer booted up, Marty went to the kitchen. The bottle of vodka taunted her as she walked by the table. She was
tempted to drink straight from the bottle, but opted for a
glass. This time, she poured nearly to the rim, drank half
of it straight down, then refilled.

She couldn't stop thinking about Rosetti, about the people

who loved him, the people he'd left behind. She thought of his wife and four grown children, and she knew this would leave a huge gap in their lives. Rosetti had taught her everything she knew about being a cop. He'd taught her even more about being a person. The kind of person she wanted to be. Sure, he was a bigmouth. He cussed too much and smoked like a chimney. But he was the kind of person you could trust with your life when the chips were down. He'd been good inside, and Marty had loved him like family. How could he just cease to exist?

In the living room, she turned on the television, hoping for news. She surfed the channels, but found only the usual mindless afternoon fare. She tried Peck's number, but got instant voice mail, telling her he was probably on the phone. She imagined most of the cops in the city were jamming the phone lines. The rest were already out trying to catch the son of a bitch who'd killed one of their own.

She wanted to be there so badly she could taste that heady need for revenge. She was one of them; Rosetti had been her partner. But Marty knew she couldn't go back. This wasn't about her. Her showing up now would only shift the focus and risk turning everything that happened in the next days into a circus.

Rosetti deserved better than that.

She tried two other cop friends, but neither answered. For an instant, she considered calling Rosetti's wife, but she knew Eileen had enough on her hands. Marty needed information. The kind of information that came from cops.

Desperate, she finally dialed another officer she'd ridden with for a short time and got him on the first ring. "Huffman," she began.

"Hogan?" He sounded surprised to hear from her.

"I'm calling from Texas. I just heard about Rosetti. Is it true?"

He blew out a curse. "No one can believe it. There's some bad stuff going down."

"I'm trying to find out what happened."

"No one knows much." He paused. "But I'm hearing some god-awful stuff."

"Like what?"

"Like some fucking gangstas got their hands on him and tortured him to death."

*Oh, Rosetti,* she thought and closed her eyes. In the distance she thought she heard the low roar of an approaching wave, then realized it was inside her head. The world around her swirled and went silent as the water tumbled her, ground her into sand. "Did they catch the bastard?"

"As far as I know we don't even have a suspect yet. Most of us think it's gang related. I mean who else is going to do that kind of crap to a cop?"

Marty didn't want to ask, but she did. "What did they do to him?"

"Aw, Hogan, you don't want to know what I'm hearing."

She did; cops always needed to hear the truth, no matter how horrific. Before she could ask again, she lost her breath and paused to catch it.

"Why Rosetti?" she asked. "He was a street cop. He didn't have much to do with gangs."

"I don't know. Some of the guys thought it might be the mob. But those guys have pretty much been dismantled."

"Will you call me if you find out anything?"

"Will do."

Marty disconnected, knowing little more than she had before calling. Leaning forward, she put her face in her hands and swallowed the sob stuck in her throat. "Rosetti, you shit. How could you do this?"

Feeling despondent and alone, she straightened and looked around the room. She didn't want to sit here and do nothing, or God forbid get drunk and feel sorry for herself.

But she knew that was exactly what she was going to do. Marty wasn't proud of it, but she could feel herself being sucked into the black abyss. A fighter jet spiraling down to the ultimate crash and burn.

Moving to the sofa, she set the laptop on her thighs and called up a search engine. She picked up her glass and drank half without coming up for air. The alcohol burned all the way down to her stomach, but she didn't let it slow her down. She could feel the pain pressing in on her, like a giant fist squeezing her chest. Marty didn't want to hurt. She didn't want to feel anything. At the moment, she wasn't even sure she wanted to be on this earth.

Outside, the wind picked up, groaning as it whipped around the eaves. She'd once read that the sound of the incessant prairie wind could make people go insane. Listening, she believed it.

She typed in "Steven Rosetti" + "Chicago Police" and hit Enter. Four reputable news sites returned hits. She selected the first link and began to read.

*Breaking news out of Chicago. Veteran police officer found dead. Gruesome details of torture emerging. For full details click here . . .*

Marty pressed her hand over her mouth, clicked and braced.

*Forty-eight-year-old Steven Rosetti, a twenty-year veteran with the Chicago PD, was found slain today just outside Palatine. The police aren't releasing details, but it has been verified that his nude body was found in a snow-covered ditch on a side road outside the city limits. The police are calling his death an apparent homicide. The officer who discovered the corpse reported the scene as "one of the most horrific sights I've seen in twenty-two years." Another police source who asked to remain anonymous said Rosetti's body bore visible signs of torture. Police are aggressively investigating the crime. No motive or suspects have yet been named.*

Disbelief and grief and a terrible sense of outrage gripped Marty with such viciousness that she couldn't breathe. Furious, she brought her fist down on the laptop, then flung it across the room.

"No!" she screamed. *"No!"*

Choking out sounds she didn't know she was capable of making, she put her face in her hands and wished she could cry.

*Clay waited until after dark to drive by her place.* He didn't know what he'd find when he got there. A cop who'd lost a partner. A person in need of a friend. A woman broken into a thousand pieces by grief. He wasn't exactly her friend, but he knew she didn't have anyone else in Caprock Canyon. Sometimes, the next best thing had to do.

He parked curbside, shut down the engine and watched the wind push a tumbleweed against a chain-link fence. He wasn't surprised to find the house dark. He knew how grief worked, and how different personalities responded to it. He didn't know Hogan well, but figured she was a leave-me-alone-or-I'll-rip-your-head-off type. Her grief would be a dark place. Still, he hesitated, wondering if approaching her now was territory he wanted to breach. But as much as he didn't want to admit it, he was concerned. The least he could do was check on her and make sure she was all right.

He got out of the Explorer, took the sidewalk to the front door and knocked. He waited a full minute, then knocked again, harder. When that didn't produce an answer, he tried the knob—and found it unlocked.

The crime rate was low in Caprock Canyon, but Hogan knew better than to leave her place unlocked. Opening the door, he stepped into the darkened living room. He was in the process of making a mental note to scold her for being lax on her personal security when he heard a creak from across the room. On instinct, Clay put his hand on his gun. With his left hand he fumbled for the light switch, flipped it on.

Marty sat cross-legged in a ragtag recliner. She wore gray sweatpants with a drawstring waist and an over-size T-shirt with Chicago PD emblazoned in blue. Her eyes were haunted—and dry, he noted. But her face was ghostly pale.

She took in the sight of him as if he were a stray dog that had come to her door in the midst of a rainstorm. Her feet were bare, and he was surprised to see her toenails painted the color of a seashell. She didn't seem like a toenail-painting type, but then he imagined she was full of all sorts of surprises.

In the four days she'd been in Caprock Canyon, he'd never seen her hair down, and the unruly length of it curling around her shoulders added another layer of surprise. She had a lot of hair, and it made her look just a little wild. On the end table next to her, a cell phone and a nearly empty bottle of vodka gave him a pretty good idea of how she'd spent the last hours. A few feet away, a laptop computer lay upended on the floor. Several keys had popped from the pad, telling him it hadn't landed there softly.

Before driving over, he'd made it a point to check the national news online. He wanted to know what he was dealing with, what he would be walking into. There was a lot of ugly information coming out of Chicago. Not only was a veteran cop dead, but his death had been long and extremely violent. When the cops didn't release details, it was bad. Clay knew firsthand how close partners could get.

"You're the last person I want to see right now," Marty said in a voice that was surprisingly strong.

"I figured that."

"I'm in no condition to talk to my boss."

He crossed to the laptop and picked it up. "I'm not here as your boss, okay?"

She said nothing.

He carried the laptop to a scratched-up coffee table, set it down and closed the lid. "You okay?"

Instead of answering, she rose, quickly, with the grace and swiftness of a ballet dancer. Clay turned to see her snag the bottle of vodka and her glass and carry both to the kitchen. Sighing, he followed.

She set the glass on the counter and filled it. Staring through the window above the sink into the darkness beyond, she raised the glass and drank deeply.

"That's not going to help," he said.

"No, but it will get me through tonight." She faced him, her expression cool and slightly defiant. "Do you have a cigarette?"

"I don't smoke."

"Rosetti used to smoke. His wife hated it, so he had to sneak. Sometimes we'd sit in the car, roll down the windows and steal a few puffs like a couple of teenagers." She took another long pull of vodka. "I could really use a smoke right now."

For the first time he noticed just how thin she was. Her shoulders were angular and slender. The drawstring pants hung over narrow hips and a flat belly. When she crossed her free arm over her midsection, Clay noticed other things about her, too. Like how pretty her hands were. That she wasn't wearing a bra. That her breasts were the size of small fruits, her nipples tiny and pointed.

Suddenly, she wasn't a cop anymore. She was a woman with a woman's heart and a woman's emotions rolled into a very attractive package. Despite the tough-guy facade, Clay saw the bottomless chasm of despondency in her eyes. He saw the deep well of vulnerability. He didn't know what he could do about any of it.

For a moment the only sound came from the moan of the wind as it buffeted the house. Silence usually didn't bother him. Tonight, it did. It was as if her grief were a living, breathing thing in the room with them. A vicious creature neither of them could trust or confront.

"I thought you might want to talk," he said.

"Or maybe you thought I might do something stupid."

"The only thing you're doing that you shouldn't be is drinking."

She laughed, but it was a hollow sound. "If drinking myself into a stupor is the worst thing I could do to myself, I think neither of us has anything to worry about."

Clay wanted to cross to her, take the glass from her and maybe dump what was left in the bottle down the sink. But he didn't. He didn't want to get too close. He knew that was stupid. She weighed little more than a hundred pounds soaking wet and was well on her way to total inebriation. But combine grief and alcohol and she was as unpredictable as a Panhandle storm.

He looked around the kitchen. There were no signs the place was lived in. No dishes in the sink. No residual coffee in the coffeemaker from the morning. No loaf of bread on the counter. "Have you eaten dinner?"

"You don't have to babysit me."

"I'm here to watch your back," he said.

"That's good, Chief. I like that." She took another long pull of vodka. "But I still want you to leave."

"I'm afraid I can't do that just yet." Clay watched her and waited. For what, he wasn't sure. But he was beginning to get the feeling that he was going to have to wait this out. That eventually the dam would burst. That the outpouring would be explosive when it did.

"I can't believe he's gone," she said after a moment.

"Do they have a suspect?"

"No."

"Cops pull together when it's one of their own. They'll find the person responsible."

"I want to be there."

"If you need some time off for the funeral, you've got it."

"I want to find the son of a bitch who did it. I want to put my gun in his mouth and pull the trigger."

"Hogan . . . Jesus."

Her eyes met his. In their depths, he saw the extent of her pain, the depth of her misery. Her dark frame of mind. "What they did to him . . . You don't do that to a cop."

"A cop doesn't take the law into her own hands, either."

Her lips curved, but her eyes remained hard. "Gets them into all kinds of trouble, doesn't it?"

She sipped, watching him over the rim. Clay stepped forward and took the glass from her. Some of the vodka spilled when she tried to grab it, but he easily held on to the glass and dumped the rest of the vodka down the drain.

"You're pissing me off," she said.

"I'm doing you a favor."

Hogan left the kitchen and strode to the living room. Clay tossed the bottle in the trash, then followed. He found her standing in the middle of the room with her back to him, her arms wrapped around her midsection. Though he couldn't see her face from where he stood, he'd never seen anyone look so damn alone.

"They tortured him," she choked out after a moment. "I can't get my head around that. It's too terrible to think about."

It was hard to see this degree of hurt and not reach out. He wanted to go to her. But Clay felt as if he were walking a minefield. Tread carefully, or risk the situation blowing up in his face.

"I'm sorry," he said, but the words sounded incredibly inept.

"I can't imagine the world without Rosetti."

"You're going to be all right."

She turned to him then, gave him that thousand-yard stare, as if she wasn't really looking at him. But he knew she was. "I can't cry."

"People grieve in different ways." It was then that Clay realized he was out of his league here. He didn't know how to deal with this complicated, hurting woman. He didn't know what to say or how to feel. "Were you and Rosetti . . ."
Because he didn't know how to finish the sentence,

because he didn't know if he should, he let the words trail.

She surprised him by laughing. "God, no. But we were friends. Even his wife liked me."

"That's something."

"He taught me everything I know about being a cop." As if realizing how that sounded in light of her recent history, she touched her temple with her fingertips. "The good stuff, I mean."

"I knew what you meant."

"He was there the day I . . . went off on that suspect."

Because Clay didn't know how to respond to that, he remained silent.

"He supported me when most of the other guys treated me like a leper."

"Cops can be a political bunch."

"He was an ass, but I loved him."

Stumped again, he said nothing, kept his distance. But he saw the crack in the dam. He knew that when it broke, the rush of emotion would be volatile. That if he wasn't careful, he was going to get caught up in it.

"I miss him."

"You're going to be okay, Hogan. You'll get through this."

She looked at him. For the first time, emotion swam in her eyes. "Don't you dare be nice to me. Goddamn it, I didn't ask you to come here."

Clay didn't realize he was going to move until he took that first, dangerous step toward her. She raised her hands as if to stop him, but he didn't stop.

He reached her in three resolute strides. Her eyes went wide. For the first time, tears glistened. But they didn't fall.

He set his hands on her shoulders. Clay wanted to believe it was comfort he offered. But he was too aware of how small and fragile her shoulders felt beneath his hands. How her entire body trembled with pent-up emotion.

He didn't know exactly when he'd begun seeing her as a woman and not a cop. But damn it, she smelled like a woman. Some shampoo-and-fruit smell so exotic and sweet his mouth watered. He looked into her eyes, and the floor seemed to shift beneath his feet. She had the longest lashes of anyone he'd ever met. A perfect mouth the color of a coral reef on a sunny day . . .

It had been a long time since he'd been this close to a woman. He'd forgotten just how powerful the draw could be. But Clay felt the magnetic pull of sexual attraction. His fingers itched to slide through all that hair. He wanted to set his palm beneath her chin and bring her lips to his. He wanted to kiss away her pain. Make her stop looking at him as if the entire world had just crashed down on her shoulders.

But while his body wanted what would in the long run cost him the most, his intellect reminded him that she was a subordinate. That she was hurting and intoxicated. Acting on any of the impulses running through his mind was a sure ticket to disaster.

It was a line he would not cross.

The first tear fell with the weight of a thousand gallons. She tried to turn away from him, but Clay held her, and wiped the tear away with the pad of his thumb.

"Go on," he whispered. "Let it out."

She tried to cover her face with her hands. He wasn't sure why, but he grasped her wrists, kept her from doing it. Maybe because she was still trying to hold all of this inside, and he knew at some point she was going to have to let go. Better for him to be here when she did. At least that way, she'd have a shoulder to cry on.

The dam broke. Lowering her head, she began to sob. Quiet sobs that were powerful enough to wrack her entire body. Clay did the only thing he could and put his arms around her shaking shoulders. It did something to him to see such a strong woman break. And it was that much more profound after seeing her play it tough for so long.

"I told you not to be nice to me," she sobbed. "This is what you get."

"Remind me to yell at you later."

"I'm sorry."

"It's okay. That's why I'm here."

He was standing too close. Clay could feel the press of her breasts against his chest. He was keenly aware of her hair against his face. Her head dropping to rest on his shoulder. The faint odor of vodka on her breath. A sweeter, more feminine scent filled his nostrils. A vague need he didn't want to feel stormed his blood and ran hot through his veins.

She raised her face to his, and her mouth brushed softly against his lips. Clay felt the contact as if it were an electrical shock. He told himself she hadn't meant to kiss him. But a warning blared in his head. A warning that told him to pull back and regroup and maybe think this through before one of them did something they would be sorry for later.

But it was already too late . . .

Putting her arms around his neck, she kissed him full on the mouth. Clay knew this was the moment when he should do the right thing and stop her. But the gentle press of her lips taunted him with a slow spiral of pleasure that wound through every nerve in his body. The intensity of that pleasure rendered him incapable of pushing her away or turning his head.

Instead, his body heated. All the blood seemed to leave his head. It rushed south so fast that for a moment he was dizzy. He crushed his mouth to hers. She tasted of woman and vodka and tears. A volatile combination he was a fool for not acknowledging.

She shifted against him, and his erection strained uncomfortably against the fly of his slacks. Need like he hadn't known for a very long time pummeled him like fists, beating down the last of his good judgment. When she opened to him, he went in deep, using his tongue to savor the warm sweetness of her mouth.

He jolted when she reached for him, gripped him through his uniform trousers. Groaning, he pushed her against the wall. Catching her straying hands, he laced her fingers with his and eased them above her head. All the while his mouth fused with hers, the contact drugging him like some illicit narcotic he could never get enough of. Moaning with need, he ground against her, and she gave, as pliant and soft as her woman's body.

Then his hands were on her breasts, small and liquid within the thin confines of her T-shirt. He could feel the pebbled nipples beneath his palms. Her breath quickened against his face, the heat of it coming from her nose in short gasps. She arched against him and his control snapped.

Clay devoured her mouth. He devoured her body with his hands. Her breasts. The curve of her hip. The juncture between her thighs. Her flesh seemed superheated when he slipped his hands beneath her T-shirt. A shiver wracked her when he brushed his fingertips across her nipples.

The next thing he knew her hands were on his belt. Anticipation jumped inside him. He acknowledged the lust inside him, and the purest form of male need. Her fingers trembled as she worked the buckle. He wanted her. Wanted her more than he wanted to draw his next breath.

But Clay wasn't some randy teenager. He was a man with a man's responsibilities and a man's sense of right and wrong. Thankfully, that sense kicked in just in time to avoid disaster. Gently, he grasped her hands and eased her to arm's length.

"Marty." Her name came out as little more than a puff of air between breaths. "We can't do this."

"I think we're doing a pretty good job."

If the circumstances hadn't been so damn serious, Clay might have smiled. But he didn't. There was nothing even remotely funny about anything that had happened in the past five minutes. She was his subordinate. A cop who'd just lost her partner. A woman who was vulnerable and hurting. Not to mention intoxicated. Her dignity was at stake. His reputation was on the line. There was honor and self-respect at stake on both sides.

Grimacing, he tilted his head and made eye contact with her. "I'm going to put you to bed."

"Alone?"

He nearly groaned. "Yeah."

"I want to go to Chicago."

"Tomorrow." Taking her arm, he guided her down the narrow hall. He passed a bathroom tiled in pink. The first bedroom was furnished with only a desk and chair. At the end of the hall he found the second bedroom, with the bed, and turned on the light. A twin-size bed with an antique-looking iron headboard dominated the room. He caught a glimpse of a butt-ugly laminate dresser and mismatched night table, a lamp someone had probably found at a garage sale twenty years ago.

He led her to the bed and pulled the covers aside. "In you go."

She crawled onto the bed without argument and slid beneath the blankets. Closing her eyes, she laid her head against the pillow. "Rosetti always was a pain in the ass," she whispered.

For a moment, Clay couldn't look away. Gone was the tough-talking big city cop from Chicago. In her place was a vulnerable woman who felt deeply and had one of the prettiest faces he'd ever laid eyes on. For a split second, he wondered what it would be like to climb into bed with her and take what he wanted . . .

"You need anything before I go?" he asked.

She didn't answer. Clay figured that was just as well. He might just give it to her. He'd handled this all wrong. Hopefully, by morning she wouldn't remember too much of what had happened.

Turning, he started toward the door. The sound of his name stopped him and he looked at her over his shoulder.

"That was a really great kiss," she said.

Clay turned off the light and walked out.

# SEVEN

Marty woke with a head-banger of a headache and a vague and troubling memory of doing something she shouldn't have. It wasn't the first time she'd started her day that way in the past six months. Every time she swore it would be the last. She'd broken the promise more times than she could count.

Sunshine streamed through the window, and she rolled over to shield her eyes. A knot in her chest reminded her of the grief she had felt the day before, and she thought of Rosetti. She remembered what had happened to him, and the pain blossomed, an awful flower blooming inside her. Loss combined with a terrible sense of finality, reminding her he was gone and she would never have the chance to speak to him again.

The alarm clock on the night table told her it was just after 10 A.M. A groan escaped her as she rolled out of bed. Holding her head between her hands, she padded down the hall, trying to remember how she'd gotten to bed.

She was midway through the living room when giant

chunks of memory from the night before came at her. The power of those memories stopped her cold. Clay Settle-meyer standing in her kitchen, looking at her as if she'd done something terrible. Clay pouring the last of her vodka down the sink. She'd been drinking and angry and hurting so badly she could barely stand it. Full self-destruct mode in all its shining glory.

Another flash of memory assailed her. Clay's hands on her body. His mouth fused to hers in a kiss so hot Marty could still feel the heat. The faint scent of his aftershave. Gentle hands on her breasts, touching between her thighs . . .

"Oh my God." Marty made it to the kitchen and leaned against the counter. Of all the things she could have done, making a pass at her boss had to be the worst. How could she be so stupid and self-destructive? How was she going to face him?

"Hogan, you are pathetic."

She glanced out the window at the windblown land-scape beyond and wondered how she was going to get through this without Rosetti to help her keep things in per-spective. If she knew him, he'd be laughing his ass off about now. Marty Hogan, the queen of bad behavior.

She lowered her face into her hands and rubbed at the ache behind her eyes. For a crazy moment, she thought about throwing all of her meager belongings into her Mus-tang and driving away. Driving until she found a place where nobody knew her face. A place where she could start fresh. But Marty knew the pain would follow her wherever she went. She was going to have to ride this one out and make it work.


*Clay sat behind his desk and tried not to think about* what had happened between him and Marty the night be-fore. But like a headache, thoughts of her crept repeatedly into his brain and refused to leave. The softness of her lips.

The vulnerability in her eyes. The pain etched into her every feature. The warm lushness of a body he'd had no right to touch.

After leaving her place the night before, he'd done something he hadn't done since the last woman who'd pried her way into his life and messed things up; he'd gone to the bar and gotten drunk. He'd known he would pay for it this morning—and by God he was—but he'd been so keyed up when he'd left Hogan's, it was either drink or end up back at her place.

He'd done the smart thing and gotten drunk.

Clay had always prided himself on having a level head. On being responsible and cautious and using the good judgment God gave him. A single dad, he didn't have a choice. Last night he'd blown that image of himself to hell and back.

The scene that played out between him and Hogan had not only been impulsive and reckless, it had been downright dangerous—a career wrecker—and morally wrong. She was his *subordinate*. A young cop who'd just lost her partner and best friend. She'd been drinking and vulnerable. Alone in a new town, she'd needed a friend.

None of those things had made any difference when she'd kissed him. No siree. The instant her mouth touched his, he'd forgotten all about taking the high road and went after her like some sex-deprived teenager.

"You're as hungover as a rug on a clothesline."

Clay nearly sloshed coffee out of his mug at the sound of Jo Nell's voice. He looked up to find her standing in the doorway to his office, staring at him the way a crazy aunt might look at her favorite nephew who happened to be just as crazy.

"I'm not hungover," he growled.

"And I haven't been smoking."

He sniffed, smelled cigarette smoke. "I guess that makes us even."

Crossing to his desk, she shoved a glass of ice water at

him with one hand and offered three suspicious-looking pills in the other. "This'll help."

"Are those legal?" he asked, wondering briefly if he really wanted to know.

"Don't worry, Chief. They're all over-the-counter. My special recipe for hangovers."

Without further ado, he scooped up the pills and downed them with the water. "Thanks."

"So what's got you tied into little knots this morning?"

"Who says I've got anything in a knot?"

"I ain't seen you look this miserable since your wife flew the coop."

Clay figured he had enough female problems at the moment without borrowing more from his ex-wife. "Don't you have work to do?"

The bell on the front door jingled, telling them someone had entered the reception area. All Clay could think was that he'd been saved by the bell. He didn't have the patience for Jo Nell's antics this morning.

"Holler if you need anything." She started toward the front.

"No more smoking," he called out behind her.

Footsteps sounded as someone started down the hall toward them. Clay couldn't see who it was from where he sat, but Jo Nell stopped and turned, her eyes widening slightly. "Good morning," she said with a little too much enthusiasm.

He heard a mumbled reply. Clay barely had time to brace before Marty stepped into the doorway of his office. She stared at him as if she'd just stepped in front of a firing squad to wait for the killing shot.

Jo Nell looked at him then back to Marty, one brow raised speculatively. "You're a little early, ain't you?"

Marty didn't take her eyes off him. "I need to speak to the chief."

Removing a pill bottle from her shirt pocket, Jo Nell tapped out three and handed them to Marty. "You look like you could use this, too," she said.

Marty held out her hand and muttered a thank-you.

"Must be something going round." Jo Nell shook her head.

"Close the door behind you," Clay snapped.

But she was smiling when the door clicked shut.

Clay hadn't been expecting Marty to show up early. He hadn't quite formulated what he was going to say to her yet. An apology, at least. Something that would excuse his behavior and allow them to work together without the discomfort of having shared inappropriate intimacies. For the life of him he couldn't figure out what that might be.

"How you feeling?" he asked.

"Better."

Automatic reply, he thought. A lie. He could tell by the way her eyes darted quickly to the right before meeting his again that she wasn't okay. But he let it go.

"Have a seat."

She took the chair opposite his desk. She looked at the Santa Fe–inspired oil reproduction on his wall and fidgeted like a kid who'd been sent to the principal's office.

Clay waited.

"I'm sorry about what happened last night," she blurted. "I was . . . out of line. It was inappropriate and—"

"Hogan."

". . . unprofessional. I was upset because of . . . Rosetti. I wasn't thinking straight. But I can assure you nothing like this will ever happen—"

"*Hogan.*"

She quieted and blinked at him.

It would have been easy at that point to lay the blame on her. He was the superior, after all. She had, in fact, made the first move. But while Clay might be a lot of things, he was not a liar. He would never let someone take the blame for something he'd played a role in.

Taking a moment to get his thoughts in order, he rose and walked to the coffee station, where he poured coffee into a cup for her and refilled his own. He handed the cup to Marty, then sat behind his desk. "Don't apologize," he said.

"I just thought—"

"You'd just found out your former partner was killed," he cut in. "You were . . ."

"Smashed," she finished.

Clay scrubbed a hand over his jaw, realizing he'd missed a good bit of stubble this morning. "Half the cops I know would have reacted the same way you did."

Her gaze skittered away, but she forced it back to his. "The drinking part, maybe."

Clay felt himself flush, but he didn't break eye contact. This was where he was supposed to tell her it hadn't been all her doing; he'd played a role in those few minutes of insanity, too. After all, it had been his hands roaming her body. "Look, I'm not excusing what happened," he said. "I didn't exactly handle the situation the way I should have."

"I don't blame you if you need to take some kind of disciplinary measure."

"If I put something in your file, I'll have to put something in mine, too. If it's all the same to you, I'd rather not."

"Oh." Her brows drew together. *"Oh."*

"Yeah."

She looked down into her coffee cup, then back at him. "So what are we going to do about it?"

"Not a damn thing."

She looked at the oil painting again, as if she wished she could escape into it. "Pretend it never happened."

"I'm sorry I handled things so badly. I think we can both agree nothing like that will happen again."

"Absolutely."

The silence grew awkward, and he asked the question he'd been dreading. "Any news from Chicago?"

A shadow passed over her eyes, but she focused on answering, on the facts. "Nothing new."

"I would imagine you won't get much until the ME's preliminary report comes out."

"Probably."

Another awkward silence descended. "I'm actually glad you came in early."

"Now, there's a surprise."

"I've been getting some feedback on your Rufus work."

"I'm feeling better already."

"Good feedback," he clarified. "Especially getting the word out to kids with the Run Away, Shout It Out, and Tell a Grown-up Program."

"Look, Chief, no offense intended, but before you tell me what a good job I've been doing, I should tell you being Rufus the crime dog is not my greatest aspiration as a cop."

"Actually, I was going to tell you I'm going to put you on the patrol roster."

"Does that mean I'm out of the Rufus doghouse?"

Clay couldn't help it. He smiled, unduly relieved that through all of this she was able to muster some semblance of humor. "The assignment wasn't meant as punishment. I wanted to give you a chance to get your feet under you, get your focus."

"Keep me away from the rest of your guys," she put in.

"That, too." Because she was charming him, he looked down at the roster and schedule in front of him. "Part-time, at first. You'll still have a few Rufus stints."

"Of course."

"Same shift. I've assigned you a patrol car. I'll let you know about the upcoming Rufus appearances."

As if realizing that was her cue to leave, she rose. "Is that it?"

Clay rose, too. "Keep me posted on any news out of Chicago."

"Will do."

She hesitated for an instant longer, then turned and walked from his office. Clay sank into his chair, wiped the sweat from his palms and hoped he could keep himself from screwing up again.

*They had followed her to the ends of the earth. Or so it* seemed. For the last hundred miles Radimir had seen nothing but an arid and scarred landscape that spread out before him like an oil painting created in an era of violence. Dotted with scrub, rock and the occasional bovine, the land was as desolate and hostile as an ancient war zone.

His head still ached from the sunset. Despite his hundred-dollar shades, the sun had drilled into his eyes for the last two hundred miles with the blinding light of an atomic bomb.

Next to him, Katja stretched like a cat and glanced out the window. "Looks like Mars."

"Might as well be."

"You are sure she's here?"

"I am sure." He glanced over at his sister. "What is the address?"

She reached into the console and unfolded the single sheet of paper. "Thirteen Brushy Creek Drive."

"Do you have the map?"

Turning on the dome light, she squinted at the sheet of paper. "It's off of Cactus Street on the west end of town, past the traffic light. Over the railroad tracks on the right."

They passed beneath a blinking yellow light. "There are tracks ahead."

Katja turned off the dome light and pointed as the rental car bumped over the tracks. "There's Brushy Creek."

He made a right, taking in as much of his surroundings as he could in the darkness. "Dismal fucking place."

"There's the house."

Radimir slowed the car, assessing the house as they idled by. "Bitch lives in a rat hole."

"No car in the driveway."

"Maybe she's working."

"Might be a good time to go into the house."

He cast her a sidelong look, wondering—not for for the first time—about her sanity. "We don't know where she is or what she's doing. She could be back at any time."

She gave him a sly smile, but her eyes flashed with cruelty. *"Ootebya nyet yayeesav."*

"I have balls," he snapped. "And I have a brain to go with them, which is more than I can say for you."

Katja threw her head back and laughed. "So you say."

Angry, Radimir hit the gas and sped past the darkened house. He'd carefully analyzed every detail of this operation; there was no way in hell he was going to let his crazy sister screw things up. She might be creative in the ways of death, but that wasn't to say her passion would not be her downfall. "This isn't the time for foolishness."

Hissing another curse in Russian, she waved him off and turned to the window. "As long as I get my time with her."

"You will." He thought of the cop in Chicago and smiled. "He gave her up readily enough, didn't he?"

"It took some doing." She nodded, her expression revealing an odd sense of respect. "He was tough. A warrior."

"It will be interesting to see just how tough the bitch is."

"No matter. I will break her. I always do."

Radimir headed out of town, toward the tiny place he'd rented before leaving Chicago. He knew it was going to be a dump. Probably worse than the place Hogan lived. He knew Katja would complain. But in the long run, there had been no other way. Two Russians in a small Texas Panhandle town would stand out too much for them to remain anonymous long enough to get the job done. People would remember their accents, their faces. And when they left Marty Hogan dead and cut to pieces, the police would eventually figure things out. He couldn't let that happen.

According to the bubba real estate agent, the house they'd rented was located on the south side of the Canadian River basin on the edge of Deaf Smith County.

"In the middle of fucking nowhere," Radimir muttered as headlights played over mesquite and prickly pear frosted with a coating of dust. The Lexus handled the dirt road without a problem, but he wouldn't want to be caught out here after a rain without a four-wheel-drive vehicle.

The road banked right, and the house loomed into view. It was a stucco structure the color of mud with a tin roof and a hundred years of grime clinging to opaque windows. A windmill and a skeletal tree stood in the front yard like a couple of long dead sentinels. Fifty yards beyond the house, two crumbling outbuildings melted into the landscape. The remnants of a decades-old wire fence lay in tangles among tumbleweed and hip-high prairie grass.

Radimir parked in front of the house, and they got out of the car. Katja looked around, a space traveler from some hokey television show who'd just landed on a planet in another solar system. "I will kill her good for this."

"In that case, I'll unload the equipment and we will figure out exactly how to do it."

*Marty had never been to a rodeo. Not because she'd de-*prived herself of the pleasure or entertainment, but because she'd never had the slightest inclination to go. She'd never been a fan of cowboys or horses or anything Western for that matter. Even as a child, while most young girls were riding bikes or pining for a horse, all Marty wanted was to ride shotgun with her dad, the cop. She was urban all the way. Give her a forest of tall buildings, a pot of bad coffee and a crime to solve, and she was a happy camper.

The Caprock Canyon Sheriff's Posse arena was as far removed from cosmopolitan as it got. Pickup trucks of every shape and size jammed the gravel parking lot. Most of the trucks hauled horse trailers, some carrying as many as six animals. Men in cowboy hats, tight jeans and belt buckles half the size of Texas milled about with the purposeful determination of a broker walking North Michigan Avenue. Little boys with gun belts and girls in pink cowboy hats played tag between the parked vehicles and RVs where their mothers sat with watchful eyes beneath the awnings. Then there were the dogs. Corgis, Australian shepherds and border collies waited patiently for their owners from the beds of pickup trucks. Marty had never seen anything like it in her life.

If it hadn't been for Clay's invitation, she never would have ventured into the dust and chaos, especially after their encounter at her place the night Rosetti had died. But she was on her dinner break with half an hour to kill. She could please her boss, and when she needed to escape she had the excuse of work. He couldn't argue with that.

Four days had passed since she'd found out about Rosetti's murder. The grief was still a giant, squeezing fist in her chest. Rosetti had been her hero. Marty's dad had taught her a lot about law enforcement when she was growing up. But Rosetti had taught her how to be a street cop. How horribly ironic that his own murder remained unsolved.

The ME's report hadn't been released yet, but from what little information she'd gathered, Rosetti had been accosted outside a diner, somehow subdued or knocked unconscious, and taken to an unknown location where the perpetrators had tortured him for several hours before killing him. His nude body had been found miles away on the outskirts of Palatine. As of this morning, the cops had no suspects and no motive.

She'd wanted desperately to jump on a jet and find the sons of bitches who were responsible. When she did, she wanted to lay down her badge and take them apart with her bare hands. But Marty knew it was the last thing she could do. At the very least she wanted to go to the funeral. She'd gone so far as to make reservations. But a call to Rosetti's widow had changed her mind. Eileen asked her not to come. The request hurt, but Marty understood. She knew that if she showed up at the funeral, the media would descend and the focus would be shifted away from paying final respects to a fallen officer and onto her. She wouldn't do that to Rosetti. She sure as hell wouldn't give the media the satisfaction of turning the event into a circus.

She walked through the parking lot, sidestepping the occasional manure pile, pausing to let horses and riders sweep past. She felt out of place in uniform. Regardless, almost every person she passed smiled, tilted a hat and said hello. She didn't think she'd ever met a friendlier group of people. What the hell were they so happy about?

"Hogan."

She turned to find Clay standing a few yards away, next to a white horse trailer that was hooked up to a blue pickup. "Hey, Chief."

Her eyes took in the length of him before she could stop herself. He wore a sky blue work shirt rolled up at the sleeves and wet beneath his arms. Faded jeans hugged lean hips and long, muscular legs. Boots that looked to be at least a hundred years old covered his feet. The hat he wore shaded his eyes, but she could still feel the intent sweep of his gaze as she crossed to him.

"Nice belt buckle," she said.

He glanced down at the buckle and smiled. "Thanks."

A brown horse with a saddle on its back and white spots on its rump stood tied to the trailer. A little girl in a purple Western shirt and matching hat stood next to the horse, looking expectantly at Clay.

"Come on, Dad. It's almost time. I gotta get him warmed up."

Only then did Marty recognize the girl as Clay's daughter. She'd met her during her Rufus stint at the elementary school. Marty had since noticed her gap-toothed photo on the corner of his desk. Still, an odd sense of surprise rippled through her. She hadn't expected this little slip of a girl to have a wild-eyed, snorting horse the size of a tank. She had to hand it to her; the kid had balls.

The girl cast an uninterested glance in Marty's direction. Marty stared back, and found herself thinking about Clay's marital status. Not that she was interested one way or another, she told herself. She just liked to stay on top of things.

Clay turned back to his daughter. "Erica, this is Marty Hogan."

The girl yanked a strap through the saddle girth before turning. She stared at Marty for a moment, as if sizing her up, trying to decide if she was friend or foe. Marty stared back, feeling more than a little out of her league. What the hell was it about kids? They were so frickin' weird.

"Hey, Rufus," Erica said.

Marty gave a very unladylike snort. She thought about giving a couple of woofs just for the entertainment value, but she didn't want to scare the horse.

Erica giggled and stuck out her hand. "I mean, Marty."

Surprised by the girl's good manners, Marty shook her hand. "Hey, cowgirl. Nice horse."

"Thanks."

"You going to win today?"

"Hope so." She looked at her father. "Dad says we got what it takes." Erica turned back to her horse and spoke over her shoulder. "Dad, can you get the bridle?"

Casting an apologetic look in Marty's direction, Clay crossed to the horse and quickly unfastened the halter. He slipped a bit into the animal's mouth and the bridle over its poll. Checking the strap that ran beneath the animal's belly, he led the horse a few steps from the trailer. "Don't forget to keep your eyes on the next barrel," he said.

"I know."

"Don't look down. Use your legs."

"Okay, okay." With the confidence of a bronc rider, she put her foot in the stirrup and swung onto the horse's back.

"Go warm him up." Clay pointed. "I'll be over by the stands."

"'Kay." Giving Marty a final look, Erica swung the horse around and they were off at a fast trot.

Clay watched her go, then looked at Marty. "She's nervous," he said.

"So is her dad."

"That obvious, huh?"

Marty had sworn she wouldn't think about the kiss, but looking into his eyes, she suddenly couldn't get it out of her head. Feeling a small rise of embarrassment, she looked around. "I've never been to a rodeo before."

He arched a brow. "Are you sure you're not from another planet?"

"Not that I know of, but my mom was kind of wild."

He laughed. "Well, you're in for a treat." His eyes skimmed over her uniform, then quickly away. "On your dinner break?"

"I thought I might educate myself on some of the local culture."

"Dugan, Smitty and Jett are over there." He motioned toward the small grandstand. "Dugan brought his wife and kid if you want to meet them."

Marty knew mingling with her fellow officers outside of work was the right thing to do, especially after such a rocky start. But she'd never been good at doing the right thing, particularly when it entailed phony smiles and a let's-just-get-along attitude she didn't feel. "Uh, well, I wasn't planning on staying that long. Maybe next time?"

Clay frowned, but to his credit, he let it go. "In that case, let's get over to the arena. They run them through pretty quickly."

Marty didn't know what that meant, but she didn't ask for clarification. He seemed a little frazzled. Maybe even more nervous than his daughter. When they reached the arena, she figured out why.

"So what's this event called?" she asked.

"Barrel racing." He pointed to three barrels positioned

in a triangular pattern, each about sixty feet apart. "It's a timed event. Rider takes a horse around the barrels as fast as he can and hopes he gets the best time."

"My kind of event."

He shot her a sideways look. "I bet."

The arena was open air and huge—probably a hundred feet wide by two hundred feet long. It was enclosed on all four sides by a white pipe fence. Bleachers bracketed two sides and were jam-packed with cowboy-hat-clad parents, sunburned moms fanning themselves and children eating hot dogs and French fries.

The announcer called a number. An instant later the gate swung open. A girl not much older than Erica blasted through on a wild-eyed white horse. Hooves kicking up dirt, horse and rider rode the pattern at a death-defying speed. It was enough to give even a seasoned cop a heart attack.

"Now I understand why you're nervous," Marty said.

"I swear, seeing her ride like that does me in every time."

"I don't blame you."

He pointed. "There she is, in the warm-up pen."

Marty wasn't easily impressed, but these kids impressed her and then some.

Clay cupped his hands on either side of his mouth. "Drive him forward! Keep a nice big pocket between you and the barrel!"

As if homed in to her father's voice, Erica nodded, never seeming to lose her focus on the animal beneath her.

"You're doing great, honey!"

Marty shot him a furtive glance. Cool-headed Clay Settlemeyer was a bundle of nerves. His hands gripped the pipe rail in front of him with such force that his knuckles were white.

"How long until it's her turn?" Marty asked.

"A minute or two. She's number eighty-four."

Marty leaned against the pipe fence and watched in awe as children as young as five years old whipped horses around the barrels at a mind-boggling speed. "They're practically babies," she said.

Clay grinned at her, and for a moment, Marty couldn't look away. The brim of his hat shaded his eyes, but she could see pinlights of excitement veiled by layers of nerves. A father's pride. "Most of them have been riding horses since they could walk. It's kind of a way of life out here." He chuckled. "They beat the pants off the adults half the time."

Marty laughed, truly amused by the thought.

"She's next. Here we go."

The gate swung open and Erica's spotted horse pranced into the arena, snorting, its head held high. The girl looked totally relaxed, focused and in control. The horse spun once, then lunged into a wild sprint for the first barrel.

"Go, honey!" Clay shouted. "Use your legs! Give him his head!"

Marty's breath caught in her throat as girl and horse streaked around the first barrel and shot toward the second. Before she could stop herself, she began shouting right along with Clay. "Get on it! Go, kid! Go! *Go!*"

The horse spun around the second barrel, leaning in, as low as a motorcycle racer around a hairpin curve, and sprinted toward the third. Erica clung to his back like a little monkey, hands forward and urging him faster, her legs rocking in time with every breathtaking stride. They rounded the third barrel and headed back toward the gate.

"Come on, honey! Go!"

Marty jumped up and down a couple of times as the horse barreled down the arena toward home. "You go, girl! *Go!*"

Next to her, Clay laughed. His eyes went to the electronic scoreboard where a time of 15.53 popped up. "She's got it!"

"That was amazing!" Marty was breathless just from watching.

He grinned at her, his eyes alight with excitement.

Marty found herself staring back, unable to look away. For a crazy moment, she thought he might lean forward and kiss her. The memory of the intimate moments they'd shared four days ago at her house flashed in her mind's eye and a little trill of excitement rippled through her.

"Uh . . ." Clay cleared his throat. "That was her best time ever."

"Is she going to win?"

"She's going to be pissed if she doesn't."

"My kind of girl."

He frowned at her, then glanced toward the parking lot where the horse trailer was parked. "Come on."

Marty had never seen this side of her boss. The side of him that was soft and lighthearted and as excited as a kid on Christmas morning. All over a freckle-faced little girl who could ride like the wind. The thought made her smile, and she found herself wondering about the girl's mother. Was Clay divorced? If so, how was it that he'd gotten custody of the kid? And why had the divorce happened in the first place? Not only did he appear to be a doting father, but he was undeniably attractive.

Once again, images of the kiss they'd shared flickered in her mind. Marty remembered the scrape of his beard against her cheek. The warmth of his breath against her face. The firm pressure of his mouth against hers. The way the combination of those things had sucked the breath right out of her lungs . . .

The realization of where her mind had taken her stopped her cold. Marty wasn't prone to noticing inconsequential details about men. It wasn't like her to fantasize. Especially in broad daylight standing next to the man in question.

Clay Settlemeyer might have a bit of charm; she'd give him that. But she had far too much going on in her life to let herself be swayed by it. Marty could not afford to make another mistake. Like it or not, her job here in Caprock Canyon was her last chance. She wasn't going to screw it up.

"Hogan, you coming?"

She gave herself a hard mental shake, realizing she'd actually stopped in the middle of the dusty parking lot with trucks and horses and cowboys rushing by. "Um . . . yeah."

He gave her a sage look as they walked side by side toward the trailer. "Any word from Chicago?"

Marty shook her head. "Nothing new."

"Keep me posted, okay?"

"Sure."

They reached the trailer where Erica sat on her horse, grinning ear to ear. "Dad, did you see that time?"

"Sure did, honey."

Marty watched as he helped her from the horse and began to unsaddle it. "That was awesome, cowgirl."

The girl leaned forward and hugged her horse around its neck. "I knew you could do it, George."

Clay met Marty's eyes and they exchanged amused smiles. Realizing she'd already spent more time here than she'd intended, she glanced at her watch. "I gotta get back to work. Let me know if you win."

The little girl walked over to Marty. "You know how to ride?"

"I know how to get bucked off."

"If you come over, I'll show you."

Marty glanced at Clay, who'd just slid the saddle from the horse's back. "She's a good teacher," he said.

She smiled at the girl, more charmed than she wanted to be. "I'll think about it."

"Heading out?" Clay asked.

"Duty calls."

"Uh huh." He set the saddle in a small compartment at the front of the trailer, then leaned against the door and crossed his arms. Erica came up next to him and he set his hand on her skinny little shoulder.

As Marty walked away, she could feel their eyes on her back, and she found herself wishing she could stay.

# EIGHT

*Marty was still thinking about Clay and his daredevil*
daughter when Jo Nell's voice crackled over the radio.
"Hogan, you out there?"

She hit the Talk button. "What you got?"

"I just took a 911 from some guy down in the canyon.
Says there's a pickup truck on the ranch road. Driver's
drunk and almost hit him."

"You got a description of the vehicle?" Glancing in her
rearview mirror, she made a U-turn on Cactus and headed
out of town.

"Ford F-150. Red. Short bed. Didn't get a plate."

"I think that narrows it down enough."

"Don't get fresh with me, young lady."

Marty grinned. "Wouldn't dream of it."

In the last week she and Jo Nell had struck up an odd
camaraderie. They weren't exactly friends, but they made
each other laugh and that was enough to break down the
barriers between them. Secretly, Marty thought it was the
smoke they'd shared one morning before the other officers

or Clay had arrived. They'd smoked and made small talk and then Marty had helped Jo Nell dispose of the evidence. They were now partners in crime, a relationship that suited both to a tee.

Racking the mike, she flipped on her emergency lights and hit the gas, pushing the speedometer a little past the limit. On the south side of town, she left the main drag and turned onto a farm-to-market road that took her to the northwest entrance of the canyon.

The road that ran through the canyon was not well traveled, but for many of the area ranchers and farmers, it was the only way to get into town without having to drive around the north or south side. The road was a narrow swath of unlined asphalt that curved down the three-hundred-foot slope to the valley floor. The base of the canyon was only a mile or so wide. On the opposite side, the road became unpaved and a series of switchbacks took motorists back up to the top.

Marty stopped the cruiser on the northwest rim of the canyon and got out. Using the binoculars all officers kept in their vehicles, she scoured the main road, the valley floor and the lesser-traveled dirt roads for a red pickup truck. Nothing moved within the desolate stretch of juniper, mesquite and copper-colored rock.

The locals called Palo Duro Canyon Texas's best-kept secret. Staring out over the rust-colored mesas that flared like Spanish skirts, Marty thought it was probably one of the best-kept secrets in the entire United States. It was the first truly beautiful place she'd seen since traveling to Texas. Not many people knew it was the country's second-largest canyon. She wondered if, perhaps, that was by design.

She found herself thinking about Clay again. Not a good sign. She wanted to believe her attraction to him was a result of stress, a state that had wreaked havoc on her life since *The Incident* six months ago. Or maybe it was the grief she felt in response to Rosetti's murder. Whatever the case, her emotions were evidently playing tricks on her. She was sad and a little lonely. That's all it was. Plain and simple.

But Marty knew there was nothing plain or simple about her feelings for her boss. She was not prone to petty attractions or infatuations. So then why the hell was she thinking about him now? Why did her heart stumble around in her chest every time she got within shouting distance of him? Why couldn't she wait until the next time she saw him?

"Because you're a freaking idiot," she muttered.

Disgusted with herself, Marty climbed back into the cruiser and picked up the mike. "Jo Nell, this is 353."

"Go ahead."

"I'm out at the canyon and don't see a soul."

"Roger that."

"I'm going to cruise down to the bridge. See what I can find." The bridge was an old wooden structure that arched over a small tributary that ultimately fed into the Canadian River. It was dry nine months out of the year, but floodwaters during the rainy season had cut a deep ravine into the earth.

"When you get back, we'll have us a smoke."

Marty grinned. "I could arrest you for that."

The older woman hung up on her.

Marty laughed outright as she racked the mike and started into the canyon. The sun disappeared behind the high rock walls as she descended the steep, narrow road, casting her in shadow. At the base of the canyon, the asphalt fell away. Her tires crunched over dirt and gravel, leaving a dusty wake that was slow to dissipate. Her windows were down, and the evening air was cool and pleasant against her face. She was tapping her fingers to a quirky Red Hot Chili Peppers tune when the cruiser jolted. The steering wheel jerked to the right, and Marty knew she'd blown a tire.

"Crap," she muttered as she pulled onto the dusty shoulder.

She killed the engine, and got out and walked around to the front of the car. Sure enough, the right front tire was as flat as a Texas wheat field. She kicked the tire, then made her way to the trunk to start the process of changing it.

Around her the canyon sang a thousand songs. Finches and titmice tittered from the branches of the low-growing mesquite and juniper. The occasional meadowlark warbled from the tall grasses. From the distant peaks of the mesas, she could hear the coyotes yipping. A hundred yards away, frogs and toads had gathered on the banks of the creek in preparation for the night. All of it was punctuated by a chorus of crickets and grasshoppers and cicadas.

For a moment, the compelling beauty rendered her to stillness. Marty could do nothing but stand there and take it all in, marveling at its unique and hostile magnificence.

Realizing the shadows were deepening, she made her way to the car and picked up her mike. "Jo Nell, this is 353, you there?"

"What now?" Jo Nell's voice crackled over the airwaves.

"I'm in the canyon. No sign of the red truck or driver."

"Probably home and sleeping it off by now."

"I've got a flat tire. I've got to put on the spare."

"You know how to do that?"

Marty rolled her eyes. "For God's sake, Jo Nell, I'm a cop."

"Just checking. I doubt Smitty knows how to and *he's* a cop."

Marty chuckled, glad she had Jo Nell to help her keep things in perspective. "I'll be there in half an hour."

"I'll have that smoke waitin'."

"Roger that." She racked the mike and walked around to the rear of the car to open the trunk. It had been a while since she'd had to change a tire, but she remembered how. She just didn't like it.

Bending, she removed the trunk panel, unlocked the spare tire and jack and carried both to the front of the car. She broke a sweat as she set the jack in place and began to pump. The wind had picked up and whispered like unruly schoolchildren through the mesquite and high grass. The coyotes were closer now, yipping and howling like hyenas. Marty knew they weren't dangerous, but the sound was enough to make the hairs on her nape stand up. Around her, the birds had gone silent, announcing nightfall's approach.

"Come on, Hogan, get a move on."

Of course, she wasn't afraid of the dark. But the rugged and desolate canyon was no place to be at night. She'd just finished jacking the car to the proper height when a dull thud in the dirt a foot or so from her right knee snagged her attention. She glanced over, noticed the remaining small puff of dust. An instant later, the unmistakable sound of a rifle's retort sent her to her feet.

"What the hell?"

Her words were punctuated by a second thud, a rise of dust and a long-distance report. Disbelief and an uneasy sense of fear shot through her. Ducking low, Marty rushed to the driver's side of the vehicle, swung open the door and grabbed the mike. "This is 353. I got a 10-33."

"What the hell's a 10-33?"

Another gunshot sounded. Closer this time. Not the distant firing of a rifle. More like a handgun. Marty couldn't believe it. "Shots fired in the canyon!"

"Someone's shootin' at ya?"

A bullet slammed into the ground, less than a foot from where she knelt. "I'm under fire!" she shouted. "Get someone out here, damn it!"

"Where are you?"

"Northwest corner on the ranch road. A hundred yards from the bridge. I'm taking goddamn fire!"

"I'll call the chief."

*Thwack! Thwack! Thwack!*

Only then did Marty acknowledge there were two shooters, firing from opposite directions. One from a distance to the southwest, the other from behind her, from where there was a clear shot. She was pretty sure the second shooter had a rifle.

She spun, vulnerable with no cover. A flash of color from the rocks seventy yards away grabbed her attention. Drawing her revolver, she dropped into a shooter's stance and fired three times in quick succession. She caught another glimpse of movement. Someone moving up the rocky face of the cliff, just off the road Marty had come down.

Tossing the mike onto the seat, Marty slid behind the wheel and slammed the door. Never taking her eyes from the place where she'd seen movement, she twisted the key, cut the wheel hard and hit the gas. The cruiser shot forward, the right front tire dropping as it came off the jack. Driving over rough terrain with a flat tire would undoubtedly ruin the wheel, but she figured it was a small price to pay to catch some drunken son of a bitch taking potshots at a cop.

She took the car up the road, closest to the place she'd seen the shooter. With dusk rapidly falling away to darkness, it was difficult to see. She squinted into the shadows, caught a glimpse of blue twenty yards up the road. She floored the gas. The car's rear tires spun as it shot forward. Her target disappeared, then reemerged ten yards from the road.

Marty took the car off-road. It bounced violently over deadfall and rocks the size of basketballs. Just when she thought she might catch him, the car bottomed out and hung up.

"Damn it." Snarling, she hit the emergency lights, threw open the door and hit the ground running.

Keeping low, ever watchful for movement, she sprinted toward the place where she'd last seen her quarry. Midway there, the unmistakable sound of a bullet ricocheting off rock stopped her cold. Ducking into a small ravine where runoff had eroded the soil, Marty squinted into the thickening darkness, her heart pounding wildly in her chest.

"Police!" she shouted. "Put your hands up and step out now!"

The only answer was the screech of a hoot owl and the mocking whisper of the wind.

She gripped the revolver with sweat-slicked hands and peered around a low-growing juniper. Visibility had dwindled, but she heard rocks sliding a few yards away, as if someone were scrambling up the steep incline. Holding her weapon steady, she muscled her way out of the ravine.

"Halt! Police! Drop your weapon! Do it now!"

Whoever it was didn't stop. She could hear him scrambling up the sheer face of the cliff. Anger and nerves pulled her in different directions as she pursued. She could hear her labored breathing over the hard thrum of her heart. A few yards ahead, she heard the shooter breaking through brush and followed the sound, guessing him to be no more than ten or fifteen yards ahead.

"Stop or I'll fire!" she shouted.

Marty raised the revolver, her finger on the trigger. There was no way she could fire blindly; as far as she knew the person running from her could be a twelve-year-old kid stupid enough to shoot at a cop.

She entered a thicket of mesquite. Branches clawed at her uniform, scratching her face, spindly fingers snagging her hair. She was making too much noise, but she could hear him in front of her, running. She was gaining ground.

Breaking from the thicket, she caught a glimpse of movement. Too late she saw the gun. Blue steel. The muzzle flash blinding her. Explosion deafening her ears. The hot whiz of a bullet inches from her left ear.

A scream tore from her throat as she spun. She lost her footing and went to her knees. The ground beneath her crumbled. The next thing she knew she was rolling down a steep embankment, branches and rocks punching her like rude fists.

Dust and grit filled her mouth and eyes. Jagged rock tore at her clothes and bruised skin. The gun flew from her hand as she tumbled ever downward. All Marty could think was that if he came for her now, she was a dead woman.

*Clay finished unhooking the horse trailer from the pickup* truck while Erica put George in his stall for the night. Around him, the meadowlarks sang their final songs of the day. To the west, a final ray of sunshine spread yellow light on the wheat field beyond his pasture. The evening was as pleasant as evenings ever were here in the Panhandle.

Leaning against the paddock gate, he looked out over his small spread at the loafing sheds, the horses grazing nearby, and the arena where he and Erica had worked so many hours in preparation for the barrel-racing season. It had taken him years, but he'd built a secure and comfortable home for his daughter.

He should have been satisfied; many a man went his entire lifetime without the gifts that had been bestowed upon him. Yes, he'd worked his ass off to get where he was. He'd made his share of sacrifices to give his daughter the kind of opportunities he'd never had. Still, sometimes there was a weight in his chest that told him something was missing.

But Clay had always been full of dreams. Foolish dreams, according to his father. Growing up in a rural area where he could hope for little more than to farm the land upon which his father and his grandfather had farmed before him, Clay had been cursed with a perpetual case of discontent. A hunger for more than had been allotted him.

Clay had sworn he would get out of Caprock Canyon. He'd sworn he would be the first Settlemeyer to graduate from college. Go to the city. Make something of himself. He'd sworn he would never settle.

Had he?

He told himself that was crazy. He had it all. A job he loved. A comfortable home. Good friends. And Erica was the love of his life. Some days he loved her so much he ached inside with the need to keep her safe and happy and secure. God knew he tried. But sometimes he wondered if he could have done a better job. He wondered if she missed having a mother.

She knew Eve had left, but she'd never asked why. Clay had never told Erica that Eve hadn't wanted her. Even if Erica asked, he wouldn't say. The truth was too harsh for a ten-year-old. He'd rather walk through fire than hurt his child.

The cell phone clipped to his belt chirped twice before he noticed. Sighing, he answered with a clipped utterance of his name.

"Chief!"

Clay knew immediately by Jo Nell's tone this was no false alarm. She was as tough as they came and didn't panic easily.

"I just got a call from Hogan," she panted. "She's in the canyon. Says someone's shootin' at her!"

He was sprinting toward the Explorer before she finished the first sentence. "Where?"

"Ranch road. Northwest side."

"I'm on my way. Call Jett and Dugan. Get them out there. Send an ambulance, too, will you?"

"Sure thing."

He hit End as the Explorer tore out of the driveway. The speedometer hit sixty as he dialed his home number. Heidi Huffschmidtt answered on the fourth ring. The Amish woman cooked and cleaned for him and Erica five days a week and worried about them getting enough to eat the other two. "Heidi?"

"Yah?"

"I have an emergency to take care of. Can you stay for a couple more hours?"

"No problem, Chief. I just put out the rhubarb pie and might just have me a piece."

"Thanks," he muttered and disconnected.

The speedometer reached ninety as he hit the highway. Picking up his mike, he put a call out to Marty. "What the hell's going on?"

An instant of static, then Jett got on the line. "I'm en route, Chief. Jo Nell said they got shots fired in the canyon."

"What's your ETA?"

"Fifteen minutes."

Clay was only five minutes away. "Loop around and enter from the southwest ranch road."

"That'll take longer."

"Yeah, but if someone's trying to run, that's where you'll intercept."

"Roger that."

Clay made the canyon in record time. He blew the stop sign at the ranch road and hit the dirt doing fifty. Midway down the northwest side, he spotted headlights and picked up his mike.

"Hogan, you there?"

Silence hissed. If she were able, Clay knew she'd respond. Why wasn't she answering?

The remains of dusk were little more than a pale gray layer of clouds lying on the western horizon. But Clay could still see. The hairs at his nape prickled when he spotted Hogan's cruiser. He could tell by the angle of the headlight beams that the vehicle was in the ditch.

Following the ranch road, he found the place where the car had left the road. "What the hell?"

Deep tire grooves marred the sandy soil. What would compel her to drive over terrain she didn't have a chance of traversing without getting stuck?

He continued on, and the cruiser loomed into view, a wrecked ship listing on a sandy beach. Clay parked a few yards away, scanning the surrounding area as he snatched up the radio. "I got a visual on Hogan's car. No sign of her."

"Roger that, Chief," came Jett's voice. "I'm coming up from the south, ETA five minutes."

"No lights or siren."

"Ten four."

Clay racked the mike. Grabbing the flashlight, he slid from his vehicle, but he didn't turn it on. He didn't want to give away his position if there was, indeed, a sniper in the canyon.

Where the hell was Hogan?

Drawing his revolver, he started toward her vehicle, praying he didn't find a nightmare. Concern scraped up his back when he spotted the driver's side door standing open. Clay peered inside. Relief slipped through him when he didn't find her. When he didn't find blood. No shattered windows. She'd left her flashlight. He made his way around the vehicle, noticed the right front tire was flat.

He scanned the surrounding scrub, listening. "Hogan!" he ventured after a moment.

"I'm here."

Clay spun, flipping on the flashlight with his thumb. The sound of breaking brush and crumbling rocks drew his eye, and he swung the beam right. Marty pushed from a stand of mesquite. Even in the dim beam from the flashlight, he saw blood on her face. A coating of dust on her uniform.

"What happened?" He didn't wait for an answer. He crossed to her, put his hands on her shoulders. Looking into her eyes, he was torn between shaking her and pulling her to him.

"Ambush." Her entire body vibrated beneath his hands.

That was the kind of word the Marines used in Iraq, not

in Palo Duro Canyon. In fact, Clay had never heard it used in relation to anything that happened in Caprock Canyon, Texas. "You okay?"

"Yeah."

She was far from okay. But at least she wasn't seriously injured. For now, that was going to have to do, because he needed answers.

"How long ago?" he asked.

"Five minutes."

"Where are they now?"

"Ran. You must have scared them off."

"Maybe you ought to start at the beginning."

"I answered a possible drunk driver call." She fell into cop mode, but her eyes went repeatedly to the steep and rocky area from which she'd emerged. "I had a flat. Got out to change the tire. Almost immediately I came under fire."

Clay gaped at her, disbelief warring with an uneasiness he didn't want to feel. But he found his own eyes scanning the ridge to his right. "Are you sure?"

"What do you mean, am I sure? How could I not be sure? I know what a rifle report sounds like."

"Calm down. All I'm asking is how you know it was a sniper and not a stray bullet from a hunter."

"Because he fired at least a dozen times. If I hadn't taken cover, I wouldn't be standing here talking to you right now." She gulped a breath and coughed. "In case you're not reading between the lines here, Chief, there's a sniper in the canyon and he shot at a cop."

A chill slid down his spine at the thought. The chill deepened to something unfathomable when he imagined someone watching them through the crosshairs of a rifle. He looked her up and down. "You sure you're all right?"

"I don't have any holes in me, if that's what you mean."

"You're bleeding."

She flinched when he reached out and touched her face.

"I slid on some loose rock and fell about twenty feet." Some of the bravado leached from her.

He scanned the shadows surrounding them, refusing to allow the uneasiness to take hold. "Any idea who?"

"Male. Blue shirt or jacket. Fast runner, so he's probably young."

Clay felt his eyes narrow. "Let me get this straight. You have no backup. You're not wearing Kevlar." He flicked her vest-free shoulder with his thumb and forefinger. "You're at an obvious disadvantage. And you gave chase?"

"If you're working up to a nice rake over the coals, it gets worse."

"I can't wait to hear it."

A breath shuddered out of her, betraying the attitude she put so much effort into projecting. "I'm pretty sure there were two shooters."

"Two?"

"On either side of the canyon. One armed with a rifle. The other with a handgun."

"And you surmised this how?"

She looked a little offended. "I know my weapons. I know what a rifle sounds like in relation to a handgun."

"Not always easy to distinguish."

"In this case, it was."

She stared at him, holding her ground. He could tell some of the adrenaline was giving way to relief. The kind of weak-in-the-knees relief that came with a disaster narrowly averted.

Clay didn't know what to think about her assertion that there were two snipers on the loose in Palo Duro Canyon and shooting at cops. It wasn't that Clay didn't trust her judgment. But Marty had been through several months of extreme stress. She'd seen a child murdered in cold blood. She'd seen her career go down the drain. She'd moved to a new town, started a new job. She'd lost her partner.

He was pretty sure she was suffering from post-traumatic

stress disorder. He ought to know. He'd been back from Kuwait for almost ten years, and some days he still felt the disorder sneaking up on him. A sound or a smell that would take him back to the night he'd pulled the trigger when he shouldn't have.

Shoving the dark memories aside, Clay gave Marty a hard look. "You sure about this?"

Her expression turned incredulous. "You don't believe me."

"I'm asking you a question."

"I'm sure."

"In that case, I've got to call the sheriff's office. They'll send a few officers, step up patrols. Get some dogs out here. Maybe organize a manhunt first daylight." He gave her an assessing look. "Did you fire your weapon?"

She nodded.

"How many times?"

"I don't remember." He knew enough about adrenaline to know that was usually the case with cops who had to fire their weapon. Most thought they'd fired less than what they really had. He wondered if that would be the case with Marty.

Twin pairs of headlights slashed through the darkness, telling him Jett and Dugan had arrived. Clay raised his flashlight so the other men could find them.

"Chief? Everyone okay?" Jett arrived out of breath.

"Everyone's fine."

Dugan trailed Jett, his flashlight bobbing with every step. "What happened?"

Marty faced the men. "Someone took a shot at me."

Jett's eyes widened. "Damn."

Dugan flashed a look at the chief she couldn't quite read. "Any idea who?"

"No." Clay looked around. "It's too dark to do anything tonight. First light, we'll see if we can find any brass."

"I dropped my gun when I fell," she said.

"Where?"

She pointed toward the stand of mesquite from which she'd emerged.

"We'll find it," Jett said.

"Folks hunt dove this time of year," Dugan put in. "You think it was a stray shot or what?"

"It wasn't a stray bullet," Marty snapped.

Clay glanced sharply at her, but addressed Jett. "Get on the horn and get Rodney out here to tow her car, will you?"

"Sure thing, Chief."

Jett left for his cruiser with a speed that told Clay he didn't want to hear what came next. Clay couldn't blame him. He had a few things to discuss with Marty. He wanted every detail and a time line. Then he needed to broach the possibility that she was suffering from PTSD. The only question that remained was how the hell he was going to do it.

# NINE

*Marty sat at the small interview table, feeling more like* a suspect than a cop and hating every second of it. Six months ago she would have laughed—and maybe even thrown out a few not-so-complimentary names—if her superior had questioned her account of what happened.

Someone had tried to kill her tonight. Two people, more than likely. The question was who and why. Was it random? Or had someone targeted her specifically? Was the incident related to something that had happened here in Caprock Canyon? Did it stem from the scuffle in the bar the other day? Or was someone angry because of what she'd done in Chicago?

One culprit that came to mind was Smitty. Marty had humiliated him in front of his coworkers, gotten him into trouble with his superior. He'd been off duty at the time. He would certainly have access to guns and know how to use them. But how did that explain the second shooter? That brought her to her next problem. Was she absolutely certain of what she'd seen?

Before she could ponder the most disconcerting question of all, the door to the interview room swung open. Marty glanced up to see Clay walk in, looking like he was about to face off with John Gotti.

"What? No rubber hose? No tape recorder? No bamboo slivers?"

"Dugan found your weapon." Setting the gun on the table, he took the seat across from her. "I read your statement."

"So you believe me?"

"I believe *something* happened in that canyon."

He may as well have slapped her. The surge of anger sent her to her feet. "I know what happened, damn it. Someone took a shot at me."

"Two people. Two weapons." He leaned back in the chair and studied her. "No hard evidence. No motive."

"It's in the report." She stared back at him, hating it that she was breathing hard, that she was uneasy. "Can I go now?"

"Sit down. I want to talk to you about something else."

Marty resisted for a moment, then lowered herself into the chair. She didn't like the way he was looking at her, the way a doctor might look at a patient in the moments before he announced some dreadful disease.

For a moment the only sound came from the buzz of the fluorescent light above. She fidgeted, realized belatedly what she was doing and stilled.

"Did you talk to a mental health professional after what happened in Chicago?"

She choked out a laugh. "Oh, for God's sake."

"Did you?"

"I was a little busy getting fired."

"I'll take that as a no."

"I don't see what that has to do with anything."

"I'm not the enemy here."

"You're undermining my credibility."

"I care about you."

His words sucked every combative word right out of her throat. She wanted to ask him how he could possibly care about her when she hadn't exactly been on her best behavior. But that would be too telling a statement. She didn't want him getting that close to knowing her frame of mind.

"What you should care about right now is that someone took a shot at one of your officers," she said.

Clay scraped a hand over his jaw and sighed. "Did you know I did a tour of duty in the Middle East?"

The question knocked her off balance. "I didn't know."

"I spent two years as an MP in Kuwait. A few months before I came home, I was involved in a shooting."

"Why are you telling me this?"

"Because you need to hear it. You need to understand I know what I'm talking about. I've been in your shoes."

"I don't know what you mean." But she got the uneasy sensation he was about to fling some unpleasant surprise her way.

"Three months before I was sent home, I shot and killed a thirteen-year-old girl."

Her vision tunneled on his face, his expression, the pain he couldn't hide in his eyes. She didn't know what to say to that, so she said nothing.

"It happened at a checkpoint. Me and another MP had the graveyard shift." He clasped his hands in front of him and looked down at them. "It was hot that night. Ninety degrees. No wind. We were smothering beneath all our equipment. Three o'clock in the morning, someone approached the checkpoint on foot. My partner was already walking up on the person, yelling at them to stop.

"They didn't stop. I couldn't stop thinking about the rash of suicide bombings, and I knew this was exactly the way it happened. I told my partner to back away, but she didn't. I started yelling at the suspect. I could see it was a female. I saw something dark in her hand. I swear to God it was a gun. When she still didn't stop, I fired my weapon."

For the first time Marty realized a sweat had broken out on his forehead. His hands were clenched in front of him, but she knew if they weren't, they would be trembling.

"I fired four shots," he said. "Every one of them hit home. For a few seconds, all I felt was relief. That there hadn't been a bomb. That both of us were still alive. That the fanatic on the ground was dead."

Clay fell silent. For several seconds he stared at his hands. Then his gaze met Marty's. "Only later did I learn that the dead woman wasn't a fanatic at all. She wasn't even a woman yet. I'd shot and killed a thirteen-year-old girl. The dark object in her hand wasn't a gun, but a bottle of water. She didn't know English. She didn't know we were telling her to stop. She'd been bringing us water."

Marty stared at him, her heart pounding. This was the last conversation she'd expected to have with him. But she thought she knew where he was heading with it.

"I'm sorry," she managed after a moment.

"Me, too. But it's done. You can't go back. You find a way to move on."

"Why are you telling me this?"

"It's relevant."

She waited, not sure she wanted to hear what he was going to say next.

"Killing that kid was tough to swallow. I screwed up. I took a life that never should have been taken. I couldn't stop thinking about it. About her. About what I could have done differently." He smiled, but it looked sharp and unnatural on his face. "I started having nightmares. Flashbacks. A smell or sound could take me right back to that moment. Finally, my commanding officer forced me to go see a shrink. A month later I was diagnosed with post-traumatic stress disorder."

Marty was already shaking her head. "I don't have PTSD."

"I want you to talk to someone." He slid a card across the desk, but she didn't pick it up.

"Shrinks are full of shit."

He smiled again, but this time she could tell he was truly amused. "Maybe."

"Then why—"

"This guy is a psychiatrist, but he did two tours in Vietnam. He was a cop in Atlanta for six years. You'll like him."

The last thing she wanted to do was talk to a shrink. But for the first time, she acknowledged that her reluctance had more to do with what he might say about her as opposed to any philosophical reason.

She picked up the card, slid it into her uniform pocket and met his gaze. "None of this changes the fact that someone took a shot at me in the canyon tonight."

"Deaf Smith County Sheriff's Office is stepping up patrols. We'll look for brass tomorrow." His gaze drilled into hers. "You're sure it wasn't a stray shot?"

"I know it wasn't."

"You do have a penchant for pissing people off. Any ideas who might have done it?"

An odd sense of relief went through her that he was at least asking questions that needed asking. The problem was she couldn't tell if he was pacifying her. "Maybe someone local didn't like what I did in Chicago and decided to take matters into their own hands."

"What else?"

"Maybe I ticked off someone at the bar the other day."

"The guy's in jail."

"Maybe he had a buddy."

"Worth checking out."

Marty debated whether to tell him the other theory that had come to mind. "Whoever did it knows how to handle a weapon."

Clay's eyes narrowed. She knew it the instant he realized where she was going. "You mean Smitty?"

She nodded. "What do you think?"

"I can't see him taking a shot at you. That's not his style, Hogan."

"I thought I should bring it up."

"Consider it duly noted." He rose. "I'll let you know if we find anything tomorrow."

"I want to be there."

"Take the day off." He softened the words with a smile. "Go to the grocery, for God's sake."

"You're giving me the day off to go to the grocery?"

"Whatever works."

"I need to be there, Settlemeyer."

"No dice."

Feeling angry and awkward, Marty got to her feet, picked up the Glock and holstered it. "Are we finished here?"

"For now."

Nodding, she started toward the door.

"Hogan."

She turned. "Yeah?"

"Make the call."

"I'll think about it," she said and walked out.


"*Dura.*"

Katja stopped pacing and glared at her brother. "The only dumb bitch around here is you."

"I told you not to fire your weapon!"

"I had her in my sights."

Radimir crossed to her and got in her face. "If that were true, she would be dead now!"

"Stop it. Your veins are popping out. You'll have a heart attack."

"Crazy woman! Are you trying to ruin everything?"

She'd been holding on to her temper. But there was only so much she could tolerate. "I have no plan to stay in this pigsty much longer." Spinning, she bent and slid her hand across the beat-up coffee table. The wrappers of the fast-food restaurant flew to the floor. "This place is not fit for a pig."

"We stay until the job is finished."

"We could have finished it tonight."

"We take her down with the stun gun, not the rifle. That was the agreement."

"I would have only wounded her. That way, I would still get my time with her."

"And filled the car with blood? Stupid woman! You fired on her and that gave her time to call the cops. You just about ruined everything."

Katja licked her lips, enjoying her brother's anger, anticipating the culmination of their trip. "Nothing is ruined."

"Now the cops are suspicious. We have to worry that maybe she knows we're here. That's going to make our job twice as difficult."

"If you're not up to it, let me know."

"Katja . . ."

"You're a slug," she snapped. "You're fat and move too slowly."

"And you are like a young lion, excited by the hunt, but inexperienced." Softening, he crossed to her. "You have to be patient."

"I want to kill her." It excited her just to say the words aloud. It was a sensation that was almost sexual in its intensity. Katja would never admit it to her brother, but she'd nearly climaxed while she'd been working on the fat cop from Chicago.

"You'll get your chance," he cooed. "But we have to be careful."

She stared into her brother's eyes, felt her respect for him waning. She'd always secretly thought he was soft. Big talk on the outside for everyone to see, but a coward where it counted. Rurik was different. He was courageous and bold, and she wished it were Radimir in prison, enduring the beatings and rape instead of her more audacious older brother.

Katja wasn't afraid of anything. Not the gangsters she'd hung with since she'd been a gangly girl. Not the police who would like nothing more than to send all of them back to Moscow. Certainly not Radimir.

"When?" she asked. "I hate this place. I'm getting bored."

"A few days." Reaching out, he smoothed her hair with his hand. "We wait for the right moment. Get her when she's alone. Use the stunner. Bring her here. When we do . . ." He shrugged. "You can spend hours with her the way you did with the fat cop in Chicago."

Warmth flooded her at the memory. "He screamed like a pig."

"So will the woman," he assured her.

"Yes, she will." Katja's lips pulled into a smile. "I'll make sure of it."


*Marty wasn't good at downtime. She defined herself by* her work. Without it, she invariably felt a little lost. As if she didn't quite know who she was or where she fit into the scheme of things.

The good news, she supposed, was that she'd gotten through the night without buying another bottle of vodka. It hadn't been easy; she should have been pleased with herself. But bad news came with the dawn.

Marty was on the phone with Peck before finishing her first cup of coffee.

"Rosetti was taken down with a stun gun." Peck sounded as if he'd been up all night. "They took him to an unknown location. Someplace private. They bound him, stripped him, and just freakin' went nuts on him."

"Cause of death?"

"No one's talking. Prelim report is due out any day now. But those sick bastards did some bad shit."

"Like what?"

"I heard they injected acid beneath his skin. Cut him. Burned him."

"My God." Marty closed her eyes. "Any leads?"

"We got squat."

"Any idea who might have done it?"

"The general consensus is that this is not the work of some amateur sociopath. The people who did this knew what they were doing. They were prepared and armed with some pretty effective tools. They knew how to inflict pain. They'd kept him conscious and aware by administering amphetamines . . ."

Unable to listen to more, Marty removed the phone from her ear. Outrage squeezed her chest, and for a moment she couldn't catch her breath. Rosetti had died a long and unimaginably savage death.

"Hogan, you there?"

She returned the phone to her ear. "You catch these sons of bitches, Peck. I mean it. Find them and bring them in."

"It's just a matter of time."

But Marty knew that wasn't always the case. She knew that if this was some kind of professional job, they could already be overseas and the crime might never be solved.

She was shaking when she hung up the phone. The coffee had turned sour in her stomach. Before even realizing what she was going to do, she found herself at the kitchen table, wishing for a bottle. Just a splash in your coffee, a little voice taunted. Just enough to get you over this rough spot.

But Marty knew alcohol would only make everything worse. Feeling sorry for herself wasn't going to bring Rosetti back. It wasn't going to help the cops in Chicago find his killer. It sure as hell wasn't going to get her through the day.

Furious with herself, with fate, she hurled her coffee cup across the kitchen. The glass shattered and left a satisfying nick in the wallpaper. Frustrated and hurting so keenly she couldn't stand to be in her own skin, she left the kitchen and headed for the bedroom, where she threw on her sneakers and sweatpants.

Two minutes later, she was out the front door. She took the first half mile at a too-fast pace, working off the anger. She welcomed the aching muscles and burning lungs; anything was better than the horror of knowing what Rosetti had gone through in his last hours.

Marty channeled her anger, used it to fuel her. She ran hard, her sneakers pounding asphalt, her arms pumping, her breaths keeping perfect time with her heart.

A mile from town, a dirt road intersected Cactus Street. Wanting to be alone, she took the ranch road at an all-out sprint. She knew she'd pay tomorrow for overtaxing muscles that hadn't been used this way for six months. But it felt good to hurt in a way that didn't have anything to do with Rosetti or her career.

The open plain with its swaying grass rolled out before her. The yellow landscape became vivid, as if a dark cloud had given way to sunshine and she was seeing it for the first time. To her right she could see the northernmost finger of Palo Duro Canyon. To her left the land sloped to the Canadian River basin. Ahead, the road snaked through the yellow plain like the slash of an artist's brush on canvas.

Marty headed toward the canyon, where the rough terrain offered a more challenging run. By the time she reached the floor, her body was spent. Six months ago, she'd been able to run five miles with ease. Not the case today.

At the foot of the narrow finger of the canyon, Marty stopped. Bending, she gripped her knees and sucked in mouthfuls of air, trying to catch her breath. She could feel her legs trembling from exertion. Her quadriceps cramped. Nausea seesawed in her gut. But the physical pain was exactly what she'd needed to clear her head.

"Get with the program," she panted.

Straightening, she looked around. The wind had kicked up, rustling the branches of the mesquite and chinaberry trees. Somewhere nearby a meadowlark called to its mate. She'd lived in Caprock Canyon for almost two weeks, but she'd taken little time to fully appreciate the stark and hostile beauty of the land.

Looking across the canyon floor, she wished for binoculars. She knew Clay, a few of his officers, and the Deaf Smith County Sheriff's Office were in the main section a few miles to the south and east, looking for casings from last night's "alleged" shooting. She wondered if they'd find anything. Or if she'd spend the rest of her time here in Caprock Canyon without credibility.

"Alleged my ass," she muttered, kicking at the dirt with the toe of her running shoe.

Clay thought she'd mistaken a hunter's stray bullet for a sniper's. He'd all but accused her of having post-traumatic stress disorder. Initially, she'd scoffed at the assertion. But while he was wrong about the shooter, was there a possibility he was right about the PTSD?

Marty didn't like the answers that came to mind. The flashbacks. The nightmares. The sights or sounds or smells that took her back to the day of the high-speed chase. The day she'd seen the little girl shot dead at point-blank range. Had she been so preoccupied with other things in her life that she'd missed the signs? Or maybe deep inside a small part of her thought she didn't deserve any help.

Marty didn't have much faith in psychiatrists, even less in the medications they doled out like Halloween candy. But maybe she'd call the guy Clay had recommended. What would it hurt to talk to him? Hell, it might even do her some good to get some of this baggage off her chest.

The sound of a car engine spun her around. Surprise rippled through her at the sight of the cruiser coming up behind her. She squinted and realized it was Dugan behind the wheel. Probably going into town for a food run. She raised her hand and waved. He waved back, but didn't stop.

She ignored the pang of hurt in her gut. Her coworkers didn't trust her. That was all right. Marty didn't have anything to prove to them or anyone else. But it hurt that he hadn't stopped just to shoot the breeze or maybe give her an update on what they had or hadn't found.

Cops could be such jerks.

She started toward town at a slow jog. She'd only gone a few yards when she heard a second vehicle behind her. Her heart did a little jig in her chest when she thought it might be Clay. Maybe they'd found casings and were heading back to town to send them to some lab for analysis. She turned. Surprise rippled through her when she saw the white Lexus climbing out of the canyon.

It was unusual to see non-farm or -ranch vehicles in this area. On impulse, she raised her hand and waved as it passed. The young couple inside stared, but they didn't wave back. Marty noticed the New York plates and wondered if they'd ventured off the interstate and gotten lost.

"Weird," she said.

Taking a final look in the direction of the canyon, she started toward town at an easy jog, wondering if she could make it all the way back without stopping.

*Turning in the front seat of the Lexus, Katja raised the* field glasses to her eyes. "We could have had her."

"Maybe."

She scowled at her brother. "Why didn't we?"

"The other cop is too close."

"The risk is half the fun."

Radimir didn't think so, but he didn't disagree. When it came to his sister, he'd learned to choose his battles. "We ambush her at the house. During the night, while she's sleeping. We have privacy. There will be less noise. She won't be missed until morning. They won't begin looking for her until afternoon." He shrugged. "You'll have more time with her."

"If we take her back to our rental place, no one will be able to hear her scream."

He thought of the cardboard box containing his sister's equipment. Syringes. Sulfuric acid. Propane torch. Roofing nails. Handcuffs. Extra rope. Despite his resolve to avenge Rurik and maybe elevate his own reputation in the process, Radimir shivered. "You'll have five or six hours. Then we drive."

Katja raised the glasses to her eyes and licked her lips. "Tonight then," she whispered.

"Yes," Radimir said. "Tonight."

# TEN

*Clay knocked, then stood back and waited, trying to ig-*nore the fact that his heart was beating too fast. He would have liked to blame it on the conversation he was about to have with Marty. But he was honest enough with himself to know it had more to do with the woman than anything he was about to say.

Needing to move, he strolled the porch, taking note of the clay pot of geraniums on the steps and the old-fashioned rocking chair on the opposite end.

The door swung open. Clay spun to see Marty standing just inside, a fluffy white towel wrapped turban style on her head. Before he could stop himself, his eyes made a quick sweep of her. She wore a denim shirt over ragtag denim shorts. No shoes. No makeup. His gaze lingered on slender, well-muscled legs. Damp tendrils curled from within the towel, and he got the impression he'd interrupted a shower.

"Bad time?"

"Not if you're going to tell me what you found today." She swung open the door.

Clay stepped inside. The house smelled of eucalyptus and lemon oil. He wasn't sure why, but it pleased him to see she'd been cleaning. That she was trying to spiffy the place up. Making herself at home.

"Sorry about the towel. I went running and just got out of the shower."

"No problem." He cleared his throat, trying not to stare at the little drop of water glittering on the slender column of her throat.

"You want some coffee?" Not waiting for an answer, she started for the kitchen.

Clay's eyes dropped to the denim stretched over her round ass. He should have known she was a runner. There wasn't much to her, but she had some muscle definition. He'd always liked that in a woman. Substance. Firm flesh. He wondered what she looked like beneath those baggy clothes . . .

"I actually made it to the grocery today."

He trailed her as far as the doorway, trying hard not to acknowledge the fact that she wasn't wearing a bra. The shirt she wore was two sizes too big, but if he looked closely, he could just make out the faint outline of her nipples . . .

*Get the hell off it, Settlemeyer,* a little voice warned.

"I like the flowers," he said in a tight voice.

"How about that rocking chair?"

"You're not going all domestic on me, are you?"

"Not a chance." Grinning, she crossed to him and shoved a cup of steaming coffee into his hand. "So what did you find?"

Not wanting the banter to end, he grimaced. "The only casings we found were yours."

Disbelief flashed in her eyes. "No way."

"There were eight of us, Hogan. We spent four hours in the sun and the wind, looking exactly where you told us to look."

"Then someone missed something." Turning away from him, she set her coffee on the table and began to pace. "Maybe the location I gave you wasn't quite right."

Clay wanted to believe her. He wanted to have faith in her. He didn't want to believe the PTSD had affected her judgment. "Are you absolutely certain what happened out there wasn't a stray shot from a hunter?"

She spun on him. "I'm sure, damn it."

"Why would someone shoot at you?"

"I don't know! Maybe it was random. An idiot with a gun. It wouldn't be the first time. Maybe—"

"Maybe you made a mistake," he said. "For God's sake, Hogan, you're human. It happens."

Her mouth tightened. "I didn't make a mistake. Damn it, I had to take cover."

Setting his cup beside hers, he raised his hands. "Look, I'm not the bad guy here. I'm telling you what we found."

"You think I have PTSD. You think that's affected my judgment."

"Tell me you don't think about that kid," he snapped. "Tell me a sound or a smell or the color of the shirt she wore that day doesn't bring it back."

"Maybe it does!" she shouted. "But that doesn't mean I don't realize it when I'm under fire!"

She started to turn away. Clay wasn't finished with this. He didn't want it to end on a bad note. Before he could stop himself, he reached for her. His fingers closed around her biceps. But evidently she wasn't ready to calm down. Snarling under her breath, she tried to twist away.

"Cut it out," he growled.

"You think I'm . . . delusional or something, and that pisses me off."

"I do not think you're delusional."

He could see her gritting her teeth, her arm trembling beneath his hand. All he could think was that he wanted to make her stop shaking. Make her stop hurting. And for a moment, she wasn't a cop to him, but a woman who'd been hurt in a thousand ways and beaten down by a system that wasn't always fair. Before he could heed the warning blaring in his head, he pulled her close and crushed his mouth to hers.

*Marty had to hand it to him; Clay Settlemeyer definitely* knew how to distract a girl. Of all the things he could have done to mollify her anger, kissing her was probably the most effective. Of course, it was also the most dangerous. But then she'd always been drawn to danger.

She responded the way any reckless woman would, and kissed him back. She matched the power of his passion with the power of her own. When he wasn't close enough, she moved against him. When he didn't groan with wanting her, she edged closer until he did.

Every thought that didn't have to do with Clay or kissing left her head. Chicago. The shooting in the canyon. Rosetti. The possibility that she could be suffering from PTSD. Marty was no longer a cop. She was a woman with a woman's needs, and at the moment those needs were spiraling out of control.

She couldn't remember the last time she'd been with a man. Probably some disastrous date where she'd tried to pretend she wasn't a cop. That she didn't drink or cuss or occasionally partake in bad behavior. There were no pretenses with Clay. He'd seen her at her worst. He'd seen her furious. Crushed with grief. Drunk. And now this. Whatever *this* was.

Need churned inside her with every erratic beat of her heart. An edgy, unbearable need that burned inside her like red-hot coals. She writhed against him. He moaned and kissed her harder. Her every sense focused on the point between them where their bodies touched. The blood rushed in her ears like a white-water rapid down the side of a mountain.

He raised his hands. His palms were hot and rough on either side of her face. When he used his tongue, Marty opened to him. She could feel her control slipping away, but she didn't care. She didn't let herself think about repercussions.

A cry escaped her when he slid his hands to her breasts. She arched when he rubbed his fingertips over her sensitized nipples. Even through the fabric of the shirt, the sensations went through her like an earthquake. She felt her panties go wet.

The next thing she knew he put his arms around her and swung her around to the kitchen table. Lifting her, he sat her down. The towel slipped from her head and hit the table. A chair clattered to the floor when he opened her knees. She gasped when he stepped between them. Not a gasp of shock, but a sound of pleasure.

His hands went to the buttons of her shirt. She felt the long, hard length of him against her cleft, moving, driving her crazy. Her shirt fell open. Her body arched involuntarily when he kneaded her breasts. The pleasure sucked her last breath from her lungs. Extinguished every last shred of logic from her brain.

Their clothes were the only things keeping them from making a very big mistake. A mistake that would complicate things for both of them. Maybe even threaten their jobs. Marty knew better than to partake in a fling with her boss. *He* knew better than to sleep with a subordinate. But the high-wire sexual tension between them whenever they were within shouting distance of each other was quite simply like nothing she'd ever experienced.

Bending, he kissed her hard and deep. She nearly came off the table when he moved against her. All she could think of was removing the barriers between them to ease the unbearable need knifing through the center of her body.

Vaguely, she was aware of their labored breaths, her heart pounding so hard she heard it echoing throughout the house.

"The door." Straightening, Clay panted out the words.

Only then did Marty realize the pounding wasn't inside her head, but at the front door. Clay stepped away. She clutched her shirt together with hands that were far from steady.

"Expecting company?" he asked.

"I don't exactly know anyone in this town," she said, surprised by the breathlessness of her voice.

"You'd better get it." He reached for her, kissed her hard on the mouth.

Despite the alarm and embarrassment zinging through her, she kissed him back, nearly lost herself in the edgy pleasure of his mouth. But the knocking sounded again.

"We're going to have to talk about this," he said.

"I know."

Quickly, Marty slid from the table and buttoned her shirt. She swept her fingers through her damp hair as she walked quickly to the front door. Clay headed for the hall, where he could hear, but not be seen. She looked through the peephole and her heart sank.

"It's Smitty." She spun to see Clay enter the living room, his face concerned.

He glanced down at the obvious bulge of his erection against his fly. "Well, this is going to be awkward."

Marty choked out a laugh that sounded a little hysterical. "What do we do?"

"My vehicle's out front. You have to answer."

Taking a deep, steadying breath, she partially opened the door. "Hey, Smitty."

He looked at her with narrowed eyes, his gaze moving past her toward the living room. "Is the chief here?"

"He was just filling me in on the search today."

"I bet."

Coming up behind her, Clay opened the door the rest of the way. "What's up, Smitty?"

Marty saw knowledge in the man's eyes. She couldn't bring herself to look at Clay. Smitty's expression was smug and knowing. She could only imagine the guilty truth etched on their faces.

"Dick Crowley's got livestock on the road again," Smitty said. "Several dozen this time. One's been hit. Car spun out. I was on my way out there and saw your vehicle." He shoved his hands into his pockets. "I tried reaching you on the radio."

"Anyone hurt?" Clay was already reaching for his keys.

"No."

"I'll meet you out there. Is anyone on the scene?"

"Not yet."

"Set up flares and cones. I'll be there in a few minutes."

Smitty's gaze went once more to Marty, then he touched the brim of his hat. "Thanks, Chief."

Marty watched Smitty jog down the sidewalk toward his vehicle. Next to her, Clay closed the door and turned to her, his expression grim. "That wasn't good," he said. "I'm sorry."

"I thought you covered pretty well."

"Smitty's no dummy."

"I'm sorry. I didn't . . ." Because she didn't know how to finish the sentence, she let the words hang.

"Me, too."

"Do you think he'll—"

"Maybe." He sighed. "I take full responsibility for this, Hogan."

"It takes two to tango."

"I'm your superior."

Marty could tell he was angry with himself. Frustrated with the situation. With her. But his erection hadn't diminished, and even now she still felt the edgy pull to him.

His gaze burned into hers. "This can't happen again."

"I know."

"I have to go."

But he didn't move, and for a crazy instant, Marty thought he was going to kiss her again. His eyes flicked to her mouth. She still tingled where he'd kissed her earlier, where he'd touched her.

"Good luck with those cows," she managed.

Clay walked out the door without responding.

* * *

*It was 10 P.M. by the time Clay made it back to the sta-*tion. He was bone tired, hungry and enormously troubled by what had happened between him and Marty. What the hell was he thinking?

But Clay knew what he was thinking. What his body was thinking, anyway. He wanted to have sex with her. The need was like a bamboo sliver beneath his skin, all edgy and painful and refusing to be ignored.

For as long as he could remember, he'd been cursed with a propensity for wanting what he couldn't have. As a younger man he'd wanted out of Caprock Canyon so badly he could feel the need eating away at him. Then along came beautiful, sultry Eve Sutherland and that goal had transformed to a vicious need that had overridden everything else in his life. When she got pregnant, the military became his ticket out. Clay had the forethought to see the big picture and gave them four years.

When he came back and Eve announced she wanted a divorce, all Clay could think was that he wanted to keep Erica. He'd been unduly relieved when Eve didn't want her . . .

Clay wasn't sure why he was rehashing his life. There was a big part of him that believed the key to leading a happy life was settling for less and learning to be satisfied with it. He was, for the most part. But now Marty Hogan with her take-no-prisoners attitude and understated loveliness threatened to turn his even-keeled world on its head.

Clay couldn't let that happen. He'd worked hard to get where he was. He was too smart to let an illicit affair with a subordinate threaten his position or reputation. People talked in small towns; he didn't want Erica hearing about her father's sexual adventures from some fifth-grade big mouth repeating what he'd heard from his parents.

But he could no longer deny his attraction to Marty. It was keen and cutting him deeper every time he laid eyes on her. When he wasn't with her, he thought of her. He relived the moments when they were together. He could conjure the sound of her laughter. The emotion in her eyes that belied the tough facade she put on for the world to see. Worse, he dreamed about her at night. Hot dreams that left him sweating and disturbed and feeling more alone than he'd ever felt in his life. He wanted to believe his infatuation with her was a phase. That it was something a sexual encounter with any willing female would cure.

But Clay had always been honest with himself. His feelings for Marty were not the kind of passing interest a man felt for a pretty woman. This went deeper than physical. He related to her on a level he didn't with most people. He understood her. That brought the problem full circle: wanting what he could never have.

Best-case scenario, a miracle would happen and she'd be reinstated in Chicago. She'd return and he'd never see her again. But Clay knew that wouldn't happen. He was going to have to deal with her. He was going to have to deal with his feelings for her. The question was how.

The good news was he didn't have to figure it out tonight. Fatigue tugged at him as he pulled into his reserved parking space at the police station. Smitty had agreed to write up the accident report. Clay had been on his way home so his housekeeper could go home to her own family when he remembered he'd left his laptop in his office. Erica needed it for school the next day.

He crossed the sidewalk. Voices met him when he shoved open the door. Clay almost called out, but the words he heard stopped him cold.

"I'm telling you. He's fucking her." Smitty's voice.

"The chief? Naw." Jett, trying to defuse a potentially explosive conversation.

"He's too smart for that," Dugan put in.

Silently, Clay closed the door behind him and stood there in the dark, listening.

"If he wasn't sticking it in her every night, there's no way he'd keep her around," Smitty said. "She's frickin' trouble, man."

"Chief is too straitlaced to get hooked up with Hogan," said Jett.

"He might be a straight shooter, but he's got a dick. If you ask me, Hogan's leading him around by it."

"You're full of crap."

Smitty laughed, but it was a mean, argumentative sound. "Look, I drove by her place completely by accident this afternoon on my way to the accident out on the highway. I hadn't been able to get him on the radio. Where do I find him? Hogan's place. What do I find when I knock on the door? I'm telling you, they had 'we've been fucking like rabbits' written all over their faces."

"No shit?" asked Dugan.

"No shit."

"Hey, Smitty, maybe that's not such a big deal," Jett put in. "Chief ain't married and neither is Hogan."

"You want to know why it's a big deal? Well, listen up and I'll tell you. That bitch comes in here all high and mighty and starts breaking our balls. The chief takes one look at those little titties of hers and takes her side."

"Settlemeyer's a fair man."

"I'll tell you about fair. Lookit. She picks a fight with some biker at Foley's Bar and gets herself decked. Settlemeyer puts her on Rufus duty. Next, she drives into the canyon and claims a sniper is shooting at her. What does Settlemeyer do? Instead of firing her for being a crazy bitch, he sends all of us out there to look for casings." Smitty laughed nastily. "A freakin' *sniper*, man. When's the last time you heard of a sniper in Caprock Canyon? If she's not a fuckin' head case, I don't know what is."

"So did you guys find brass?" Jett, trying to change the subject.

"The only one shooting in the canyon was her. Settlemeyer kept us in that canyon all damn day and we still didn't find nothin'."

"Lots of area to cover for just a few guys."

"I say she made the whole thing up." Smitty paused to chuckle. "Hey, maybe she's got that disease. That Munchausen's syndrome where people do weird shit for attention."

Clay stood stone still in the reception area and willed his temper to cool. What he really wanted to do was walk into the break room and wipe the floor with Smitty's face. But he knew decking one of his officers would probably cause more problems than it would solve.

That didn't mean he couldn't fire him; this wasn't the first time Smitty had stepped over a line. A dozen other moments scrolled through Clay's mind. He'd documented some, but not all. But he had enough to fire him without the threat of litigation.

He didn't remember leaving the reception area. Conversation went quiet as he traversed the hall and headed toward the break room, and he realized the men heard him coming. He walked in to find Smitty standing next to the refrigerator, holding the door open. Jett was slumped in a chair at the break room table. Dugan stood at the sink, looking down at the mug he'd been rinsing, but his hands were frozen in place. None of the men met his gaze.

Clay focused on Smitty. "You look like you just saw a ghost."

The younger man's gaze darted to Jett, then to Dugan, as if looking for help, but neither man dared look at him.

"We were just goofing off." Smitty stuttered on every word.

"You seem to be doing a lot of that lately."

Smitty stared.

Clay pointed. "In my office. Now."

Giving Jett and Dugan final, reproachful looks, Smitty

closed the refrigerator and started down the hall. Clay's heart was pounding as he followed.

They reached the office. Clay slammed the door and pointed to a chair. "Sit down."

"Chief—"

"Shut up and sit down."

"I don't know what you heard, but—"

Clay went behind his desk. Too angry to sit, he yanked open the drawer, pulled out Smitty's personnel file and threw it on the desktop. "Since you evidently don't want to take that chair, I can fire you just as well standing up."

"Aw, Chief, don't do that."

"I heard every word."

"Hey, I know it must have sounded bad, but we were just messing around."

"Neither Jett nor Dugan said a damn thing, so don't try to put any of this on them."

"This is bullshit."

"Yeah, it is." Clay snatched a sheet from the file. "You were already on probation. You blew it tonight. I want your locker cleaned out in the next five minutes. Whatever's left will be mailed to you. You'll have your check by the end of the week."

Smitty gaped at him, his face turning a deep hue of red. "You can't do this."

"It's done. Now get your things. If you can't manage, I'll do it for you."

"You *are* fuckin' her, aren't you?"

Clay could hear his molars grinding. Before he could stop himself, he rounded his desk. An odd light entered Smitty's eyes, but he stepped back. Clay knew the other man was baiting him. Egging him on. But his temper was lit, and for a moment he thought slugging him would be worth whatever troubles it brought down on his head later.

"I'll take your gun and badge," Clay said evenly.

"Fuck you." Snarling, Smitty tore the badge from his

shirt, leaving a hole the size of a quarter. "And fuck her."
He yanked the revolver from his holster and tossed both
onto the desk.

"Get out before I throw you out."

Smitty jabbed a finger at him. "You ain't heard the last
of this, Settlemeyer."

Clay imagined himself grabbing the other man's shirt
and slamming him against the wall. The sound of his head
crashing against the Sheetrock would have satisfied the
dark anger pumping through him.

But Clay didn't move. He knew once he crossed that line
he would be no better than the man standing before him.

Hissing an expletive, Smitty turned on his heel. He
slammed both hands against the door and sent it flying
open. Jett stood at the doorway to the break room, looking
wary, probably wondering if he was next. Smitty snarled at
him, then headed toward the front door.

For the span of a full minute, neither man moved. Clay
could feel the nerves coming off Jett. After a while, he
made eye contact with him. "Where's Dugan?"

Jett blinked a dozen times before answering. "Uh, he
left."

Clay almost smiled, but he didn't.

The younger man's Adam's apple bobbed twice in
quick succession. "Smitty gone?"

"Keep it under your hat for now, will you?"

"Yessir."

"I'll get Dugan on the radio and ask him to do the
same."

Jett didn't move.

Realizing the young officer feared for his job, Clay
sighed. "Looks like I've got some paperwork to do. There
any coffee?"

"Uh, it's old."

Clay started toward the kitchen, setting his hand on
Jett's shoulder as he passed. "That'll do."

# ELEVEN

*"Dad, don't forget about the barrel race this weekend."*

Clay glanced away from his driving to look at his daughter, who sat in the passenger seat beside him. She looked like a rough-and-tumble kid in her faded blue jeans, Western shirt and scuffed tennis shoes. But the signs of maturity were beginning to show through the pigtails and freckles. It was her birthday today; he couldn't believe she was ten years old. In a few more years puberty would set in. The thought put a pang in his gut powerful enough to make his palms sweat on the steering wheel. A pang that was part fear, part grief and part pride.

"How could I forget?"

She shot him a determined look. "I'm going to win this time."

"If you stay focused, keep George focused and run clean, you have a good chance, honey."

"I want to beat Mary Lou Finkbine."

He arched a brow. He was a firm believer that there was nothing wrong with a little competitive spirit. But he wanted his daughter to strive to win for the right reasons. "Why do you want to beat Mary Lou so badly?"

"She beat me last time and she says George looks like a mule."

Knowing his daughter wouldn't see an insult to her horse as even remotely humorous, Clay bit back the smile that tried to emerge. "You know better than that, right? George is a fine horse and you're an excellent rider."

She looked down at her sneakers. "I guess."

"That horse has worked his heart out for you. You've worked hard, too, honey. All you can do is your best. Just concentrate on that. You can't control what other people say or do."

She raised her eyes to his. Within their innocent depths, he saw something he'd never seen before. Adult pain. Childhood curiosity that had become adult questions.

"Mary Lou said some other stuff, too," she said.

Concern flitted through him. Erica was usually vocal and open with him on just about any subject. Clay had never known her to hold back. "Like what?"

"She said Mom left you for another man because he had a bigger wallet."

A spear of pain shot through Clay's chest. "What did you say?"

"I told her she was full of crap because you're the police chief and no one cares about some stupid wallet."

Small towns, he thought with dismay, and smiled through the pain. "I'll talk to her mom, honey."

"Don't tell her I told you."

"I won't."

Wondering about fifth-grade dynamics, Clay watched as she gathered her books and shoved them into her backpack. She was the most precious thing in the world to him. He loved her so much it hurt just to look at her some days.

She'd asked about Eve several times in the last year. When she'd been younger, it had never been an issue. Now

Erica was becoming curious. And Clay was going to have to come up with an answer that wouldn't break her heart.

She climbed out of the Explorer.

"Don't forget your math paper." Leaning across the seat, Clay picked up the fallen paper and handed it to her.

"Oh."

"And don't forget my smooch."

Grinning, she jumped back in the vehicle and gave him a smacking kiss on the cheek. She did the same thing every morning when he dropped her at school, and it melted his heart a little bit more every time.

"Do we get to eat ice cream at the Dairy Dream tonight?" she asked.

"Mrs. Huffschmidtt is fixing fried chicken."

"Chicken is boring."

Ten years old going on sixteen, he thought, and sighed. Pretty soon he was going to be light-years out of his element. "She made you a cake, too."

Erica grinned. "Really?"

"Chocolate." He kissed her cheek. "Happy birthday, honey."

"Thanks, Dad." She pulled back and sobered. "I'm going to beat Mary Lou this time."

"Get through your math test first."

"I'm going to get an A."

Clay didn't doubt it. Erica was one of the most determined people he'd ever met. "See you at three o'clock," he said.

Sliding from the vehicle, she waved, looked both ways and crossed the street at an all-out run. Clay watched her join another little girl on the sidewalk, where they walked side by side into the school.

He couldn't put off telling her about Eve much longer. He'd decided a long time ago he would never malign his ex-wife. But he wouldn't lie, either. That left him with the quandary he'd struggled with since the day she'd left them.

How could he tell his daughter her own mother hadn't wanted her, without breaking her heart?

The question gnawed at him as he drove toward the police station. Having parked in his reserved spot, he left the Explorer and headed for the front door. Midway there, he spotted Marty's car a few spaces down and his thoughts shifted to her. He squashed the small thrill of anticipation that rose in his chest at the thought of seeing her. He wasn't going to let himself become a victim of his own sex drive, for God's sake. Especially after what had happened between them the day before.

Marty might be a decent person. She might even be a decent cop. But Clay had had enough trouble in his life to recognize it when it looked him in the eye. Marty Hogan had trouble written all over that pretty body of hers, in big red letters. He didn't need another challenge. He needed to focus on Erica, on being a good father and running the police department the way it should be run.

But whether he wanted to admit it or not, things were starting to get complicated, something Clay had tried to avoid most of his adult life. And while he should have been thinking about Smitty and how he was going to break the news of his departure from the department to the rest of the team, his mind was on Marty and that earth-shattering kiss.

He entered to find Jo Nell sitting behind her desk looking like the cat that had just swallowed the canary. Next to her, Marty sat on the edge of the desk with a similar expression on her face. Jett stood next to Marty, looking like he'd been holding his breath for at least a minute.

Clay realized why when Jo Nell coughed and a puff of smoke blew out. "Oh, for chrissake." Sniffing, he smelled cigarette smoke and realized Jo Nell had not only drafted Marty into her secret smoking society, but Jett as well.

"Chief, we were just . . ."

"I know what you were doing." Trying not to be amused,

he didn't pause on the way to his office. "Doesn't anybody have any respect for the law around here?"

He poured coffee, then wandered back into the reception area. Marty knelt at the four-drawer file cabinet, filing reports. Her uniform slacks stretched taut over her rear end, and for a moment he couldn't take his eyes off those dangerous curves.

At the desk, Jett and Jo Nell were discussing the benefits of using the ten-code system for dispatch. An air purifier purred atop Jo Nell's desk. Next to it, some sort of scented candle emanated the aroma of sugar cookies. Clay didn't condone smoking, but he was secretly pleased to see that Marty had been accepted by Jett and Jo Nell.

He cleared his throat. "If I can have your attention for a moment."

All eyes turned toward him. Clay looked at Jett, wondering if he'd told the rest of the department about Smitty's termination. "Do they know?" he asked.

Jett shook his head.

Good boy, Clay thought, and continued. "I thought I should let you know. Smitty is no longer with the department."

"You fired Smitty?" Jo Nell exclaimed.

Clay frowned. "I didn't say I fired him. He left the department. That's all you need to know."

Jo Nell looked at Jett. "I can't believe he fired Smitty."

"Jo Nell," Clay warned.

"We ain't idiots, Chief," she said without rancor. She glared at Jett and gave him an elbow to the ribs. "You knew and didn't tell us."

Jett ducked his head.

Wanting to avoid gossip, Clay moved to change the subject. "I also wanted all of you to know there's a rodeo this weekend out at the Sheriff's Posse arena. Erica's running barrels. All of you are invited. Food's on me."

"I just love watching her beat the pants off the boys." Jo

Nell brought her hands together. "It's her birthday today, ain't it?"

Clay sighed. "Yeah." But he could tell their collective attention was still on Smitty.

"What's Smitty going to do now?" Jett asked. "It's not like there's another law enforcement agency nearby."

"I don't know," Clay said. "Not my problem."

Marty's gaze met Clay's. "What if he shows up?"

Just looking at her, his heart rate spiked. The memory of the kiss they'd shared flashed in his brain. His fingers tingled with the memory of her flesh. To his dismay a warm rush of blood headed south.

Damn it.

"You mean here?" he said in a thick voice.

"I mean anywhere."

Clay knew what she was asking. He also knew Marty was capable of taking care of herself. She was a cop, after all. But Smitty had a temper on him, and a mean streak to boot. He liked to drink. And he knew how to handle a gun. A powder keg that might just explode if a disgruntled Smitty decided to blame his recent termination on Marty.

"I wouldn't put it past him," Jo Nell put in.

Clay frowned, his eyes level on Marty. "You call me at the first sign of trouble, and I'll take care of it."

She nodded.

Hopefully, if a furious Smitty did make an appearance, Marty wouldn't try to take matters into her own hands. And Clay would be able to get there fast enough to keep that powder keg from exploding into something ugly.

*Driving back to the station, Marty wondered if a cop had* ever died of boredom. Back when she'd worked Chicago's South Side, nearly every day was chock-full of events most cops would categorize as exciting. Robberies. Burglaries. Violent domestic disputes. Murder. She used to wonder what the world was coming to. Tonight, she'd longed for just a fraction of the action.

She'd longed even more for the easy camaraderie she'd shared with Rosetti. His funeral had been two days ago. Since Marty couldn't be there, she'd used a good bit of her paycheck to send a massive spray of fall flowers with an anonymous note that read: "A good cop. An even better man. You were loved. And you will be missed." Rosetti probably wouldn't have appreciated it in the least, so she'd done it for herself.

The Chicago PD was working tirelessly to find the killers who'd taken out one of their own. When overtime limits were hit, many of the cops worked on their own time. To their credit, the brass looked the other way and let them do what they needed to do. Morale was low, but the cops had pulled together for this and made things happen. A potential break came when forensics produced fibers on the duct tape that had been used to muffle Rosetti's screams. But the fibers were common and netted nothing more than a dead end.

For the thousandth time, Marty wished she were there, talking to the other cops, beating on doors, doing something—anything—to track down the bastards and bring them to justice. Instead, she was rounding up wayward livestock, writing tickets to grandmothers on their way to bridge and, well, fantasizing about her boss.

Of the three recent pastimes, the latter bothered her most. Marty was not an overly sexual creature. She could count on two fingers the number of relationships she'd had as an adult. She couldn't remember the last time she'd been kissed—pre–Clay Settlemeyer, anyway. She sure as hell couldn't remember the last time she'd had sex. Celibacy suited her. Helped her stay focused on the important things and steer clear of the turmoil that came with relationships.

But damn, the man knew how to kiss. Marty felt sure he was probably just as adept in other areas, too. A real overachiever when it came to knowing just where to . . .

She caught herself a moment too late to stop the shiver that rippled through her like warm water down her back. "Get over it," she muttered as she pulled into a parking space next to Clay's Explorer.

She tried hard to ignore the way her heart jigged in her chest as she got out of the cruiser. She told herself she'd been hoping he wasn't there. But a very big part of her thrilled at the thought of seeing him again.

The intellectual side of her brain knew this could never go anywhere. Sexual tension did not a relationship make. If all went as planned, she'd land a better job and leave Caprock Canyon behind inside of a year.

That didn't keep her palms from going damp as she opened the door. Jo Nell sat behind her desk. She grinned when Marty entered, held up an unsmoked cigarette, mouthed the word "Later," then hand signaled to the chief's office to let her know he was there.

Marty nodded and headed toward the break room for a soda. She couldn't keep her eyes from flicking toward Clay when she passed his office. He frowned at her as she walked by. "Hogan."

Marty returned his scowl and kept moving. "Chief."

"Tell Jo Nell to hold my calls for a while, will you?"

"Sure thing." To Marty's dismay the minuscule exchange was enough to start an infusion of heat that ran straight down her middle and went all the way to her toes.

She was standing next to Jo Nell's desk with her hand in a bag of chips and a soda in the other when the front door opened. An elegant-looking woman with platinum blond hair and the biggest green eyes Marty had ever seen entered with a gust of wind infused with Chanel No. 5 perfume. Marty's first impression was that she must be lost. Or maybe had car problems. Evidently on her way from Los Angeles to New York or something. But then people who looked like her usually didn't take cross-country road trips. They flew first class on some private jet.

She wore fitted ivory slacks that showed off nicely rounded hips and a tiny waist. An ivory-colored jacket covered a sleek black tank that dipped low enough to show ample cleavage and ivory skin. Her makeup looked professionally done, an array of smoky, shimmering colors blended together and applied with the brush of some talented *artiste*. A woman at the height of her beauty—and she knew it.

Jo Nell didn't look impressed. "You lost?"

The woman crossed to the desk, scrunched up her nose as she took in Jo Nell's slightly wrinkled, slightly disheveled form. "I know exactly where I am, actually." Her gaze swept to Marty, lingered an instant too long, then went back to Jo Nell. "Is Clayton in?"

Marty took her hand out of the chip bag and resisted the urge to wipe the salt and crumbs on her uniform slacks. She'd never been unduly impressed by a pretty face or the girly trimmings that went along with it. But this woman was beautiful and poised and seemed so out of place in Caprock Canyon that her curiosity was piqued.

"He's on the phone with some bigwig." Jo Nell looked at the woman over her bifocals. "Who's askin'?"

"His wife."

# TWELVE

*His wife.*

Marty felt the word like a punch between the eyes. She'd had no idea Clay was married. He'd never mentioned a wife. He didn't wear a ring. Certainly not when he'd been kissing her and putting his hands all over her body.

Marty had wondered about Erica's mother, but she'd never gotten the details. She assumed Clay was divorced. Or, perhaps, widowed, since most often the wife got the children when marriages went bad.

She told herself it didn't matter. She told herself she wasn't shocked. That she wasn't disappointed. To admit either of those things would be to acknowledge there was something going on between her and Clay that didn't have to do with sexual attraction. They'd engaged in a couple of hot kisses; that was all. End of story. But the overly simplistic elucidation didn't explain why she suddenly felt nauseous and deflated.

Why hadn't Clay mentioned this woman?

Across the room, Jo Nell reached for the phone to buzz Clay.

The blonde intervened. "I'll just pop in and surprise him if you don't mind."

Jo Nell didn't hang up. "Chief don't like surprises."

"Oh, he'll like this one." The woman smiled, showing the whitest teeth Marty had ever seen. "Trust me."

*Just when Clay thought the day couldn't get any worse,* it did. Tenfold. He'd just gotten off the phone with Smitty's lawyer, who was threatening to file suit against the city of Caprock Canyon and the police department for unlawful discharge—when his worst nightmare entered his office without knocking.

The sight of Eve Sutherland nearly toppled him from his chair. He hadn't seen or heard from her for six years. He'd been operating under the assumption that he would never have to deal with her again. Evidently, she had other ideas.

She hadn't changed much since she'd walked out on him all those years ago. If anything, she was even prettier. The kind of pretty that sucked the oxygen right out of a man's lungs and turned his brain to mush. He'd been only twenty-two years old when they met, and Clay hadn't stood a chance against that kind of beauty. It was the one and only time in his life when he'd gone against his every instinct and risked it all for the love of a woman. In the end he'd paid dearly for his lack of judgment.

Six years was a long time, but Clay hadn't forgotten that punch-in-the-gut pain he'd felt when she'd walked out. The sense of betrayal. But Eve's departure wasn't the worst of what she'd done. She hadn't just left him, after all. She'd left their four-year-old little girl, too. A little girl who'd asked about her mother a hundred times since.

Clay stood. "Eve."

"Clayton." She extended a long, elegant hand.

For an instant he thought she expected him to kiss it. He hesitated a moment before giving her hand a single, firm shake. "It's been a while."

"Too long."

"What are you doing here?"

A shadow passed over her eyes. Her full mouth compressed slightly. At one time Clay had known her so well. Or thought he had. But he remembered enough to realize hers was a practiced reaction designed to get the desired response. He didn't want to think about what that might be.

"J.B. died," she said softly. "Two months ago. A heart attack."

"I'm sorry."

She closed her eyes in a silent thank-you. "I've been taking stock of my life."

"We do that sometimes when tragedy strikes."

Her gaze met his, beseeching him for something she hadn't yet asked. But he knew she would. She was working up to it. And he was afraid to hear it.

But her gaze was so compelling he felt his resolve weakening. The way it had all those years ago every time he looked at her.

"I want to see Erica," she said.

Clay felt the words as if she'd thrown a glass of ice water in his face. He didn't know what to say. Didn't know how to express the emotions coiling and flexing inside him. An uneasy mix of anger and regret and a bone-chilling fear that he might lose something precious. The only thing he knew for certain was that he didn't want his daughter in the middle of it.

"You left," he said after a moment. "You didn't want her."

She had the grace to wince, but Clay wondered if that was practiced, too. She was so damn slick. So perfect and poised and credible.

"I've made mistakes," she said. "Lots of them. Walking out on her is the biggest regret of my life."

"What's done is done. I don't want her hurt."

"I'm not going to hurt her."

"You already have. More than you know."

"I have the right to see my own daughter."

"You gave up that right when you left. When you married someone else and left me to raise her."

"I didn't relinquish my rights to her. Not legally."

"What the hell is that supposed to mean?"

"That means you let me see her or I'll get an attorney."

"Is that the way it's going to be?"

"I don't want it that way, Clayton. But I want to see my daughter. You owe me that much."

"I don't owe you a goddamn thing." His heart knocked against his ribs like the piston of an engine that had been run without oil. All he could think was that this woman was going to try to take away the thing that meant most to him in the world. A little girl he'd built his life around.

"Let me see her, Clayton. I can come to the house. While you're there. You can . . . supervise the visit. I just want to see her."

He stared at her for what felt like an eternity, seeing beyond the outward beauty to the selfish woman beneath. He wondered if she'd always been that way. If he'd been so blinded by lust, by that first, heady taste of love, that he hadn't seen her for what she was. A taker. A user.

"I'll ask Erica," he said. "It's her decision."

"She'll see me. Won't she?" She pouted. "Or have you told her something unpleasant about me?"

"I haven't told her a damn thing. That's not to say she hasn't asked." He gave her a hard look. "Maybe while you're here, you can explain to her why you didn't want her."

"That's not the way it was."

"That's exactly the way it was, Eve."

She pursed her lips, seemed to gather herself. "I was

hoping we could be . . . friendly. Do this together. Let the past go."

"Let bygones be bygones?" Sarcasm drenched the words, but Clay didn't care. He knew he was being a bastard. But he'd had a lot of time to think about what Eve had done. Not only to him, but to Erica. He'd had a lot of time to think about why she'd done it. And he'd decided a long time ago he would never forgive her.

"I'll talk to Erica," he repeated.

"I guess that's all I can ask."

"Yeah, it is."

Squaring her shoulders, she met his gaze with the level intensity of a pious minister looking down upon a fallen parishioner. "I'm staying at the Pioneer Motel."

When Clay said nothing, she gave him a small smile then turned to leave.

The moment she walked out the door, he let out the breath he'd been holding. He couldn't believe Eve was back. That she was asking to see Erica. What the hell was he supposed to do?

More than anything, he wanted to protect Erica. He wanted to keep her happy and secure and safe. As far as he was concerned, Eve threatened all of those things.

But that didn't give him the right to keep his daughter from knowing her mother. He was pretty sure that if he asked her, Erica would want to talk to Eve. Naturally, she was curious. That didn't mean Clay had to like it.

The only reason Erica had no ill feelings toward Eve was because Clay had never put them there. He'd never said a negative word about Eve, though he could have filled a book with them. How the hell was he supposed to handle this?

"One disaster at a time," he muttered and wished fervently it were that simple.

\* \* \*

*Marty knew she was taking the news far too personally.*
After all, she and Clay were not involved. Damn it, they
weren't. They'd partaken in a couple of blood-burning, skin-
melting kisses during a time of high stress. That was all.

She couldn't believe he was married. She couldn't believe he hadn't told her. That she'd been too stupid to ask.
Men could be such whores.

Those were the thoughts running through her mind
when she stopped at Foley's Bar and picked up a quart of
vodka. Just for a nightcap, she told herself. A little something to take the edge off. She gave herself points for not
buying cigarettes. But a woman had to draw the line somewhere. One of these days Marty was going to get her act
together.

Just not tonight.

Dusk was being swallowed by darkness as she parked
the Mustang and took the sidewalk to the front door. She
was thinking about that first, anesthetizing drink as she let
herself inside. A hot bath. A candle if she could find one.
And that Norah Jones CD, if it hadn't melted on the drive
from Chicago to Texas.

In the kitchen, Marty uncapped the bottle, grabbed a tall
glass from the cupboard and poured. The first long pull reminded her that she really didn't like the taste of vodka.
But then this wasn't about pleasure. It was about getting
through the night, forgetting her troubles for a little while,
and this was the only way she could think of to get the job
done.

In the bathroom, she turned on the water, then found
some bubble bath beads someone who didn't know her
very well had gotten her for Christmas. She dumped a
handful beneath the running water. Back in the bedroom,
she set her pistol on the night table. Next came the holster
and boots, both of which stayed on the floor. She worked
off her uniform shirt and bra and paused to take another
drink of salvation.

She carried the glass to the bathroom and set it on the edge of the tub. She found a never-opened candle in the nightstand and lit it with a pad of matches from Foley's Bar. The chipped soap tray on the sink made a good candleholder, and she set it on the commode. She kicked off her pants and flung them into the hall, making a mental note to pick them up later.

The initial notes of Norah Jones floated in the air as she walked into the bathroom wearing only her panties. Steam filled the room. Marty breathed in the scent of vanilla and musk and tried not to think about Clay or the sudden appearance of his wife. She assured herself none of it meant anything to her. *He* didn't mean anything. She barely knew him. He was only her boss. A small-town hick cop to boot. But none of that explained the kick-in-the-stomach reaction she'd felt when the woman walked through the door.

Marty slipped out of her panties and stuck a toe into the bubbles. The water was too hot, but that was exactly what she needed. A hot bath. A few drinks. A movie on the tube, if she could find something decent. And then the oblivion of sleep.

The mirror snagged her gaze. She wiped away the condensation with her hand. The image staring back at her gave her pause. She saw a woman with a wild mane of cinnamon-colored curls that had long been in need of a decent cut. She was a little too thin, a little too pale. Her mouth was too full. She had the deeply troubled eyes of an ugly shelter dog that didn't have a hope in the world of ever getting adopted.

Eve Sutherland was beautiful. She was classy. Elegant. She knew how to dress. How to style her hair. How to wear makeup. And she definitely had bigger boobs.

"What the hell are you doing?" she whispered.

Turning away from the mirror, she stepped into the tub and sank into bubbles up to her chin. She concentrated on relaxing her tense muscles. On clearing her mind of all the clutter that had accumulated throughout the last few months. When that failed, Marty sat up and reached for the glass. She drank deeply, knowing it was a mistake. But if she was good at anything, mistakes were her specialty.

The initial rush of alcohol hit her brain, blurred her thoughts. Norah's smooth-as-silk voice lulled. Leaning back in the water, Marty closed her eyes.

She wasn't sure how long she lay there, floating in an alcohol-induced haze. Ten minutes. Maybe twenty. The water was just starting to get cold. She was thinking about getting out when the light above the sink buzzed. When she opened her eyes, she found herself plunged into darkness.

"Now what?" she muttered.

Alarm rattled through her, but it was dampened by the alcohol and her dark frame of mind. Muttering a curse, she stood and fumbled for the robe she'd left hanging on the door hook. She'd just snugged the belt around her waist when a noise from beyond her bedroom froze her in place.

Marty stood stone still, listening. She hadn't lived there long, but she knew the house well enough to know the muffled bump she'd heard wasn't a normal sound. That could only mean one thing: there was someone in the house.

Her heart jackknifed in her chest. Who the hell would be here? Surely the landlord would have knocked. She'd been dozing, but not fully asleep. She would have heard it. Whoever it was, they shouldn't be there.

Of course, she wasn't in any position to do much about it. Her gun lay on the night table, out of reach. She was wet and wearing only her robe.

The bathroom door stood open a foot. Silently, she leaned against the wall and tried to see through the tiny crack near the hinge. Her eyes had adjusted to the darkness and she could just make out the shape of the bed. The lamp. The rectangle of light from the window.

She wanted her gun. Had the noise she'd heard come from the bedroom? Or was someone trying to break in?

Knowing she had only seconds to act, that she would be safer armed than not, she slipped around the door. Every sense on red alert, she headed straight for the night table.

A sound from the hall to her right sent a paralyzing blast of adrenaline through her. Marty lunged toward the night table. But she wasn't fast enough. A rock-solid body crashed into her. A linebacker sacking a quarterback. Marty reeled sideways and went down hard. Her left shoulder hit the floor. Her head bounced. Stars burst in front of her eyes. No time to feel the pain or dizziness. If she didn't get a handle on the situation, the son of a bitch was going to hurt her.

Her training kicked in as he lurched to his feet. A thin man. Blue jeans. She smelled the stink of sweat and chewing gum. Rolling onto her back, she drew her knees up to her chest and mule-kicked him with both feet.

The man let out a satisfying grunt. Marty didn't wait to see whether or not she'd knocked him down. Scrambling to her feet, she lunged to the nightstand, slammed her hand down on the gun. Instinct put her finger on the trigger.

Spinning, she raised the weapon and fired.

# THIRTEEN

*Clay stood in his darkened study and wished with all of his heart that he didn't have to do what he was about to do. But there was no way around it. He was going to have to tell Erica her mother was here. That she wanted to talk. And he hated it.*

He knew his little girl well. Usually, he knew exactly how she would react to a situation or question or problem. This time, he didn't have a clue.

Erica had started asking about her mother when she was six. Clay had always answered truthfully, but as vaguely as possible. He'd never told his daughter Eve had chosen her new lover over them. Now that Eve was back and wanting to see Erica, he wondered if he should have been more forthright.

"Damn," he muttered, scrubbing his hands over his face.

His ex-wife wasn't the only woman weighing heavy on his mind this evening. As had become the norm in the last week, Marty was in the forefront, dominating his every waking thought. He didn't quite know what to make of his feelings for her. The one and only time he'd felt this way about a woman was when he was twenty-two years old, as dumb as the day was long—and falling headlong for Eve Sutherland.

She'd been the most stunning woman Clay had ever laid eyes on, a slender, platinum-haired beauty with eyes the color of an Amarillo sky and a voice as rich and sultry as the Louisiana bayou.

Marty Hogan was her polar opposite in every way. She was brash and reckless with a hint of tough that ran all the way to her core. All of those things were tempered with a self-destructive streak that made her all the more vulnerable. But Marty was also a cop. She could shoot with the skill of an Army Ranger sniper and take down a man twice her size. And yet Clay still felt the need to protect her. As much from herself as from the pain that had followed her here from Chicago.

Despite the fact that he'd only known Marty for a short time, he felt connected to her in a way that went deeper than anything he'd ever felt for Eve. He'd been in the same dark place Marty was in now. Somehow, that linked them. Made them kindred spirits.

Clay had sworn he wouldn't, but he was getting caught up in things. In Marty. He spent far too much time thinking about her, the rest of the time fantasizing about her. Not a good frame of mind for a man who'd sworn never again. Damn it, he had Erica to think of. His career. His own peace of mind.

Shoving thoughts of Marty aside for the dozenth time that evening, Clay forced his attention back to the matter at hand and rose. He found Erica in her room, sitting cross-legged on the bed, a novel open on her lap.

"I thought you were going to do homework," he said.

"I already did." She looked down at the book and grinned. "I couldn't wait to see how Jimmy rescued the stallion from the island."

Reading a horse story. He should have known. It was her newest passion. In fact, anything having to do with horses fascinated her. He entered the room. "I need to talk to you for a minute."

"Sure, Dad." She scooted over to make room for him on the bed.

He sat and looked into his daughter's eyes. So innocent of mind and pure of heart. How could he do this? "You know how sometimes you ask about your mom?"

"Her name was Eve and she was pretty and you and her were married, but you had to get divorced." She nodded. "Jenny Watson's mom and dad are divorced because they kept getting into arguments."

"That happens sometimes, honey." Clay drew a deep breath and then plunged. "Your mother is here to see you. She wants to talk to you."

Seeming very adult, she thought about it a moment, then nodded. "Is she nice?"

"She'll be very nice to you."

She shrugged. "Okay."

Just like that. His daughter opened her mind, her heart. No questions asked. In that moment Clay ached with love for her. "We're in the living room. I'll make some hot chocolate."

"'Kay." Unfolding her legs, she hopped off the bed. "Dad?" Her voice was too quiet.

"Yeah, honey?"

"Why did she leave us?"

The words cut him with the proficiency of a blade. For his daughter's sake, Clay tried not to wince. "You can ask your mom that if you want to."

"'Kay," she said and they started toward the living room.


*Clay found Eve pacing the length of the living room like* a sleek and elegant cat. She'd changed clothes and now wore fitted red slacks and a matching jacket over a white silk blouse. A glittering red stone sparkled at her cleavage. Earrings the size of hen's eggs dangled from her lobes.

She turned when they entered the room. Her face lit into a smile at the sight of her daughter. "Erica!"

The girl took several steps into the room, looked back once at Clay. He held his ground at the doorway. Eve walked briskly toward the girl, leaned down and threw her arms around her.

"Darling, it's so good to see you. My goodness, how you've grown!"

Erica kept her arms at her sides. She looked embarrassed, but Clay knew she was shy about being the center of attention sometimes, particularly when it came to strangers. Unless she was running a barrel race, she was a low-key kind of kid.

Eve shoved her to arm's length and looked her up and down. "My God, you're beautiful."

Erica grinned. "So are you."

Eve beamed. "Thank you, darling."

Silence stretched for the span of a heartbeat. Eve rose and crossed to the sofa, where a shopping bag stuffed with pink tissue paper sat. "I bought you something. For your birthday."

The girl's eyes lit up with the sincerity only a child could manage. "For me?"

"Of course. Let's sit down."

Mother and daughter sat together on the sofa. Erica in her holey sneakers and Eve in her Via Spiga spikes. Picking up the shopping bag by its handle, Eve offered it. "Here you go."

Erica dug into the bag with unencumbered enthusiasm. She pulled out a pink ostrich-skin purse with a short strap and a bling-bling latch.

"It's from Paris," Eve said.

"Paris, Texas?"

"Paris, France."

"Wow." Erica held it up as if it were a baby alligator that was known to bite. "It's pretty."

"I knew you'd like it. I thought about you the whole time I was there, wondering what to buy you."

Erica opened the purse and looked inside, exploring the gift. Clay was astute enough to see Erica had about as much use for a purse as she did a Ferrari. Unless, of course, she could use it as a saddlebag. The thought made him smile.

Leaving them to get acquainted, Clay went to the kitchen, where he made hot chocolate for Erica. He poured coffee for himself and Eve. Setting the three cups on a tray, he carried them to the living room in time to hear Erica broach the subject she'd been dying to talk about.

". . . and I'll show you George."

"George?"

"Yeah. He's an appy.".

"An appy?"

"Appaloosa," Clay put in, noticing Eve's dumbfounded expression.

"Oh, of course. An appy. Right. But this is quarter horse country, isn't it?"

"My dad and I like Appaloosas." Erica dismissed the question. "Anyway, we've been running barrels, but he's hard in the bridle. I've been reading books and trying to get him softened up. Last weekend we ran fifteen seconds."

Jumping up from the sofa, Erica went for her mug of hot chocolate. "Oh, wow, Dad, this looks yummy."

He set the tray on the coffee table. Eve shot him a grateful look and picked up her coffee. "So are you in fifth grade now?" she asked.

"Yeah." Erica slurped whipped cream. "As soon as we finish our drinks, we can go look at George. He's so cute. I'm teaching him to kiss."

"Oh." She glanced at Clay. "You must have inherited your love of horses from your dad."

"He thinks George is a brat," Erica said.

"He is," Clay put in.

"A cute brat." Erica gave him an impish grin, then turned

her attention back to her mother. "Anyway, we can go look at him if you want."

"Of course."

Clay glanced at Eve's spiked shoes and tried not to smile as he picked up his coffee and sipped. Ever since Eve had shown up, he'd been fighting the fear that his ex-wife would insert herself into their lives and try to take Erica away from him. That she would try to woo his little girl with all her glitter and sophistication. Clay didn't want to share Erica, especially with a woman who'd discarded her like an old doll she'd lost interest in.

His thoughts were interrupted by the chirp of his cell phone. Unclipping it from his belt, he checked the display. Surprise whispered through him when he saw Marty's number. He hit the Talk button. Before he could say a word, her voice crashed over the line.

"This is Hogan. I've got shots fired. My house. Someone broke in . . ."

Concern slammed into his chest like a cannonball. "Are you all right?"

"I'm . . . fine."

"Anyone hit?"

"I don't know."

Clay was already in the kitchen, snagging his keys off the counter. "Where is he now?"

"Gone."

"I'm on my way. Sit tight."

When he reached the living room, Erica and Eve had both risen. Clay didn't want to leave Erica with Eve. But Mrs. Huffschmidtt had already gone for the day, and Marty was in trouble. He didn't have a choice.

"Can I talk to you for a moment?" he said to Eve.

"Of course."

He went to the kitchen, aware that she followed. At the center island, he turned to her. "There's an emergency in town. Can you stay for a couple of hours?"

He couldn't believe it when she looked undecided for a moment. "Oh, of course. We'll use this time to get better acquainted."

He stared hard at her, aware that his heart was beating too hard. "Watch your mouth around Erica."

She looked offended. "I would never say anything to hurt her."

He leaned close, his voice falling to a whisper. "Don't even think about going anywhere with her. If you so much as open your car door, I'll know about it and I'll come looking for you. When I find you, I'll make you sorry you came back."

Her flawless complexion reddened. "How dare—"

"You got that?" he cut in.

"Yes."

Clay left the kitchen, went to Erica and pressed a kiss to her head. "Sorry kiddo. Gotta go."

"It's okay."

"It's late, so don't go anywhere, okay?"

"'Kay."

"Take her out to see George."

"I will."

At that Clay turned and ran out the door.

*He hit sixty miles per hour at Cactus Street and blew the* stoplight at the main intersection of the tiny downtown area. He had no idea what he'd find when he got to Marty's house, but a dozen scenarios rampaged through his mind, and none of them were good.

Home-invasion type crimes did not happen in Caprock Canyon. Neither did sniper shootings. What the hell was going on? Did she have a disgruntled boyfriend who'd followed her to Texas? Had Smitty decided to make good on the hatred Clay had seen in his eyes? Or was there something more ominous in the works? Clay didn't know the answers to any of the questions, but he intended to find out.

Marty's house was totally dark when he arrived. The hairs at his nape prickled uncomfortably as he parked curbside. Grabbing the flashlight, he hit the ground running, took the steps in a single leap. His hand rested on the butt of his weapon as he traversed the porch. Clay didn't bother knocking and entered the living room.

"Hogan?"

Silence screamed for a fraction of a second too long. Clay reached out and hit the light switch, but nothing happened. "Hogan!"

"I'm here."

He shifted the beam to see her at the hall, walking toward him. The first thing he noticed was that she was wearing a robe. Her hair was wet. Her expression told him she was very frightened. "You okay?" he asked, knowing from the look on her face she wasn't.

"I'm fine."

"Where's the perp?"

"I don't know. Out the back, maybe."

"Armed?"

"I didn't see a gun."

The urge to run his hands over her and make sure she was all right was strong, but Clay resisted. In the short time he'd known her, they'd been through a few intense situations, but he'd never seen her like this. "Stay put."

Drawing his weapon, he entered the kitchen. The back door stood open, the screen door beyond closed. Clay pushed it open and stepped outside, listening, his eyes scanning the shadows around the small shed. Keeping the flashlight turned off, he started toward the shed. He tried the door, found it locked. The windows were intact. His boots crunched over dry grass as he walked around the structure. But there was no sign anyone had been there.

Turning on the flashlight, he walked the path back to the house, checking for footprints. He found them at the bedroom window. A hefty dose of anger went through him at the thought of some Peeping Tom son of a bitch watching Marty and getting his rocks off. But he knew that was a purely male response. The cop in him thought there might be more going on than either of them realized.

He entered the house through the front door just as the lights flashed on. He found Marty coming in through the back door in the kitchen.

"The fuse was unscrewed," she said.

"I'm not surprised." Clay grimaced. "I found footprints. By your bedroom window."

For the first time he was able to get a good look at her. She was ghastly pale beneath the fluorescent light and clutched the lapels of the robe together with white-knuckled hands. Bright red abrasions glowed on both knees. She looked small and vulnerable out of uniform. And despite the circumstances, incredibly lovely.

· "I need to get dressed." She turned toward the living room.

Clay stopped her. "Marty, did he . . ." Unable to complete the sentence, he let the words trail.

"No," she said quickly. "I fought him hard and managed to get my weapon."

Clay nodded. Questions buzzed in his head like a thousand live wires. "Get dressed. I'm going to call this in. Get Jett out looking." He pulled out the phone, hit some numbers. "Any idea what he looked like?"

She shook her head. "Once the lights went out, I couldn't see a thing. You might have Jett check nearby hospitals because I may have gotten lucky and shot the son of a bitch."

Clay briefed Jett on the situation and sent him on patrol. He walked into the living room expecting to find Marty there, but the room was empty. "Hogan?"

"Just a sec," came her voice from the bedroom.

Clay wandered to the hall, found the door to her bedroom closed. "You okay?"

She came out. "Better."

He frowned at the sight of her in uniform. "What do you think you're doing?"

"My job."

"Your job right now is to sit down and tell me what happened."

Crossing to the night table, she picked up her holster and proceeded to buckle it at her hips. Clay stopped her with a hand on her arm. "You're not going to do this."

"Some son of a bitch invaded my home and attacked me and you expect me to sit back and let him go?"

He took the holster from her hands and returned it to the night table. "Come here."

"I need to work this."

"I mean it, damn it." Taking her arm, he ushered her into the living room and gently pushed her onto the sofa. "Now, sit."

"We're wasting time." She started to rise, but he eased her back down by putting his hand on her shoulder.

Sighing, she leaned back and folded her arms. "Please tell me you at least have Jett out looking."

Clay nodded, lowered himself to the adjacent chair and put his elbows on his knees. Across from him, she was trying to get back into cop mode, trying even harder to appear calm and in control. But he could tell by her body language she wasn't any of those things. "Tell me what happened."

She looked away briefly, then met his gaze head-on. "I was taking a bath. The lights went out. I grabbed my robe. Walked into the bedroom." A breath shuddered out of her. "He hit me like a ton of bricks. Took me down to the floor." The words were tumbling out of her now. Too fast, running together. "We struggled. I kept my head, but he was . . . incredibly strong. I knew my only chance of getting control of the situation was my weapon. I'd left it on the night table. I kept trying to break away. When I finally did, I grabbed it and fired."

"You think you hit him?"

"I don't know. I looked, but there wasn't any blood."

"How many times did you fire?"

"I emptied the clip."

Good girl, he thought, as he got out his notebook. "Was he armed?"

"I didn't see a weapon."

But Clay knew that didn't mean the perp didn't have one. All that told him was that the intruder hadn't planned to kill her right off the bat. He'd had other things planned, but what? "Did you get a feel for his size? Height? Weight?"

"He didn't have a lot of bulk. He was more wiry. Muscular. Thin, but not bony or frail. He was like a damn rock."

"Clothes?"

Her brows went together. Clay wondered what it would be like to go to her and smooth away the wrinkle between them with his fingers . . .

"He was wearing a jacket. I felt it when we were struggling. Denim. Maybe a T-shirt underneath. I don't know about his pants."

"What about hair?"

"Not long because I tried to yank it out. That's about all I can tell you."

"Color?"

She shook her head.

"Facial hair?"

"I don't know."

"Did he have a smell? Booze breath? Cigarettes? Maybe he'd just pumped gas?"

"He smelled like gum." Her eyes widened as if she'd just thought of it. "Mint. Spearmint, maybe. I remember thinking he had pretty fresh breath for a shit-eating perp."

Despite the seriousness of the situation, Clay smiled as he scribbled in the notebook, details he would need in order to put out a description with the county and file his report. "Did he say anything?"

"That's one of the things that was so weird about it. He

didn't say a word. Didn't call me names. Didn't cuss. Didn't grope."

"Maybe he was afraid you'd recognize his voice."

Marty said nothing.

Clay tried again. "Was there anything familiar about him?"

Her eyes narrowed. "You thinking it was Smitty?"

"Or someone else you might know. Maybe someone who followed you from Chicago?"

"A fan from my perp-beating days?"

"Old boyfriend. Admirer. Stalker. You know how it goes."

"I didn't have any of those things."

"You sure?"

"How could I not be sure?"

"What about Smitty?"

She shook her head, but Clay thought it was more of an I-don't-know kind of shake as opposed to an adamant no. "You think he's capable of something like this?"

"I think Smitty walks a fine line." Clay sighed. "There have been a couple of incidents."

"He definitely didn't like me." She gave him a wry smile that looked out of place on her pale face. "He's a bully and a pig, but I can't see him doing something like this."

"In any case, I'll make it a point to talk to him. Feel him out."

She nodded.

"Hogan, when I got here tonight, your doors were unlocked. What the hell were you thinking?"

"Guess I'm getting lax since moving here to Mayberry, where the crime rate, by the way, is—and I quote the chief—'next to nothing.'" She gave him a knowing look. "I guess that excludes home invasions and sniper attacks."

Clay had debated whether or not to bring up something else that had been eating at him. A niggling at the back of his brain that wouldn't go away. He'd learned when that happened to pull it out and take a look at it. He figured he owed it to Marty to lay down his theories no matter how fervently she didn't want to hear them.

"You have any other ideas?" he asked.

Her gaze skittered to the right, a sure sign that she had an idea of what he was thinking. "Like what?"

He let the silence work for a moment, watched her fidget, then opened the Pandora's box neither of them had wanted to touch. "Since you seem reluctant to broach the subject, I will."

"I know what you're thinking," she said. "We're a thousand miles from Chicago."

"That's why God invented cars and airplanes. So people could travel long distances to do dirty deeds."

"Is that what you think this is about?"

"I think it's something we need to consider, don't you?"

"Look, I've had my share of crackpots and idiots contact me about what happened. Most people just want to voice their opinion or tell me what they think of me or call me a few names. But nothing like this has ever happened."

"Is the perp still in jail?"

"No one's told me different."

"In other words you haven't checked."

"The guy killed a kid, Clay. He can't be out."

"Stranger things have happened." He scribbled a note to put a call in to the Federal Bureau of Prisons, then he gave Marty a level stare. "I think that, for whatever reason, someone has targeted you. Let's face it, to anyone who saw that video, you're not exactly cop of the year."

He could see her mind spinning through the arguments she could use to debate the theory. "I think that's a stretch."

"How do you explain the shots fired in the canyon? Who the hell broke into your house and attacked you tonight?"

"I don't know! It could have been random."

"Random crimes with that level of violence don't happen here."

She gave him a wry smile, but her expression reminded

him of a kitten that had just been kicked by a cruel child. "At least not until I came along, huh?"

"For God's sake, Marty, this isn't some lowlife trying to scare you. This is a dangerous individual with a serious agenda. We're talking home invasion. The kind of crime that gets people killed. He had to have wanted you pretty badly to go to those lengths."

Her throat bobbed twice. "He could have had me tonight. I was down. It would have been easy—" When her hands trembled, she set them on her knees and pushed, as if she could push away the memory. "There was a moment when I thought it was over. I thought he was going to kill me."

Rising abruptly, she stalked to the kitchen to stare out the window above the sink. God help him, he knew better, but Clay went after her. Coming up behind her, he set his hands on her shoulders. "I'm not going to let anything happen to you." Despite his words of reassurance, he could feel her shoulders trembling beneath his fingertips. "Marty."

Slowly, she turned to him. Wiping her eyes with the back of her sleeve, she looked up at him. "I'm a cop," she whispered. "I'm not supposed to be scared."

Clay detected vodka on her breath, but didn't mention it. He knew they were playing with fire. He knew he was probably the one who would get burned. But the need to protect rose to mingle with another need that wasn't so black-and-white. A need that was part affection and a whole lot sexual. It gripped him every time he so much as thought of her— which seemed to be every couple of minutes.

"Come here," he whispered.

"I don't think that's a very good idea."

"Because of what happened last time?"

"Because you're married."

Sincere surprise sent his brows up. "Married?"

"That, too." Using the cuff of her shirt, she wiped at the tear on her cheek. "Look, no offense but I've got enough problems without getting tangled up in someone else's marriage."

"I'm divorced."

"The woman who came to see you today claims to be married to you."

"We've been divorced for six years."

"You're sure about that?"

He laughed and used her words from earlier when he'd asked her a dumb question. "How could I not be sure?"

"Some men get confused about those kinds of details."

"Ah, Hogan, you're such a cynic."

"Safer that way."

"Since when do you play it safe?"

"Even I have my limits."

Since she evidently wasn't going to willingly get any closer to him, Clay went to her. Alarm flashed in her eyes. She went rigid when he put his arms around her. "Jesus, Hogan, you're tense."

"That home invasion stuff does me in every time."

"Or maybe it's me."

She smiled. "Don't give yourself too much credit, Chief."

"Ouch."

She came against him with the warm softness of a summer breeze. "Thanks for getting here so quickly."

Clay mentally braced when she slid her arms around his shoulders. "Just doing my job."

But it was a lie. He accepted that, as the slow spiral of pleasure wrapped around him, like some illicit narcotic. He didn't know what to do next. His feelings for Marty had officially become a problem.

The one thing he knew for certain was that someone was trying to hurt her. Clay had to find out why. He had to find out who. And then he had to stop them.

*From the cloak of darkness and the safety of distance*, he watched them through the binoculars. Through the kitchen window of her house, he saw that Marty Hogan was a lot closer to the chief of police than he'd ever imagined. An interesting development to say the least. One he could certainly find a way to use to his advantage.

He'd almost had her tonight. One more second and he would have used the stun gun. But he'd underestimated her. She'd been tougher and stronger and faster than he'd anticipated. He'd been careless, and it had nearly cost him his life.

It wouldn't happen again.

The bullet had creased the flesh of his forearm. The wound wasn't serious, but the pain infuriated him. It angered him even more that the American cop—a *woman*—had bested him. She wouldn't be so lucky next time.

Of course, he or Katja could take her out with a single bullet from a half mile away. A full-metal-jacket boat tail out of the Dragunov sniper rifle and Marty Hogan would no longer be a problem. He and his sister would already be on their way back to Brighton Beach.

But neither Radimir nor Katja would be satisfied with a quick and painless death for the woman who'd destroyed their brother's life. The Red Mafia didn't work that way; their reputation hadn't been built on easy death. No, he and Katja would make an example of Hogan, the way they had with the other Chicago cop, who'd stood back and done nothing while their brother sustained a beating severe enough to put him in the hospital. In the end, the cop had screamed like a pig at slaughter.

Marty Hogan would do the same. Radimir would make sure her screams echoed across the land until her vocal cords burst. He would make sure her blood stained the earth until her veins ran dry. He would make his mark on this town. He would take her life in a way no one would ever forget. Maybe post photos on the Internet so everyone would remember the Redfellas were a force to be reckoned with.

And when Radimir and Katja left this godforsaken part of Texas, Rurik would be avenged.

# FOURTEEN

*Clay pulled away an instant before the situation got out* of hand. It took every bit of discipline he possessed, but he took another step back, hoping the distance would help. When it didn't, he turned and started toward the living room.

He heard Marty behind him, but he didn't turn to look at her. He wasn't sure what he might do if he did. Go to her. Wrap his arms around her. Kiss her. Or maybe he'd go for the gold, take her down to the floor and sink into all that heat . . .

Before he knew it, he was out the door and striding across the porch. He berated himself all the way to the Explorer, then slid inside. This wasn't like him. Clay was far too cautious to get caught up in this kind of situation. Marty Hogan was the last kind of woman he needed in his life. She was reckless and brash and thumbed her nose at the rules. Clay just happened to be fond of rules. He was fond of boundaries and personal restraint, responsibility.

When it came to Marty, all those things he prided

himself on possessing went out the window right along with his self-respect.

Cursing beneath his breath, he snatched up the radio and called Jett. The other man picked up immediately. "Yeah, Chief."

"Any sign of our guy?"

"I've been driving around town for half an hour now. Found a couple of neckers in the park. Ramsey Decker was drunk again and sleeping in the Dumpster by the church. Nothing out of the ordinary."

"What about hospitals?"

"Called a couple in Amarillo, but they haven't reported any gunshot wounds."

"I've got a partial description." Clay relayed what little Marty had been able to give him.

"Roger that," Jett said. "Hogan okay?"

"Yeah, just shaken up."

"Any idea who attacked her?"

"Could be about that Chicago thing." Clay paused. "Smitty crossed my mind."

"You think he'd do something like that?" Jett sounded dubious.

"No, but I'm concerned enough to have a talk with him."

"You want me to cruise around awhile longer?"

Clay looked at his watch. It was 10 P.M. Jett had been on duty for almost twelve hours. "Go on home."

"I'm not going to argue with that."

Clay racked the mike and cursed. He set his hands on the wheel. For a moment he was tempted to start the car and drive away. But he couldn't do that to Marty. He couldn't do it to himself. If something happened to her, he'd never be able to live with himself.

Clay had never been the kind of man to run away from his problems. Marty Hogan might be a problem, but she worked for him. She was his officer. A cop. But that wasn't what bothered him most about the whole thing. It was the woman part that was eating him from the inside out. Not just any woman, but an attractive woman wreaking havoc on his willpower.

Self-preservation told him to steer clear. But the part of him that was a man first could not deny the fact that she was in danger. That he was the only one in a position to keep her safe.

"God *damn* it." He rapped his fist hard against the steering wheel, then swung open the door and got out of the cruiser. He stood there for a moment, debating. But his decision was made.

Someone had come to *his* town and attacked one of *his* officers. They'd crossed a line. Clay couldn't let his personal feelings for Marty get in the way of doing the right thing. He owed it to her. Owed it to himself. He was in it up to his chin, and he wouldn't walk away until he got to the bottom of this.

Listening, he stood silent and still and looked around. There were plenty of hiding places around the house. The hedge of overgrown juniper on the south side. The cluster of pampas grass in the side yard. The squat piñon pine. The shed at the rear.

The hairs on his neck stood up. Clay stared into the vast darkness of the field to the west and wondered if someone was out there, watching, waiting, planning . . .

*Planning what?*

"Who are you?" he whispered.

Only the night answered, with the hiss of wind through the tall prairie grass.

He found Marty sitting in the kitchen, applying a Band-Aid to her abrasion. "How's the knee?" he asked.

"Just skinned."

But he knew she would be bruised in the morning. He wondered where else she'd been hurt but hadn't mentioned. "I want you to walk me through what happened."

She nodded. "I told you. I was in the tub, and I heard something."

Glancing over his shoulder, he started down the hall, not stopping until he was in the bathroom. The candle sitting on the commode had nearly burned all the way down. Next to it, a tumbler half-full of what he assumed was vodka sat in testimony to what she'd been doing.

She spotted the glass at the same time he did. He gave her points for not trying to hide it or offering hollow explanations. He wondered why she'd bought another bottle. For an instant, he considered dumping it. But Clay knew it wouldn't do any good in the long run. Short-term, he could dump a hundred bottles down the drain. In the long haul, she was going to have to do it on her own.

"I was half-dozing when the lights went out."

"He unscrewed the main fuse."

She nodded. "I got out of the tub. Grabbed my robe. I'd just stepped into the bedroom when he slammed into me from the side."

"Both doors were unlocked?"

She looked sheepish for a moment and nodded. "I know. Stupid."

"What happened next?"

"We struggled. I mule-kicked him and managed to grab my weapon on the night table." She gave him a steady look. "And I engaged the son of a bitch."

"Did he wear gloves?"

"Yeah. I felt them. Leather, I think."

"That means this was premeditated. Not some Peeping Tom acting on impulse. This guy put some thought into it, came here with something specific in mind."

"Yeah, well, he got more than he bargained for, didn't he?"

Her tough talk didn't convince him she was impervious to what had happened. He'd seen the way she was shaking when he arrived. He'd seen the fear in her eyes and the pale cast of her skin. Both of those things were all the more powerful because he knew it was a rare state for her. "The overriding question is why," he said. "And will he be back?"

She crossed the room and blew out the candle. "If he tries, I've got another box of ammo and a nice little .22 mini Magnum I've been dying to try out."

Clay sighed. "Hogan . . ."

"Oh, I forgot. I'm a woman. I'm not allowed to fight back because I might break a nail or become hysterical. Thanks for reminding me."

"Cut it out. This has nothing to do with your being a woman." It was a lie and they both knew it, but Clay would be damned if he'd admit it. There were some double standards that were in place because they needed to be. "You can't stay here tonight."

"I'm a trained police officer. I'm armed—"

"You're a target."

"Would you be saying that to Jett?"

"You're damn straight I would."

"Just exactly where do you expect me to sleep?"

Clay had already considered his options; he didn't like any of them. The motel wouldn't be much safer than her house if the nameless, faceless goon came calling in the middle of the night. He'd thought about Jo Nell, but his dispatcher was getting on in years and wouldn't be much help if something happened. If there had been any other officer available at that moment, Clay would have utilized him.

To his dismay, there wasn't. Jett had just pulled a double shift. Dugan was off tonight. Clay was going to have to rely on himself. "The way I see it we have two choices."

"I can't wait to hear them."

"I can sit in my Explorer all night and keep an eye on your place. Or you can follow me home and stay in my guest room."

Marty snorted. "That'll get the tongues wagging."

"You have a better idea?"

"Look, Chief, I appreciate what you're trying to do, but I don't think that's a good idea."

"Unless you come up with a better plan in the next two minutes, you don't have a choice."

"Is that an order?"

"Let's just call it a suggestion from a friend."

That seemed to deflate her resistance, but only marginally. Clay knew it wouldn't last. "Look," he said reasonably, "I don't relish the idea of sitting in my damn vehicle for the next eight hours. Pack your bag. We'll go to my house and figure this thing out."

"You're treating me like some helpless female."

"Hogan, for God's sake, will you stop being so damn oversensitive about that? I don't like this any better than you do. But if you want to pretend the situation isn't dangerous, you're a bigger fool than I thought."

Pressing her fingertips to her temples, she sighed. "Okay. You win. I'll let you treat me like a frightened bimbo. But if you think I'm going to let you keep me from being a cop and doing what I do best, you're sadly mistaken."

"Whatever." Clay motioned toward the bedroom. "Pack. I'm going to take some photos of those footprints outside. We leave in ten."


*Marty was so angry she barely paid attention to the* clothes and toiletries she threw into her overnight bag. Not at Clay so much; she knew he was just doing his job. The person she was really angry with was the son of a bitch who was causing all this trouble. The person who'd shot at her in the canyon and, tonight, attacked her in her home.

Since, she'd been wracking her brain, trying to figure out who had it in for her. Like Clay, she'd considered Smitty. But she honestly didn't think a home-invasion type attack was his style. He was more bark than bite. The kind of guy who liked to shoot off his mouth and push people around. But when it came down to firing on a fellow cop, Marty didn't think he was up to the job.

If not Smitty, then who?

The question ate at her as she zipped her laptop into its case. She considered past arrests. Like a lot of cops, she'd made plenty of enemies in the years she'd worked Chicago's South Side. Retaliation from an inmate upon his release from prison was always a concern. Marty couldn't count the number of times she'd appeared in court to testify against some gangsta or lowlife. While some of them might have long memories, Chicago was their world. She couldn't see any of them leaving their turf to follow her all the way to Texas.

That left the debacle from six months ago. As vehemently as Marty didn't want to consider it, she was starting to believe someone had targeted her because of what she'd done. It wouldn't have been hard to track her, thanks to an overzealous media. Her photograph and her move to Caprock Canyon had been blasted over the airwaves for everyone to see.

Had some police brutality zealot targeted her? Or did someone with ties to the suspect she'd abused on that terrible day decide to reap revenge on a cop gone bad?

"Ready?"

She startled at the sound of Clay's voice. Straightening, Marty hefted her bag onto her shoulder, lifted her laptop case, and turned to face him. "I'm ready to find and catch this guy."

He frowned. "I don't think that's going to happen tonight."

"I may not catch him, but with a little help from the computer I might be able to ID him."

"Jesus, Hogan, are you always such a type A personality?"

"What do you think?"

"I think this guy's in trouble if you get your hands on him." Giving her a crooked smile, he took her bag. "That was a joke."

"Oh."

He shook his head. "Come on. We'll take the Explorer."

Marty had driven by Clay's place once or twice while on patrol. It was, after all, her responsibility to familiarize herself with the town and its citizenry. But the truth of the matter was she'd been curious. About where he lived. How he lived. She'd been curious about *him*.

She was so caught up in her thoughts, she didn't realize they weren't heading toward his place until he turned into the gravel lot of Foley's Bar.

"Don't tell me we're stopping in for a beer," she said.

He motioned toward a newish red Chevy pickup parked next to a Ford F250 flatbed. "Smitty's truck."

An odd sense of excitement kicked in her gut at the sight of Smitty's vehicle. The kind of excitement a cop felt in anticipation of some action. "He's probably not going to buy us drinks."

Frowning, Clay put the Explorer in park and shut down the engine. "That truck wasn't here when I drove by the first time."

"You think he's the one who paid me a visit tonight?"

"I think it's a possibility worth checking out." He opened his door.

Marty slid from the Explorer. "Clay, I didn't get a good look at him."

He met her in front of the vehicle. "Look, I know Smitty. And I think his reaction will tell us what we need to know."

The only sound came from the crunch of their shoes over gravel and the deep-bass rumble of too-loud music and bad acoustics as they started toward the entrance. Marty was glad she'd changed into her uniform. She would never admit it to Clay, but she didn't think she could face Smitty dressed in her civvies. Sometimes the uniform really was a coat of armor.

Clay opened the door. The blast of music hit Marty in the face with the force of a concussion grenade. The odors of cigarette smoke and spilled beer mingled with the darker smells of dirty hair and cheap cologne. She spotted Nola hustling up drinks behind the bar. A group of biker types congregated at the pool tables in the back. Two women wearing pinch-front straw hats, matching tank tops and bling-bling belts dirty danced in front of the jukebox.

Smitty slumped on a stool at the bar, where a longneck Bud sat next to a salt-crusted shot glass and a spent lime. He wore blue jeans and a denim jacket.

"You said the guy was wearing a denim jacket." Clay motioned with his eyes toward Smitty.

Marty stared at the man on the bar stool, trying to mentally superimpose him over the vague image of the man who'd accosted her back at the house. She couldn't pinpoint the exact reason, but the images didn't jibe.

"I don't know," she said.

But Clay was already pushing through the crowd, making his way toward Smitty. Trying hard to ignore the jab of trepidation in her gut, Marty took a deep breath and followed.

The music paused, and an instant later a classic Pink Floyd tune floated through the air like marijuana smoke. Clay reached Smitty and touched him on the shoulder.

"Smitty."

The man turned on the stool and gave Clay a red-eyed glare. When his gaze slid to Marty, the rise of hostility was powerful enough to send a quiver of uneasiness through her. "Well, if it ain't the fuckin' caped crusaders."

"Can it," Clay said. "I need to talk to you. Outside. Now."

Drunks were an unpredictable lot. Judging from the way he leaned on the bar when he stood, that wasn't the

8

first longneck Smitty had had tonight. It sure as hell wasn't the first shot of tequila.

Smitty wiped his mouth on his sleeve. "What are you going to do, fire me again? Or maybe you're going to cuff me and let your female Rambo take a cheap shot."

"Don't make this hard," Clay said.

Smitty snarled something about rutting whores beneath his breath and started for the door.

"He's a real charmer," Marty said.

Clay shot her a firm look. "I'll do the talking. I want you to take a good long look at him and tell me if he was in your house tonight."

"Okay."

She trailed both men to the door, trying hard not to notice the eyes burning into her back. For the first time she wondered how much of her past had gotten around town. If the people in this bar knew what she'd done. If they condemned her for it. Or maybe Smitty had put some convenient spin on his recent termination.

The air was cooler and cleaner outside. Smitty walked as far as the corner of the building, then turned to face them. Even in the semidarkness, Marty could see the ruddiness of his complexion. The anger sparking hot in his eyes. The hostility oozing from every pore.

"What do you want?" he asked.

Clay stopped a scant foot away from him, invading the other man's space just enough to let him know he was in charge. "I want to know where you were tonight."

"You gotta be kidding." He thrust a finger at Marty. "What did she do? Make up another story about me?"

"Answer the question," Clay said.

"I ain't gonna answer shit until you tell me why I gotta."

"We can do this here, and when we're done you can go back in and finish your drink. Or we can do it at the station, where I can ruin your night and probably the rest of your week. Your choice."

Smitty struggled with that for a moment. Marty could see his alcohol-fuzzed brain working through his options. He must have seen something in Clay's eyes because he decided to cooperate. He shoved his hands into his pockets and shook his head. "I got back from Plainview about an hour ago."

"Why were you in Plainview?"

"I had an interview."

"At the police department?"

Smitty's mouth tightened. "Yeah."

"You come straight here?"

"Yeah."

"Were you alone?"

"I don't take my fuckin' mother on interviews with me, if that's what you're asking."

Clay frowned. "Can anyone in Plainview vouch for you?"

Smitty blinked as if realizing for the first time he might have to prove his whereabouts. "The sergeant. Frank Chaney." His eyes narrowed. "Why are you questioning me?"

"Someone broke into Hogan's house tonight," Clay said.

Smitty looked at her and grinned. He looked like a mongoose that had outmaneuvered a cobra and had the snake clenched in its jaws. "She probably mouthed off to the wrong person."

"Or maybe you blame me for your getting fired," she shot back.

Smitty hissed another expletive and moved toward her. Clay stopped him with a forearm across his chest. Before the other man stepped back, Marty caught a whiff of cheap tequila and onions.

"Don't do anything stupid," Clay warned. "Or you won't be starting that new job."

Sneering, the other man jabbed a finger toward her. "She's a mouthy bitch."

Clay glanced at Marty, the question clear in his eyes. She didn't like Smitty and knew the feeling was mutual, but in her gut she knew he wasn't the one who'd attacked her. She gave Clay a minute shake of the head.

"Enjoy the rest of your evening," Clay said.

Smitty made a sound of disgust. "Fuck you and fuck her."

Shaking his head, Clay turned away.

Marty took a final look at Smitty. He stared back, his hands clenched into fists at his sides. "You might consider an anger management class," she said.

"Or maybe I'll just take you down a few notches with my fist."

Marty stopped and turned toward him. "How about right now?"

"Hogan. Jesus." Clay hooked his finger around her belt loop and pulled her back. "I can't take you anywhere, can I?"

She fell into step beside him, thinking about Smitty and what had happened. Midway to the Explorer, Clay broke the silence. "What do you think?"

"He didn't do it."

He cut her a sharp look. "You sure?"

"He smells like onions," she said. "The guy who broke in smelled like chewing gum."

"He could have gone for a burger after he attacked you."

"I looked closely at Smitty, Clay. It wasn't him."

"That leaves us with a problem."

Clay hit the locks and Marty climbed into the Explorer. "If Smitty didn't do it," she said, "who did?"


Clay lived on the opposite side of town, in a single-story redbrick ranch. Marty was still thinking about Smitty when Clay turned into the gravel driveway. The Explorer's headlights played over a red steel barn, a horse trailer parked next to it and a big Ford F250. A sleek Jaguar lounged adjacent the garage door.

"Nice wheels," she said.

"Not mine."

"Don't tell me Erica drives."

Clay parked and shut down the engine. "My ex-wife is here."

Marty wouldn't have been more surprised if he'd taken out his flashlight and hit her on the forehead with it. She wondered just how ex his former wife really was. "Cozy."

"I wouldn't go that far." Getting out of the Explorer, he picked up her bag and they started toward the side door, where a yellow porch light welcomed them. Clay used his key and they stepped into a kitchen.

The first thing Marty noticed was the smell of some savory dish she couldn't name. Her stomach rumbled, reminding her she'd skipped both lunch and dinner.

It was a big, airy room with painted white cabinetry above a granite countertop and a pale turquoise backsplash. It was also spotless. "You didn't tell me you were such a good housekeeper," she said.

"I'm not. Mrs. Huffschmidtt cooks and cleans for us five days a week."

"Oh." She looked around. "Nice."

What made the house special was the undeniable fact that someone had made it into a home. It was neat and clean with a comfortable amount of clutter that spoke highly of Mrs. Huffschmidtt the housekeeper—and Clay, too.

"Dad!"

Marty turned to see Erica dash into the room. "Hey, Marty."

"Hey."

The girl trotted to Clay. "I took Eve out to the barn to see George and she stepped in a pile of poop."

Eve appeared at the doorway just as an unladylike snort

erupted from Marty. Realizing it probably wouldn't go over well with Clay's ex-wife, Marty attempted to disguise her amusement with a cough, but she didn't think she succeeded.

Erica giggled and put her hand over her mouth.

Clay frowned at both of them, then turned his attention to his ex-wife. "Did you get your shoe cleaned off all right?"

Everyone looked down at her extraordinarily impractical heels. "Yes." Her eyes slid to Marty, sank into her like fangs, then moved on to Clay. "Did you get the emergency taken care of?"

"Everything's fine." He cleared his throat. "Eve, I'd like for you to meet Marty Hogan, my newest officer."

The elegant woman crossed to Marty with the poise of a Paris runway model and extended her hand, but her eyes were cool. "Pleased to meet you."

Clay glanced at Marty. "This is Eve Sutherland, Erica's mother."

Marty gave her hand an extra-firm grip. "Likewise."

Eve's perfectly plucked brows pulled together. "You look familiar, Marcy."

"Marty," she corrected.

"Have we met?"

"Not until today." This was the part Marty hated most. The part when the person she was meeting recognized her from the footage they'd seen on television and had to decide if she was a hero or a bad cop.

"I'm sure we've met at some point. Where are you from?"

The urge to lie was strong. But Marty had long since learned there was no running from the truth. Somehow it invariably caught up with her. "Chicago."

"Oh." Eve put her fingers beneath her chin as if considering, then her brows shot up. "*Oh. That* Marty Hogan. Well, I guess that answers my next question."

"What question is that?" Marty asked.

"Now I know why you came to Caprock Canyon." Eve's gaze went to Clay. "I didn't realize you were that hard up for officers."

Subtly, he positioned himself between the two women. "Eve . . ."

When she returned her gaze to Marty, a small, nasty smile played at the corners of her mouth. "He's always had a weakness for cops down on their luck."

Marty stared at her, aware that her heart rate was up, that her hands were clenched. She didn't know what to say or how to feel. She thought about jumping down that slender, elegant throat with a verbal barrage the woman would not soon forget.

But for the first time in a long time, Marty cared what someone thought of her. Not only Clay, she realized, but Erica, too.

Instead of responding, Marty turned to Erica. "How's it going, buckaroo?"

The name elicited a smile. "What are you doing here?"

"Oh, just some police business."

"Did you bring your Rufus the Police Dog suit?"

"Ah, not tonight." Remembering the gift she'd picked up for the girl's birthday, Marty reached into her duffel and pulled out the small bag. Since she didn't know the first thing about wrapping or bows, she'd stuck it in a colorful little bag from Fox's Pharmacy. She had to admit it looked pretty good for a woman who hadn't a clue about those kinds of things.

"Happy birthday."

The little girl took the bag. "Thanks."

"So how old are you?"

"Ten."

"Wow, that's really old."

"Is not." Erica reached into the bag. Her eyes lit up when she pulled out the figurine. "Oh my gosh! I love it!"

The figurine was of an Appaloosa horse, dashing around a barrel with a little girl in a cowboy hat astride. It wasn't expensive—just made of resin—but the horse looked just like George and Marty had known Erica would love it.

Spinning, she shoved the figurine at Clay. "Dad!"

Marty couldn't remember the last time such a simple moment meant so much to her. Kids might be weird little creatures, but they were honest. There were no pretenses. No complicated games. And their joy was incredibly genuine.

"Hey, that's nice." Clay picked up the figurine and glanced at Marty. "Where did you find it?"

"I ordered it online."

"Thanks, Marty."

Before Marty realized what the girl was going to do, Erica jumped toward her and threw her arms around her. "It's perfect. I love it. I really do."

Marty allowed herself to be hugged, but for the life of her she couldn't think of anything to say.

"It's charming," Eve put in. "It reminds me of those adorable little plastic horses I collected as a child. The farm store used to sell them for five dollars." Her gaze swept to Clay. "Remember those?"

Marty extricated herself from Erica's arms. Ignoring Eve, she turned her attention to Clay. "Is there someplace I can set up my laptop? I need to get to work."

"Aren't you going to have ice cream and cake?" Erica asked.

Clay looked at Marty. "It's chocolate."

Marty didn't want to stick around, chocolate or not. She wasn't so dense that she didn't sense Eve's not-so-subtle hostility. She wished she hadn't agreed to come here. "I really have to get to work, log in to some databases for research."

When Erica started to protest, Clay set his hand on his daughter's shoulder. "We're working on a case, honey."

Erica looked confused for a moment. "Is she spending the night with us?"

Clay cleared his throat. "We, uh, had a big case come up. Officer Hogan has some computer research to do. I told her she could use the guest room."

To back him up, Marty raised her laptop and tapped it. "See?"

"A case?" Eve cut in. "How fascinating. Are your other officers spending the night, too? Or just . . . Marcy?"

Clay's jaw went taut. "Eve, thank you for staying with Erica during the emergency. I think we've got everything under control now."

The other woman glared at Marty. "Oh, I'll just bet you do."

"I'll walk you out." He glanced at Erica. "Honey, will you show Marty to the guest room and help her get her laptop set up?"

"Sure, Dad." The little girl looked at Eve, but the woman's attention was still focused on Marty and Clay.

Marty didn't know exactly what was going on between Eve and Clay, but the one thing she did know was that his ex-wife was a cold-hearted bitch. If Erica hadn't been there, Marty would have told her so.

"Come on, Marty."

Surprising her, Erica took her hand and tugged her toward the door. Marty let the girl guide her through the living room and down the hall. They ended up in a small, comfortable bedroom furnished with pine furniture, Southwestern art and a floor-to-ceiling shelf filled with books.

"This is kind of our office." Erica walked in and motioned toward the shelf. "A desk folds down there. Sometimes Daddy sets up his laptop."

"Do you have Internet?"

"Yeah, but I'm not allowed to get on it. Daddy thinks there are too many predators and naked people doing weird stuff."

Marty hid a smile as she set her duffel on the bed. Her respect for Clay heightened. "You know what Rufus says about the Internet, right?"

Erica grinned. "Shout It Out and Tell a Grown-up."

"That's right."

Marty was ready to get to work. The first thing she was going to do was look into the background of the suspect she'd assaulted in Chicago. She was going to look at his family members and friends and see if anything popped.

The little girl lingered. "You want me to help you set up your computer?"

"Aren't you going to have ice cream and cake?"

"Yeah, but Dad's probably still talking to . . . Eve." She hesitated on the last word as if not quite sure what to call her.

"How long has it been since you saw your mom?"

"A long time. I was just a little kid when her and my dad got divorced."

Marty wasn't sure why that made her sad, but it did. She unzipped her laptop. "Okay, so how do I get online?"

*"Your taste in women has certainly . . . evolved."*

"I'm not going to discuss this with you."

"I'm not criticizing. She's . . . cute. In a girl-next-door kind of way. Are you fucking her yet?"

Clay stood next to the Jaguar and resisted the urge to shove his ex-wife into it headfirst. No matter how he answered the question, she would believe what she wanted to believe. "You haven't changed, have you?"

She responded with a half smile. "Come on. I wasn't that bad to start with, was I?"

"I guess that depends on your perspective."

"We had some good years."

He wondered if her good years were the ones when he'd been in Kuwait and she'd been in Midland with her oilman. "We did one thing right. We created Erica."

"She's everything I imagined she would be."

"I don't know what I'd do without her."

The words hung like the stench of spent powder after a killing shot. For a moment the only sound came from the chorus of crickets and the whisper of wind through the junipers that grew alongside the driveway.

"I'm sorry I hurt you," she said.

He wondered if she was sorry she hurt their innocent little girl, if she'd given her child so much as a single thought in the years she'd been away.

"I want to get to know her." Raising her eyes to his, she reached out, brushed her fingertips over his sleeve. "I'd like to get to know you again, too."

Clay was not naive. He knew where this was going. Eve was an incredibly attractive woman. Whey they'd first met, he'd been nothing more than a twenty-two-year-old hayseed plowboy with big dreams and even bigger ambitions. He hadn't been prepared for his first taste of love, and he hadn't stood a chance against her charms. He'd fallen hard and fast and out-of-control in love. But his love for her had been as blind as his ambition, as mindless as his lust. Too late, he'd realized there was a thin layer of something dark and ugly beneath that pretty facade.

"That's a losing proposition," he said. "For both of us."

She stared at him intently, her head slightly cocked. "I don't think so."

The next thing he knew she had him against the car. Her mouth sought his, hungry and wet and achingly familiar. Six years ago he would have sold his soul for this moment. He would have given his blood, his last breath, for the chance to touch her, to hear the sound of her voice or the whisper of her sighs. He'd spent half of his adult life in love with her, the other half hating her.

For an instant, Clay felt the old draw grip him, like the nectar of a Venus flytrap luring a fly to its death. Setting his hands against her shoulders, he shoved her to arm's length. For the span of several seconds, they stared at each other.

"You've become cautious," she said after a moment.

"I've just gotten smarter in my old age."

"Is it her?"

He knew she was referring to Marty. He wasn't going to give her the satisfaction of an answer. "It's you." He opened the car door for her.

She reached out and stopped him by touching his sleeve. "We could still be good together."

"If that's why you came back, it's a wasted trip."

A humorless smile curved one side of her mouth. "You always were a self-righteous bastard."

"And you're still a manipulative bitch."

"Touché." Straightening her jacket, she looked around. "What about Erica?"

"I won't stop you from seeing her, if that's what you're asking."

"But you won't make it easy for me, will you?"

"This isn't about me. It sure as hell isn't about you. It's about Erica and her happiness."

"I won't make her unhappy."

"I know." Touching his hat, he motioned her into the car. "I won't let you."

# FIFTEEN

Marty sat at the desk in the small guest room, with her laptop open, and stared at the screen where she'd typed in the name Rurik Ivanov. She'd been hard at it for going on two hours, checking several federal and state law enforcement databases. So far she was batting zero.

She'd made inquiries with the Citizens and Law Enforcement Analysis and Reporting System known to most cops as CLEAR, the Illinois State Police Street Gang Information Center, the Law Enforcement Information Network, or LEIN, and a few others. For security purposes, a couple of sites required authorization, which wouldn't be finalized until morning.

Nothing was happening fast enough; frustration simmered inside her. She wasn't exactly sure what she was looking for. But sometimes a cop didn't know what small, unexpected piece of information would break a case until she saw it.

She'd begun her investigation by looking for convicted felons known to associate with Ivanov. She'd then switched tactics and searched for past employers. She searched for shady organizations that had gotten involved in the police brutality brouhaha. Organizations whose members were known to occasionally take the law into their own hands. She was following up on that when, by accident, she discovered Ivanov had siblings. The brother, Radimir, was an ex-con. Normally in this kind of case, Marty wouldn't take a serious look at a female. But the sister, Katja Ivanov, was not your everyday female. She had an arrest record—and ties to organized crime.

Katja had been arrested two years earlier during a bust, with a group of individuals known to be involved in the Russian Mafia out of Brighton Beach, New York. Charges against her were ultimately dropped. But Marty had found a connection, however tenuous.

She stared at the screen, a snake of cold, hard fear slithering up her spine. She couldn't believe that more than six months had passed and no one had made the connection between Rurik Ivanov and the Russian mob. But then she'd been fired shortly after the fiasco. She'd lost most of her law enforcement tools, including access to various databases. Her superiors had been so busy covering their political asses, they hadn't bothered with more than a cursory look at Rurik Ivanov. No one else had cared. They'd been more concerned with the sensational story of a cop gone bad.

Was Rurik Ivanov a member of the Red Mafia? Even if he wasn't a bona fide member, did he have ties?

A chill swept over her body at the thought. The Russian Mafia was renowned for unbridled brutality. Torture. Mass murder. High visibility when it was convenient. Maximum terror.

The next thought that struck her made her nauseous. Marty leaned back in her chair and put her hand over her stomach. Had the Russian mob murdered Rosetti? The possibility sickened her. It was their trademark style. Rosetti had been on the scene the day Marty beat Ivanov.

Why hadn't anyone considered the connection? Why hadn't she?

But she knew the answer to that, too. For the most part, the Russian Mafia didn't operate out of Chicago. They were in the Northeast, particularly New York and New Jersey.

"Shit," she whispered. *"Shit."*

A sudden gust of wind against the window sent her to her feet. She reached for her sidearm, only to remember she'd locked it up because of Erica. Marty didn't scare easily, but she could feel the uncharacteristic zing of fear running through her blood. She needed to talk to Clay. They needed to contact the FBI, the Chicago PD, and the Brighton Beach PD.

Backing away from the laptop, she left the guest room. The house was semi-dark, the only light coming from the bulb above the stove. Marty entered the kitchen and looked around. The clock told her it was just past midnight. Erica was in bed. Clay probably was, too. She didn't think this could wait until morning.

In the back of her mind she wondered if Eve was still here. If maybe she and Clay had sneaked off to bed to make up for lost time. She knew better than to let her thoughts go in that direction. She had no claim on Clay. She had no right to be jealous. She did not do jealous.

"You are *such* a liar," she whispered.

"Who are you talking to?"

Gasping, she spun to see him standing in the living room, just inside the French door that led outside to the patio. He wore a pair of faded jeans and a Caprock Canyon PD T-shirt, both of which hugged his lean frame like kidskin.

"A little jumpy tonight, aren't you?" he asked.

Blowing out a breath, she crossed to him. "You'll be jumpy, too, when I tell you what I found."

"Want a beer?"

For the first time she noticed the longneck in his hand. "Uh . . . sure."

He shot her a look she couldn't quite decipher. "I'm fresh out of vodka."

"That's too bad because we're probably going to need it after you hear what I've got to say."

She went out to the patio while he got their beers. A candle burned on a small table, and she smelled citronella. Around her the night was so silent it seemed preternatural. No traffic. No jets overhead. Not even a barking dog. The only sounds came from the crickets and the hiss of wind through the prairie grass in the field beyond.

She turned when the door whispered open. "You're not going to believe this," she said.

Clay set a beer in front of her and took the adjacent chair. "I'm afraid to ask."

"The perp I . . . went off on has ties to the Russian Mafia out of Brighton Beach."

Clay set his beer down hard. "What?"

"He's got siblings. A sister, Katja, and brother, Radimir, both with ties."

"Where did you get this information?"

"I did an ad hoc search using NCIC 2000 and a couple of other databases."

He came forward in his chair, set his elbows on the table. "Are you sure about this?"

"I wouldn't be scaring the hell out of both of us if I wasn't sure. What I don't know is if it's connected to me."

"Son of a bitch." Clay scrubbed a hand over his jaw. The sound of his palm scraping over stubble was an intimate one. "Do either of the siblings have a rap sheet?"

"Sister has an arrest record. Charges were later dropped. But you know how that goes. A person can lead a life of crime and beat the system every time."

He seemed to consider that for a moment. "So it's possible she was just in the wrong place at the wrong time."

"Maybe. But you know what they say about making assumptions."

"What about the brother?"

"He was involved in a chop shop operation and did a year at the Fishkill Correctional Facility in Beacon, New York."

"Small-time."

"We both know small-time leads to big-time."

He frowned at her. "Your partner, Rosetti, was he there the day you got into it with that suspect?"

She closed her eyes, jerked her head.

"This could explain what happened to him."

The fear she'd felt earlier was giving way to cold determination. More than anything Marty wanted to catch the people who'd done this to Rosetti. "I want to move on this, Clay," she said. "I owe him."

"What happened to him . . . it wasn't your fault. You know that, don't you?"

"I still owe him. He'd do it for me."

Clay shook his head. "You can't take on the Russian Mafia all by yourself."

"I can do my part."

"Marty, this is bad news."

"What are we going to do?"

"I'll call in the Feds first thing in the morning. You call your people in Chicago, get things rolling up there. Do you know anyone in Brighton Beach?"

She shook her head. "No, but I can put a call in to the department. I'm sure they have an organized crime or gang unit that can help us."

"Do that first thing in the morning. And I mean first thing. We've got to jump on this quick."

"We're out of our league on this thing, aren't we?"

"By a couple of light-years."

"Is there anything else I can do tonight?"

He glanced at the cell phone clipped to his jeans. "It's twelve thirty. All you can do now is stay on the research end. See if you can connect any more dots."

"Okay." She felt better now that she'd shared the news with Clay. Sitting here with him, somehow the Russians didn't seem quite so frightening. At least she and Clay had a plan.

For the first time Marty noticed there were two other beer bottles on the table, telling her he'd been at it for some time. She thought about Eve and wondered if that was good or bad. "Are you drowning your troubles or celebrating?" she asked.

"Let's just say I've had more than my share of surprises today."

She considered that a moment. "So, do you want her back, but she doesn't want you?"

"I want her gone but she doesn't want to leave."

"Oh." Marty thought about it a moment. "I can't see you two together."

"Why not?"

"She's . . ."

"A bombshell and I'm a small-town cop." He gave a wry smile. "That was always the problem. I just never saw it."

"I was going to say she's plastic. You're the real deal, Settlemeyer."

"You know what they say about opposites."

"I'm not sure I agree with that."

"She's the mother of my child."

"So how did that happen?"

He arched a brow.

She laughed. "I mean how did you two . . ."

"Hook up?" Clay took a long pull of beer, his gaze going to the dark field beyond. "We were young. I was . . . stupid. She wasn't. We were both ambitious."

"There's nothing wrong with ambition."

"Let's suffice it to say in a town the size of Caprock Canyon it can cause some frustration." Leaning back in the chair, he drank again, then set the bottle in his lap. "No Settlemeyer had ever gone to college," he said. "That was my goal. I wanted to blow this town and make something of myself."

"Nothing wrong with that."

He smiled, but there was little humor in it. "I was twenty-two when I met Eve. She'd just turned eighteen, but even then she was the most sophisticated, beautiful woman I'd ever laid eyes on. It happened so damn fast. She was like . . . I don't know . . . a drug. I couldn't get enough."

"I think it's called lust."

He laughed outright. "Everyone wondered why she was living in Caprock Canyon. I mean, she could have gone to New York to model or maybe to LA to try to break into acting."

"So why didn't she?"

"I got her pregnant. I was . . . in awe that we were going to have a child. But there was still a part of me that was disappointed because I was pretty sure I wasn't going to make it to college. I was starting to accept the possibility that I wasn't even going to make it out of Caprock Canyon."

Marty stared at him, captivated. He hadn't shared this part of himself with her. Suddenly, she wanted to know everything there was to know. "Caprock Canyon's not so bad."

"It is when you're twenty-two and ready to conquer the world."

"So what happened?"

"I worked the farm with my dad during the day. I worked at the tire center at Wal-Mart in Amarillo in the evenings. I knew things weren't going to happen the way I wanted them to if I didn't do something to change them. So I joined the army."

"They pay for college," Marty said.

He nodded. "I gave them four years. I missed Erica's birth. Her first words. Her first steps. I came home as often as I could. Every time, Eve seemed to be a little more discontented, a little more frustrated with the way her life was going." He took a drink of beer. "We lived in a trailer home at the time. Our living conditions weren't great. We didn't have shit. I told her it was only temporary, that the sacrifices we made would be worth it later. Once I'd put in my four years with the military, we could move to Dallas and buy a house. I could go to college. She could pursue whatever career she chose.

"But I think by that time she'd lost faith in me. She was lonely and discontented, spent a lot of money we didn't have. She got . . . restless."

"What happened?"

"When I came home for good, things were all right for a while. I was glad to be home. After being gone so long, I knew there would be an adjustment period. But after a few months I couldn't deny there were problems. We fought a lot over stupid things that didn't matter. Then one night we got into it pretty bad. She told me she'd met someone. Some older guy from Midland. He was wealthy. She wanted a divorce."

Marty could only imagine how much that hurt. Coming home after four hard years of serving your country only to learn the person you loved had moved on to someone else. "I'm sorry."

"Losing her," he said, "wasn't the worst of it. I swear all I could think of was losing Erica. Somehow, she'd become the center of my life. She was sweet and smart and so innocent I could barely bring myself to touch her some days. I was afraid I would somehow taint her."

"Was there a custody battle?"

Clay shook his head, looked down at his beer. "Eve didn't want her."

The emotional recoil surprised her. Marty had never been a fan of kids. But in the small span of time she'd known Erica, she'd realized the girl was special. She was loving and open, and even Marty couldn't imagine her own mother not wanting her. "At least she didn't fight you for her," she said.

His laugh was bitter. "Somehow her not wanting Erica was worse. I mean, I was terrified Eve was going to take her away from me. I couldn't sleep for worrying about it. Then I get this letter. A frickin' letter telling me she didn't want her. As if Erica were some homeless puppy Eve had adopted, then changed her mind about."

"A letter," Marty murmured. "That's pretty cold."

"That's her style. When things got messy, she always took the easy way out." He raised his gaze to hers. Even in the darkness Marty saw the remnants of pain in his eyes, and for the first time since she'd known him he looked older than his thirty-three years. "How could someone not want such a good and beautiful four-year-old little girl?" he asked.

In her gut, Marty thought she knew. But for the sake of fairness she wouldn't say it. She didn't know Eve Sutherland. "Maybe the guy from Midland didn't want children," she offered.

"I never asked. I'll probably never know. To tell you the truth, I think Erica and I are better off not knowing."

"You never told Erica?"

"I couldn't. How do you tell a little girl her mom didn't want her?"

Marty nodded. "And now Eve is back and wanting to know her daughter."

"I told her I'd leave it up to Erica."

"That's more than fair."

He drank some of the beer and set the empty bottle on the table. "It's a mess."

"Does she have legal rights?"

"I don't know. Probably."

Marty considered that a moment. "And now she wants to jump your bones. Package deal. Takes a lot of nerve."

He chuckled. "Jesus, Hogan, why don't you just say what's on your mind?"

"Sorry. In case you haven't noticed, I have a big mouth sometimes."

"I've noticed." He contemplated her, his stare so direct she had a difficult time holding it, but she did. "What about you?" he asked.

"What about me?"

"Do you want to jump my bones?"

Marty couldn't help it; she laughed. But her heart was pounding. She couldn't stop thinking about what had happened between them the other night. "Are you drunk, Chief?"

"Getting there." He lifted his beer and checked how much was left, then returned his gaze to hers. "It isn't the beer talking. I've been thinking about getting you into bed since I kissed you."

"You're not half-bad in the kissing department."

"That's a relief. How did I rate on a scale of one to ten?"

"You're pretty close to being a ten."

"So I could stand some improvement."

"Or practice."

"Is that a yes or no?"

"A stall tactic mostly."

"So do you want to go into my bedroom and work off some of this tension?"

Marty's heart jigged in her chest. The blood turned hot in her veins. She could feel the liquid heat leaching through her body, pooling low. Temptation tugged her in one direction, caution in another. "I think this is where I'm supposed to take your beer away from you."

"Looking out for my dignity, huh?"

"And mine."

"Premeditation isn't your style, is it? For you it's all about spontaneity."

"And the rush, of course."

One side of his mouth curved. "If I were to come over there and kiss you, you might change your mind."

She swallowed, her head spinning, her body beginning to ache. He stared intently at her, but Marty didn't dare look at him. She knew if she did, one of them would do something stupid. "Or I'd just stop thinking altogether. Once that happened, we'd both be in trouble."

Conversation lagged, but the silence wasn't unduly awkward. Marty drained her beer and set the bottle on the table before her. For several minutes they sat in amicable silence and watched the moon rise over the plain.

Clay broke the silence with the words Marty didn't want to hear. "If you're right about these ties you found to the Russian Mafia, we've got serious problems. You don't want to take chances with these people. Until we get to the bottom of this thing, you can't stay here."

"I know." Thinking of Erica, of the safe and wholesome life Clay had made for her here, she rose. "I shouldn't even be here now."

He rose simultaneously. "I'm not going to let you leave now."

"What about—"

"We'll get up early. We'll go to the station and work this thing. See what we can find out. Then we'll get you set up in a hotel in Amarillo."

It was the last place Marty wanted to go, but she knew she didn't have a choice in the matter. "And in the interim?"

He shrugged. "We watch our backs."

"Do you have an alarm system?"

He shook his head. "Most home alarms in this town have four paws and a tail."

"Or a hollow-point bullet."

"You armed?"

"I locked the gun in my ammo box." She cleared her throat. "Because of Erica."

"She knows about firearm safety. You keep your weapon handy tonight. Don't worry about Erica."

"I hope we're wrong about this."

"Me, too."

Nodding, Marty looked out over the moonlit prairie grass swaying in the breeze. Caprock Canyon seemed like one of the most benign places on earth. But for the first time, she sensed danger in the stark and hostile beauty of the high plains. She felt its presence as if it were a physical being, drawing ever closer, stalking her.

*I'm ready for you,* she thought.

And she prayed that when the time came, she would be.

*Katja drove all the way to Hereford for cigarettes and a* cheap bottle of vodka. She didn't have to go that far; she could have bought both at the gas station off the interstate a few miles away. But if she hadn't gotten out of the fucking dump they'd been staying in, she was going to go stark raving insane. Or maybe she'd just put a bullet in her brother's empty head.

She'd already smoked four cigarettes and was working on the fifth when she walked through the door.

Radimir glared at her from his place on the sofa, where evidently, he'd been watching some late-night television crap. "Where the hell have you been?"

For a moment, she thought about shooting him. "What business is it of yours?"

"I've been worried!"

"Worried that I might kill the bitch cop without you, maybe." Laughing, she shoved the pack of cigarettes at him. "Have a smoke."

He slapped the pack out of her hand. "You don't take the vehicle and drive away without letting me know. It's fucking three o'clock in the morning!"

Katja turned on him. "I'm sick of sitting around and doing nothing. I came here to kill the cop who ruined our brother's life. If you're too much of a *manda* to finish the job, just say the word. I could have had that bitch a dozen times in the last few days."

Radimir threw his head back and laughed. Katja didn't like being laughed at, especially when she didn't know the punch line. But she joined him. "What's so funny?"

"There's been a new development, sister."

"What?" She feigned shock. "You grew balls?"

He shot her a nasty look. "The hillbilly police chief and our lady cop are fucking."

Katja's mind spun through all the ways the information could help them, landing on nothing concrete. "So?"

"So we use that to get to Hogan. They could be onto us."

"They don't know anything."

"How can you say that? You shot at her in the can—"

"And she kicked your ass tonight," she said teasingly.

"She was armed!" But Radimir looked sheepish and angry, like a little boy who'd been spanked by his mommy in front of his friends. "In any case, we have to be careful. And we have to move soon."

Katja considered the new development. "She was probably at his house tonight."

"You drove by her place?" he asked, incredulous.

"Half an hour ago."

Radimir sighed, resigned to the fact that his sister would continue to tempt fate no matter how vehemently he complained.

"I was bored."

Bending, he scooped up the pack of cigarettes, wondering what she might have done had Hogan been there. If she would have killed the lady cop without him. He shook out a cigarette and stuck it in his mouth. "The cops are going to be careful from here on out. Hogan won't be easy to get to. I've been thinking about it, and I have a new plan."

"What plan?"

"Listen up, sister," he said. "It will suit your appetites perfectly."

# SIXTEEN

*At six thirty the next morning, Marty sat in the spare of-*
fice at the police station with the phone plastered to her ear.
She'd been on hold with the Brighton Beach PD for going
on ten minutes and her patience was wearing thin.

In his office down the hall, Clay had already been in
contact with the local FBI office in El Paso, Texas, where
he was assigned Rubin Valdez, the special agent in charge
of the American Criminal Enterprise Program. The ACEP
umbrella encompassed, among other things, violent gangs
and organized crime.

Valdez had plugged all the information Marty dug up on
the Ivanov siblings into several law enforcement databases,
promising to get back to Clay with information by the end
of the day. Depending on the outcome of the inquiries,
Valdez had a tentative visit planned for the end of the
week. Marty didn't think that was thorough enough or fast
enough, but then she'd never been patient when it came to
results.

She worked through breakfast, totally unaware of the

passage of time. She was surprised to hear from her brother, Jack, midmorning. "I hear you're in deep shit," he said without preamble.

Jack was an Army Ranger, stationed in Iraq. Because she didn't want him to worry, she hadn't told him about the attempts on her life. "No more than usual."

"Don't lie to me, little sister. I just talked to Peck in Chicago. Why the hell didn't you give me a heads-up on this?"

Marty's hands stilled on the keyboard. She hadn't liked leaving Jack in the dark about Rosetti and the attempt on her life, but she knew he would worry. In the middle of a war zone, he had enough on his plate; she didn't want him to lose his focus. "There isn't anything you can do. I didn't want you to worry."

"I'm now officially worried, so you can stop with the omission of facts." He paused, and the distance between them scratched over the line. "Have you talked to Peck?"

"No."

"In that case, I'll fill you in on the latest, so listen up. He talked to one of his State Police buddies down in Peoria a few minutes ago. A farmer found a body in his cornfield last week. The body was IDed this morning. Belongs to Aaron Christopher Meade. He's a trooper who disappeared three weeks ago."

She reached for coffee that had long since gone cold. "What does that have to do with me?"

"Meade had just transferred from Chicago PD to the state. He was on the scene the day you were involved in that car chase."

The mug of coffee stopped midway to her lips. The vague memory of something pushed at her brain. She'd heard that name before. "How did he die?"

"This is all going down right now. No one in Peoria is releasing any information. But Peck's buddy talked to one of the techs with the ME's office. All he was able to tell me was that the body was nude. There were obvious signs of torture. Decapitation."

"My God." She set down the mug of coffee, her mind spinning with implications. "Are you sure?"

"I wouldn't be calling you to tell you to keep your eyeballs peeled if I wasn't sure. Marty, this can't be a coincidence. Two cops involved in that chase are dead. You need to watch your back."

She found herself looking out the window, at the passing cars, the pedestrians on the street, and she was only marginally reassured by the firm press of her holster against her hip. "Thanks for the heads-up."

"I don't like this, Marty. If these sons of bitches want revenge and followed you to Texas, it could get bad."

"I'll keep you posted."

"I gotta go, sis. Love you."

"Love you, too. Be careful."

"Always."

Marty dropped the phone into its cradle as she rose. Rounding the desk, she headed toward Clay's office.

She opened the door without knocking. "I have news."

"Why don't you come in," he said dryly, then spoke into the phone. "I've got to go." He hung up.

Marty took the chair. "I just heard from my brother in Baghdad. Another cop was murdered. He was—"

"Baghdad?"

"My brother, Jack, was a cop in Chicago," she said impatiently. "He joined the army after 9/11. But he keeps in touch with his cop buddies. Anyway, Jack was talking to one of the cops from Chicago about Rosetti and found out there was yet another cop who was on the scene the day of the chase who was murdered."

"Murdered how?"

"Tortured to death. Just like Rosetti."

"When did this happen?"

"Three weeks ago. The cop had just transferred from

Chicago PD to the state. He was working in the Peoria area. That's why it took so long for me to connect it to what happened in Chicago and Rosetti."

That got Clay's attention. He stared at her. She could see his mind working through this terrible new development, putting the pieces of the puzzle together, not liking the way they fit. "Was he involved in the beating?"

"No, but I just now remembered where I've heard his name before. There was a news clip that ran shortly after the incident. A television cameraman just happened to zoom in when this young cop was laughing. To the outside eye, it might have looked as if he was being insensitive about the beating."

"Shit." Clay rubbed at an invisible spot between his eyes. "Why didn't we know about this sooner?"

"The body was only recently found and identified," she said.

"How long had he been missing?"

"Three weeks."

"So they murdered him three weeks ago."

She nodded.

"That means they could be anywhere by now."

Sensing where this was going, Marty said nothing.

"That means they could be here." Clay rose slowly. "I can't keep you on patrol."

"What?" Marty rose with him.

"I'm going to have to put you on administrative leave."

"You can't do that."

"Do you want me to repeat it? Put it in writing for you?"

"Don't shut me down now. I want to work this. Damn it, I can help."

"I know it goes against your grain, Hogan, but we're out of our bailiwick here."

Marty couldn't believe it. Of all the things he could have done, this was the worst. Asking her to take a backseat while one, maybe two, cop killers hunted down their next victim. Her. "I'm not going to sit this out."

"If you want to keep your job, you will." Steel laced his voice. She could see it in his eyes, too. An icy resolve that hadn't been there before.

For a crazy instant she was tempted to lay her revolver and badge on his desk. But she knew it was her pride talking, her emotions. She wasn't going to let this finish off what was left of her career. But she wasn't going to sit back on her heels, either. One way or another, she was going to bring these cop killers to justice.

"You're overreacting," she said, forcing a calm she didn't feel into her voice.

"Yeah? Why don't you tell Rosetti that?"

She winced at the mention of her friend's name, and it took her a moment to find her voice. "You're being unfair."

"I'm being cautious, which is a lot more than I can say for you." He pointed at her. "As far as we know you're at the top of a cop killer's hit list."

Fear tingled from her nape and went all the way down her spine. A cold, uncomfortable sensation she didn't want to feel. She hated being afraid. But Marty knew how ugly death could be. She didn't want to end up like Rosetti or Meade. But she didn't want to run, either. To do that was to deny who she was. And she was a cop first and foremost.

"I'm not going to run and hide," she said.

"You're not running. You're following orders."

"Would you do this if I were male?"

"Don't play the sexist card. It's insulting."

Frustrated and angry, Marty threw up her hands. "Clay, damn it, I'm not some hysterical civilian. I've had SWAT training, for God's sake. I know how to handle a weapon and I know how to handle myself."

"You saying Rosetti didn't handle things?"

She had to hand it to him; he knew just where to hit and

just how much force to use. "Rosetti didn't know someone wanted him dead."

Stepping around the desk, Clay put his hands on the arms of her chair and got in her face. "So what are you going to do? Draw down on every person you pass in the street? What about the canyon? What if they don't miss next time?"

"I'll wear a vest," she shot back.

"That'll solve everything," he said sarcastically. "Except maybe a head shot."

"Damn it, Clay, a cop's job is inherently dangerous. That doesn't mean we tuck our tails between our legs and run away."

"And you're inherently stubborn!"

Marty could feel her heart rate cranking, her temper following suit. "Don't do this. Please. I need to be involved. I need to work."

Straightening, he crossed to a metal cabinet and yanked it open. "You're going to check into a hotel and you're going to stay put until I tell you otherwise."

"This is unfair."

"Life's unfair." Without warning, he pulled out a Kevlar vest and tossed it at her. "Deal with it."

"You need my help."

"I need your cooperation."

Marty looked down at the vest in her hands. The urge to throw it at him was powerful, but she resisted. She knew a tantrum wouldn't help the situation. But more than anything she wanted to work this case. She wanted to nail the sons of bitches who'd murdered Rosetti.

"What about you?" she asked.

"I'm going to gather my resources, pull out all the stops and do my job." He looked at her and softened marginally. "You can work the computer end of it. Run information through some of the law enforcement databases. Make calls."

Even with that small scrap of responsibility, Marty felt a surge of excitement. She leaned forward, too excited, like a kid in the seconds before the recess bell.

"But I don't want you on patrol. I've already assigned your cruiser to Dugan."

Frustration crawled into her chest and squeezed so hard she thought she might choke. She despised feeling so helpless, and for the first time she understood how some cops turned rogue. "I can't believe you're relegating me to the sidelines."

Clay glanced at his watch. "I've got to go."

"Where?"

"I'm going to have Jett drive Erica over to my sister's house in Tucumcari."

"Tucumcari?"

"New Mexico. It's a couple of hours from here."

For the first time she realized fully the extent of his worry, the weight of his responsibility, and another quiver of fear went through her. "Do you think they'd go after Erica?"

"I think these people are capable of anything. I think they'll do anything they think might be effective."

Grabbing his keys off his desk, he started toward the door. "I'll be back in half an hour. If you want to help, call the sheriff's office and get an update. Field my calls. My radio's on. I'll be back as soon as I can."

Jo Nell appeared at his office doorway as he started toward the door, her narrowed eyes going from Marty to Clay. "I'm starting to feel like a mushroom, kept in the dark and fed horseshit. What's going on?"

Marty looked at Clay, wondering if they should fill her in or if this was one of those times when others were better off not knowing the details.

"Since Hogan won't be leaving until I get back, she can fill you in." Clay looked from Marty back to Jo Nell. "She's on administrative leave. If she tries to walk out that door, shoot her."

Jo Nell frowned. "What'd she do now?"

"I didn't do anything," Marty said defensively.

"Yeah, and I don't smoke."

Shaking his head, Clay walked out the door.

Marty stood in the hall, feeling like a grounded teenager.

"What's got you two so wound up, anyway?" Reaching into a box of tissues, Jo Nell removed a hidden pack of cigarettes and offered one to Marty. "Aside from being in heat."

Marty accepted the smoke and the two women lit up. Quickly, she explained what she and Clay had discovered about Katja and Radimir Ivanov.

"Those people are bad news," Jo Nell said. "I saw that movie *The Departed*. I know what they do."

"That was the Irish Mafia, not the Russians."

"Mafia is Mafia. Don't matter if they're commies or micks. Dead is dead and that's what'll happen if you don't do what the chief says." Jo Nell snapped on the air cleaner unit, and the motor began to buzz. "The chief is right. You need to stay put."

Marty knew she was right. But sitting this out wasn't going to be easy. Having fallen from grace six months ago, she was desperate for a chance to prove herself.

"They murdered my partner," she said. "My best friend."

"So you going to give them what they want and let them murder you, too?" Jo Nell huffed. "Now there's some poetic justice."

"Give me some credit, will you?" Bursting with frustration, Marty began to pace. "I'm a cop, not some desperate housewife."

"No one thinks that about you, Marty. The chief just gets a little protective sometimes. That's how you know he cares. Don't that matter to you?"

She stopped pacing and turned to look at the wrinkled little creature sitting behind the desk, holding a cigarette as if she were Lauren Bacall giving Humphrey Bogart a piece of her mind. "It matters," she said.

"Then do what the hell he says and let the rest go. If anyone can nail these Mafia pukes, it's the chief. He might be small town, but that don't mean he ain't good at what he does."

Marty crossed to the desk and stubbed out the half-smoked butt.

Jo Nell did the same, then pulled out a can of citrus-scented air freshener and sprayed. "You scared?" she asked.

"No." It was an impulse answer and not wholly true. Thinking of Rosetti, she amended it. "Yeah, I'm scared."

"Smart person knows when to be scared."

"No one's ever accused me of being smart."

"Smart-mouthed, maybe." But the older woman smiled.

Marty couldn't return the smile; frustration had her gut in a vise. Needing to do something productive, she started toward her makeshift office. "I need to make some calls," she said.

"Let me know if I can help," Jo Nell called to her back. "At least we're safe here."

Even though they were in the police station, this was one time when Marty felt anything but safe.

*"I don't want to go to Aunt Debbie and Uncle Jack's."*

Clay glanced down at the pink overnight case Erica was forcefully tossing jeans and T-shirts into and sighed. "Why not? You love Debbie and Jack."

"I don't want to miss the barrel race on Sunday."

"There'll be another race, honey."

"Dad, please—"

"It'll only be a couple of days. Three days max." He sat on the bed. "Aunt Deb says you can sleep with Ripley." Ripley was his sister's obese but very sweet tomcat.

"Why can't you come, too?"

"I have to work, honey. We think there might be some bad guys in the area. I want to make sure they don't try to hurt someone I care about."

Her eyes widened. "You mean me?"

Clay nodded, maybe because he couldn't bring himself to say the words aloud. He'd debated on how much to tell her. But Erica was mature and smart for a ten-year-old. If he tried to sugarcoat the truth or feed her some passable lie, she would call him on it. As a cop, he'd always been a firm believer that an informed child was a safer child. In this day and age, it wasn't always prudent for a parent to protect a child too much. Kids needed the truth even when it was ugly.

"I still don't want to go," she said.

Clay firmed his voice. "The decision's been made. You're going and that's final. No more arguing."

"It's not fair."

The words made him think of Marty. She hadn't been happy about being relegated to the sidelines. But as a cop, she realized the dangers. She might be willing to accept the risks, but Clay wasn't.

Erica slammed her overnight bag closed and yanked at the zipper, using a bit too much force. Clay reached out to help, but she pulled it away.

At the bedroom door, Jett leaned against the jamb with his arms crossed over his chest, looking as out of his element as a priest in a girls' locker room. "Anything I can do, Chief?"

Clay shook his head. "You got the map?" He'd downloaded a map with directions to his sister's place in Tucumcari.

Jett patted his breast pocket. "Right here."

"When you get back, we'll meet with the Deaf Smith Sheriff's Office. I'm going to brief them on the situation and share everything we have on Ivanov, so they can step up patrols in the area."

"Hogan?"

"I yanked her off patrol."

Jett smiled. "Bet she's not happy about that."

"Bet you're right."

Both men shared a moment of amusement before the gravity of the situation kicked back in.

Erica finished with her overnight bag, slid it off the bed and dropped it on the floor.

Sighing, Clay bent and kissed the top of her head. "Call me on my cell when you get to Aunt Deb's, okay?"

She rolled her eyes. "Fine."

He turned to Jett. "If you run into any problems on the way, call me."

"Will do."

"If Deb invites you inside, tell her you have to get back. She can't cook worth a damn, anyway."

Smiling, Jett picked up the overnight case. "No problem."

"I'll see you in about four and a half hours."

*Marty was on hold with the New York State Police and* tapping her finger forcefully against her desktop when outside her office door some subtle, intangible shift snagged her attention. For the last half hour, the switchboard and phones and background noise of the radio had been nothing more than babble. The chief checking in from his place. Dugan patrolling the canyon. Jo Nell's country music.

Giving the phone-hell music only half her attention, she listened for Jo Nell. Marty's cop's instincts jumped to attention when she discerned stress in the woman's voice. Hanging up the phone, she walked to the reception area to see Jo Nell sitting behind her desk, her face white as pasteurized milk.

"I just got the weirdest dispatch from Dugan," Jo Nell said.

"What about?"

"He radioed that he'd pulled someone over in the canyon when the radio went dead."

Both women jumped when Marty's police radio cracked to life.

"This is 452!" came Dugan's voice. "I got fuckin' shots fired in the canyon!"

Marty hit her radio. "What's your twenty?"

"FM 3553!" Terror laced the man's voice as he screamed into the mike. "I'm under heavy fire! *Shit!*"

Marty could hear the *pop! pop! pop!* of gunfire over his quickened breaths. Adrenaline rushed her system.

"Get out of there!" Clay's voice cracked over the radio.

"I'm pinned. Wrecked out." He screamed a curse. "I'm returning fire, but I need help down here!"

"I'm on my way," Clay said.

Clay's place was on the other side of town from the canyon. Marty hit her mike. "What's your ETA?"

"You stay put, god damn it," Clay ordered.

He was at least ten minutes away. Marty was five at most. Scant minutes that could mean the difference between life and death when you were in dire straits.

Putting her face in her hands, Marty walked to the chair opposite Jo Nell's desk and sat down hard. Dugan screamed into the mike. Marty closed her eyes against his cries for help. The need to assist her fellow officer hammered at her. Frustration and impotence ate at her. She'd felt that jumpy need before. Something happened inside a cop's head when one of their own was in trouble. An overriding instinct to back up a brother in blue. An instinct that sometimes overrode all else, even common sense.

Feeling helpless, Marty looked at Jo Nell. "I can't stand it. I'm going."

"Chief ain't going to like it."

"Dugan's out there all alone."

"Don't do it."

She didn't remember getting to her feet. She was midway to the door when Jo Nell called out her name. "At least take this."

Marty spun, caught the Kevlar vest with one hand.

"Do an old lady a favor and put it on."

The gesture touched Marty with unexpected force. Modesty forgotten, she turned away, tore off her uniform shirt and donned the vest.

"Be careful," Jo Nell called out as Marty went through the door.

Marty was still buttoning up when she jammed herself behind the wheel of her Mustang and rammed the car into gear. Her tires screeched when she hit the gas and sped south on the main road. A sense of urgency flooded her, and the speedometer cranked up to ninety miles per hour when she passed the city limit sign.

Around her the wind kicked up swirls of dust, driving sand and small debris against the windshield like a sandblaster. Tumbleweeds careened across the road like shy, bony mammals. On the radio station, the announcer bemoaned a high wind warning with downslope gusts as high as seventy miles per hour in the western counties. Marty barely heard it above the whine of the engine and the roar of her heart.

Ever aware that Dugan had gone silent, Marty entered the canyon at nearly one hundred miles per hour. The Mustang fishtailed as she made the turn onto FM 3553. Despite the dust, visibility was relatively good, and she spotted Dugan's vehicle on the shoulder two hundred yards ahead. The strobes flashed blue and white, giving the dusty air an eerie countenance.

She picked up the radio. "I'm 10-23," she said, letting Clay know she'd arrived on the scene.

"Hogan, what the hell are you doing?" The anger came across loud and clear over the scratch and hiss of the radio.

"I got a visual on Dugan's car."

He cursed. "Roger that."

"You there, Dugan?" Her eyes scanned the ridges and heavy brush as she drew closer to the abandoned cruiser.

Silence hissed over the radio.

Racking the mike, Marty stopped twenty yards from the cruiser and shut down her engine. Drawing her weapon, she opened her car door and got out. "Dugan!"

No answer.

Despite the fact that she was sweating beneath her uniform, gooseflesh raced down her back. Leaning into her car, she hit the siren for a second to let him know she'd arrived, in case he'd taken cover in the rocks above.

When he didn't immediately appear, she knew something was wrong. A prickly sensation crept over the back of her neck like the trace of a cold finger.

Squinting against the dust and wind, Marty thumbed off the safety and approached the cruiser with caution.

"Any sign of Dugan?" came Clay's voice over her radio.

Marty hit her lapel mike. "Negative."

"I'm almost there."

"Roger that."

Marty stopped a few feet from the car. Weapon poised to fire, she sidled to the right so she could see through the open driver's-side door without getting too close.

Dugan lay slumped across the seat. Blood oozed from a hole the size of her fist in the back of his head. It dripped from the seat and pooled on the floor. His pale, red-spattered hand still gripped his revolver. His eyes were open and glazed. Blowback from the horrific head wound covered the inside of the passenger door.

The roar of wind through the mesquite and juniper drowned out the scream that sounded inside her head. Visions of the young girl she'd seen shot to death six months earlier flashed vividly in her mind's eye. Blood matted in blond hair. A wound big enough to put your fist through.

"Oh God. Dugan. Ohmigod." Her first instinct was to

help him. Touch him. Assess him. But Marty knew she was too late. His staring eyes and blue black lips told her he was already gone.

Panic bubbled inside her as she stumbled back. In some small corner of her mind it registered that she was standing in the midst of a crime scene. That the shooter could be nearby. That she could be in the crosshairs of a rifle at this very moment.

Her fingers shook violently as she hit her lapel mike. "Dugan's down!" she cried. "I need an ambulance! Get someone out here now!"

She looked around wildly, her eyes scanning the surrounding scrub and rock and open land. It wasn't an ideal place for an ambush, but it was desolate. Someone could shoot from a distance then get the hell out.

Clay cursed. "Get out of there!"

Marty ran toward her Mustang. Vaguely, she was aware of Clay's voice coming over her radio. She was midway there when movement in her peripheral vision caught her eye. Someone in the gully that ran alongside the road. Bringing up her weapon, she spun. "Police! Step out with your hands up now!"

But it was panic more than authority she heard in her voice. Ducking low, keeping her weapon level, Marty backed toward the cover of her car.

Relief flitted through her when a bullet didn't come. Using one hand, she opened the car door, stepped behind it. An instant before she slid behind the wheel, she saw a flash of red from the passenger seat. Stupid, she thought as she stumbled back from the vehicle.

She caught a glimpse of dark hair, a pale face and a flash of chrome as a woman leveled a semiautomatic pistol at Marty's chest. "This is for my brother, you fuckin' bitch."

Marty didn't hear the gunshot. The impact hit her like an invisible baseball bat slamming into her chest. She flew backward. The breath left her lungs in a rush. All she could think was that she wasn't ready to die.

The force knocked her four feet from the vehicle. The ground hit her square in the back. She tried to suck in a breath. Pain seized her chest. Her vision blurred. She tried to move, ended up making an undignified sound.

In the distance Marty heard the sound of a police siren. Vaguely, she was aware of movement a few feet away. Turning her head, she saw blue-jean-clad legs and dust-covered high-heeled boots as the shooter fled.

*Hurry,* she thought, and prayed her would-be killer didn't finish the job before Clay arrived.

# SEVENTEEN

*Clay hit the lights and siren as he barreled toward the* scene, praying a vociferous approach would buy him precious seconds. He couldn't get the sound of gunfire out of his head. The panic in Marty's voice. The fear clutching his heart.

He spotted the vehicles the instant he turned onto the farm-to-market road. Dugan's cruiser sitting on the shoulder at a tilted angle. The driver's-side door open. Hogan's Mustang was parked behind it. The driver's-side door open.

The world crashed to a halt around him when he spotted her lying a few feet from the vehicle. "Hogan!" he shouted. *"Marty!"*

The Explorer skidded to a halt ten feet from her car. Clay drew his weapon and hit the ground running. He saw cinnamon-colored hair against the parched earth. The blue of her uniform. For a horrible instant he thought she was dead, found himself looking for blood. Then she groaned and hope leapt into his heart.

"Hogan." He slid to a stop and landed on his knees beside her. "What happened?"

"Bitch . . . shot me."

"How bad are you hurt?"

"Vest," she ground out and opened her eyes.

Clay was nearly overcome with relief. That she was alive. That she was able to speak. "A female?"

"Yeah."

He glanced over his shoulder, scanned the immediate vicinity. "Where?"

"Don't know. She must have . . . heard siren . . . and run. Could still be here. Be careful."

He looked around. Though he saw no movement, he knew that didn't mean the shooter wasn't nearby, hoping to finish the job.

"Be still," he said, "I need to move you to cover." Bending slightly, he looped his hands beneath her arms. She groaned when he dragged her to the cover of the Explorer.

"Stay put."

Pistol leading the way, he approached Dugan's cruiser from the driver's side. He saw the blood first. A river of it on the seat and dripping into the carpet like a macabre oil slick. The sight of his dead officer hit him like power punch to the gut.

"Aw, Dugan," he whispered. "Aw, no."

He scanned the surrounding countryside. The rocks to the south. The stand of mesquite and juniper to the east. The gully that ran alongside the road. The vast yellow plain. Clay saw no movement, no flash of color or glint of light. He glanced down at the tire tracks in the dust. He was able to identify Dugan's and Hogan's. A third set headed into the canyon.

In that instant, a small, angry part of him wanted to jump into the Explorer and go after the bitch. He wanted to hunt her down and put a bullet between her eyes. But

Marty lay injured just a few yards away. Another officer was dead.

Straightening, Clay fumbled for his cell phone, hit the speed dial for the Deaf Smith County Sheriff's Office. "This is Caprock Canyon. I've got a 10-35. I repeat 10-35. Officer down. Need assistance at FM 3553, south rim of the canyon." He thought of Dugan and swore. "All available units. Use extreme caution."

He clipped the phone to his belt. Back at the Explorer, Marty had struggled to her hands and knees. She was looking at him, her hair loose and spiraling around her face. Her eyes were dark with fear, her complexion so pale it was almost translucent. He started toward her, looking for blood on her uniform.

"Dugan?" she asked.

Clay dropped to his knees beside her and shook his head. "How bad are you hurt?"

"Vest protected me." Her face screwed up. "Knocked the wind out of me."

Emotion washed over him with such force that he couldn't speak. He ran his hands over her shoulders and down the sides of her rib cage, praying he wouldn't find blood. "Did you get a look at the shooter?"

"Female. Mid-thirties. Brown. Brown. Shot me with a chrome Sig Sauer." Marty shifted, tried to get her legs under her.

"Vehicle?"

"I didn't see one."

She struggled to her feet, raised her gaze to his. "If you hadn't shown when you did, she would have killed me."

Wrapping his fingers around her biceps, he gently pulled her to him. "I'm glad you're okay."

Clay staved off another wave of emotion by clamping his jaws together so hard his teeth ground. The sirens of approaching emergency vehicles blared in the distance.

Unable to speak, he raised his hand and touched her temple. Gazing into her eyes, he traced his fingertips over her cheekbone to her lips.

"I told you not to leave the station," he whispered.

"Dugan was in trouble."

"If I didn't like you so much, I'd fire you."

She closed her eyes. "I like you, too, Settlemeyer."

"You're too damn brave for your own good, you know that?"

"That's what cops do."

He wanted to yell at her for disobeying a direct order. For almost getting herself killed. He wanted to kiss her. Wanted even more to crush her body to his and never let her go. This wasn't the time or place for any of that.

Instead, he brushed the hair from her eyes, stepped away from her and tried like hell not to think of how this might have turned out if she hadn't worn that vest.

*Clay and a Deaf Smith County Sheriff's deputy by the name of Justin* followed the tire tracks into the canyon, but lost the trail once the dirt road became paved. They ascertained the driver had gone north, but it was impossible to determine where she'd gone after that.

As he worked the scene, Clay couldn't stop thinking about Marty and how easily he could have lost her today. The thought put an uneasy fear right in the center of his chest.

Of course she'd wanted to work the scene, but he'd refused to allow it. When she argued, he'd sicced one of the paramedics on her, a buff gal Clay had known since sixth grade. Ruby ushered Marty into the ambulance like a world-class cutting horse penning a recalcitrant calf. There, she checked her for broken ribs and other possible injuries.

Clay spent half an hour photographing Dugan and the

scene where the shooting had occurred. He'd seen a lot of terrible things in the years he'd been a cop, even more as an MP. He'd seen death up close and personal more times than he wanted to think about. Still, this shocked him. And it hurt.

One of his officers was dead. Dugan had been a good man. He'd been a husband. A father. Clay hadn't been close to him; still, it hurt. It hurt so badly that several times he had to walk away just so he could catch his breath.

Once the ambulance removed the body for transport to the hospital morgue, Clay spent another twenty minutes walking the immediate area. He talked to Sheriff Shawn McNulty and was relieved to know a forensics team from Lubbock had been called in to take tire tread imprints. Once they were finished, the images entered into the computer, they would be run through several law enforcement databases in an effort to determine the make of the car and ascertain where the tires had been purchased. You never knew when you might catch a break.

Clay wanted to drive Marty to Amarillo and get her checked into a hotel until this nightmare was over. But duty called, and he asked one of the sheriff's deputies to do it. Marty wasn't happy about it. But then most cops didn't make very good victims.

With the crime scene in good hands, Clay left to do the one thing he hated more than anything else in the world. The responsibility of breaking the news of Dugan's death to his wife fell upon his shoulders. He bore that weighty responsibility in stoic silence. He called the Lutheran minister, Larry Gilmore, on his way into town and requested his presence at Dugan's house.

Clay parked curbside and waited for the minister. Dugan lived in a modest frame house on a narrow street shrouded with fruitless mulberry trees and neatly trimmed boxwood shrubs. A PT Cruiser sat in the driveway next to a kid's red wagon full of blooming geraniums.

A few minutes later, Gilmore pulled in behind Clay. Clay disembarked and wished like hell he didn't have to do this.

"Looks like she's home," the pastor said.

"Yeah." Clay knew it was selfish of him, but he didn't want to go inside. He did not want to be the one to shatter this woman's life.

His feet felt as if they were weighted by concrete as he took the sidewalk toward the front door. He was aware of Gilmore beside him, but the minister's presence offered little comfort. Some moments were so dark nothing offered even a glimmer of light. This was one of those times.

Sweat slicked his back as he rang the doorbell. His heart hammered steady and hard against his rib cage as he waited. He could hear the TV on inside. The pound of footsteps against hardwood floors, and then the door swung open.

Teresa Dugan's smile fell as she took in the sight of Clay and Pastor Gilmore. Clay saw knowledge swim into her eyes followed by a rush of fear, of denial.

"Where's Jimmy?" Her eyes swept past them toward the cruiser in the driveway. "Where's he at?"

Setting his hands on her shoulders, Clay stepped inside. "We need to talk to you about Jimmy."

"Just tell me where he is."

Clay forced the words he didn't want to say. "Jimmy was killed in the line of duty tonight."

*"What?"* She jerked back. "No. I don't believe you."

Pastor Gilmore stepped forward. "I'm afraid it's true, Teresa. I'm so very sorry."

She turned away. Her hands shook as they covered her face. A horrific sound of grief tore from her throat. Clay could feel that same grief sounding in his chest, a silent scream of outrage and denial and the unfairness of death.

She spun back to him, her gaze going from Pastor Gilmore to Clay. "There's got to be some kind of mistake."

Clay shook his head. "I wish this was a mistake, honey, but it's not. Jimmy's gone. I'm sorry."

"How could this happen?" Hugging herself, she began to pace. "How did he die?"

Clay could feel his emotions shutting down. There were some things a man was better off not feeling. He couldn't afford to join this woman in her grief and outrage. He had a cop killer to find.

"He was shot and killed tonight," he heard himself say.

"*Shot?*" She spat a sound that was part gasp, part sob. "How could he have been shot?"

"We don't know exactly how it happened. He was in the canyon. In his cruiser. We're still investigating."

"Oh my God no! Oh God no! Jimmy!" Sobs choked her. "Not my Jimmy."

Pastor Gilmore placed his hand on her shoulder. "I'm going to call your mother, Teresa."

The woman was so engulfed in grief, she didn't acknowledge the minister. "Jimmy can't be gone. He just can't."

The pastor unclipped his cell phone. "Teresa, honey, what's your mama's number? I'm going to call her and ask her to come over if that's all right with you. You need family right now."

The woman blinked at him through tear-filled eyes as if he were speaking in a language she didn't understand. The pastor repeated his question, and she finally choked out the number.

"Who did it?" she asked after a moment. "Who shot my Jimmy?"

Clay crossed to her, set his hands on her shoulders and squeezed gently. "We don't know yet, but we're looking."

"Find him!" she screamed. "*Find him and make him pay!*"


*Twenty minutes later Clay sat in his cruiser and* scrubbed his hands over his face. Teresa Dugan's mother had arrived. Jimmy's mother had shown up a few minutes later. Clay had fielded more questions, some of them angry. There was a part of him that felt he deserved their anger. Jimmy Dugan, after all, had been his officer.

Clay couldn't dwell on his own shortcomings or the grief that had his chest in a vise. He had a cop killer to find. A town to protect. If he was going to do either of those things, he had to focus on the living, not the dead.

But he felt sick inside as he pulled the Explorer onto the street. Around him, afternoon sun bathed Caprock Canyon in golden light. Two boys passed a football back and forth, oblivious to the bottomless grief occurring just down the street. But the innocence of his town had been shattered, its citizens under siege.

The steel resolve to protect what was his engulfed him. He looked at his watch and thought of Erica. She and Jett would be arriving at his sister's house before long. He was glad he'd sent her away where she would be safe.

He wondered how Marty was handling Dugan's death. Relegated to a hotel room in Amarillo, alone with her thoughts, she was more than likely bouncing off the walls. He understood her need to be involved, but he didn't share it. She'd taken a bullet in the chest from the same gun that had killed her counterpart. If it hadn't been for the Kevlar vest, Clay would be dealing with two dead cops instead of one. The thought frightened him in a way that was as black and cold as death itself.

He'd almost lost her tonight. Funny and infuriating Marty. The quirky, stubborn cop from Chicago who charmed and tempted him at once. She made him smile when no one else could. Made him want her when he knew better. She could send his blood pressure into the red zone without even trying. Just thinking of her comforted him in a way he hadn't been comforted in a very long time.

He wanted her now.

Clay looked at his watch again. He should go back to

the crime scene, but he knew there was little he could do there. The forensic team from Lubbock would be working the scene by now. The sheriff's department would still be there. He could drive to Amarillo and see if Marty had remembered anything new. Some minute detail that might help the investigation.

But Clay knew that was a flimsy excuse. The truth of the matter was he wanted to see her. He wanted to hear her voice, touch her, talk to her. He wanted all of those things more than he wanted his next breath.

The need ate at him as he pulled onto Cactus Street. He could be in Amarillo in twenty minutes if he hurried . . .

Clay didn't let himself debate the matter as he sped past the city limit sign and headed toward Interstate 40. He didn't let himself think about right or wrong or that he might be getting in too deep. He wouldn't let himself feel anything until she opened her hotel room door and he saw her face.

When that happened, Clay knew he would feel too much.

And as surely as the sun made its daily trek toward the western horizon, he knew he'd regret it.

# EIGHTEEN

*Marty had never been a fan of hotels. Wound up tight* and pissed off to boot, she liked this one even less. The Executive might be Amarillo's finest, but twenty minutes after being dropped off by a Deaf Smith County sheriff's deputy, she was bouncing off the walls.

To make matters worse, the painkiller the doctor had given her for her bruised ribs was starting to fuzz up her head. How the hell was she supposed to think when the pills turned her brain to mush?

She'd given a detailed statement to the sheriff's office at the scene that included a decent description of the female. She'd gotten a good look at the weapon and was able to narrow down the make of the firearm. She even remembered the shooter's words.

*This is for my brother, you fuckin' bitch.*

The woman's voice echoed in Marty's head for the hundredth time. She was utterly certain the ambush in the canyon was related to what happened in Chicago. Rurik

Ivanov's sister? Katja? The Russian Mafia was renowned for using female assassins.

*This is for my brother . . .*

Graphic images of the ambush flew at her like bloody shrapnel. Dugan's staring eyes. The pool of blood, black and shiny on the car seat. The cold determination in the female shooter's eyes. Death trailing a cold finger down Marty's spine.

No matter how many times she'd dealt with violence in her years as a police officer, a visit from the grim reaper never failed to scare the hell out of her. Marty could still feel the primal grip of horror when she'd stared down the barrel of the Sig. For the span of several seconds she'd been frozen in place, unaware of anything around her except for the on-rush of terror. If the shooter had gone for a head shot instead of a body shot, Marty would be lying on a slab at the morgue.

Upon arriving at the hotel, she'd immediately opened her laptop and begun making notes, hoping that in the next hours she would recall details that might help later. But her concentration was skewed. She couldn't stop thinking about Dugan. She couldn't quiet the little voice inside her head telling her she was the one who'd brought violence to this peaceful town.

Marty stopped short of blaming herself for Dugan's death. She wouldn't do that to herself. After all, police work was inherently dangerous. She hadn't murdered him; Katja and Radimir Ivanov had. But the knowledge did little to ease the lead weight of guilt building in her chest.

Cursing, she paced the hotel room, trying not to wince when her bruised ribs protested. The X-ray taken at the clinic had determined none were broken. But her entire body ached. A hot shower had eased some of the achiness. But when she peeled off her uniform shirt, she was shocked to see a bruise the color and consistency of an overripe eggplant just below her right breast.

It irked her that she hadn't been able to get off a shot. If she'd reacted more quickly, a cop killer would be in custody. Or dead. Caprock Canyon would once again be safe and serene. Rosetti's murder would be solved. And Marty wouldn't be stuck in this godforsaken hotel, locked out of the most important case of her career.

"Damn you, Settlemeyer," she muttered.

Frustration gnawed at her. She despised being penned up like some stupid cow. At her wits' end, she crossed to the liquor cabinet, swung open the door and peered inside. Two tiny bottles of vodka sat on the shelf. Marty hesitated an instant before snatching up both. She knew better than to mix prescription painkillers with alcohol, but she didn't let herself think of repercussions as she poured the vodka into a glass and topped it with ice.

She wanted to believe the frustration and anger over being cut from the investigation were what had her tied into little knots. That was black-and-white. Simple. To the point. She could deal with that.

It was those gray areas that got her.

Her feelings for Clay were as murky and unexplored as the depths of some underwater cave. From the very start, Marty had denied her feelings for him, tried to deny the sharp-edged attraction. But she'd failed on all counts. A tough defeat for a woman who liked to win.

She thought about him twenty-four hours a day, seven days a week. She dreamed of him at night. Hot, sweaty dreams that left her breathless and aching and wishing for things that could never be. Her heart jumped every time he looked at her. He made her laugh. A laughter that was real and came from a warm place deep inside her. He made her feel good inside. Made her feel good about herself. About who she was.

And then there was the lust.

Marty had never been prone to sexual infatuations. Her barely existent sex drive had kept her out of trouble most of her adult life. Up until now she could take it or leave it. Most often, she'd rather work than go through the rigmarole of the dating scene.

Then along came Clay, and everything she'd ever believed about herself went out the window. She felt like a sixteen-year-old in the throes of her first puppy love. It was an obsessive feeling that threatened her control, and she didn't like it one bit. The question was, what the hell was she going to do about it?

"Nothing," she muttered.

She'd just taken that first dangerous sip of vodka when a knock sounded on the door. She spun, her hand going automatically to where her pistol would have been strapped to her hip. But she'd taken it off with her uniform when she'd showered. Crossing quickly to the night table, she set down the glass, picked up the weapon and thumbed off the safety. All the while her mind spun with images of thugs from the Russian mob bursting into the room, taking her to their lair, where they would spend hours gleefully torturing her the way they had Rosetti . . .

Her heart was pounding when she walked to the door and put her eye to the peephole. A different kind of tension gripped her when she saw Clay standing in the hall, alone and stone-faced. For the span of several heartbeats, Marty just stood there, looking at him, wondering why he was there and what she was going to do about it.

Taking a deep breath, she opened the door. Clay's eyes met hers, then swept to the weapon in her hand. He said nothing, but she saw the approval in his gaze.

"Did you get the shooter?" Marty stepped aside and motioned him in.

Clay shook his head and entered. "No."

"It's them," she said. "The Red Mafia. The sister, at least. Gotta be."

"Maybe."

His voice was soft and low, but something edgy simmered

just beneath the quiet facade. She knew him well enough to realize he was the one who'd broken the news of Dugan's murder to his wife, and her heart went out to him. It was a terrible thing for any cop. But she knew the death of one of his officers would be particularly hard for a man like Clay. Not only did he hurt for the man he'd lost, but he blamed himself.

"You okay?" she asked.

He looked at her for a long time, his expression inscrutable, his mouth pulled into a taut, unhappy line. "No."

"You talked to Dugan's wife?"

"Yeah."

"That must have been tough. I'm sorry."

"How about you?" He looked around the room. "You okay?"

"I'd be a lot better if I could get out there and work this case."

"You know I can't let you do that."

"I know you need all the manpower you can get."

"You're the target."

"You think I'm going to let them get their hands on me?"

"I think there could be a situation where you don't have a choice."

"Oh, come on! I'm not stupid. I'm not vulnerable. I'm a trained police officer."

He spotted the glass on the night table, picked it up, sniffed and frowned. "Jesus, Hogan."

"I'm going crazy sitting here doing nothing."

He turned to her, his eyes narrowing. "So you mix booze and pills? Like that's going to solve all your problems."

Anger drilled through her chest with such force that for a moment she couldn't draw a breath. "Someone tried to kill me today. They got one of your other officers. So what do you do? You lock me in this goddamn hotel room like some kind of pet dog that gets in the way."

"You're here for your own safety."

"I'm here so you can feel good about yourself."

The instant the words were out she knew they were a mistake. She'd pushed the wrong button too hard and at just the wrong moment. For a crazy moment, she imagined him slapping her. But if Marty had ever known anything for certain in her life, it was that Clay Settlemeyer was not a violent man.

That wasn't to say he didn't have a temper. His lips peeled back from straight white teeth. Marty wasn't easily frightened, but for an instant, she wanted to turn and run. Of course, she didn't.

The next thing she knew his hands were on her shoulders, pushing her back. Her spine hit the wall hard enough to make her wince. "You're here because I care about you, god damn it! I don't want anything to happen to you. Why is that so damn hard for you to get through that stubborn brain of yours?"

Her breaths were coming so short and fast that for a moment she couldn't speak. It was as if every emotion that burst forth stuck in her throat and clogged her voice. "Everything that's happened is my fault. I need to fix it, but you won't let me."

"You can't fix it. You're a target, for God's sake. I'm not going to lose another cop. You got that?"

His words drained some of the anger and frustration from her. "I got it."

For a moment he stood there, holding her against the wall, his breaths rushing between clenched teeth. "This isn't just about you."

Looking into his eyes, Marty saw the extent of his pain. And she realized fully how awful it must have been for him to walk into Dugan's house and tell his wife her husband would never be coming home.

"I'm sorry," she said.

"All I'm asking is for you to lay low until this is over." His voice came low and rough. The voice of a man on the edge of some emotional precipice and poised to jump.

"You can't blame yourself for what happened to Dugan," she said.

"I'm the chief of police. Who else is going to take responsibility?"

"The bitch who shot him."

Clay's expression softened. His grip on her shoulders relaxed. Some of the tension leached from his body. "Thanks for saying that. I needed to hear it."

He fell silent, but he didn't move away from her. Marty sensed he wanted to say more, but the silence stretched into something unwieldy and awkward. When Marty could bear it no longer, she started to pull away.

Clay stopped her by shifting closer and looking into her eyes. "I told myself I came here to see if you'd remembered anything else about the ambush." His gaze searched hers. "It was a lie. I came here because I needed to see you. I needed to be with you. Like this."

He didn't warn her, and Marty was so caught up in his words, she didn't see it coming. One moment she was listening, watching him hurt, hurting *for* him, and the next he was crushing his mouth to hers.

The shock of pleasure clashed with the pain and jolted her all the way to her toes. For an instant, all she could do was absorb the kiss. As the essence of him sank into her, she opened to him and kissed him back with equal ferocity.

It was as if she'd tossed gasoline onto a fire. His hands went to the sides of her face. Vaguely, she was aware of his calloused palms scraping her cheeks. The need streaking hot and out of control through her body. Her intellect cried out for her to stop before they reached the flashpoint.

But Marty knew they'd reached that summit the instant Clay walked into the room. The instant she looked at him and saw the pain and guilt etched into his every feature.

Pulling back, he made eye contact with her. His hands trembled slightly as he reached for the hem of her sweatshirt and drew it over her head. Marty wasn't wearing a bra, and a shiver swept through her as the cool air met the heated flesh of her breasts. Her nipples hardened and ached. She could feel that same ache flutter low in her pelvis.

"Aw, Marty, you're bruised." Grimacing at the bruises on her rib cage, Clay drew back. "I shouldn't—"

"Don't stop." The words were out before she could think them through. She knew if she had, she would have ended this. But Marty needed this with a desperation she'd never before experienced. A desperation that was part physical, part emotional and part so soul-deep it frightened her.

His gaze held hers an instant longer, then he reached out and ran his fingers over the bruised flesh. His touch was feather light, but the contact sent a shiver barreling through her. "This is where you were hit?"

She nodded.

"Hurt?"

"I'm tougher than you think."

"You don't look very tough right now."

"Yeah, well, you should see me break bricks over my head."

He smiled. "I should be working, but I couldn't stop thinking about you. About what happened. About what might have happened. If I'd lost you . . . that way . . ." Breaking off, he shook his head. "It would have done me in."

His eyes darkened with an emotion she couldn't quite read. Fear of what might have been. The reality that life wasn't always fair. That death could be an indiscriminate son of a bitch.

"I had to see you," he said.

"I'm glad you're here."

He leaned close and brushed a kiss across her mouth. "I want you. I've wanted you since the day I talked to you on the phone." He kissed her a second time. "I want you like this. Beneath me. I want to be inside you."

Marty's mind reeled with the devastating effects of the

kiss, his words and the flurry of emotions that followed. All she could think was that she hadn't known. She'd never seen Clay like this. He was a private man, and as closed off emotionally as a person could be. He kept his thoughts to himself; held his feelings close to his chest.

Her body joined the chorus when he deepened the kiss. Lust vibrated from bone to muscle to sizzle just beneath her skin. She could feel herself melting, going wet between her legs.

He kissed her like his life depended on it. As if she were slipping away and he would never get another chance. Marty tasted desperation and need. Both were tempered by the underlying hint of fear, but she didn't know if it was coming from him or her or both.

Clay ran his hands down her sides, past her waist, and stopped at the fly of her jeans. Marty knew what would happen next. Her intellect told her to stop. This was not the right time for them to explore whatever feelings were exploding between them. Clay had lost an officer tonight. Marty had come very close to losing her life. She didn't know if this was a reaction to high stress or if they would end up like this no matter what the situation.

But his kisses drugged her. The physical pull to him was too powerful. When he unzipped her jeans and worked the denim over her hips, Marty didn't stop him. Her heart was like a locomotive in her chest when he ran his hand over her pelvis. She gasped when his fingertip penetrated the curls at her vee. That gasp turned into a keening sound when he slid two fingers into her and went deep.

All the while he kissed her. Sensation after sensation rolled over her until she could think of nothing except his mouth against hers, his magical fingers moving inside her. Marty opened to him and rode his hand. It had been so long since she'd been this close to another person. Since she'd been held by a man. No man had ever held her the way Clay did.

He kissed her hard. Vaguely, she was aware of the wall at her back. His body flush against hers. The dull ache of her bruised ribs. Her heart exploding in her chest. But at the forefront of it all, a wild pleasure leapt in her blood, heated her skin, drove her to near madness.

She wrapped her arms around his neck and kissed him with wild abandon. A spark stoking a flame and threatening an inferno. Clay responded in kind. She could feel the steel rod of his erection against her cleft, and the need clamped down on her like a vise.

"Not here," he whispered, pulling back slightly.

"Here." Marty fumbled with the buttons of his uniform shirt. "Now."

"The bedroom . . ."

"There, too." She flung his shirt to the floor, set her hands on the rock-hard flesh of his belly.

Clay opened his fly, stepped out of his slacks. Marty caught a glimpse of dark hair on a muscular chest, a flat belly and the thrust of his penis, and a thrill of pure feminine admiration went through her. He was magnificent. He was kind. And he wanted her.

The next thing she knew his mouth was on hers, devouring the last of her thoughts. The sound of their labored breathing kept pace with the hard pound of Marty's heart. She was aware of his breath warm against her cheek. The hard length of his body against hers. The spicy scent of his aftershave titillating her senses.

"I don't want to hurt your ribs," he ground out.

She was beyond the ability to speak. It was as if her body took on a mind of its own. A mind that was determined to love this man and partake in the emotional joy and physical pleasure being with him would bring.

A gasp escaped her when he lifted her, hooked his arms around the backs of her knees and propped her against the wall. A keen sensation of vulnerability assailed her, but the feeling was short-lived. A cry escaped her when he slid into her and went deep. Her head went back and bumped the wall. Grasping his shoulders she arched into him. Once. Twice.

"Aw God," he hissed. "Marty. Marty."

The orgasm slammed down on her like an avalanche. Sensation after sensation tore down her defenses and rocked her mind. She heard his name, realized she was shouting it. All the while her body took her to a place she'd never been before. And Marty knew that when she emerged, she wouldn't be the same.

The world would be a different place.

And neither of them could ever go back to the way they were before.

*Erica looked out the window at the dust devils and scrub* and wished she wasn't on her way to Debbie and Jack's. Sure, they were fun and she had a great time whenever she was there. Debbie always had lots of good stuff to eat. Uncle Jack liked to watch all those shoot-'em-up movies that Erica liked, too. And then there was Ripley the big fat cat.

But visiting this weekend meant she would have to miss one of the biggest barrel races of the year. If she didn't go, Mary Lou Finkbine was going to win. It just wasn't fair.

Turning on her iPod, Erica decided she was mad at her dad. This was all his fault. He was always telling her what to do. He was always being so strict. She was the only girl in her class who wasn't allowed to wear makeup yet. Not even a little bit of lip gloss. Why did he have to be so over-protective?

Martina McBride was belting out a song about dreams and an angel spreading her wings when the car jolted suddenly and swerved. Alarmed, Erica looked over to see Officer Jett turn the steering wheel hard. The next thing she knew the car flew off the road and headed toward the ditch.

"Hang on!" Officer Jett shouted.

Erica dropped her iPod and hung on for dear life.

# NINETEEN

*Clay told himself this was all about lust. It was about* physical pleasure. The warmth and comfort and physical release only a woman could offer a man. He could handle that. Simple. Black-and-white with none of those confusing gray areas.

Too bad it was all a lie.

He told himself he'd come here to have sex with Marty. He'd wanted her. Wanted to fuck her. He wanted to get off and then get the hell out.

But deep inside, he acknowledged there was so much more to his being here than sex. He'd *needed* her in ways he could never put into words. He'd needed to hear her voice. He'd needed to touch her and hear her laughter. He'd needed all of those things with a viciousness that shredded every last ounce of resistance he'd had.

As desperately as he'd wanted this to be an uncomplicated case of lust, there was nothing simple about any of what had happened between them. In fact, the situation was so damn complicated it scared him. Somehow emotions had gotten involved. Not only his, but hers. He knew how easily hearts could be bruised, how easily they shattered, how long and arduous the healing process could be. The situation could turn into disaster if he didn't tread carefully. But how could he be cautious when Marty called out to every reckless, impulsive cell in his body?

He carried her to the bedroom, stumbling because her legs were wrapped around his hips and he was sunk deep into the wet heat of her. Heat so intense his entire body sizzled with it. *Lust,* he reminded himself as he lay her down on the bed. *This is just lust at work.* But when she raised her eyes to his, he felt it like a knife slicing his heart to pieces. His world shifted on its axis. And in that instant they were the only two people left on earth, and the moment between them was all that mattered.

In the back of his mind a smidgen of responsibility reminded him he should use some kind of protection. But Clay didn't have a condom. It wasn't like he ever had sex on the spur of the moment. He hadn't stopped to buy a box, because then he would have had to admit this was premeditated. That he'd planned it.

He should stop this now. Take stock. Think it through. Stop being so goddamn reckless.

But he needed her the way a free diver needs air after a deep and dangerously long dive. He could not deny himself that life-giving breath, that burst of oxygen to his brain. Without Marty he would surely die. And for once in his life he chose feeling over thinking. He chose recklessness over caution. The fickle slant of his own heart over the wisdom life experience had bestowed.

He knelt on the bed, walked on his knees toward her. She sat up, hair wild and cascading, and got to her knees. The first kiss devastated him. The second shattered every perception he'd ever had about himself. All the while need and an urgency he could not deny drove him closer to some dangerous edge and an inevitable fall.

Easing her back, he climbed over her. She lay against the pillows, opened to him. He could see her belly trembling. Her lips. Her thighs. Her hands as she reached for him. The blood rushing through his veins sounded like a tornado ripping around outside the hotel. Beautiful and deadly and destructive. A force too powerful to deny.

"Tell me we're not going to be sorry for this later," she said.

Clay saw a vulnerability he didn't want to see in her eyes. She deserved an answer, but he didn't have one. He couldn't say the words because he couldn't lie. Not to her. Not at this moment. The one thing he did know was that when all was said and done, one or both of them would be sorry for it.

She started to speak a second time. He silenced her with a kiss. When she turned her head and whispered his name, he drove into her. He knew it was wrong. That it was selfish. Maybe even cruel. But he wanted this moment to be honest and true. He owed it to her. He owed it to himself.

Even when neither of those things was easy to hear.

Bracing his arms on either side of her, he stared down at her, loving the feel of being inside her, loving even more the sweet sound of his name on her lips. He moved within her, long, steady strokes, and watched her climax. Felt his own completion rushing over him in a tumble of sensation and emotion he couldn't begin to control.

He held back as long as he could. He wanted this moment to last. But he knew it wouldn't. Growling low in his throat, he spilled his seed into the deepest reaches of her body. He steeled himself against her cries as they echoed inside him.

And he resigned himself to the inevitable crash that would follow, and the cruel reality of what he had to do next.

\* \* \*

*Clay crept from the bed and stepped into his uniform* slacks. At the bar, he snatched a tiny bottle of whiskey from the shelf, poured it into a tumbler and drank it straight down.

He knew better than to try to drown his troubles with alcohol. He had a long night ahead of him. With a cop killer on the loose, he needed to keep his wits about him. Stay on his toes. He needed to work around the clock until the son of a bitch was caught.

So then why was he here?

That was the question that bothered him most. The one he hadn't been able to adequately answer. Or maybe he just didn't want to examine the answer too closely.

He was midway through the second bottle when he heard Marty emerge from the bedroom. He turned, steeled himself against the sight of her standing there in a robe that was two sizes too big. Her eyes were large and dark against her pale complexion. Her cinnamon-colored hair spiraled wildly around her face. She was beautiful and sexy, and for a moment all he could think of was the precious moments they'd spent making love every way a man and a woman could.

She looked at the glass in his hand and started toward him. "If I didn't know better, I might think I was starting to rub off on you."

For a moment he was afraid she would touch him. Clay wasn't sure what he'd do if she did. Take her down to the floor and make love to her until neither of them could think or speak or screw this up. He wanted her; he couldn't deny that. But this was the last place he should be tonight. "I don't mix with pills."

She hesitated, then crossed to the small refrigerator and removed a bottle of water. "I guess I had that coming." She took a long drink, watching him over the rim, her eyes wary. "I'm not sure why you felt the need to say it."

"You needed to hear it."

"You're not my keeper."

"I'm a cop. And your boss."

"Is that what you are? My boss?"

Clay stomped down the anger starting to churn inside him. She didn't deserve his anger; she wasn't the source. But she was probably going to be the target. "I'm your friend."

A minute ripple went through her. "Oh. A *friend.* I'm glad you clarified that for me, Clay, because after what we just did, I could get the wrong idea."

"If you're as smart as I think you are, you won't read anything into what just happened that isn't there."

He could tell by the way she winced that he'd scored a direct hit. It should have made him feel better; he didn't want to deal with this awkward moment-after. But it made him feel like hell.

"Maybe I'm a little dense, but when two people make love the way we just did, I was under the impression that they're usually more than just friends."

"Is that what you want?"

"That's what I'd like to talk about."

"What do you expect me to say, Marty? That I love you? That I want to marry you? That I want you to be the mother of my children?"

"Don't you dare make fun of me," she snapped. "I don't deserve that."

"You deserve the truth. And the truth of the matter is I like you. I'm attracted to you. But you're one of the most reckless, impulsive and self-destructive people I've ever known."

"Don't forget my reputation as a rogue cop," she interjected. "And my violent temper."

"Look, the last thing you need in your life is a complicated relationship."

"I guess what I really need is a *pal.*"

"I'm being honest when I tell you I want to be your friend."

"Are we talking the kind of friends who have sex

occasionally or a strictly platonic-relationship kind of friend?" she asked sarcastically.

"I don't think it's a very good idea for this to happen again."

"Funny, you didn't seem to feel that way a few minutes ago when you were—"

"Don't turn what happened between us into something ugly. It wasn't."

"Then what was it?"

"It was a response to an incredible amount of stress."

She set the water bottle on the bar so hard a few drops spurted out the top. "Why did you come here tonight?"

"Because I needed . . ." *You.* Clay came within an inch of saying the one word he didn't want to say. The word that would seal his fate. Her fate. He didn't want to do that to either of them. Not tonight. Not until they'd both had time to sort through their feelings and decide how to handle what had happened between them. "Something," he finished.

"I see." Anger sharpened her gaze. "Well, here's a word of advice for you, Clay. The next time you need *something*, go to Eve. I'm sure she'd be more than happy to accommodate you."

Clay could feel the vein in his neck throbbing. He hated this, hated arguing with her, hurting her. He was angry, and for the first time since Eve had left him with a little girl to raise and not a clue how to do it, he was confused. Worse, he was hurting and he didn't want to examine the reason for his pain too closely because he knew he wouldn't like what he found.

"I have to go." Striding briskly to the table, he snatched up his holster and weapon and started toward the door.

Clay hesitated an instant before opening it. In some small corner of his mind he wanted her to call out to him. He wanted to turn to her and tell her the time they'd spent together meant something. He wanted to tell her he cared.

But the thought of doing any of those things scared him even more than knowing he had to leave. Holding that thought, he stepped into the hall and closed the door behind him.

*Marty refused to cry. Not over a man. Hell, she hadn't* even fallen to that contemptible level back in high school when Rick Reigelsperger told her she was too ugly to take to the prom.

But in all of her twenty-nine years, she couldn't remember ever hurting like this. Not like this.

She finished the vodka first, then started on the whiskey. She knew she was indulging in self-destructive behavior. She knew it was stupid and pathetic. But it was as if he'd sliced her open from end to end and left her holding herself together with inept, bloody hands.

She would rather have been angry. At least she understood anger. She could channel it and turn it into something positive. With hurt, it seemed all she could do was walk around bewildered and gut-punched. Not her style at all.

She hadn't a clue what had just happened between her and Clay. He'd purposefully hurt her, and she didn't understand why. Maybe because his life was so neat and hers was so messy. He was used to being in control and laying down the law. In classic Marty fashion, she refused to let herself be controlled, and she never followed the rules. Talk about incompatible.

The anger was starting to take hold; that was good. The vodka was fuzzing up her brain; that was even better. She was so much better at being a cop than she was a cop's lover.

It was at that moment that she saw clearly what had happened. The reality of it scared her a hell of a lot more than being at the top of the Red Mafia's hit list.

Marty had fallen in love with Clay.

She'd done the one thing she was destined to ruin. She didn't know how to be in love. Didn't have a clue how to have a healthy relationship with a good man. Yet she'd opened her heart and handed it to him on a big, tarnished platter. She'd made herself vulnerable in a way that gave him the ultimate power over her. A man who, evidently, thought she was good enough to sleep with but drew the line at anything more.

"Oh my God."

The truth of it staggered her. Sent a knife blade of panic slicing through the center of her chest. How could she have let herself do something so incredibly stupid?

Pressing her fingers to her temples, Marty sat down hard on the bed. She put her face in her hands and wished she was wrong. But the pain twisting her heart into knots was proof positive that she wasn't.

"Oh, Hogan, what have you done?" she whispered.

She jumped when the phone on the night table jangled. Her first thought was that Clay was calling to apologize. That he'd had time to think about everything he'd said.

Taking a deep breath, she answered with a curt utterance of her name.

Every nerve in her body went taut at the sound of the female voice with the Russian accent. She knew immediately it was the woman who'd shot her.

Katja Ivanov.

Marty looked stupidly down at the phone, but there was no caller ID. No way to identify the caller or determine where she was calling from. "Who is this?"

"You know who I am."

"You flatter yourself, asshole. I'm going to hang up if you don't tell me—"

"You hang up and I will cut this child's heart from her chest," she hissed.

Marty went perfectly still. *Child?* Confusion swirled,

but she felt an underlying sense of terror building just beneath the surface. "What are you talking about?"

She heard the phone being jostled about. "Marty! I'm scared! I want my *dad*!"

Everything went cold inside her at the sound of Erica's voice. It was as if her blood had been transfused with ice. Somehow this vicious bitch had gotten her hands on Erica. Clay's sweet little girl who could ride like the wind and feared nothing. But hadn't Clay sent her to his sister's house in New Mexico for safekeeping? Had this savage thug somehow intercepted them?

Cold, hard terror took her breath away. But a new and unyielding fury buffeted the fear. She could feel it burgeoning inside her like a festering sore, and she vowed in that instant that she would not let that child die. She would do whatever it took to save her.

She could hear her own breathing echoing over the line, and she put her hand over the receiver so the woman on the other end wouldn't hear that telltale sound of panic. She closed her eyes, struggled to get a grip. When she finally spoke, her voice was strong. "What do you want?"

"You."

"Why?"

"Meet me and we will discuss the matter."

"You want to kill me. Why would I meet with you?"

"This is why."

The high-pitched shriek of a child's terror and pain barreled through the line. Marty put a hand over the mouthpiece to cover the choking sob that burst from her lips. Oh dear God, they were hurting Erica. She couldn't fathom such cruelty. But as a cop, she knew better; she'd seen the results. In the back of her mind, visions of the little girl she'd witnessed being shot and killed in Chicago flashed in grotesque detail.

"Don't hurt her." This time her voice trembled.

"You will meet with me."

"Yes." Marty's mind spun through her options. "But you have to let her go."

"In due time."

"It's not too late to end this. I'll help you get away. If you don't want that, I'll make sure you get a fair—"

Erica screamed. It was the terrible sound of a wild animal that seemed to go on and on. Marty closed her eyes tightly, wished she could cover her ears, shut down her heart. But the little girl was the one thing she couldn't steel herself against. "I'll do whatever you want. Just don't hurt her."

"These are the rules. If you want this girl to live, you will follow them to the last detail. Are you listening?"

"Yes."

"Put your cell phone and your revolver in your overnight bag. Go downstairs and leave the bag with the concierge. Tell him someone will be picking it up. If we do not see you in the lobby in five minutes, we will kill the girl."

Marty hesitated, her mind scrambling wildly. She needed more time. There was no way she could walk into this without notifying Clay. Before she could answer or come up with anything to say, Erica screamed again.

"Stop it!" Marty cried. "I'll do it."

"You'll find a white PT Cruiser parked in the first space on the east side of the lot. Take Interstate 40 west toward Vega."

Vega was a small town off the interstate forty-five minutes from Amarillo. "Where am I going?"

"There will be a phone on the passenger seat. Once you're on the highway, I will call you with instructions."

Marty was already stepping into her jeans. "Why are you doing this?"

The woman continued as if she hadn't heard her. "My associate had better find your cell phone and weapon in that bag or I will kill this child. I will *hurt* her, and her blood will be on your hands. Do you understand?"

"Yes."

"Someone will be watching you at all times. In the lobby. On the highway. If you do anything stupid, I will cut out this little girl's heart and send it to you in the mail. Am I clear?"

The threat was punctuated by Erica's screams. "*Marty! Help me! I want my daaaaaaaaddy!*"

"*Erica.*" Marty gripped the phone hard. "Honey, I'm on my way. You're going to be okay."

The woman came back on the line. "You have four minutes left."

"If you hurt her," she snarled, "I swear I'll hunt you down and kill you with my bare hands."

The line went dead. Fury and terror tore down her carefully constructed wall of control. Marty could hear her heart hammering. Panic clawing like a small, sharp-toothed animal trapped inside her belly.

She checked her watch. Five thirty. Only half an hour had passed since Clay left. Such a small span of time for the entire world to change . . .

Without setting down the phone, she punched in the numbers for Clay's cell. Each ring clanged like a tuning fork against a broken bone. "Answer, damn it!"

A curse slid from her lips when his voice told her to leave a message. "The Russians have Erica," she began. "Katja Ivanov, I think. Maybe her brother. They're going to kill her if I don't meet with them. I'm going. Undisclosed location. All I know is I'll be heading west on I-40 toward Vega. I'll be in a white PT Cruiser. I'll have my personal cell." She recited the number. "There are at least two of them. One will be watching me, but I'll try to get a message to you. Clay, they said they'd kill her if I didn't come alone. I didn't know what else to do."

She paused, wanting to say more. Wanting desperately to tell him she was going to get his daughter back. But Marty couldn't lie. She didn't know if she would be able to save Erica. She wasn't even sure she could save herself.

Hanging up, she quickly finished dressing. Jeans. Sweatshirt. Dumping her overnight bag on the bed, she unloaded her revolver and placed it in an inside pocket. Next came the cell phone Clay had given her. Three minutes left.

Marty had no illusions about what the Russians would do once she showed up. She knew they would kill her. Probably Erica, too. There was no way in hell she could show up unarmed and without communication. She still had her personal cell phone. She didn't know how she could use it if, indeed, someone would be following her close enough to see what she was doing. But she had to find a way.

She had the .22 mini Magnum. It was a five-shot revolver. Minimal stopping power. The good thing about the weapon was it was small enough to conceal.

In her years of working in law enforcement, Marty had found guns hidden in all sorts of places. She knew the Russians would search her. That is, if they didn't just put a bullet in her head the moment she arrived. But Marty sensed they wanted to spend some quality time with her. The way they had with Rosetti.

The thought made her shudder, and a stark, electric stab of terror shot through her. All she could think was that she wasn't brave enough to do this. Not alone. Not without backup.

But there was no backup. And she didn't have a choice. They were going to kill that little girl. Marty already had one child's murder branded into her brain. She couldn't let it happen again.

Lifting her sweatshirt, she shoved the mini Mag into her bra. Though the gun was small, it wasn't minuscule enough for such an obvious place. She knew they'd find it in her waistband or crotch or boot.

Urgency and panic buffeted her, and for a moment she could do nothing but stand in the middle of the room and shake while the seconds ticked by. She had to conceal the weapon in a place they wouldn't find it and pray to God she could get to it when the time came. She glanced at the bed, saw a hair band lying next to her purse.

Snatching up the elastic band, she finger-combed her mane of hair and twisted it into a knot at the top of her head, securing it with the band. For the first time in her life, she was glad for her mass of unruly locks. Sliding the mini Mag from its leather holster, she worked it into her hair between the knot and her scalp. On a person with normal hair, the weapon would have been visible and fallen out. But on a woman cursed with enough hair to keep a wig shop in business for a week, it was the perfect place.

Gun concealed, she glanced at her watch. Two minutes. Snatching up the remaining cell phone, Marty slid it into the front of her pants. Not the most comfortable hiding place, but the only one she could think of where she stood a chance of getting to it when she needed it. If they decided to strip-search her, it would be over.

She picked up the hotel phone, hit Redial, cursed when she got Clay's voice mail. Not knowing what else to do, she dialed Jo Nell. The woman picked up on the first ring with her usual "Caprock Canyon PD."

"Don't talk. Just listen. The Russians have Erica—"

"*What?* Oh good Lord in heaven!"

"They're going to kill her if I don't meet them."

"Ohmigod-you-can't-do-that!"

"Find Clay. Now. Tell him. I left a message on his cell. Tell him to listen to it. I have to go."

"*Marty!*"

Closing her eyes against the panic she heard in the other woman's voice, she hung up. Marty was on her own.

A glance at the clock told her she had one minute left. Praying she wasn't making a fatal mistake, she grabbed her overnight bag, flung open the door and ran into the hall, hoping the elevator would get her to the lobby on time.

*  *  *

*"What do you mean they never showed?"* An uneasy fear seesawed in Clay's gut as his sister told him Jett and Erica hadn't yet arrived. He'd called to speak with Erica, only to learn she'd never reached her destination. "They should have been there half an hour ago."

"Maybe they had car problems," his sister offered.

"I'll call you back." Clay disconnected and pulled the Explorer into the parking lot of the Super Value grocery. He gripped the steering wheel, terrible possibilities slamming into him with the force of a wrecking ball. Not giving himself time to examine those possibilities, he hit the speed dial for Jett's number. Three rings and the phone went to voice mail.

"Where the hell are you?" he asked and hung up.

His mind whirled with feasible explanations. Jett had taken a wrong turn that put him behind schedule. An accident on the highway had delayed them. But every reasonable explanation was nullified by a dozen terrible ones.

Clay dialed the New Mexico State Highway Patrol. He spoke to the supervisor and asked if there had been any accidents on the interstate between the Texas state line and Tucumcari. The supervisor promised to check and call him back ASAP.

Next he called the Texas State Highway Patrol and asked if there had been any accidents between Amarillo and the New Mexico state line. He was on hold for less than a minute when the dispatcher told him there had been nothing reported in the last few hours.

He dialed the Deaf Smith County Sheriff's office and asked the same question. This was the last county before the New Mexico state line. Relief and edgy concern took turns punching him when he was told no accidents had been reported.

He'd just hung up when his cell beeped, telling him someone had left a message while he'd been on the phone.

Praying it was Erica, he quickly called up the message. His blood ran cold when he listened to Marty's voice.

*The Russians have Erica . . .*

The click as the message ended sounded like a death knell in his ears. Utter disbelief transformed into a wild, riotous terror as her words sank into a brain that didn't want to believe. For a moment, he thought he would throw up.

*The Russians have Erica.*

Clay knew enough about the organization to know they would kill her without hesitation and without regret.

When his hands began to shake, he set them on the wheel, gripped it hard. Fear screamed inside him. Panic echoed. For a moment, he was paralyzed. His little girl was in mortal danger. She'd been kidnapped, maybe while he'd been in bed with Marty. The crush of guilt took his breath away. Dear God in heaven, he didn't know how to save her.

Clay stumbled from the vehicle. His cell rang again, and he snapped it open.

*"Chief!"* Terror rang in Jo Nell's voice. "Marty called. They have Erica! Lord God Almighty, Marty's going to meet them!"

"Jesus." Clay got back in the Explorer, started the engine. "Keep trying Jett. Patch him through to me the second you get him." But he didn't even know if his officer was still alive.

"I'm on it."

"I'm going to get the sheriff's office involved. Alert Amarillo SWAT, will you?" Flipping on his emergency lights, he tore out of the parking lot and headed toward the sheriff's office.

Having something to do seemed to calm her. "Anything else?"

"You might try praying," he said and disconnected.

# TWENTY

In the hotel lobby, Marty left the overnight bag with the concierge. She scanned the few people milling about—the businessman checking in at the registration desk, the couple sitting nose to nose at the bar, the family sitting together in the small atrium lobby—but no one face stood out from the others. No time to linger.

She found the PT Cruiser in the parking lot exactly where the caller had told her it would be. The thought that the car could be booby-trapped floated uneasily through her mind as she opened the door and slid behind the wheel. It wasn't enough to keep her from proceeding.

Having located the key in the visor, she started the engine. A cell phone lay on the passenger seat. For a crazy instant, Marty considered snatching it up and calling Clay. She was scared. For herself. For Erica. But Marty knew if the Russians were watching, they might make good on their threat and kill the girl. In the back of her mind she thought maybe she could dial unnoticed once she was on the interstate, while the phone lay on the seat out of view.

Taking the service road, she headed west and merged onto the interstate at the first entrance ramp. As usual, traffic was light in the city of Amarillo. At the city limits sign, she took the speedometer to seventy and set the cruise control.

All the while she kept her eyes on the cars around her. A blue Chevy pickup truck. A silver Toyota. Several semirigs. She wasn't sure exactly what she was looking for, so she watched for other vehicles following too closely. A driver or passenger paying too much attention to her. A car keeping perfect pace with hers.

But as Marty headed west toward Wildorado and Vega, she saw nothing unusual. Traffic shifted; drivers passed and exited and slowed. Where the hell were they?

Just past Bushland, she carefully worked the cell phone from her pants with her right hand. Without looking down, she hit the speed dial for Clay. She didn't have her ear bud; she couldn't raise the phone to her ear. She was going to have to assume he would pick up.

"Clay," she said, trying not to move her lips. "I'm westbound on I-40 just past Bushland in a white PT Cruiser. Plate number Zero Five Victor Adam Frank Four."

She jolted when the cell phone on the seat next to her trilled. Leaving the line open on her cell, she reached for the other and put it to her ear. "Yeah."

"I see you found the car."

"Where am I going?" she asked, hoping Clay was on the other phone, listening.

"Exit at County Road 53. Go north until you hit dirt and keep going."

Marty repeated his instructions loud enough so that if Clay were listening on the other phone he would be able to hear her.

"Drive for three miles and stop."

She started to respond, but the caller disconnected. "Clay, I'm to drive three miles and stop."

The exit came up fast. As she left the highway, Marty risked picking up her cell phone. Her heart sank when she found that the call had ended. Had Clay picked up? Had he heard anything she'd said? Had she even left a message?

The questions pummeled her as she turned onto the county road and headed north. Ahead, the massive white turbines of the Wildorado wind farm loomed. Dozens of them rose out of the earth like the sun-baked bones of long-dead behemoth creatures. Around her, the area was as desolate and flat as Death Valley, a mix of pasture and farmland dissected by barbed wire and the occasional dirt road.

A quarter mile in, asphalt gave way to dirt. Marty drove as slowly as she dared, in the hope Clay had gotten the directions she'd repeated and was on his way. She prayed he would find them. The area was so desolate, no one would hear them scream.

The fear that had been hibernating inside her began to thaw. A terrible and cold sensation spread from her chest to her limbs. She knew it was counterproductive to dwell on all the terrible things that could happen. But Marty knew she was driving to her death. She knew they would probably kill Erica, too. A sweet and innocent little girl with her entire life ahead of her. The injustice of that was almost too much to bear.

There had to be a way to give Clay her destination. That was when she remembered she could take photos with her cell phone. It was equipped with a browser and e-mail capabilities. One shot of the giant structures and Clay would know where to go. If she could covertly shoot a few pics and send them to Jo Nell, Clay could be here in minutes.

Marty glanced down at the odometer. The Russian had told her to drive three miles, which she had. Stopping the car, she turned off the engine. Without giving herself time to debate, she reached for her cell phone. Holding it low, she studied the main menu, put it to memory. She hit the Address Book feature and called up Jo Nell's e-mail address: jojo@caprockpd.org.

The other cell phone trilled. Heart lurching, Marty reached for it, hit Talk. "Yeah."

"Get out of the car and walk."

"Where's the girl—"

The line went dead. Cursing, Marty tossed the phone onto the seat. Gripping her own cell in her left hand, she opened the car door. Her legs trembled as she got out and looked around. She could smell the Wildorado feedlot to the southwest from where she stood. Around her, the wind had kicked up, moaning like the sound effects of some film noir. Tumbleweeds barreled across the open fields to huddle like shy, frightened animals against barbed-wire fences. Beyond, the arms of the windmills chopped through the air like the rotor blades of a massive helicopter.

Ever conscious of the mini Magnum against her scalp and the cell phone clutched in her left fist, Marty started down the road. The wind buffeted her, kicked dust into her eyes, but she didn't stop. She sensed them watching her as she drew closer to the wind farm. She wondered if they had binoculars. Or if they gazed at her through the scope of a high-powered rifle. The thought of crosshairs focused on her chest made her shiver despite the sweat pouring down her back.

A hundred yards from the gate to the wind farm Marty took her last chance. Twisting her left arm slightly, she pointed the cell phone camera lens at the turbines and hit Enter three times. Unable to look at the phone, she had no way of knowing if she'd captured the images. The only thing left to do was e-mail them to Jo Nell without being seen and pray to God they found their way to Clay.

Marty continued to walk, trying to move naturally. All

the while she tried to recall the menu buttons that would e-mail the pics to Jo Nell. It was tough to do without looking at the phone. A swirl of dust pelted her. It wasn't enough to diminish visibility, but she used the moment to raise her left hand as if she were shielding her eyes. She looked directly at the menu. Using her thumb she hit Select, Send To, and then she pressed J to bring up Jo Nell's e-mail address. As she lowered her hand to her side, she hit Send.

There was no way she could do more without risking being seen. If they caught her with the cell phone, there was no telling what they might do. If they realized she'd summoned help, they might just put a quick bullet in her head as well as Erica's and get the hell out.

Swinging her arm slightly as she walked, Marty let go of the phone. She heard it land in the high grass behind her and to her left, but she didn't look back.

She was truly on her own now. There were no more chances. If Clay didn't receive the e-mails, both she and Erica were as good as dead.


*Jo Nell sat behind her desk sipping a diet Dr Pepper and* munching on a Snickers bar, trying in vain not to think about Erica and Marty. The Russian Mafia in Caprock Canyon. She couldn't believe it. This was the worst thing that had ever happened in the sixteen years she'd been with the police department. God help that sweet little child. God help them all.

She found an inkling of comfort by telling herself that if anyone could get through this, Marty Hogan could. The city slicker from Chicago might be a little rough around the edges, but she had that cat-always-lands-on-her-feet thing going. Marty Hogan was as tough as they came.

That didn't mean the chief wasn't sick with worry. Jo Nell had never seen him like this. As pale and grim as a damn corpse. She didn't know the whole story, but she knew not all of that worry was reserved for Erica. There was something going on between him and Marty. Jo Nell didn't know what it was, but she'd known enough men in her sixty-two years to know it was serious.

She was listening to Gretchen Wilson belt out "Redneck Woman" when her e-mail program notified her of incoming mail. Taking a swig from the can, she reached for the mouse and clicked.

Three e-mails with attachments from M. Hogan landed in her in-box. Jo Nell set down the can. "What the hell?"

Last she'd heard, Marty was on her way to meet the kidnappers. No one knew where she was going. The chief was bouncing off the walls. She looked down at her switchboard to find he was still on the phone with the Feds. Jo Nell figured if there was ever a good time to interrupt, this was it.

Rising quickly, she rounded her desk, jogged to the chief's office and shoved open the door. He glared at her from behind his desk.

"I just got an e-mail from Hogan," Jo Nell said.

Clay hung up without saying anything to the caller and rose. "What? When?"

"Just now."

He was already coming around his desk. Jo Nell trotted back to hers. Sliding behind her computer, she turned the monitor so he could see. "There're attachments."

"Open them."

Jo Nell clicked the first e-mail. "No text."

"Try the attachment."

She double clicked. The photo managing software booted. In the next instant an image she didn't recognize filled the screen. "What the hell is it?"

Clay's heart beat hard and fast as he rounded her desk. Kneeling, he squinted at the screen. "It's outdoors."

"I see grass and sky."

He lifted his finger. "Looks like part of a barbed-wire fence here."

"What's that in the background?"

He couldn't tell. "Go to the next one."

Jo Nell clicked. Another image filled the screen. This time the photo was too dark to make out much. Clay discerned yellow grass. Brown, dusty earth. Barbed-wire fence. And something smooth and white that looked like part of an aircraft blade.

"Is that a plane prop?" Jo Nell asked. "Could they be at the airport or a landing strip?"

"That doesn't look like any prop I've ever seen." Urgency tugged hard at him. Fear was a lead weight in his chest. He couldn't stop thinking about Erica and what she must be going through. How terrified she must be. He thought of Marty and couldn't get the horrific images of what they had done to her partner in Chicago out of his head.

"Click on the next one," he said.

Jo Nell clicked. "This one's better."

Clay stared at the image. He saw the same yellow grass. Tumbleweeds trapped against a locust post and barbed-wire fence. Beyond, part of a smooth white structure stood out in stark contrast against a blue sky.

He stared. Recognition sparked in his brain. At some point, he'd seen that structure before. But where?

"I don't get this," Jo Nell said.

"Marty is trying to tell us where she is."

"We know she's outside. No traffic. What the hell is that white thing?"

A memory materialized. A story in the *Amarillo Globe News* about a wind farm project. "The Wildorado wind farm."

"You think that's where she's meeting them?"

Clay was already sprinting toward his office. "Call the sheriff's office and Amarillo SWAT. Give them the twenty. Expedite. No lights. No sirens."

"Got it." She snatched up the phone.

Clay's hands shook as he jammed the key into the gun cabinet. He grabbed the AR-15 and an extra magazine and started toward the door. Jo Nell wished him luck as he crossed through the reception area and went out the door, but he didn't respond.

Clay figured it was going to take a hell of a lot more than luck to get the two people he loved most in the world out of this alive.

# TWENTY-ONE

*Gravel and dirt crunched beneath her boots as Marty* approached the gate. From twenty feet away she noticed the rusty chain and padlock securing it, the *No Trespassing* sign swinging in the wind. She considered stopping and waiting. But the caller had told her to keep going, so she put her toes on the first rail, swung her leg over the top of the gate and jumped down on the other side.

Around her the wind turbines groaned, a sound so low and hushed it was nearly drowned out by the whistle of the wind through the power lines. As she approached the first turbine, she tried hard to quiet the little voice telling her the e-mails she'd sent hadn't gone through. If that was the case, there was no way in hell she was going to walk away from this. Best-case scenario, they would kill her quickly. Worst case, she would go the route Rosetti had gone.

Marty couldn't think of a more horrific way to die.

She felt the weight of her own death pressing down on her as she walked past the first turbine. She could feel her legs shaking, her heart pounding out pure adrenaline. She was keenly aware of the mini Magnum jammed into the hair atop her head, but the small weapon was little comfort in light of what she faced. Unless the Russians presented Erica right away, and Marty got a clean shot at the person holding her, the gun probably wouldn't do much good.

That wasn't taking into consideration all the variables. Like how she would get to the weapon without being gunned down. And there was a possibility Erica wasn't even here. Then what? The answers eluded her. The only thing she knew for certain was that she didn't want to die, and she didn't want that innocent girl to die.

Her heart beat heavily in her chest as she proceeded toward the second turbine. She felt as if she were being stalked by some bloodthirsty predator. A sense of danger hung in the air like the stink of cordite after a shot. Fear infused every cell in her body. The urge to turn and run was strong. But Marty had Erica to think of. Even if the Russians killed them both, at least the little girl wouldn't be alone.

She thought of Clay, and unexpected tears burned at the backs of her eyes. The stolen moments they'd spent together in her hotel room flashed in her mind's eye. Their lovemaking had been one of the most emotionally moving experiences of her life. Only now did she realize what it meant to love someone heart, body and soul. It was the ultimate irony that she would die now that she'd finally found him.

It didn't escape her that her love for him had brought violence into his life. Into his child's life. It would destroy Clay to lose Erica. His daughter was the center of his world. Without her, he would be pitched into a never-ending darkness.

The thought broke her heart.

Wiping her eyes with the back of her sleeve, Marty shifted her focus to her environment. The size of the turbines was astounding. The diameter of the base was so large a dozen men could easily hide behind it. The surrounding landscape was a flat plain interrupted only by the occasional cholla cactus or scraggly mesquite, providing little cover. There was no doubt in her mind they were watching her.

"I'm here!" she shouted. "Where are you?"

The wind and the low groan of the turbines mocked her with otherworldly sound. To her left a small herd of cattle grazed the prairie grass. The peacefulness of the scene stood in stark contrast to the terror bubbling just beneath the surface.

The sound of tires crunching through gravel spun her around. Dizzy with adrenaline and fear, Marty watched as a white Lexus idled up to the gate and stopped. The driver got out. A young man with brown hair and dark eyes, she noted. The blue steel of a handgun jutted from his waistband. In his right hand he carried bolt cutters and used them to sever the chain.

He shoved the gate open with his foot, got back into the car and drove through it. Marty's heart pounded her ribs like a piston when the car stopped a few feet from her. The man was alone. No female cohort. No Erica.

*Where the hell was Erica?*

Marty could hear her breaths coming short and fast as the man got out. He pulled a semiautomatic revolver from his waistband as he approached her.

"Ah, you came," he said in a slight accent.

"You didn't leave me a choice." Marty looked more carefully at the car. A rental. Four-door. *The one she'd seen in the canyon the day she'd been jogging.* "Where's the girl?"

"In a safe place."

"You were supposed to bring her."

He lifted a shoulder, let it drop. "So I was."

"What about your sister? Katja?"

Surprise flicked across his expression. "Nearby."

"In that case tell the bitch her shooting sucks."

Amusement infused with cruelty glinted in his pale blue eyes. "She could not have known you were wearing a vest."

"I'm a cop. What do you expect?"

"Ah, a smart aleck."

"I hope that doesn't hurt your sensibilities."

"Oh, but Katja will be pleased with you."

The words unnerved her, and for a moment her heart beat so hard she couldn't speak.

His gaze raked over her. Marty felt it as if his eyes were laser beams burning streaks on her skin. "Put your hands up."

Marty did as she was told. "I know who you are. Radimir Ivanov."

"We can forgo introductions, then." Quickly and impersonally, he ran his hands over her, checking her bra, the waistband of her pants. "Spread your legs."

She did so and he spent a minute feeling up and down her legs, and her boots, the seat and crotch of her jeans.

"I'm clean," she said. "I followed your instructions. Now let the girl go."

"Take off your shirt."

"What?" Rolling her eyes, Marty forced a laugh. "I'm not going to do a damn thing until you—"

His fist shot out so quickly she didn't have time to brace. The impact of the punch snapped her head back. The momentum knocked her sideways so forcefully she lost her footing and went to her knees.

"Take off the goddamn shirt, you American bitch cop."

Marty didn't want to take off her shirt. She didn't know what he had in mind; she didn't want to make herself any more vulnerable than she already was. Her mind spun through options, but there were none.

Meeting his gaze, she got to her feet, hooked her fingers beneath the hem of her sweatshirt and pulled it over her head. She'd worn a sport bra, so it was more functional than revealing. Still, she hated feeling so exposed.

She tasted blood as she tossed the shirt onto the ground at his feet. "I'm not armed."

"Good thing for you." His gaze swept slowly down her body. "Are you alone?"

"Yes."

"Does anyone know you're here?"

"No."

"Take off your pants."

She tried not to cringe when he licked his lips. "Not until you show me the girl."

"You are in no position to bargain."

"Let her go, and I'll do whatever you want."

He jammed the pistol into her face. "Take off your goddamn pants."

Marty knew there was a high probability that he was going to shoot her no matter what she said or did. She also realized Erica and the female Russian might not show up at all. That her life would end here and now at the hands of this man. The best she could hope for at this point was to buy some time.

Never taking her eyes from his, she unsnapped her fly, eased her jeans over her hips and down her legs, and stepped out of them.

The man grinned. "Stupid sow."

Marty could feel herself trembling, and she knew he could see her knees quaking. She didn't want to give him the satisfaction of knowing she was scared. "Where's the girl?"

The man's eyes moved beyond her. Slowly, Marty turned. Twenty yards away a slender, dark-haired woman wearing jeans and a light blue blouse stepped out from behind the base of the nearest wind turbine. Next to her, Erica stood as stiff and pale as a mannequin. Katja Ivanov clutched a handful of the child's hair in her left fist. In her right, the chrome Sig she'd shot Marty with in the canyon gleamed in the sunlight.

"Erica, are you all right?" Marty yelled.

"I'm scared." The girl began to sob.

"It's going to be all right, honey."

The woman started toward them, her hand clenching the girl's hair. Marty wanted to pull out the mini Mag and put a slug right between her eyes. Instead, she turned to the man. She looked into his eyes. "You've got me. I know you're going to kill me. Let the girl go. You gave me your word."

A stone of dread dropped into her gut when he didn't answer. *Please, God, don't let them hurt this child.*

Looking past her, he spoke to the woman in Russian. Katja gestured angrily and hissed a reply as she approached them. Next to her, Erica stood stone still, her eyes red from crying. Dust coated her face, and Marty could see where tears had left clean stripes in their wake. She wore jeans and a red blouse. No shoes.

Marty caught the girl's eye as she and the woman walked past her toward the man. "It's going to be okay."

"I want my daddy."

"I know, hon—"

The blow came out of nowhere. Smashing across her back like a baseball bat slamming in a home run. Marty felt the air rush from her lungs. Pain streaked down her sciatic nerve all the way to her toes. Momentarily paralyzed, she stumbled forward, fell hard on her stomach.

*"Marty!"* Erica screamed at the top of her lungs. "Stop it! Don't hurt her!"

"Shut up."

Marty was only vaguely aware of the exchange. Her vision went black and white as she got her hands beneath her. An undignified sound squeezed from her throat as she flopped onto her side, raised her head and made eye contact with Katja.

"That's for my brother." The woman clutched an expandable baton in her right hand. Police issue. In the back of her mind, Marty wondered if it was Rosetti's . . .

She was aware of Erica crying quietly. The urge to go to the little girl was strong, but Marty resisted. For now, her goal had to be getting the girl to safety. To do that, she was going to have to play her cards right. There was no room for error.

"Your brother shot a kid," Marty ground out as she got her knees beneath her.

Katja's fingers shifted on the baton. "Lying pig."

Marty braced as the baton went up. For an instant, she thought about going for the gun hidden in her hair. But it was premature. Both Russians were armed with handguns. With Erica so close, it was too risky. If she could get them to send Erica away, she might be able to take them.

The blow caught her left shoulder hard enough to make her arm go numb. Pain fired and streaked to her hand. Marty rolled, her face grinding into dust and gravel hard enough to bruise her cheek. She lay there, gasping, her fingers twitching uncontrollably.

"You killed our brother." Contempt blazed in the woman's eyes. "You beat him. Humiliated him. Sent him to prison. They rape him every day."

Rolling onto her side, Marty looked at her. "He blew a kid's brains out," she panted. "I . . . lost it."

"You lost it." Katja's lips peeled back. The baton went up.

Marty turned, curled into a ball. It didn't help. The baton struck the small of her back with bone-crunching force. She heard her spine crack. Pain burned down her left buttock and exploded at the back of her knee.

As if from a great distance, she heard Erica crying. Marty closed her heart to it. She had to stay focused, figure out a plan. If the situation didn't improve, she was going to have to take her chances and go for the gun.

Or else risk getting beaten to death.

"Enough!"

Marty looked over her shoulder to see Radimir grab his sister's arm. "You are wasting time we do not have."

The woman never took her eyes off Marty. "I want to kill her."

Marty rolled onto her side. Pain wracked her shoulder and back, but she ground her teeth and struggled to her hands and knees. "Let the girl go, and you can do whatever you want with me."

Radimir looked at Erica. The girl shrank away, but he grabbed her arm, yanked her toward him, then shoved her toward the gate. "Run, you little bitch."

Erica stood vacillating for a moment, crying, her terrified eyes flicking from the man to Marty.

*"Run!"* Marty screamed. *"Run!"*

A hysterical laugh tore from Marty's throat as the little girl spun and stumbled to a sprint. "Go! Faster! Don't stop!"

She watched the girl duck between strands of barbed wire and head for an open field to the east. Erica had a chance. She was going to make it.

Marty wasn't too sure about herself.

"Why did you let her go?" Katja snarled.

"We have to get out of here." He motioned to Marty. "She's a fucking cop. She probably told someone where she was going."

"I want to take her with us."

"No, Katja. It ends here."

Marty watched the exchange with interest. The challenge in the woman's eyes told her there was discord within the ranks. A chink in their armor. If she could find a way to use that to her advantage, she might be able to gain the upper hand.

Marty struggled to her feet. Her pants and sweatshirt lay on the ground a few feet away. She wanted her clothes. At least her pants.

"I want to get dressed," she said.

The woman leveled her sidearm at her. "You don't need clothes in hell, *svinya* bitch." She glared at her brother. "Get the chain, Radimir. Hurry up."

*Chain?*

The word made Marty cringe; she wondered what the hell they were going to do with a chain. Her nerves crawled as she watched the man stride to the car and open the trunk. Next to him the female leaned in. Dread swamped Marty when the woman withdrew a rifle. A Dragunov, she realized. A deadly sniper rifle made for accuracy and distance. More than likely the gun that had been used that night in the canyon. The question was, who was she going to kill with it?

Marty's blood turned to ice when Katja raised the rifle and trained it on Erica, a hundred and fifty yards away and moving fast.

The Dragunov would be faster.

*Oh dear God no.*

The mini Magnum pressed insistently against her scalp. Marty stared at the girl's form, her heart pounding. She stared at the Russian woman, evil personified. She visualized herself going for the gun. Right hand, fingers jamming into her hair, yanking it out. Her finger on the trigger. She would take out the female first. A single shot to the chest. Then she would drop slightly. Shift the muzzle to the male. Aim for the chest, the largest target. Take him out with two shots. She could do it.

Her eyes followed Erica. *Run!* Her brain chanted the word like a mantra. The girl was two hundred yards away now. Running as fast as her legs would take her. The Dragunov could still reach her. Death could reach out and snatch her young life away before she ever heard the shot.

Marty wasn't going to let that happen.

An eerie calm descended inside her head. Closing her eyes, Marty grappled for focus, for resolve, and reached for her gun.

*It had been a long time since Clay was truly terrified.* Since he'd experienced the kind of terror that paralyzed a man from the inside out and left him as ineffectual as a spent cartridge. He felt that terror now, like a cancer rampaging through his body, tearing him down, leaving him in a place that was as black as death.

He parked the Explorer a mile from the interstate, grabbed the rifle and binoculars, and set out at a dead run toward the wind farm.

The surrounding land was flat and sparsely vegetated, offering very little in the way of cover. How the hell was he going to get close enough to stop this?

He'd put an emergency call out to the Deaf Smith Sheriff's Department and Amarillo SWAT, warning first responders to approach with caution. No lights. No siren. Clay hadn't waited for them. He knew if he did, they would try to force him to sit this one out. They'd tell him he was too personally involved. There was no way in hell Clay could sit back and do nothing.

They had no way of knowing Erica wasn't the only person he cared for who was in mortal danger. Marty was the target, after all. Erica had merely been a convenient way of reeling her in. Clay knew enough about the Russian Mafia to know they had no compunction about killing children. All he could do was pray they spared his child. That they spared the woman he'd come to love.

His boots pounded the hard-packed surface of the dirt road. He ran until his lungs threatened to ignite. Until his heart verged on bursting. A mile or so from the wind farm, he stopped. His breaths ripped from his throat as he raised the binoculars. He was trembling so violently he could barely hold the field glasses steady. But he saw enough to realize he was facing a tactical nightmare.

Marty stood twenty feet from a white Lexus. The Russians had stripped off her clothes. More than likely to make sure she wasn't armed, but also to demean. He knew how it worked. "Hang tight, Hogan," he whispered.

Where was Erica?

He shifted the binoculars, swept the area. His heart stopped when he spotted her. A hundred and fifty yards to the east, Erica was running through a cow pasture. Her arms pumped, keeping perfect time with her legs. Even from two miles away and through field glasses, Clay could see the terror in her eyes. Were they letting her go?

"Baby, run. Oh, honey, run."

Every cell in his body screamed for him to jump up and run to her. But Clay knew that would be not only ineffectual, but suicidal.

He shifted the binoculars back to the Lexus. Katja Ivanov stood near the open trunk. She'd withdrawn a rifle. From this distance Clay couldn't ascertain the model, couldn't predict its range. The male, Radimir, stood at the rear of the Lexus, looking in the trunk. Clay couldn't see what he was doing. God only knew what else they had stashed inside.

He thought about trying to set up a shot. Take out the biggest threat first: the woman. Then quickly take out the male. But the AR-15 wasn't accurate at this distance. He didn't have a tripod to stabilize the muzzle. His own hands were far from steady. He had to get closer.

Heart pounding, he looked around. His best hope lay with the bar ditch that ran alongside the road. It was barely three feet in depth and width. But it was his only cover.

Looping the binoculars around his neck, he ran to the bar ditch. It was going to be tough going; the ditch was filled with tumbleweeds and rock. Bending at the waist, he gripped the rifle and broke into a run toward the wind farm.

*Marty watched Katja put her eye to the scope, set her* finger against the trigger and prepare for the shot. In her peripheral vision, she saw Radimir still rummaging in the trunk.

Marty brought up her right hand, jammed her fingers

into her hair, yanked out the gun. Hair tore from her scalp, but she barely felt the smart. She trained the gun on the woman. Katja glanced over her shoulder. Saw the gun. Her eyes went wide.

Gotcha, Marty thought and pulled the trigger.

*Pop! Pop! Pop!*

The woman dropped the rifle and reeled backward. Red bloomed on her shirt, a bloody rose opening deadly petals. A sound tore from her throat. She went down, landed in the dust on her back.

Marty shifted the gun. Through a fog of adrenaline and terror, she saw Radimir turn, the blue steel of a gun in his hand. She heard a gunshot, and fired blindly. Once. Twice.

The bullet struck her right hand. The slash of a sickle opening her palm from finger to thumb. Marty screamed as pain shocked her system, climbed to her shoulder. The mini Magnum flew from her hand. She looked down, saw blood and mangled skin.

A sudden rush of nausea sent her to her knees. Choking back sickness and sobs of shock and pain, she grasped her wrist with her left hand and tried to stanch the flow. Blood continued to drip from her fingertips onto the dusty ground.

*"Katja!"*

Marty looked up to see the man rush to his sister and help her to a sitting position. The woman was conscious, but pale and sweating. Blood soaked the entire front of her shirt.

"She fucking shot me!" she screamed.

"You will be all right." The man helped her to her feet. "Come. We must go."

"Kill her!" Her face contorted in rage and pain, Katja thrust a shaking finger at Marty. *"Kill her!"*

"Go to the car!" he ordered.

The woman screamed in agony as he lifted her to her feet. But she never took her eyes off Marty. "Kill her," she said. "Use the chain. The way we planned."

"Get in the car!"

He yanked open the passenger door of the Lexus and shoved her onto the seat. He reclined the seatback slightly, touched her face gently with his knuckles, then slammed the door.

His eyes were black with fury when they fell upon Marty. "You will pay for shooting my sister."

Sweating and nauseous, Marty looked out across the open plain. Erica was nowhere in sight. Even though Marty was pretty sure she was going to die, the realization that she'd saved the girl's life bolstered her.

She risked a look at the man. "Your sister is gut-shot. You need to get her to a hospital or she'll die."

"She will go to prison if I take her there." He nodded as if convincing himself he was right. "She would prefer death."

Marty had always envisioned herself dying at a ripe old age in some retirement home, playing bridge or poker, being a pain in the ass to the orderlies. Standing in this open field with two people whose mission in life was to kill her, she could feel death taunting her with dark threats, ridiculing her like a cruel jokester.

"The girl will go to the police," she said.

He smiled. "In that case, we will begin," he said and started toward her.

# TWENTY-TWO

*The sound of the first gunshot hit his brain with the vio-*lence of a bomb. Clay fell to his knees, jammed the binoculars to his eyes and watched helplessly as Marty opened fire on the woman. Hope leapt in his chest when Katja Ivanov fell.

That hope shriveled when the man drew down on Marty and fired.

Horror punched him when Marty went to her knees. "Aw, Marty, no," he heard himself say. "God, no."

Cursing, he swung the field glasses to where he'd last seen Erica. Relief turned his bones to rubber when he realized his daughter had reached the fence on the opposite side of the pasture. Probably heading for the nearest farmhouse. She was out of range. Safe for now.

He swung the glasses back to Marty. He saw blood on her hand and knew she'd been shot. He squinted, trying to figure out where the bullet had hit her.

Clay got to his feet, hit his lapel mike. "This is 02. I'm 10-23."

"Chief?" came Jo Nell's voice. "You okay?"

"I'm fine. I need someone to pick up Erica. She's on foot. South of County Road 53. North of the Interstate. Expedite. No siren. No lights."

She started to speak, but Clay muted his mike. Keeping as low as possible, he broke into a wild sprint in the bar ditch. He was three quarters of a mile from where the Lexus sat. Too far to get off a shot. Eight hundred yards was the maximum accurate range of the AR-15. He had to get closer.

Stumbling over rocks, crashing through jams of tumbleweeds, Clay sprinted as fast as his legs would take him. Around him the wind moaned through the fence posts and barbed wire. The prairie grass whispered and taunted.

*They're going to kill her.*

He couldn't get the image of Marty out of his head. Blood on her hand. Practically nude. The dull sheen of hopelessness in her eyes. "Hang on," he said between gritted teeth.

Images of everything they'd shared back at the hotel scrolled in his mind's eye. The rush of emotion that followed wrenched a sound of pure regret from his throat. It was then that he realized he'd done the one thing he'd sworn he wouldn't.

He'd fallen in love with her.

*Marty had always heard that when a person suffered a* gunshot wound, they went into shock. Shock was supposed to dull the pain, and the mind's reaction to it. Only now did she realize the theory was a crock of shit.

Her injured hand hurt like nothing she'd ever experienced. A jagged pain ripped up her arm as if some ravenous flesh-eating creature were tearing away at it with sharp teeth. She looked down and shuddered at the sight. The bullet had gone straight through. Both the palm and top of her hand were a bloody mess of damaged tissue. Her fingers were numb; she couldn't move any of them. A hell of a lot of good a gun would have done her at that moment.

Blood flowed from the wound and dripped off her fingertips. She could feel her entire body responding to the massive wound. Her limbs quaked violently. Sweat poured down her neck and back. Fear was a clenched fist in her gut.

She wanted desperately to believe Clay had received her e-mails. That he was en route. That the scene would soon be surrounded by various law enforcement agencies. The man with the gun would surrender without incident. An ambulance would rush her to the hospital, where some skilled surgeon would restore full use of her hand.

But Marty held no such illusions.

This wasn't going to end nicely. There was a high probability she would not survive. The thought swung open a gate, and a sort of desperate panic gushed forth. She didn't want to die. Not like this. She thought of Clay, pictured him in her mind's eye. The way he'd looked the day of the rodeo, cheering his daughter on. The way he looked when he'd kissed her, when he'd touched her, made love to her. For a moment she was able to draw comfort from those images.

But the realization that she would probably never see him again twisted something inside her, as if a giant hand reached into her chest and wrenched her heart. She wished she'd told him she loved him, even if he hadn't wanted to hear it. She wished he'd told her the same, even if he didn't mean it.

Choking back sobs, Marty glanced toward the Lexus. From where she stood, she could see the back of Katja's head in the passenger seat and wondered how badly she was injured. If she was still a threat.

Radimir yanked a length of heavy chain from the trunk. One end of it fell to the dusty ground with a thump.

Kneeling, he looped the other end around the undercarriage of the car.

The chain was about twenty feet in length. Newly bought, because it was still shiny and rust free. Holding the other end in his hand, he started toward her. He was muttering in Russian. He looked shaken as he approached. Marty had a pretty good idea what he was going to do, and the thought terrified her so thoroughly that for a moment she was frozen. She had two choices: Run and risk getting shot in the back. Or fight him and try to gain control of his weapon.

Neither option seemed feasible. If she made a run for it and he opened fire, he probably wouldn't miss. She wasn't strong enough for a physical altercation. The shock and pain from the gunshot wound had weakened her. Her pulse skittered thready and fast. She felt dizzy and nauseous and so scared she could barely catch her breath.

"Don't do this," she heard herself say.

"Shut the fuck up."

Movement beyond him snagged her attention. Marty looked up to see the woman emerge from the car and stumble toward them, her body bent in pain. Blood soaked the lower portion of her blouse on the right side and leached down to soak the front of her jeans. Her face was the color of paste. Blood leaked between her fingers where she pressed her hand against her abdomen. Her hate-filled eyes landed on Marty. Her lips pulled back into a snarl.

"Chain her ankle," she spat to the man.

He gave his sister an assessing look. "Get back in the car, Katja."

"I want to watch."

Shaking his head, he turned to Marty. "Get on the ground."

"She needs to go to the hospital," Marty tried.

"Get on the ground or I'll put a hole in your other hand!"

Willing to risk a bullet in the back rather than face a torturous death by dragging, Marty spun and propelled herself into a run. She had made it three steps when she heard an ominous *whoosh!* The chain hit the backs of both knees, buckling them on impact. Pain exploded up and down her legs.

A scream tore from her throat as she fell to her hands and knees in the dust. The chain rattled behind her. She twisted to face the man. Leaning back on her elbows, she lashed out with both feet. But she wasn't fast enough.

Catching her right foot with both hands, he quickly wrapped the chain around her ankle and secured it with a shackle bolt. "Now you pay," he said. "For Rurik. For Katja."

He started toward the car. Sneering, the woman moved closer and spat. "See you in hell."

Marty jerked against the chain. Using her left hand, she tried to unscrew the shackle bolt, but her hand was shaking too violently. Frustration ate at her when it wouldn't budge. He'd screwed it down tight. She dug frantically at the shackle. "Come on," she choked. "Come *on*."

The car doors slammed. Desperate and terrified, Marty crawled toward the undercarriage of the car. If she could unhook the chain there and run, she might be able to get away. She reached for the slip hook with her left hand, rocked it back and forth.

The engine started. Marty worked frantically to release the hook, but it was jammed tight over the link. Her fingers shook so hard, she lost precious seconds. In the back of her mind, she remembered reading about a case in Texas where an African-American man was dragged to death by racists. She remembered thinking what a horrific death that was. Never in her wildest dreams had she imagined the same thing happening to her.

An instant later, the transmission clicked. The engine revved. *Oh, dear God, this can't be happening.* "No!" she screamed. "No! Stop! *Stop!*"

The tires spun, spewing dust into her eyes. Gravel flew at her like bullets. The car fishtailed and shot forward. Marty grabbed the chain with her uninjured hand. An instant later the chain jerked taut so violently she lost her grip. The next thing she knew her leg was yanked out from under her. She landed on her back. Her head struck the ground hard enough to daze. Gravel tore into her skin as she was dragged across the ground. Pain ripped down her back as the ground abraded her flesh. She tried to twist and grab the chain, but the ride was too violent.

An animalistic scream tore from her throat as the earth raked her body. Ahead, the car turned sharply. Like a child playing crack the whip, Marty felt her body being snapped in a different direction, then tumbling end over end into the bar ditch.

Tufts of grass, gravel and dusty earth ate at her flesh. Rocks struck hard enough to bruise bone. All she could think was that this was the end. There was no way she could survive this.

The car's engine revved and picked up speed. Marty rolled, caught a glimpse of a perfect blue sky overhead. Beyond, the yellow grass of the open plain. She thought of Clay and choked out a sob. She thought of Rosetti and an odd sense of acceptance calmed her.

Closing her eyes, she descended into darkness.

*Clay saw the cloud of dust and knew immediately the* Lexus was coming his way. Dropping to the ground in the bar ditch, he raised the binoculars. His only thought was for Marty. Where was she? Had they shot her and left her body for him to find?

The thought shook him so profoundly that for a moment he couldn't hold the field glasses steady. He struggled to calm himself, regain his concentration. When he squinted into the binoculars and focused, he couldn't believe the sight that accosted him.

Radimir Ivanov was driving. Katja was in the passenger seat. A terrible sense of horror and outrage descended when he saw something being dragged behind the car. He wanted to believe the vehicle had picked up a piece of debris or maybe a tumbleweed.

But he knew that wasn't what had happened.

Clay had seen some terrible things in his lifetime. But he'd never seen anything as horrific as the sight of Marty being chained and dragged.

For an instant the sheer atrociousness of it froze him in place. Nausea filled his mouth with bile. He spat, struggled to keep his head. Knowing he had to act now to save her life, he slid the rifle into position and set his eye against the scope. He focused, considered shooting out the tires. But while that would stop the car, it would leave the most dangerous element—the driver—free to do harm.

The car was half a mile away and closing fast. Clay set the crosshairs on the driver's head. He concentrated on his breathing. Somehow, his body remembered his military training. His breathing slowed. His hands steadied. On exhale, he squeezed the trigger.

He took two shots. The gun recoiled against his shoulder. Clay didn't move his eye from the crosshairs. The windshield splintered. The car swerved wildly, then skidded toward the bar ditch to stop abruptly nose-down.

He scrambled to his feet. Holding the rifle ready to fire, he sprinted toward the car. A hundred yards away he saw the female disembark. "Police! Get on the ground!" he screamed. "Do it now!"

She reached into the car, came out with a rifle. Clay put his weapon to his shoulder. For an instant the child he'd shot and killed in Kuwait flashed in his mind's eye. Dark hair. Slight build.

He pulled the trigger. The woman's body jerked. The weapon slipped from her hands. Clay sprinted toward her as she went to her knees, then fell facedown into the dust and lay still. The driver was slumped over the steering wheel. Blood and brain matter caked the back of his head. He was no longer a threat.

Clay's breaths tore raggedly from his throat as he raced toward Marty. She lay still as death twenty feet behind the car. A tangled heap of bruised and bleeding flesh.

"Marty! Aw, God." A sound of pure outrage burst from his lips as he streaked toward her. Somehow his hand found his mike. "Officer down!" He barely recognized his own voice. "I need a medivac! Wildorado wind farm!"

He reached her, dropped to his knees, horrified by the sight of blood and torn flesh. She lay on her side, arms stretched out above her, as if she'd been trying desperately to grab on to something that would stop her. The chain was wrapped around her right ankle. The steel had cut deep grooves into her flesh. Her ankle looked broken.

"Aw, honey. Marty. Jesus."

He wanted to touch her, but he was afraid. He wanted to move her, roll her onto her back, cover her nudeness, but he was terrified he might hurt her. He settled for putting his finger against her carotid artery. A sound of relief squeezed from his throat when he found a pulse. It was rapid and thready, but she was alive.

She was *alive.*

"Marty. Honey, it's Clay. Can you hear me?"

A sound that was part groan, part whisper slid from her mouth. "Alive . . ." She shifted, pulled her arms closer to her body. The movement caused her face to screw up. "Hurts."

"Don't try to move," he said.

"How . . . bad?"

"You're going to be okay. There's a chopper on the way."

Her eyes fluttered open. Clay just about lost it when she

focused on him, and he saw recognition in her eyes. "I'm here, honey."

"I'm . . . in a bad way."

"You're banged up, but you're going to be okay."

"Erica?"

"Deaf Smith County picked her up. She's fine."

She closed her eyes tightly, then met his gaze. "The Russians?"

"Male is dead. Female is down."

"Bastards . . . killed . . . Rosetti."

"They're not going to be hurting anyone else."

She raised her head slightly, wincing, and looked down at her battered body. "My . . . clothes."

Clay set the rifle on the ground and quickly worked off his shirt and covered her with it. "I've got you covered. Don't worry."

"Easy . . . you to say."

He choked out a laugh. "Where are you hurting?"

"Everywhere." She shifted again and moaned. He could tell she was taking stock of her injuries. "My ankle. Right hand."

For the first time Clay noticed the gunshot wound. A clean in-and-out through the palm. "It shouldn't be long until the chopper's here."

Unable to stand the sight of the chain around her ankle, he scooted down, loosened the shackle bolt. She cried out when he removed it. "Any back pain?" he asked.

She nodded.

"Can you feel your feet?"

"They hurt."

For a moment the only sound came from the blare of music from the car radio and the whisper of wind through the prairie grass.

"Can't believe . . . I'm alive." Marty's voice cracked on the last word.

Clay looked at her to see tears streaming from her eyes,

leaving tracks in the smudges of blood and dust on her face. "I'm awful glad you made it."

"Rosetti . . . my fault."

"Rosetti was killed by the mob. You don't get credit for that."

"If I hadn't—"

"Rosetti wouldn't blame you," he cut in. "In fact, I think he'd be pretty damn proud."

She closed her eyes tightly. Giant tears squeezed between her lashes. Clay ached to pull her into his arms. He wanted to hold her and soothe her and make the pain go away. He wanted to comfort her, stanch her tears and heal her with his love.

He sat down next to her. "Do you think you could do me a favor?"

"Depends . . ."

"This one's easy. I just need to hold on to your hand for a little while."

Marty tried to laugh, but ended up coughing. "Don't get . . . sentimental on me, Settlemeyer."

"Too late."

Lifting her uninjured hand, she placed it in his. Clay ran his fingers over her bloodied knuckles and broken nails, and tried hard not to think about what almost happened.

Raising her hand to his lips, he kissed her knuckles, her palm, her wrist. "Better," he whispered.

The distinct *whop! whop! whop!* of a chopper's rotors sounded above the whistle of the wind through the fence. Clay looked eastward where the yellow land stretched as far as the eye could see. A brightly painted Bell 407 stood out in stark contrast against the blue sky.

"They're almost here." Gently he squeezed her hand. "You're going to be all right."

But when he looked down, Marty had already closed her eyes.

# Twenty-three

*"You shouldn't be smoking."*

Sitting in the visitor chair adjacent to Jo Nell's desk, Marty frowned. "At this moment, that's a very hypocritical statement."

The older woman set her smoldering cigarette in the ashtray. "I didn't just get out of the hospital."

"Maybe we should both quit sneaking around like this."

"Maybe we should." Jo Nell flipped on the air cleaner fan and set the can of freshener on her desk.

Marty grinned. "But it's so fun to piss off the chief."

Jo Nell grinned back. "We'll just have to find another way to do it."

Six days had passed since that terrible day at the wind farm. Marty spent three of those days lying in a hospital bed, hitting the morphine pump, staving off nightmares, and trying not to relive any of it.

She learned from the nurses that Clay hadn't left her side for the first twenty-four hours. The only time he'd left the second day was to spend time with Erica, who'd been understandably traumatized by the ordeal.

The doctor told Marty she was very lucky to be alive. She'd suffered a broken ankle, a concussion and too many contusions, abrasions and bruises to count. It could have been so much worse. The gunshot wound on her right hand had missed bone, but damaged at least one tendon. The surgeon had done what he could to repair it, but he couldn't say for certain if she would regain full use of her hand. In typical Marty fashion, she argued the point. Only time would tell if she'd ever be able to shoot again.

Radimir Ivanov hadn't been so lucky. The Russian national died from a gunshot wound to the head. Clay's bullet, fired from a distance of almost eight hundred yards, had taken him out instantly. The Texas Rangers were called in to investigate the use of deadly force. Clay welcomed the Rangers, confident he'd done the only thing he could. Police procedure had been followed not only by the Caprock Canyon PD, but also by the Deaf Smith County Sheriff's Office.

Katja Ivanov spent four days in critical condition in the intensive care unit under heavy guard at an Amarillo hospital. She was expected to make a full recovery. Marty wanted to be glad the woman would live to see her punishment; more than likely Katja would be convicted of multiple crimes and spend the rest of her life in prison. But Marty had looked into the woman's eyes. And she'd seen pure evil. She wasn't sure the world was better off with Katja Ivanov in it.

Clay had explained to Marty how the kidnapping happened. Radimir Ivanov had discovered where Clay lived by following him from the police station to his house. The Russian had then staked out the house. When Jett and Erica left for Tucumcari, Radimir was waiting and followed them. Just west of Vega, he shot out one of the tires, causing the cruiser to run off the road. Even though Jett had been knocked unconscious in the crash, the Russian had shot him and left him for dead. The bullet had entered his chest, but somehow bypassed all the vital organs. Jett had lost nearly half his blood volume, but he'd survived. He was recovering in a Lubbock hospital and already complaining about the food. Last Marty had heard, he would be released in a couple of days.

That brought her to Erica. The little girl had been severely traumatized by the kidnapping and subsequent treatment she'd endured at the hands of the Ivanovs. According to Clay, she suffered with nightmares nearly every night. She was afraid to be alone or sleep in her own bed. She'd been crawling into his bed at night, and he didn't have the heart to make her go back to her room.

The counselor in Amarillo seemed to help. With time, he felt Erica would bounce back. Marty took comfort in the fact that the girl was in Clay's gentle and loving hands. As far as Marty was concerned, anyone who could ride a horse as fearlessly as that girl would triumph over just about any hardship.

Marty knew she would heal, too, though not nearly fast enough to suit her. Her body hurt, a dozen different pains that were deep and dark and seemingly never-ending. Despite it, she'd already weaned herself off the painkillers the doctor gave her. He'd told her to use them; she had a long road ahead. Like most advice, Marty took it with a grain of salt. He didn't know her. Didn't know how fast she could heal or that much of it would be done through the sheer force of her will. Her ankle might be broken, but she'd already made a wager with Jo Nell that she'd be running inside of five weeks.

She took another drag off the cigarette, leaned back in the chair and looked around the small, cramped reception area of the police station. The tap of Jo Nell's fingers against the computer keyboard mingled with the smooth-as-silk voice of George Strait floating from the radio on the sill. It was good to be back, she thought. It was good to be out of the house and with people. The normalcy of it fed something ravenous inside her. The need to work. To be who she was. A cop.

But Marty wasn't so naive to believe the ordeal she'd gone through at the hands of Katja and Radimir Ivanov hadn't left her with other wounds that weren't visible to the eye. Like Erica, she suffered with nightmares. Every night since the ordeal, she'd wakened terrified, her body slicked with sweat, the threat of death like a fist clenching her throat. She dreamed of Rosetti, too. The horrific death he'd suffered. She'd traded places with him once or twice in those dark dreams. But like any other problem that cropped up in her life, Marty would deal with it. She would overcome it. Kick it. Trounce it. And in the end, she would prevail. Like Erica, she just needed a little time.

The front door swung open. Marty saw Clay's cowboy hat, and she hissed a warning. Simultaneously, both women jumped to action, snubbing out their smokes, fanning the air. By the time he stepped inside, Marty was nonchalantly disposing of the evidence while Jo Nell went to work spritzing the air with citrus freshener.

"Oh, for Pete's sake," Clay growled.

"Morning, Chief," Jo Nell said without looking up from her computer. "Early, ain't ya?"

"This is a public building," he said. "You're not supposed to be smoking."

When Marty and Jo Nell exchanged what-the-hell-are-you-talking-about looks, he shook his head and pointed at Marty. "You're supposed to be at home, recuperating."

Marty was trying to think of a comeback that wouldn't reveal her frame of mind when Jo Nell spoke for her. "She can re-cooperate just as well here."

"In that case." Clay motioned to his office. "We've got some things to discuss."

Swallowing hard, Marty grabbed her crutches and heaved herself to her feet.

"Don't let him put you on desk duty," Jo Nell whispered as Clay disappeared into his office.

"I heard that," he called out.

Marty got her crutches beneath her arms and leaned. "With a broken ankle and a bum hand, I don't know where else he could put me."

"Tell him you'll take Rufus duty."

"I hate Rufus duty."

"You're the best Rufus we ever had."

"Until I bite someone. It could happen."

Jo Nell laughed outright. Marty chuckled as she made her way toward Clay's office. He'd left the door halfway open. She pushed it the rest of the way with her elbow and peeked inside. He sat behind his desk with a file in front of him. A ripple of uneasiness went through her when she saw that it was her personnel file.

"Come in." He looked up at her, his expression indecipherable. "Close the door behind you."

Knowing that wasn't a good sign, Marty shut the door, then shuffled in and took the chair opposite his desk.

"How are you feeling?" he began.

"Pretty good, actually." She set her crutches against his desk.

Leaning back in the chair, he gave her his full attention and frowned. "Considering you were dragged behind a speeding car for a hundred yards six days ago, you have a broken ankle and a penetrating gunshot wound in your right hand, I would say 'pretty good' is a stretch even for you."

"Maybe a little."

"You'd tell me you were fine if your head was on fire, wouldn't you?"

"I'd probably ask you for a fire extinguisher."

"You're not as tough as you think."

"You should see me bite the caps off beer bottles."

Clay smiled, but sobered quickly. "You saved Erica's life. I want to thank you for that. What you did took guts."

"It was also against policy."

"Sometimes policies can't cover real-world events. I think the Texas Rangers will see it that way."

She thought so, too. But it was still a huge relief hearing it from Clay.

Silence descended, as thick and stifling as heat in the throes of a Texas Panhandle summer. Marty fidgeted. He was making her nervous. Looking at her as if she might break if he stared too hard or too long. Dancing around the real reason he'd brought her in here.

He tapped his pen against the file. "You having nightmares?"

She recoiled in surprise, and her mind scrambled for an appropriate answer that wouldn't reveal just how shaky she felt. "I've had a couple of weird dreams—"

"Nightmares?"

She fixed her stare on her crutches and gave a reluctant nod.

"You've been through a couple of pretty traumatic ordeals in the last six months."

She lifted her gaze to his. "You're not going to give me the PTSD speech again, are you?"

He didn't smile. "I'm working up to it."

"Don't."

"Why not?"

"It makes me feel . . . vulnerable. I don't like it."

"I understand, but we need to discuss it. Deal with it."

Looking into his eyes, she knew it was true, but it didn't make the process any easier.

"Anything else? Anxiety attacks? Panic attacks? Anything like that?"

She lifted her shoulder, let it drop. "I have a little bit of anxiety at times."

"Okay."

"Sometimes at night, I wake up scared." She tried to laugh, but didn't quite manage. "That sounds stupid."

"It sounds like a normal reaction to what you went through."

For the span of several minutes, neither spoke. It was so quiet Marty could hear the switchboard ringing in the reception area. When she felt strong enough, she risked making eye contact with him, and she wondered if he had any idea how she felt about him. If he knew it was the thought of him that had gotten her through the worst of the last few days.

He'd been there for her, but she didn't know if it was out of a sense of duty or something more. She didn't know where she stood with him, and that troubled her almost as much as the lingering effects of what happened at the wind farm.

"I've got tendon damage in my right hand," she blurted. "I can't shoot. I don't know if I'll ever be able to use my hand again. I'm terrified you don't want a cop on your payroll who can't fire her weapon." The words poured out before she could stop them.

He nodded. "I've known at least one soldier whose shooting hand was injured. He surprised everyone when he became proficient using his left hand."

She blinked at him, surprised. And, even though his statement was designed to give her hope, she suddenly felt unbearably vulnerable, fragile. Not because her future with this department was in this man's hands, but her heart. The realization terrified her so thoroughly that her good hand began to shake.

"So how bad are the nightmares?" he asked.

"Bad."

"Flashbacks?"

"Sometimes." She didn't want to talk about this. But Marty knew he was going to force the issue. She tried to maintain eye contact with him, but her gaze skittered of its own accord to the window.

"Sometimes our minds need time to heal just like broken bones and bruised skin," he said.

"You're not going to fire me, are you?"

Clay smiled. "Hogan, this department wouldn't be nearly as interesting without you in it."

Deep inside she'd known Clay was too much of an upstanding guy to do anything so unjust. Still, the fear was inside her, eating at her like a cancer.

"I want you to call the psychiatrist we talked about," he said. "I want you to make an appointment, talk to him."

"Is that an order?"

He caught her gaze with his and held it. "It's a request from a friend. In case you're not reading between the lines here, I care about you, Marty. I care about you a lot more than I should. I want you to heal, inside and out."

She hadn't cried throughout the entire ordeal. She didn't know why tears chose that moment to betray her. "I knew you were going to do this."

"Do what?"

"Be nice to me. Make me cry. You can be such a jerk, Settlemeyer."

"And here I thought I was being sensitive."

Marty choked out a laugh, but the tears refused to stop. For the span of several minutes she stared down at the floor and struggled to rein in her spiraling emotions.

"I know you don't want to hear this," he said after a moment, "but I'm going to put you on medical leave for a little while."

Meeting his eyes, she wiped frantically at the tears on her cheeks. "You're right. I don't want to hear that."

"Just for a couple of weeks. That'll give you time to start physical therapy and have a few sessions with the shrink."

"I'm not very good at taking time off, physical therapy usually just frustrates me, and I hate shrinks."

"I knew you'd be cooperative."

She lowered her face to her good hand, rubbed at her temple with her fingers. Marty knew he was right. She needed time to heal. She wanted to believe the knot in her gut was because he'd forced the issue. But she was honest enough with herself to admit the tears had more to do with the man than anything else. Before that terrible day at the wind farm, they'd begun something that could have been special. Something that had been left unfinished. Something that had become a lifeline in the midst of a dark and violent sea.

Marty had been around the block enough to realize he was going to let what they'd started fade away. He would save her the embarrassment, the discomfort, of telling her there was no way a relationship could work. It would save her a lot of heartache. She should be thankful he was being kind and fair about it. She should be glad he wanted to be her friend. Even if she was never able to fire a weapon again, he'd all but promised her a place with the Caprock Canyon PD.

It wasn't enough.

"I want you to know your job is safe," he said. "Whenever you're ready to return to work, it'll be here for you."

"I appreciate that." Grappling for her crutches, Marty struggled to her feet. "I have to go."

"Hogan."

She started toward the door at a clip far too fast for a woman reliant on crutches. She knew it was cowardly to run at a time like this, but she didn't stop.

"Wait."

Before she could get the door open, he rounded his desk, came up behind her and touched her shoulder. "Please."

"I need to go," she said.

"I need you to stay."

When she didn't respond, he squeezed gently. "I'm not very good at this. But we need to talk. About us."

"I don't think I can handle this right now," she managed.

"I need to say this." When she still didn't look at him, he wrapped his fingers around her biceps and eased her around until they were facing each other. Dipping his head, he caught her gaze. "Please."

She stared, hating it that she'd given him the power to hurt her. "You don't have to spell it out. I get it."

"Judging from the way you're looking at me, I don't think you do."

For the first time since Clay had known her, she was being cautious. And *he* was the one being reckless. The irony of that didn't elude him, but it made him smile.

"I thought we should talk about what happened between us," he began. "At the hotel."

She looked up at him, and Clay felt the floor shift beneath his feet. She was the only woman in the world who could do that to him. Make the world move with nothing more than a look. She could turn him inside out with a smile or touch and just the sound of her voice.

"Look," he began, "I don't know how to say it, so I'm just going to lay it out."

She braced as if expecting him to fling something hurtful and unpleasant her way, and it took every bit of discipline he possessed not to pull her into his arms and kiss away the physical pain and the emotional hurt he saw in her eyes.

"I'm crazy about you," he said.

She stared at him as if he'd just announced he was a member of the Russian Mafia and had brought her here to do away with her once and for all. He wondered how it could come as such a surprise to her. But then he was a master at concealing his feelings, even better at hiding from the truth.

"As a matter of fact," he added, "I'm pretty sure I'm falling in love with you."

\* \* \*

Marty *had taken kickboxing lessons as a teenager and* sustained many a well-aimed blow. Clay's words struck her in much the same way, a high-impact assault right between the eyes. She stared at him, her heart turning somersaults in her chest, all the while his words echoing in her ears like a love song she couldn't get out of her head.

*I'm pretty sure I'm falling in love with you.*

It was the last thing she'd expected him to say. She was so shocked that for the span of several eternal seconds, she couldn't say anything. When she finally did, her voice was breathless. "I gotta hand it to you, Chief. You really know how to keep a girl on her toes."

"It's a full-time job with you."

"That's why you find me so irresistible."

"One of many reasons." His expression became thoughtful. "I didn't realize it until the night in the hotel. It scared the hell out of me."

"That's why you were . . ."

"A jerk?" He offered a wry smile. "Yeah. I panicked, I guess. I kept thinking how things ended with Eve. I was afraid I was getting in over my head with you."

"Speaking of Eve . . ." Not totally sure she wanted to know the status of his relationship with his ex-wife, Marty let her words trail.

"Eve went back to Midland day before yesterday. Left a note."

"Like before."

"Nothing like before." His jaw muscles tightened. "I told her I was in love with you."

The words elicited a sensation in her stomach she likened to the first momentous plunge of a roller-coaster ride. "I'll bet that went over well."

"She got it."

"Is Erica okay with that?"

He lifted his shoulder, let it drop. "She will be. I'm sure Eve will keep in touch. She'll probably send birthday cards and expensive gifts at Christmas from Europe or wherever."

"You've got a lot of baggage in the woman department, Settlemeyer."

He grimaced. "You're nothing like her, Marty. You're honest and beautiful and flawed, and those aren't even the things I love about you most. It was never like this with Eve. Not even close. And I was a fool for not recognizing it. I'm sorry."

"It's not like either of us has a lot of experience in that area."

"When I almost lost you, I knew." He set his fingers against his chest. "I knew it here. Where it counts."

Lifting his hand to her face, he brushed a strand of hair from her cheek. "I love you."

A hundred emotions rippled through her, each overlapping the other, growing larger and more powerful. She looked into his eyes, and for the first time in a long time, she felt special and lucky and . . . cherished. "Me, too," she whispered. "I knew the first time you kissed me."

"That good, huh?"

"Don't get cocky."

"Come here."

Shifting her weight to her uninjured foot, Marty let her crutches clatter to the floor. She hopped once. Twice. He reached for her, put his arms around her and pulled her against him.

He kissed her hard on the mouth. "Such a risk taker."

"Not so much," she whispered. "I knew you'd be there to catch me."